Praise for #1 *New York Times* bestselling author

NORA ROBERTS

"Nora Roberts is among the best."   —*Washington Post*

"Roberts has a warm feel for her characters and an eye for
the evocative detail."   —*Chicago Tribune*

"America's favorite writer."   —*New Yorker*

"When Roberts puts her expert fingers on the pulse of
romance, legions of fans feel the heartbeat."
—*Publishers Weekly*

"You can't bottle wish fulfillment, but Nora Roberts
certainly knows how to put it on the page."
—*New York Times*

"Roberts' style has a fresh, contemporary snap."
—*Kirkus Reviews*

Dear Reader,

We've brought together two best-loved Nora Roberts classics: *Megan's Mate*, the fifth story in the Calhoun Women series, and *Best Laid Plans* from the Jack's Stories duology. Both feature strong women looking for a solid foundation on which to build their homes—literally and figuratively!

In *Megan's Mate*, Calhoun sister-in-law Megan O'Riley has moved to Maine with her young son to start a new life. No one has ever dared to scale the walls Megan's built around her heart—until boat captain Nate Fury sets his sights on her. Nate is eager to win Megan's trust and her love. Maybe he can help her believe in happy-ever-afters again?

Some men make your pulse hammer, your heart rise and fall. Abra Wilson found that architect Cody Johnson was just such a man. Though he was utterly distracting, Cody was the kind of charmer Abra refused to fall for. But her *Best Laid Plans* go awry when Cody has other ideas…

Happy reading!

The Editors

Silhouette Books

NORA ROBERTS

A PLACE TO CALL HOME

Includes *Megan's Mate* & *Best Laid Plans*

Silhouette Books

SILHOUETTE™

Recycling programs for this product may not exist in your area.

A Place to Call Home

ISBN-13: 978-1-335-42601-7

Copyright © 2023 by Harlequin Enterprises ULC

Megan's Mate
First published in 1996. This edition published in 2023.
Copyright © 1996 by Nora Roberts

Best Laid Plans
First published in 1989. This edition published in 2023.
Copyright © 1989 by Nora Roberts

For questions and comments about the quality of this book, please contact us at CustomerService@Harlequin.com.

Silhouette
22 Adelaide St. West, 41st Floor
Toronto, Ontario M5H 4E3, Canada
www.Harlequin.com

Printed in U.S.A.

CONTENTS

MEGAN'S MATE

For the Washington Romance Writers,
my extended family

Chapter 1

She wasn't a risk-taker. She was always absolutely sure a step was completed before she took the next. It was part of her personality— at least it had been for nearly ten years. She'd trained herself to be practical, to be cautious. Megan O'Riley was a woman who double-checked the locks at night.

To prepare for the flight from Oklahoma to Maine, she had meticulously packed carry-on bags for herself and her son, and had arranged for the rest of their belongings to be shipped. It was foolish, she thought, to waste time at baggage claim.

The move east wasn't an impulse. She had told herself that dozens of times during the past six months. It was both a practical and an advantageous step, not only for herself, but for Kevin, too. The adjustment shouldn't be too difficult, she thought as she glanced over to the window seat where her son was dozing. They had family in Bar Harbor, and Kevin had been beside himself with excitement ever since she'd told him she was considering moving near his uncle and his half brother and sister. And cousins, she thought. Four new babies had been born since she and Kevin had first flown to Maine, to attend her brother's wedding to Amanda Calhoun.

She watched him sleep, her little boy. Not so little anymore, she realized. He was nearly nine. It would be good for him to be a part of a big family. The Calhouns were generous, God knew, with their affection.

She would never forget how Suzanna Calhoun Dumont, now Bradford, had welcomed her the year before. Even knowing that Megan had been Suzanna's husband's lover just prior to Suzanna's marriage, had borne Baxter Dumont a child, Suzanna had been warm and open.

Of course, Megan was a poor example of the classic other woman. She hadn't known Suzanna even existed when she fell for Baxter. She'd been only seventeen, naive, and ready to believe all the promises and the vows of undying love. No, she hadn't known Bax was engaged to Suzanna Calhoun.

When she'd given birth to Baxter's child, he'd been on his honeymoon. He had never seen or acknowledged the son Megan O'Riley had borne him.

Years later, when fate tossed Megan's brother, Sloan, and Suzanna's sister Amanda together, the story had come out.

Now, through the twists and turns of fate, Megan and her son would live in the house where Suzanna and her sisters had grown up. Kevin would have family—a half brother and sister, cousins, and a houseful of aunts and uncles. And what a house.

The Towers, Megan mused. The glorious old stone structure Kevin still called a castle. She wondered what it would be like to live there, to work there. Now that the renovations on The Towers Retreat were completed, a large portion of the house served as a hotel. A St. James hotel, she added thoughtfully, the brainstorm of Trenton St. James III, who had married the youngest Calhoun, Catherine.

St. James hotels were known worldwide for their quality and class. The offer to join the company as head accountant had, after much weighing and measuring, simply been too good to resist.

And she was dying to see her brother, Sloan, the rest of the family, The Towers itself.

If she was nervous, she told herself it was foolish to be. The move was a very practical, very logical step. Her new title, accounts manager, soothed frustrated ambitions, and though money had never been a problem, her new salary didn't hurt the ego, either.

And most important of all, she would have more time to spend with Kevin.

As the approach for landing was announced, Megan reached over, brushed a hand through Kevin's hair. His eyes, dark and sleepy, blinked open.

"Are we there yet?"

"Just about. Put your seat back up. Look, you can see the bay."

"We're going to go boating, right?" If he'd been fully awake, he might have remembered he was too old to bounce on his seat. But he bounced now, his face pressed to the window in his excitement. "And see whales. We'll go on Alex's new dad's boat."

The idea of boating made her stomach turn, but she smiled gamely. "You bet we will."

"And we're really going to live in that castle?" He turned back to her, her beautiful boy with his golden skin and tousled black hair.

"You'll have Alex's old room."

"And there's ghosts." He grinned, showing gaps where baby teeth had been.

"So they say. Friendly ones."

"Maybe not all of them." At least Kevin hoped not. "Alex says there's lots of them, and sometimes they moan and scream. And last year a man fell right out of the tower window and broke all his bones on the rocks."

She shuddered, knowing that part was sterling truth. The Calhoun emeralds, discovered a year before, had drawn out more than a legend and romance. They'd drawn out a thief and a murderer.

"That's over with now, Kevin. The Towers is safe."

"Yeah." But he was a boy, after all, and hoped for at least a little danger.

There was another boy who was already plotting adventures. It felt as though he'd been waiting forever at the airport gate for his brother to arrive. Alex had one hand in his mother's, the other in Jenny's—because, as his mother had told him, he was the oldest and had to keep his sister close.

His mother was holding the baby, his brand-new brother. Alex could hardly wait to show him off.

"Why aren't they here yet?"

"Because it takes time for people to get off the plane and out the gate."

"How come it's called a gate?" Jenny wanted to know. "It doesn't look like a gate."

"I think they used to have gates, so they still call them that." It was the best Suzanna could come up with after a frazzling half hour at the airport with three children in tow.

Then the baby cooed and made her smile.

"Look, Mom! There they are!"

Before Suzanna could respond, Alex had broken away and made a beeline toward Kevin, Jenny hot on his heels. She winced as they barely missed plowing into other passengers, then raised a resigned hand to wave at Megan.

"Hi!" Alex, having been schooled in airport procedure by his mother, manfully took Kevin's carry-on. "I'm supposed to take this 'cause we're picking you up." It bothered him a little that, even though his mother claimed he was growing like a weed, Kevin was still taller.

"Have you still got the fort?"

"We got the one at the big house," Alex told him. "*And* we got a new one at the cottage. We live at the cottage."

"With our dad," Jenny piped up. "We got new names and everything. He can fix anything, and he built me a new bedroom."

"It has pink curtains," Alex said with a sneer.

Knowing a brawl was dangerously close, Suzanna neatly stepped between her two children. "How was your flight?" She bent down, kissed Kevin, then straightened to kiss Megan.

"It was fine, thanks." Megan still didn't know quite how to respond to Suzanna's easy affection. There were still times she wanted to shout, *I slept with your husband. Don't you understand? Maybe he wasn't your husband yet, and I didn't know he would be, but facts are facts.* "A little delayed," she said instead. "I hope you haven't been waiting long."

"Hours," Alex claimed.

"Thirty minutes," Suzanna corrected with a laugh. "How about the rest of your stuff?"

"I had it shipped. This is it for now." Megan tapped her garment bag. Unable to resist, she peeked down at the bright-eyed baby in Suzanna's arms. He was all pink and smooth, with the dark blue eyes of a newborn and a shock of glossy black hair. She felt the foolish smile that comes over adults around babies spread over her face as he waved an impossibly small fist under her nose.

"Oh, he's beautiful. So tiny."

"He's three weeks old," Alex said importantly. "His name is Christian."

"'Cause that was our great-grandfather's name," Jenny supplied. "We have new cousins, too. Bianca and Cordelia—but we call her Delia—and Ethan."

Alex rolled his eyes. "Everybody had babies."

"He's nice," Kevin decided after a long look. "Is he my brother, too?"

"Absolutely," Suzanna said, before Megan could respond. "I'm afraid you've got an awfully big family now."

Kevin gave her a shy look and touched a testing finger to Christian's waving fist. "I don't mind."

Suzanna smiled over at Megan. "Want to trade?"

Megan hesitated a moment, then gave in. "I'd love to." She cradled the baby while Suzanna took the garment bag. "Oh, Lord." Unable to resist, she nuzzled. "It's easy to forget how tiny they are. How wonderful they smell. And you..." As they walked through the terminal, she took a good look at Suzanna. "How can you look so terrific, when you had a baby only three weeks ago?"

"Oh, bless you. I've been feeling like such a frump. Alex, no running."

"Same goes, Kevin. How's Sloan taking to fatherhood?" Megan wanted to know. "I hated not coming out when Mandy had the baby, but with selling the house and getting things in order to make the move, I just couldn't manage it."

"Everyone understood. And Sloan's a terrific daddy. He'd have Delia strapped on his back twenty-four hours a day if Amanda let him. He designed this incredible nursery for the babies. Window seats, cubbyholes, wonderful built-in cupboards for toys. Delia and Bianca share it, and when C.C. and Trent are in town—which, since The Retreat opened, is more often than not— Ethan's in there, too."

"It's wonderful that they'll all grow up together." She looked at Kevin, Alex and Jenny, thinking as much about them as about the babies.

Suzanna understood perfectly. "Yes, it is. I'm so glad you're here, Megan. It's like getting another sister." She watched Megan's lashes lower. Not quite ready for that, Suzanna surmised, and switched subjects. "And it's going to be a huge relief to hand over the books to you. Not only for The Retreat, but for the boat business, too."

"I'm looking forward to it."

Suzanna stopped by a new minivan, unlocked the doors. "Pile in," she told the kids, then slipped the baby out of Megan's arms. "I hope you say that after you get a look at the ledgers." Competently she strapped the baby into his car seat. "I'm afraid Holt's a pathetic record keeper. And Nathaniel…"

"Oh, that's right. Holt has a partner now. What did Sloan tell me? An old friend?"

"Holt and Nathaniel grew up together on the island. Nathaniel moved back a few months ago. He used to be in the merchant marine. There you go, sweetie." She kissed the baby, then shot an eagle eye over the rest of the children to make sure seat belts were securely buckled. She clicked the sliding door into place, then rounded the hood as Megan took the passenger seat. "He's quite a character," Suzanna said mildly. "You'll get a kick out of him."

The character was just finishing up an enormous lunch of fried chicken, potato salad and lemon meringue pie. With a sigh of satisfaction, he pushed back from the table and eyed his hostess lustfully.

"What do I have to do to get you to marry me, darling?"

She giggled, blushed and waved a hand at him. "You're such a tease, Nate."

"Who's teasing?" He rose, grabbed her fluttering hand and kissed it lavishly. She always smelled like a woman—soft, lush, glorious. He winked and skimmed his lips up to nibble on her wrist. "You know I'm crazy about you, Coco."

Cordelia Calhoun McPike gave another delighted giggle, then patted his cheek. "About my cooking."

"That, too." He grinned when she slipped away to pour him coffee. She was a hell of a woman, he thought. Tall, stately, striking. It amazed him that some smart man hadn't scooped up the widow McPike long ago. "Who do I have to fight off this week?"

"Now that The Retreat's open, I don't have time for romance." She might have sighed over it if she wasn't so pleased with her life. All her darling girls were married and happy, with babies of their own. She had grandnieces and grandnephews to spoil, nephews-in-law to coddle, and, most surprising of all, a full-fledged career as head chef for the St. James Towers Retreat. She offered Nathaniel the coffee and, because she caught him eyeing the pie, cut him another slice.

"You read my mind."

Now she did sigh a little. There was nothing quite so comforting to Coco as watching a man enjoy her food. And he was some man. When Nathaniel Fury rolled back into town, people had noticed. Who could overlook tall, dark and handsome? Certainly not Coco McPike. Particularly not when the combination came with smoky gray eyes, a cleft chin and wonderfully golden skin over sharp cheekbones—not to mention considerable charm.

The black T-shirt and jeans he wore accented an athletic, rangy body—broad shoulders, muscular arms, narrow hips.

Then there was that aura of mystery, a touch of the exotic. It went deeper than his looks, though the dark eyes and the waving mane of deep mahogany hair was exotic enough. It was a matter of presence, she supposed, the culmination of what he'd done and what had touched him in all those years he traveled to foreign ports.

If she'd been twenty years younger... Well, she thought, patting her rich chestnut hair, maybe ten.

But she wasn't, so she had given Nathaniel the place in her heart of the son she'd never had. She was determined to find the right woman for him and see him settled happily. Like her beautiful girls.

Since she felt she had personally arranged the romances and resulting unions of all four of her nieces, she was confident she could do the same for Nathaniel.

"I did your chart last night," she said casually, and checked the fish stew she had simmering for tonight's menu.

"Oh, yeah?" He scooped up more pie. God, the woman could cook.

"You're entering a new phase of your life, Nate."

He'd seen too much of the world to totally dismiss astrology—or anything else. So he smiled at her. "I'd say you're on target there, Coco. Got myself a business, a house on land, retired my seabag."

"No, this phase is more personal." She wiggled her slim brows. "It has to do with Venus."

He grinned at that. "So, are you going to marry me?"

She wagged a finger at him. "You're going to say that to someone, quite seriously, before the summer's over. Actually, I saw you falling in love twice. I'm not quite sure what that means." Her forehead wrinkled as she considered. "It didn't really seem as if you'd have to choose, though there was quite a bit of interference. Perhaps even danger."

"If a guy falls for two women, he's asking for trouble." And Nathaniel was content, at least for the moment, to have no females in his life. Women simply didn't come without expectations, and he planned to fulfill none but his own. "And since my heart already belongs to you…" He got up to go to the stove and kiss her cheek.

The tornado blew in without warning. The kitchen door slammed open, and three shrieking whirlwinds spun through.

"Aunt Coco! They're here!"

"Oh, my." Coco pressed a hand to her speeding heart. "Alex, you took a year off my life." But she smiled, studying the dark-eyed boy beside him. "Can this be Kevin? You've grown a foot! Don't you have a kiss for Aunt Coco?"

"Yes, ma'am." He went forward dutifully, still unsure of his ground. He was enveloped against soft breasts, in soft scents. It eased his somewhat nervous stomach.

"We're so glad you're here." Coco's eyes teared up sentimentally. "Now the whole family's in one place. Kevin, this is Mr. Fury. Nate, my grandnephew."

Nathaniel knew the story, how the scum Baxter Dumont had managed to get some naive kid pregnant shortly before he married Suzanna. The boy was eyeing him now, nervous but contained. Nathaniel realized Kevin knew the story, as well—or part of it.

"Welcome to Bar Harbor." He offered his hand, which Kevin took politely.

"Nate runs the boat shop and stuff with my dad." The novelty of saying "my dad" had yet to wear thin with Alex. "Kevin wants to see whales," he told Nathaniel. "He comes from Oklahoma, and they don't have any. They hardly have any water at all."

"We've got some." Kevin automatically defended his homeland. "And we've got cowboys," he added, one-upping Alex. "You don't have any of those."

"Uh-huh." This from Jenny. "I got a whole cowboy suit."

"Girl," Alex corrected. "It's a cowgirl, 'cause you're a girl."

"It is not."

"Is too."

Her eyes narrowed dangerously. "Is not."

"Well, I see everything's normal in here." Suzanna entered, aiming a warning look at both of her children. "Hello, Nate. I didn't expect to see you here."

"I got lucky." He slipped an arm around Coco's shoulders. "Spent an hour with my woman."

"Flirting with Aunt Coco again?" But Suzanna noted that his gaze had already shifted. She remembered that look from the first time they'd met. The way the gray

eyes measured, assessed. Automatically she put a hand
on Megan's arm. "Megan O'Riley, Nathaniel Fury,
Holt's partner—and Aunt Coco's latest conquest."

"Nice to meet you." She was tired, Megan realized.
Had to be, if that clear, steady gaze put her back up.
She dismissed him, a little too abruptly for politeness,
and smiled at Coco. "You look wonderful."

"Oh, and here I am in my apron. I didn't even freshen
up." Coco gave her a hard, welcoming hug. "Let me fix
you something. You must be worn-out after the flight."

"Just a little."

"We took the bags up, and I put Christian in the
nursery." While Suzanna herded the children to the
table and chatted, Nathaniel took a good long survey
of Megan O'Riley.

Cool as an Atlantic breeze, he decided. A little frazzled and unnerved at the moment, he thought, but not
willing to show it. The peach-toned skin and long, waving strawberry blond hair made an eye-catching combination.

Nathaniel usually preferred women who were dark
and sultry, but there was something to be said for all
that rose and gold. She had blue eyes, the color of a
calm sea at dawn. Stubborn mouth, he mused, though
it softened nicely when she smiled at her son.

A bit on the skinny side, he thought as he finished off
his coffee. Needed some of Coco's cooking to help her
fill out. Or maybe she just looked skinny—and prim—
because she wore such a severely tailored jacket and
slacks.

Well aware of his scrutiny, Megan forced herself
to keep up her end of the conversation with Coco and
the rest. She'd grown used to stares years before, when

she was young, unmarried, and pregnant by another woman's husband.

She knew how some men reacted to her status as a single mother, how they assumed she was an easy mark. And she knew how to disabuse them of the notion.

She met Nathaniel's stare levelly, frostily. He didn't look away, as most would, but continued to watch her, unblinkingly, until her teeth clenched.

Good going, he thought. She might be skinny, but she had grit. He grinned, lifted his coffee mug in a silent toast, then turned to Coco. "I've got to go, got a tour to do. Thanks for lunch, Coco."

"Don't forget dinner. The whole family will be here. Eight o'clock."

He glanced back at Megan. "Wouldn't miss it."

"See that you don't." Coco looked at her watch, closed her eyes. "Where is that man? He's late again."

"The Dutchman?"

"Who else? I sent him to the butcher's two hours ago."

Nathaniel shrugged. His former shipmate, and The Towers' new assistant chef, ran on his own timetable. "If I see him down at the docks, I'll send him along."

"Kiss me goodbye," Jenny demanded, delighted when Nathaniel hauled her up.

"You're the prettiest cowboy on the island," he whispered in her ear. Jenny shot a smug look at her brother when her feet touched the floor again. "You let me know when you're ready for a sail," he said to Kevin. "Nice meeting you, Ms. O'Riley."

"Nate's a sailor," Jenny said importantly when Nathaniel strolled out. "He's been everywhere and done everything."

Megan didn't doubt it for a minute.

* * *

So much had changed at The Towers, though the family rooms on the first two floors and the east wing were much the same. Trent St. James, with Megan's brother, Sloan, as architect, had concentrated most of the time and effort on the ten suites in the west wing, the new guest dining area and the west tower. All of that area comprised the hotel.

From the quick tour Megan was given, she could see that none of the time and effort that had gone into the construction and renovations had been wasted.

Sloan had designed with an appreciation for the original fortresslike structure, retaining the high-ceilinged rooms and circular stairs, ensuring that the many fireplaces were working, preserving the mullioned windows and French doors that led out onto terraces, balconies, parapets.

The lobby was sumptuous, filled with antiques and designed with a multitude of cozy corners that invited guests to lounge on a rainy or wintry day. The spectacular views of bay or cliffs or sea or Suzanna's fabulous gardens were there to be enjoyed, or tempted guests to stroll out onto terraces and balconies.

When Amanda, as hotel manager, took over the tour, Megan was told that each suite was unique. The storage rooms of The Towers had been full of old furniture, mementos and art. What hadn't been sold prior to Trent's having invested the St. James money in the transformation now graced the guest rooms.

Some suites were two levels, with an art deco staircase connecting the rooms, some had wainscoting or silk wallpaper. There was an Aubusson rug here, an old tapestry there. And all the rooms were infused with the legend of the Calhoun emeralds and the woman who had owned them.

The emeralds themselves, discovered after a difficult and dangerous search—some said with the help of the spirits of Bianca Calhoun and Christian Bradford, the artist who had loved her—resided now in a glass case in the lobby. Above the case was a portrait of Bianca, painted by Christian more than eighty years before.

"They're gorgeous," Megan whispered. "Stunning." The tiers of grass green emeralds and white diamonds almost pulsed with life.

"Sometimes I'll just stop and look at them," Amanda admitted, "and remember all we went through to find them. How Bianca tried to use them to escape with her children to Christian. It should make me sad, I suppose, but having them here, under her portrait, seems right."

"Yes, it does." Megan could feel the pull of them, even through the glass. "But isn't it risky, having them out here this way?"

"Holt arranged for security. Having an ex-cop in the family means nothing's left to chance. The glass is bulletproof." Amanda tapped her finger against it. "And wired to some high-tech sensor." Amanda checked her watch and judged that she had fifteen minutes before she had to resume her managerial duties. "I hope your rooms are all right. We've barely scratched the surface on the family renovations."

"They're fine." And the truth was, it relaxed Megan a bit to see cracked plaster and gnawed woodwork. It made it all less intimidating. "Kevin's in paradise. He's outside with Alex and Jenny, playing with the new puppy."

"Our Fred and Holt's Sadie are quite the proud parents." With a laugh, Amanda tossed back her swing of sable hair. "Eight pups."

"As Alex said, everyone's having babies. And your Delia is beautiful."

"She is, isn't she?" Maternal pride glowed in Amanda's eyes. "I can't believe how much she's grown already. You should have been around here six months ago. All four of us out to here." She laughed again as she held out her arms. "Waddling everywhere. The men strutting. Do you know they took bets to see if Lilah or I would deliver first? She beat me by two days." And since she'd bet twenty on herself, it still irritated her a little. "It's the first time I've known her to be in a hurry about anything."

"Her Bianca's beautiful, too. She was awake and howling for attention when I was in the nursery. Your nanny has her hands full."

"Mrs. Billows can handle anything."

"Actually, I wasn't thinking about the babies. It was Max." She grinned remembering how Bianca's daddy had come running in, abandoning his new novel on the typewriter to scoop his daughter out of her crib.

"He's such a softie."

"Who's a softie?" Sloan strode into the room to swing his sister off her feet.

"Not you, O'Riley," Amanda murmured, watching the way his face softened like butter as he pressed his cheek to Megan's.

"You're here." He twirled her again. "I'm so glad you're here, Meg."

"Me too." She felt her eyes tear and squeezed him tight. "Daddy."

With a laugh, he set her down, slipped his free arm around his wife. "Did you see her yet?"

Megan feigned ignorance. "Who?"

"My girl. My Delia."

"Oh, her." Megan shrugged, chuckled, then kissed Sloan on his sulking mouth. "Not only did I see her, I held her, I sniffed her, and have already decided to spoil her at every opportunity. She's gorgeous, Sloan. She looks just like Amanda."

"Yeah, she does." He kissed his wife. "Except she's got my chin."

"That's a Calhoun chin," Amanda claimed.

"Nope, it's O'Riley all the way. And speaking of O'Rileys," he continued, before Amanda could argue, "where's Kevin?"

"Outside. I should probably go get him. We haven't even unpacked yet."

"We'll go with you," Sloan said.

"You go. I'm covering." Even as Amanda spoke, the phone on the mahogany front desk rang. "Break's over. See you at dinner, Megan." She leaned up to kiss Sloan again. "See you sooner, O'Riley."

"Mmm…" Sloan gave a satisfied sigh as he watched his wife stride off. "I do love the way that woman eats up the floor."

"You look at her just the way you did a year ago, at your wedding." Megan tucked her hand in his as they walked out of the lobby and onto the stone terrace steps. "It's nice."

"She's…" He searched for a word, then settled on the simplest truth. "Everything. I'd like you to be as happy as I am, Megan."

"I am happy." A breeze flitted through her hair. On it carried the sound of children's laughter. "Hearing that makes me happy. So does being here." They descended another level and turned west. "I have to admit I'm a little nervous. It's such a big step." She saw her son scramble to the top of the fort in the yard below, arms raised high in victory. "This is good for him."

"And you?"

"And me." She leaned against her brother. "I'll miss Mom and Dad, but they've already said that with both of us out here, it gives them twice as much reason to visit twice as often." She pushed the blowing hair from her face while Kevin played sniper, fighting off Alex and Jenny's assault on the fort. "He needs to know the rest of his family. And I…needed a change. And as to that—" she looked back at Sloan "—I tried to get Amanda to show me the setup."

"And she told you that you couldn't sharpen your pencils for a week."

"Something like that."

"We decided at the last family meeting that you'd have a week to settle in before you started hammering the adding machine."

"I don't need a week. I only need—"

"I know, I know. You'd give Amanda a run for the efficiency crown. But orders are you take a week off."

She arched a brow. "And just who gives the orders around here?"

"Everybody." Sloan grinned. "That's what makes it interesting."

Thoughtful, she looked out to sea. The sky was as clear as blown glass, and the breeze warm with early summer. From her perch at the wall, she could see the small clumps of islands far out in the diamond-bright water.

A different world, she thought, from the plains and prairies of home. A different life, perhaps, for her and her son.

A week. To relax, to explore, to take excursions with Kevin. Tempting, yes. But far from responsible. "I want to pull my weight."

"You will, believe me." He glanced out at the clear sound of a boat horn. "That's one of Holt and Nate's," Sloan told her, pointing to the long terraced boat that was gliding across the water. "The *Mariner*. Takes tourists out for whale-watching."

The kids were all atop the fort now, shouting and waving at the boat. When the horn blasted again, they cheered.

"You'll meet Nate at dinner," Sloan began.

"I met him already."

"Flirting a meal out of Coco?"

"It appeared that way."

Sloan shook his head. "That man can eat, let me tell you. What did you think?"

"Not much," she muttered. "He seemed a little rough-edged to me."

"You get used to him. He's one of the family now."

Megan made a noncommittal sound. Maybe he was, but that didn't mean he was part of hers.

Chapter 2

As far as Coco was concerned, Niels Van Horne was a thoroughly unpleasant man. He did not take constructive criticism, or the subtlest of suggestions for improvement, well at all. She tried to be courteous, God knew, as he was a member of the staff of The Towers and an old, dear friend of Nathaniel's.

But the man was a thorn in her side, an abrasive grain of sand in the cozy slipper of her contentment.

In the first place, he was simply too big. The hotel kitchen was gloriously streamlined and organized. She and Sloan had worked in tandem on the design, so that the finished product would suit her specifications and needs. She adored her huge stove, her convection and conventional ovens, the glint of polished stainless steel and glossy white counters, and her whisper-silent dishwasher. She loved the smells of cooking, the hum of her exhaust fans, the sparkling cleanliness of her tile floor.

And there was Van Horne—or Dutch, as he was

called—a bull in her china shop, with his redwood-size shoulders and cinder-block arms rippling with tattoos. He refused to wear the neat white bib aprons she'd ordered, with their elegant blue lettering, preferring his rolled-up shirts and tatty jeans held up by a hank of rope.

His salt-and-pepper hair was tied back in a stubby ponytail, and his face, usually scowling, was as big as the rest of him, scored with lines around his light green eyes. His nose, broken several times in the brawls he seemed so proud of, was mashed and crooked. His skin was brown, and leathery as an old saddle.

And his language... Well, Coco didn't consider herself a prude, but she was, after all, a lady.

But the man could cook. It was his only redeeming quality.

As Dutch worked at the stove, she supervised the two line chefs. The specials tonight were her New England fish stew and stuffed trout *à la française*. Everything appeared to be in order.

"Mr. Van Horne," she began, in a tone that never failed to put his back up. "You will be in charge while I'm downstairs. I don't foresee any problems, but should any arise, I'll be in the family dining room."

He cast one of his sneering looks over his shoulder. Woman was all slicked up tonight, like she was going to some opera or something, he thought. All red silk and pearls. He wanted to snort, but knew her damned perfume would interfere with the pleasure he gained from the smell of his curried rice.

"I cooked for three hundred men," he said in his raspy, sandpaper-edged voice. "I can deal with a couple dozen pasty-faced tourists."

"Our guests," she said between her teeth, "may be

slightly more discriminating than sailors trapped on some rusty boat."

One of the busboys swung through, carrying plates. Dutch's eyes zeroed in on one that still held half an entrée. On *his* ship, men had cleaned their plates. "Not too damn hungry, were they?"

"Mr. Van Horne." Coco drew air through her nose. "You will remain in the kitchen at all times. I will not have you going out into the dining room again and berating our guests over their eating habits. A bit more garnish on that salad, please," she said to one of the line chefs, and glided out the door.

"Can't stand fancy-faced broads," Dutch muttered. And if it wasn't for Nate, he thought sourly, Dutch Van Horne wouldn't be taking orders from a dame.

Nathaniel didn't share his former shipmate's disdain of women. He loved them, one and all. He enjoyed their looks, their smells, their voices, and was more than satisfied to settle in the family parlor with six of the best-looking women it had been his pleasure to meet.

The Calhoun women were a constant delight to him. Suzanna, with her soft eyes, Lilah's lazy sexuality, Amanda's brisk practicality, C.C.'s cocky grin, not to mention Coco's feminine elegance.

They made The Towers Nathaniel's little slice of heaven.

And the sixth woman… He sipped his whiskey and water as he watched Megan O'Riley. Now there was a package he thought might be full of surprises. In the looks department, she didn't take second place to the fabulous Calhouns. And her voice, with its slow Oklahoma drawl, added its own appeal. What she lacked, he mused, was the easy warmth that flowed from the other women.

He hadn't decided as yet whether it was the result of a cold nature or simple shyness. Whatever it was, it ran deep. It was hard to be cold or shy in a room filled with laughing people, cooing babies and wrestling children.

He was holding one of his favorite females at the moment. Jenny was bouncing on his lap and barraging him with questions.

"Are you going to marry Aunt Coco?"

"She won't have me."

"I will." Jenny beamed up at him, an apprentice heartbreaker with a missing front tooth. "We can get married in the garden, like Mom and Daddy did. Then you can come live with us."

"Now that's the best offer I've had in a long time." He stroked a callused finger down her cheek.

"But you have to wait until I get big."

"It's always wise to make a man wait." This from Lilah, who slouched on a sofa, her head in the crook of her husband's arm, a baby in her own. "Don't let him rush you into anything, Jenny. Slow is always best."

"She'd know," Amanda commented. "Lilah's spent her life studying slow."

"I'm not ready to give up my girl." Holt scooped Jenny up. "Especially to a broken-down sailor."

"I can outpilot you blindfolded, Bradford."

"Nuh-uh." Alex popped up to defend the family honor. "Daddy sails the best. He can sail better than anybody. Even if bad guys were shooting at him." Territorial, Alex wrapped an arm around Holt's leg. "He even got shot. He's got a bullet hole in him."

Holt grinned at his friend. "Get your own cheering gallery, Nate."

"Did you ever get shot?" Alex wanted to know.

"Can't say that I have." Nathaniel swirled his whiskey. "But there was this Greek in Corfu that wanted to slit my throat."

Alex's eyes widened until they were like saucers. From his spot on the rug, Kevin inched closer. "Really?" Alex looked for signs of knife wounds. He knew Nathaniel had a tattoo of a fire-breathing dragon on his shoulder, but this was even better. "Did you stab him back and kill him dead?"

"Nope." Nathaniel caught the look of doubt and disapproval in Megan's eyes. "He missed and caught me in the shoulder, and the Dutchman knocked him cold with a bottle of ouzo."

Desperately impressed, Kevin slid closer. "Have you got a scar?"

"Sure do."

Amanda slapped Nathaniel's hand before he could tug up his shirt. "Cut it out, or every man in the room will be stripping to show off war wounds. Sloan's really proud of the one he got from barbed wire."

"It's a beaut," Sloan agreed. "But Meg's is even better."

"Shut up, Sloan."

"Hey, a man's gotta brag on his only sister." Enjoying himself, Sloan draped an arm around her shoulders. "She was twelve—hardheaded little brat. We had a mustang stallion nearly as bad-tempered as she was. She snuck him out one day, determined that she could break him. Well, she got about a half a mile before he shook her off."

"He did not shake me off," Megan said primly. "The bridle snapped."

"That's her story." Sloan gave her a quick squeeze. "Fact is, that horse tossed her right into a barbed-wire fence. She landed on her rump. I don't believe you sat down for six weeks."

"It was two," she said, but her lips twitched.

"Got herself a hell of a scar." Sloan gave her butt a brotherly pat.

"Wouldn't mind taking a look at it," Nathaniel said under his breath, and earned an arched-eyebrow look from Suzanna.

"I think I'll put Christian down before dinner."

"Good idea." C.C. took Ethan from Trent just as the baby began to fuss. "Somebody's hungry."

"I know I am." Lilah rose.

Megan watched mothers and babies head upstairs to nurse, and was surprised by a quick tug of envy. Funny, she mused, she hadn't even thought of having more babies until she came here and found herself surrounded by them.

"So sorry I'm late." Coco glided into the room, patting her hair. "We had a few problems in the kitchen."

Nathaniel recognized the look of frustration on her face and fought back a grin. "Dutch giving you trouble, darling?"

"Well…" She didn't like to complain. "We simply have different views on how things should be done. Oh, bless you, Trent," she said when he offered her a glass. "Oh, dear, where is my head? I forgot the canapés."

"I'll get them." Max unfolded himself from the sofa and headed toward the family kitchen.

"Thank you, dear. Now…" She took Megan's hand, squeezed. "We've hardly had a moment to talk. What do you think of The Retreat?"

"It's wonderful, everything Sloan said it would be. Amanda tells me all ten suites are booked."

"It's been a wonderful first season." She beamed at

Trent. "Hardly more than a year ago, I was in despair, so afraid my girls would lose their home. Though the cards told me differently. Did I ever tell you that I foresaw Trent in the tarot? I really must do a spread for you, dear, and see what your future holds."

"Well…"

"Perhaps I can just look at your palm."

Megan let go with a sigh of relief when Max came back with a tray and distracted Coco.

"Not interested in the future?" Nathaniel murmured.

Megan glanced over, surprised that he had moved beside her without her being aware of it. "I'm more interested in the present, one step at a time."

"A cynic." He took her hand and, though it went rigid in his, turned it palm up. "I met an old woman on the west coast of Ireland. Molly Duggin was her name. She said I had the sight." His smoky eyes stayed level with hers for a long moment before they shifted to her open palm. Megan felt something skitter down her spine. "A stubborn hand. Self-sufficient, for all its elegance."

He traced a finger over it. Now there was more than a skitter. There was a jolt.

"I don't believe in palmistry."

"You don't have to. Shy," he said quietly. "I wondered about that. The passions are there, but repressed." His thumb glided gently over her palm's mound of Venus. "Or channeled. You'd prefer to say channeled. Goal-oriented, practical. You'd rather make decisions with your head, no matter what your heart tells you." His eyes lifted to hers again. "How close am I?"

Much too close, she thought, but drew her hand coolly from his. "An interesting parlor game, Mr. Fury."

His eyes laughed at her as he tucked his thumbs in his pockets. "Isn't it?"

* * *

By noon the next day, Megan had run out of busy-work. She hadn't the heart to refuse Kevin's plea to be allowed to spend the day with the Bradfords, though his departure had left her very much to her own devices.

She simply wasn't used to free time.

One trip to the hotel lobby had aborted her idea of convincing Amanda to let her study the books and files. Amanda, she was told by a cheerful desk clerk, was in the west tower, handling a small problem.

Coco wasn't an option, either. Megan had halted just outside the door of the kitchen when she heard the crash of pots and raised voices inside.

Since Lilah had gone back to work as a naturalist in the park, and C.C. was at her automotive shop in town, Megan was left on her own.

In a house as enormous as The Towers, she felt like the last living soul on the island.

She could read, she mused, or sit in the sun on one of the terraces and contemplate the view. She could wander down to the first floor of the family area and check out the progress of the renovations. And harass Sloan and Trent, she thought with a sigh, as they tried to get some work done.

She didn't consider disturbing Max in his studio, knowing he was working on his book. As she'd already spent an hour in the nursery playing with the babies, she felt another visit was out.

She wandered her room, smoothed down the already smooth coverlet on the marvelous four-poster. The rest of her things had arrived that morning, and in her per-haps too-efficient way, she'd already unpacked. Her clothes were neatly hung in the rosewood armoire or folded in the Chippendale bureau. Framed photos of her family smiled from the gateleg table under the window.

Her shoes were aligned, her jewelry was tucked away and her books were stored on the shelf.

And if she didn't find something to do, she would go mad.

With this in mind, she picked up her briefcase, checked the contents one last time and headed outside, to the car Sloan had left at her disposal.

The sedan ran like a top, courtesy of C.C.'s mechanical skills. Megan drove down the winding road toward the village.

She enjoyed the bright blue water of the bay, and the colorful throngs of tourists strolling up and down the sloped streets. But the glistening wares in the shop windows didn't tempt her to stop and do any strolling of her own.

Shopping was something she did out of necessity, not for pleasure.

Once, long ago, she'd loved the idle pleasure of window-shopping, the careless satisfaction of buying for fun. She'd enjoyed empty, endless summer days once, with nothing more to do than watch clouds or listen to the wind.

But that was before innocence had been lost, and responsibilities found.

She saw the sign for Shipshape Tours by the docks. There were a couple of small boats in drydock, but the *Mariner* and its sister ship, the *Island Queen*, were nowhere to be seen.

Her brows knit in annoyance. She'd hoped to catch Holt before he took one of the tours out. Still, there was no reason she couldn't poke inside the little tin-roofed building that housed the offices. After all, Shipshape was now one of her clients.

Megan pulled the sedan behind a long, long T-Bird convertible. She had to admire the lines of the car, and the glossy black paint job that highlighted the white interior.

She paused a moment, shielding her eyes as she watched a two-masted schooner glide over the water, its rust-colored sails full, its decks dotted with people.

There was no denying the beauty of the spot, though the smell and look of the water was so foreign, compared to what she'd known most of her life. The midday breeze was fresh and carried the scent of the sea and the aromas of lunch from the restaurants nearby.

She could be happy here, she told herself. No, she *would* be happy here. Resolutely she turned toward the building and rapped on the door.

"Yeah. It's open."

There was Nathaniel, his feet propped on a messy and ancient metal desk, a phone at his ear. His jeans were torn at the knee and smeared with something like motor oil. His mane of dark mahogany hair was tousled by the wind, or his hands. He crooked his finger in a come-ahead gesture, his eyes measuring her as he spoke on the phone.

"Teak's your best bet. I've got enough in stock, and can have the deck finished in two days. No, the engine just needed an overhaul. It's got a lot of life left in it. No problem." He picked up a smoldering cigar. "I'll give you a call when we're finished."

He hung up the phone, clamped the cigar between his teeth. Funny, he thought, Megan O'Riley had floated into his brain that morning, looking very much as she did at this moment. All spit and polish, that pretty rose-gold hair all tucked up, her face calm and cool.

"Just in the neighborhood?" he asked.

"I was looking for Holt."

"He's out with the *Queen*." Idly Nathaniel checked the diver's watch on his wrist. "Won't be back for about an hour and a half." His cocky mouth quirked up. "Looks like you're stuck with me."

She fought back the urge to shift her briefcase from hand to hand, to back away. "I'd like to see the books."

Nathaniel took a lazy puff on his cigar. "Thought you were on vacation."

She fell back on her best defense. Disdain. "Is there a problem with the books?" she said frostily.

"Couldn't prove it by me." In a fluid move, he reached down and opened a drawer in the desk. He took out a black-bound ledger. "You're the expert." He held it out to her. "Pull up a chair, Meg."

"Thank you." She took a folding chair on the other side of the desk, then slipped dark-framed reading glasses from her briefcase. Once they were on, she opened the ledger. Her accountant's heart contracted in horror at the mess of figures, cramped margin notes and scribbled-on Post-its. "These are your books?"

"Yeah." She looked prim and efficient in her practical glasses and scooped-up hair. She made his mouth water. "Holt and I sort of take turns with them—that's since Suzanna tossed up her hands and called us idiots." He smiled charmingly. "We figured, you know, with her being pregnant at the time, she didn't need any more stress."

"Hmmm…" Megan was already turning pages. For her, the state of the bookkeeping didn't bring on anxiety so much as a sense of challenge. "Your files?"

"We got 'em." Nathaniel jerked a thumb at the dented metal cabinet shoved in the corner. There was a small, greasy boat motor on top of it.

"Is there anything in them?" she said pleasantly.

"Last I looked there was." He couldn't help it. The more prim and efficient her voice, the more he wanted to razz her.

"Invoices?"

"Sure."

"Expense receipts?"

"Absolutely." He reached in another drawer and took out a large cigar box. "We got plenty of receipts."

She took the box, opened the lid and sighed. "This is how you run your business?"

"No. We run the business by taking people out to sea, or repairing their boats. Even building them." He leaned forward on the desk, mostly so he could catch a better whiff of that soft, elusive scent that clung to her skin. "Me, I've never been much on paperwork, and Holt had his fill of it when he was on the force." His smile spread. He didn't figure she wore prim glasses, pulled-back hair and buttoned-up blouses so that a man would yearn to toss aside, muss up and unbutton. But the result was the same. "Maybe that's why the accountant we hired to do the taxes this year developed this little tic." He tapped a finger beside his left eye. "I heard he moved to Jamaica to sell straw baskets."

She had to laugh. "I'm made of sterner stuff, I promise you."

"Never doubted it." He leaned back again, his swivel chair squeaking. "You've got a nice smile, Megan. When you use it."

She knew that tone, lightly flirtatious, unmistakably

male. Her defenses locked down like a vault. "You're not paying me for my smile."

"I'd rather it came free, anyhow. How'd you come to be an accountant?"

"I'm good with numbers." She spread the ledger on the desk before opening her briefcase and taking out a calculator.

"So's a bookie. I mean, why'd you pick it?"

"Because it's a solid, dependable career." She began to run numbers, hoping to ignore him.

"And because numbers only add up one way?"

She couldn't ignore that—the faint hint of amusement in his voice. She slanted him a look, adjusted her glasses. "Accounting may be logical, Mr. Fury, but logic doesn't eliminate surprises."

"If you say so. Listen, we may have both come through the side door into the Calhouns' extended family, but we're there. Don't you feel stupid calling me Mr. Fury?"

Her smile had all the warmth of an Atlantic gale. "No, I don't."

"Is it me, or all men, you're determined to beat off with icicles?"

Patience, which she'd convinced herself she held in great store, was rapidly being depleted. "I'm here to do the books. That's all I'm here for."

"Never had a client for a friend?" He took a last puff on the cigar and stubbed it out. "You know, there's a funny thing about me."

"I'm sure you're about to tell me what it is."

"Right. I can have a pleasant conversation with a woman without being tempted to toss her on the floor and tear her clothes off. Now, you're a real treat to look

at, Meg, but I can control my more primitive urges—
especially when all the signals say stop."

Now she felt ridiculous. She'd been rude, or nearly
so, since the moment she'd met him. Because, she admitted to herself, her reaction to him made her uncomfortable. But, damn it, he was the one who kept looking
at her as though he'd like to nibble away.

"I'm sorry." The apology was sincere, if a trifle stiff.
"I'm making a lot of adjustments right now, so I haven't
felt very congenial. And the way you look at me puts
me on edge."

"Fair enough. But I have to tell you I figure it's a
man's right to look. Anything more takes an invitation—of one kind or the other."

"Then we can clear the air and start over, since I can
tell you I won't be putting out the welcome mat. Now,
Nathaniel—" it was a concession she made with a smile
"—do you suppose you could dig up your tax returns?"

"I can probably put my hands on them." He scooted
back his chair. The squeak of the wheels ended on a
high-pitched yelp that had Megan jolting and scatter-
ing papers. "Damn it—forgot you were back there."
He picked up a wriggling, whimpering black puppy.
"He sleeps a lot, so I end up stepping on him or running the damn chair over his tail," he said to Megan as
the pup licked frantically at his face. "Whenever I try
to leave him home, he cries until I give in and bring
him with me."

"He's darling." Her fingers were already itching to
stroke. "He looks a lot like the one Coco has."

"Same litter." Because he could read the sentiment
in Megan's eyes perfectly, Nathaniel handed the pup
across the desk.

"Oh, aren't you sweet? Aren't you pretty?"

When she cooed to the dog, all defenses dropped, Nathaniel noted. She forgot to be businesslike and cool, and instead was all feminine warmth—those pretty hands stroking the pup's fur, her smile soft, her eyes alight with pleasure.

He had to remind himself the invitation was for a dog, not for him.

"What's his name?"

"Dog."

She looked up from the puppy's adoring eyes. "Dog? That's it?"

"He likes it. Hey, Dog." At the sound of his master's voice, Dog immediately cocked his head at Nathaniel and barked. "See?"

"Yes." She laughed and nuzzled. "It seems a bit unimaginative."

"On the contrary. How many dogs do you know named Dog?"

"I stand corrected. Down you go, and don't get any ideas about these receipts."

Nathaniel tossed a ball, and Dog gave joyful chase. "That'll keep him busy," he said as he came around the desk to help her gather up the scattered papers.

"You don't seem the puppy type to me."

"Always wanted one." He crouched down beside her and began to toss papers back into the cigar box. "Fact is, I used to play around with one of Dog's ancestors over at the Bradfords', when I was a kid. But it's hard to keep a dog aboard a ship. Got a bird, though."

"A bird?"

"A parrot I picked up in the Caribbean about five years ago. That's another reason I bring Dog along with me. Bird might eat him."

"Bird?" She glanced up, but the laugh froze in her

throat. Why was he always closer than she anticipated? And why did those long, searching looks of his slide along her nerve ends like stroking fingers?

His gaze dropped to her mouth. The hesitant smile was still there, he noted. There was something very appealing about that touch of shyness, all wrapped up in stiff-necked confidence. Her eyes weren't cool now, but wary. Not an invitation, he reminded himself, but close. And damn tempting.

Testing his ground, he reached out to tuck a stray curl behind her ear. She was on her feet like a woman shot out of a cannon.

"You sure spook easily, Megan." After closing the lid on the cigar box, he rose. "But I can't say it isn't rewarding to know I make you nervous."

"You don't." But she didn't look at him as she said it. She'd never been a good liar. "I'm going to take all this back with me, if you don't mind. Once I have things organized, I'll be in touch with you, or Holt."

"Fine." The phone rang. He ignored it. "You know where to find us."

"Once I have the books in order, we'll need to set up a proper filing system."

Grinning, he eased a hip onto the corner of the desk. Lord, she was something. "You're the boss, sugar."

She snapped her briefcase closed. "No, you're the boss. And don't call me 'sugar.'" She marched outside, slipped into her car and eased away from the building and back into traffic. Competently she drove through the village, toward The Towers. Once she'd reached the bottom of the long, curving road that led home, she pulled the car over and stopped.

She needed a moment, she thought, before she faced anyone. With her eyes closed, she rested her head against the back of the seat. Her insides were still jittering, dancing with butterflies that willpower alone couldn't seem to swat away.

The weakness infuriated her. Nathaniel Fury infuriated her. After all this time, she mused, all this effort, it had taken no more than a few measuring looks to remind her, all too strongly, that she was still a woman.

Worse, much worse, she was sure he knew exactly what he was doing and how it affected her.

She'd been susceptible to a handsome face and smooth words before. Unlike those who loved her, she refused to blame her youth and inexperience for her reckless actions. Once upon a time, she'd listened to her heart, had believed absolutely in happy-ever-after. But no longer. Now she knew there were no princes, no pumpkins, no castles in the air. There was only reality, one a woman had to make for herself—and sometimes had to make for her child, as well.

She didn't want her pulse to race or her muscles to tense. She didn't want to feel that hot little curl in her stomach that was a yearning hunger crying to be filled. Not now. Not ever again.

All she wanted was to be a good mother to Kevin, to provide him with a happy, loving home. To earn her own way through her own skills. She wanted so badly to be strong and smart and self-sufficient.

Letting out a long sigh, she smiled to herself. And invulnerable.

Well, she might not quite achieve that, but she would be sensible. Never again would she permit a man the power to alter her life—and certainly not because he'd made her glands stand at attention.

Calmer, more confident, she started the car. She had work to do.

Chapter 3

"Have a heart, Mandy." Megan had sought her sister-in-law out the moment she returned to The Towers. "I just want to get a feel for my office and the routine."

Cocking her head, Amanda leaned back from her own pile of paperwork. "Horrible when everyone's busy and you're not, isn't it?"

Megan let out a heartfelt sigh. A kindred spirit. "Awful."

"Sloan wants you to relax," Amanda began, then laughed when Megan rolled her eyes. "But what does he know? Come on." Ready to oblige, she pushed back from the desk, skirted it. "You're practically next door." She led the way down the corridor to another thick, ornately carved door. "I think you've got just about everything you'll need. But if we've missed something, let me know."

Some women felt that frisson of excitement and anticipation on entering a department store. For some, that sensory click might occur at the smell of fresh paint, or the glint of candlelight, or the fizz of champagne just opened.

For Megan, it was the sight of a well-ordered office that caused that quick shiver of pleasure.

And here was everything she could have wanted.

The desk was glorious, gleaming Queen Anne, with a spotless rose-toned blotter and ebony desk set already in place. A multilined phone and a streamlined computer sat waiting.

She nearly purred.

There were wooden filing cabinets still smelling of lemon oil, their brass handles shining in the sunlight that poured through the many-paned windows. The Oriental rug picked up the hues of rose and slate blue in the upholstered chairs and love seat. There were shelves for her accounting books and ledgers, and a hunt table that held a coffeemaker, fax and personal copier.

Old-world charm and modern technology blended into tasteful efficiency.

"Mandy, it's perfect."

"I'd hoped you'd like it." Fussing, Amanda straightened the blotter, shifted the stapler. "I can't say I'm sorry to be handing over the books. It's more than a full-time job. I've filed everything, invoices, expenses, credit-card receipts, accounts payable, et cetera, by department." She opened a file drawer to demonstrate.

Megan's organized heart swelled at the sight of neatly color-coded file folders. Alphabetized, categorized, cross-referenced.

Glorious.

"Wonderful. Not a cigar box in sight."

Amanda hesitated, and then threw back her head and laughed. "You've seen Holt and Nate's accounting system, I take it."

Amused, and comfortable with Amanda, Megan patted her briefcase. "I *have* their accounting system." Unable to resist, she sat in the high-backed swivel chair. "Now this is more like it." She took up a sharpened pencil, set it down again. "I don't know how to thank you for letting me join the team."

"Don't be silly. You're family. Besides, you may not be so grateful after a couple of weeks in chaos. I can't tell you how many interruptions—" Amanda broke off when she heard her name bellowed. Her brow lifted. "See what I mean?" She swung to the door to answer her husband's shout. "In here, O'Riley." She shook her head as Sloan and Trent trooped up to the door. Both of them were covered with dust. "I thought you were breaking down a wall or something."

"We were. Had some more old furniture to haul out of the way. And look what we found."

She examined what he held in his hands. "A moldy old book. That's wonderful, honey. Now why don't you and Trent go play construction?"

"Not just a book," Trent announced. "Fergus's account book. For the year of 1913."

"Oh." Amanda's heart gave one hard thud as she grabbed for the book.

Curiosity piqued, Megan rose to join them in the doorway. "Is it important?"

"It's the year Bianca died." Sloan laid a comforting hand on Amanda's shoulder. "You know the story, Meg. How Bianca was trapped in a loveless, abusive marriage. She met Christian Bradford, fell in love. She decided to take the children and leave Fergus, but he found out. They argued up in the tower. She fell through the window."

"And he destroyed everything that belonged to her."

Amanda's voice tightened, shook. "Everything—her clothes, her small treasures, her pictures. Everything but the emeralds. Because she'd hidden those. Now we have them, and the portrait Christian had painted. That's all we have of her." She let out a long breath. "I suppose it's fitting that we should have this of his. A ledger of profit and loss."

"Looks like he wrote in the margins here and there." Trent reached over to flip a page open. "Sort of an abbreviated journal."

Amanda frowned and read a portion of the cramped handwriting aloud.

"Too much waste in kitchen. Fired cook. B. too soft on staff. Purchased new cuff links. Diamond. Good choice for opera tonight. Showier than J. P. Getty's."

She let out a huff of breath. "It shows just what kind of man he was, doesn't it?"

"Darling, I wouldn't have brought it out if I'd known it would bother you."

Amanda shook her head. "No, the family will want it." But she set it down, because her fingers felt coated with more than dust and mold. "I was just showing Megan her new domain."

"So I see." Sloan's eyes narrowed. "What happened to relaxing?"

"This is how I relax," Megan responded. "Now why don't you go away and let me enjoy myself?"

"An excellent idea." Amanda gave her husband a kiss and a shove. "Scram." Even as she was hurrying the men along, Amanda's phone rang. "Give me a call if you need anything," she told Megan, and rushed to answer.

Feeling smug, Megan shut the door of her office. She was rubbing her hands together in anticipation as she crossed to her briefcase. She'd show Nathaniel Fury the true meaning of the word *shipshape*.

Three hours later, she was interrupted by the thunder of little feet. Obviously, she thought even before her door crashed open, someone had given Kevin the directions to her office.

"Hi, Mom!" He rushed into her arms for a kiss, and all thoughts of balancing accounts vanished from her mind. "We had the best time. We played with Sadie and Fred and had a war in the new fort. We got to go to Suzanna's flower place and water millions of plants."

Megan glanced down at Kevin's soggy sneakers. "And yourselves, I see."

He grinned. "We had a water battle, and I won."

"My hero."

"We had pizza for lunch, and Carolanne—she works for Suzanna—said I was a bottomless pit. And tomorrow Suzanna has to landscape, so we can't go with her, but we can go out on the whale boat if you want. You want to, don't you? I told Alex and Jenny you would."

She looked down at his dark, excited eyes. He was as happy as she'd ever seen him. At that moment, if he'd asked if she wanted to take a quick trip to Nairobi and hunt lions, she'd have been tempted to agree.

"You bet I do." She laughed when his arms flew around her and squeezed. "What time do we sail?"

At ten o'clock sharp the next morning, Megan had her three charges on the docks. Though the day was warm and balmy for June, she'd taken Suzanna's advice and brought along warm jackets and caps for the trip out into the Atlantic. She had binoculars, a camera, extra film.

Though she'd already downed a dose of motion-sickness pills, her landlubber's stomach tilted queasily as she studied the boat.

It looked sturdy. She could comfort herself with that. The white paint gleamed in the sun, the rails shone. When they stepped on board, she saw that there was a large interior cabin ringed with windows on the first deck. For the less hearty, she assumed. It boasted a concession stand, soft-drink machines and plenty of chairs and benches.

She gave it a last longing look as the children pulled her along. They wouldn't settle for a nice cozy cabin.

"We get to go to the bridge." Alex strutted along importantly, waving to one of the mates. "We own the *Mariner*. Us and Nate."

"Daddy says the bank owns it." Jenny scrambled up the iron steps, a red ribbon trailing from her hair. "But that's a joke. Dutch says it's a crying shame for a real sailor to haul around weak-bellied tourists. But Nate just laughs at him."

Megan merely lifted a brow. She had yet to meet the infamous Dutchman, but Jenny, clever as any parrot, would often quote him word for word. And all too often, those words were vividly blue.

"We're here." Alex burst onto the bridge, breathless with excitement. "Kevin, too."

"Welcome aboard." Nathaniel glanced up from the chart he was studying. His eyes fastened unerringly on Megan's.

"I was expecting Holt."

"He's helming the *Queen*." He picked up his cigar,

clamped it between his teeth, grinned. "Don't worry, Meg, I won't run you aground."

She wasn't concerned about that. Exactly. In his black sweater and jeans, a black Greek fisherman's cap on his head and that gleam in his eye, he looked supremely competent. As a pirate might, she mused, upon boarding a merchant ship. "I started on your books." There, she thought, the ground was steady under her feet.

"I figured you would."

"They're a disorganized mess."

"Yeah. Kevin, come on over and take a look. I'll show you where we're heading."

Kevin hesitated, clinging to his mother's hand another moment. But the lure of those colorful charts was too much for him. He dashed over, dozens of questions tripping off his tongue.

"How many whales will we see? What happens if they bump the boat? Will they shoot water up from that hole on their back? Do you steer the boat from way up here?"

Megan started to interrupt and gently tell her son not to badger Mr. Fury, but Nathaniel was already answering questions, hauling Jenny up on one hip and taking Alex's finger to slide over the lines of the chart.

Pirate or not, she thought with a frown, he had a way with children.

"Ready to cast off, Captain."

Nathaniel nodded to the mate. "Quarter speed astern." Still holding Jenny, he walked to the wheel. "Pilot us out of here, sailor," he said to her, and guided her eager hands.

Curiosity got the better of Megan. She inched closer to study the instruments. Depth sounders, sonar, ship-to-shore radio. Those, and all the other equipment, were as foreign to her as the cockpit of a spaceship. She was a woman of the plains.

As the boat chugged gently away from the docks, her stomach lurched, reminding her why.

She clamped down on the nausea, annoyed with herself. It was in her mind, she insisted. A silly, imaginary weakness that could be overcome through willpower.

Besides, she'd taken seasickness pills, so, logically, she couldn't be seasick.

The children cheered as the boat made its long, slow turn in the bay. Megan's stomach turned with it.

Alex was generous enough to allow Kevin to blow the horn. Megan stared straight out the bridge window, her eyes focused above the calm blue water of Frenchman Bay.

It was beautiful, wasn't it? she told herself. And it was hardly tilting at all.

"You'll see The Towers on the starboard side," Nathaniel was saying.

"That's the right," Jenny announced. "Starboard's right and port's left."

"Stern's the back and the bow's in front," said Alex, not to be outdone. "We know all about boats."

Megan shifted her eyes to the cliffs, struggling to ignore another twist in her stomach. "There it is, Kevin." She gripped the brass rail beneath the starboard window for balance. "It looks like it's growing right out of the rock."

And it did look like a castle, she mused as she watched it with her son beside her. The turrets spearing up into the blue summer sky, the somber gray rock glistening with tiny flecks of mica. Even the scaffolding and the antlike figures of men working didn't detract from the fairy-tale aura. A fairy tale, she thought, with a dark side.

And that, she realized, was what made it all the more alluring. It was hardly any wonder that Sloan, with his love of buildings, adored it.

"Like something you'd expect to see on some lonely Irish coast." Nathaniel spoke from behind her. "Or on some foggy Scottish cliff."

"Yes. It's even more impressive from the sea." Her eyes drifted up, to Bianca's tower. She shivered.

"You may want to put your jacket on," Nathaniel told her. "It's going to get chillier when we get out to sea."

"No, I'm not cold. I was just thinking. When you've heard all the stories about Bianca, it's hard not to imagine what it was like."

"She'd sit up there and watch the cliffs for him. For Christian. And she'd dream—guiltily, I imagine, being a proper lady. But propriety doesn't have a snowball's chance in hell against love."

She shivered again. The statement hit much too close to home. She'd been in love once, and had tossed propriety aside, along with her innocence.

"She paid for it," Megan said flatly, and turned away. To distract herself, she wandered over to the charts. Not that she could make head or tail of them.

"We're heading north by northeast." As he had with Alex, Nathaniel took Megan's hand and guided it along the chart. "We've got a clear day, good visibility, but there's a strong wind. It'll be a little choppy."

Terrific, she thought, and swallowed hard. "If you don't come up with whales, you're going to have some very disappointed kids."

"Oh, I think I can provide a few." She bumped against him as bay gave way to sea. His hands came up to steady her shoulders, and remained. The boat might have swayed, but he stood solid as a rock. "You want to brace your feet apart. Distribute the weight. You'll get your sea legs, Meg."

She didn't think so. Already she could feel the light coating of chilly sweat springing to her skin. Nausea rolled in an answering wave in her stomach. She would not, she promised herself, spoil Kevin's day, or humiliate herself, by being sick.

"It takes about an hour to get out, doesn't it?" Her voice wasn't as strong, or as steady, as she'd hoped.

"That's right."

She started to move away, but ended by leaning dizzily against him.

"Come about," he murmured, and turned her to face him. One look at her face had his brows drawing together. She was pale as a sheet, with an interesting tinge of green just under the surface. Dead sick, he thought with a shake of his head. And they were barely under way.

"Did you take anything?"

There was no use pretending. And she didn't have the strength to be brave. "Yes, but I don't think it did any good. I get sick in a canoe."

"So you came on a three-hour trek into the Atlantic."

"Kevin had his heart set—" She broke off when Nathaniel put a steadying arm around her waist and led her to a bench.

"Sit," he ordered.

Megan obeyed and, when she saw that the children were occupied staring out the windows, gave in and dropped her head between her legs.

Three hours, she thought. They'd have to pour her into a body bag in three hours. Maybe bury her at sea.

God, what had made her think a couple of pills would steady her? She felt a tug on her hand.

"What? Is the ambulance here already?"

"Steady as she goes, sugar." Crouched in front of her, Nathaniel slipped narrow terry-cloth bands over her wrists.

"What's this?"

"Acupressure." He twisted the bands until small metal studs pressed lightly on a point on her wrist.

She would have laughed if she hadn't been moaning. "Great. I need a stretcher and you offer voodoo."

"A perfectly valid science. And I wouldn't knock voodoo, either. I've seen some pretty impressive results. Now breathe slow and easy. Just sit here." He slid open a window behind her and let in a blast of air. "I've got to get back to the helm."

She leaned back against the wall and let the fresh air slap her cheeks. On the other side of the bridge, the children huddled, hoping that Moby Dick lurked under each snowy whitecap. She watched the cliffs, but as they swayed to and fro, she closed her eyes in self-defense.

She sighed once, then began to formulate a complicated trigonometry problem in her mind. Oddly enough, by the time she'd worked it through to the solution, her stomach felt steady.

Probably because I've got my eyes closed, she thought. But she could hardly keep them closed for three hours, not when she was in charge of a trio of active children.

Experimentally, she opened one. The boat continued to rock, but her system remained steady. She opened the other. There was a moment of panic when the children weren't at the window. She jolted upright, illness forgotten, then saw them circled around Nathaniel at the helm.

A fine job she was doing, she thought in disgust, sitting there in a dizzy heap while Nathaniel piloted the ship and entertained three kids. She braced herself for the next slap of nausea as she took a step.

It didn't come.

Frowning, she took another step, and another. She felt a little weak, true, but no longer limp and clammy. Daring the ultimate test, she looked out the window at the rolling sea.

There was a tug, but a mild one. In fact, she realized, it was almost a pleasant sensation, like riding on a smooth-gaited horse. In amazement, she studied the terry-cloth bands on her wrists.

Nathaniel glanced over his shoulder. Her color was back, he noted. That pale peach was much more flattering than green. "Better?"

"Yes." She smiled, trying to dispel the embarrassment as easily as his magic bands had the seasickness. "Thank you."

He waited while she bundled the children, then herself, into jackets. On the Atlantic, summer vanished. "First time I shipped out, we hit a little squall. I spent the worst two hours of my life hanging over the rail. Come on. Take the wheel."

"The wheel? I couldn't."

"Sure you could."

"Do it, Mom. It's fun. It's really fun."

Propelled forward by three children, Megan found herself at the helm, her back pressed lightly into Nathaniel's chest, her hands covered by his.

Every nerve in her body began to throb. Nathaniel's body was hard as iron, and his hands were sure and firm. She could smell the sea, through the open windows and on him. No matter how much she tried to concentrate on the water flowing endlessly around them, he was there, just there. His chin brushing the top of her head, his heartbeat throbbing light and steady against her back.

"Nothing like being in control to settle the system," he commented, and she made some sound of agreement.

But this was nothing like being in control.

She began to imagine what it might be like to have those hard, clever hands somewhere other than on the backs of hers. If she turned so that they were face-to-face, and she tilted her head up at just the right angle...

Baffled by the way her mind was working, she set it to calculating algebra.

"Quarter speed," Nathaniel ordered, steering a few degrees to port.

The change of rhythm had Megan off balance. She was trying to regain it when Nathaniel turned her around. And now she was facing him, her head tilted up. The easy grin on his face made her wonder if he knew just where her mind had wandered.

"See the blips on the screen there, Kevin?" But he was watching her, all but hypnotizing her with those unblinking slate-colored eyes. Sorcerer's eyes, she thought dimly. "Do you know what they mean?" And his lips curved—closer to hers than they should be. "There be whales there."

"Where? Where are they, Nate?" Kevin rushed to the window, goggle-eyed.

"Keep watching. We'll stop. Look off the port bow," he told Megan. "I think you'll get your money's worth."

Still dazed, she staggered away. The boat rocked more enthusiastically when stopped—or was it her system that was so thoroughly rocked? As Nathaniel spoke into the P.A. system, taking over the mate's lecture on whales, she slipped the camera and binoculars out of her shoulder bag.

"Look!" Kevin squealed, jumping like a spring as he pointed. "Mom, look!"

Everything cleared from her mind but wonder. She saw the massive body emerge from the choppy water. Rising, up and up, sleek and grand and otherworldly. She could hear the shouts and cheers from the people on the deck below, and her own strangled gasp.

It was surely some sort of magic, she thought, that something so huge, so magnificent, could lurk under the whitecapped sea. Her fingers rose to her lips, pressed there in awe as the sound of the whale displacing water crashed like thunder.

Water flew, sparkling like drops of diamond. Her camera stayed lowered, useless. She could only stare, an ache in her throat, tears in her eyes.

"His mate's coming up."

Nathaniel's voice broke through her frozen wonder. Hurriedly she lifted the camera, snapping quickly as sea parted for whale.

They geysered from their spouts, causing the children to applaud madly. Megan was laughing as she hauled Jenny up for a better view and the three of them took impatient turns with the binoculars.

She pressed herself to the window as eagerly as the children while the boat cruised, following the glossy humps as they speared through the sea. Then the whales sounded, diving deep with a flap of their enormous tails. Below, people laughed and shouted as they were drenched with water.

Twice more the *Mariner* sought out and found pods, giving her passengers the show of a lifetime. Long after they turned and headed for home, Megan stayed at the window, hoping for one more glimpse.

"Beautiful, aren't they?"

She looked back at Nathaniel, eyes glowing. "Incredible. I had no idea. Photographs and movies don't quite do it."

"Nothing quite like seeing and doing for yourself." He cocked a brow. "Still steady?"

With a laugh, she glanced down at her wrists. "Another minor miracle. I would never have put stock in anything like this."

"'There are more things in heaven and earth, Horatio.'"

A black-suited pirate quoting Hamlet. "So it seems," she murmured. "There's The Towers." She smiled. "Off the port side."

"You're learning, sugar." He gave orders briskly and eased the *Mariner* into the calm waters of the bay.

"How long have you been sailing?"

"All my life. But I ran off and joined the merchant marine when I was eighteen."

"Ran off?" She smiled again. "Looking for adventure."

"For freedom." He turned away then, to ease the boat into its slip as smoothly as a foot slides into an old, comfortable shoe.

She wondered why a boy of eighteen would have to search for freedom. And she thought of herself at that age, a child with a child. She'd cast her freedom away. Now, more than nine years later, she could hardly regret it. Not when the price of her freedom had been a son.

"Can we go down and get a drink?" Kevin tugged on his mother's hand. "We're all thirsty."

"Sure. I'll take you."

"We can go by ourselves," Alex said earnestly. He knew they were much too big to need an overseer. "I got money and everything. We just want to sit downstairs and watch everybody get off."

"All right, then, but stay inside." She watched them rush off. "They start spreading their wings so soon."

"Your boy's going to be flying back to you for a long time yet."

"I hope so." She cut herself off before she voiced the rest: *He's all I have.* "This has been a terrific day for him. For me, too. Thanks."

"My pleasure." They were alone on the bridge now, the lines secured, the plank down and the passengers disembarking. "You'll come again."

"I don't think I could keep Kevin away. I'd better go down with them."

"They're fine." He stepped closer, before she could evade. "You know, Meg, you forget to be nervous when the kids are around."

"I'm not nervous."

"Jumpy as a fish on a line. It was a pure pleasure watching your face when we sighted whale. It's a pure pleasure anytime, but when you're laughing and the wind's in your hair, it could stop a man's heart."

He took another step and backed her up against the wheel. Maybe it wasn't fair, but he'd think about that later. It was going to take him a good long time to forget the way she'd felt, her back pressed against him, her hands soft and hesitant under his.

"Of course, there's something to be said about the way you're looking right now. All eyes. You've got the prettiest blue eyes I've ever seen. Then there's all that peaches-and-cream." He lifted a finger to her cheek, skimmed it down. She felt as though she'd stepped on a live wire. "Makes a man crave a nice long taste."

"I'm not susceptible to flattery." She'd wanted to sound firm and dismissive, not breathless.

"Just stating a fact." He leaned down until his mouth was a whisper from hers. "If you don't want me to kiss you, you'd better tell me not to."

She would have. Absolutely. If she'd been able to speak. But then his mouth was on hers, warm and firm and every bit as clever as his hands. She would tell herself later that her lips had parted with shock, to protest. But it was a lie.

They opened greedily, with a surge of hunger that went deep, that echoed on a groan that a woman might make who had her first sampling of rich cream after years of thin water.

Her body refused to go rigid in denial, instead humming like a harp string freshly plucked. Her hands dived into his hair and urged him to take the kiss deeper.

He'd expected a cool response, or at least a hesitant one. Perhaps he'd seen a flash of passion in her eyes, deep down, like the heat and rumble in the core of a volcano that seems dormant from the surface.

But nothing had prepared him for this blast of fire.

His mind went blank, then filled with woman. The scent and feel and taste of her, the sound of the moan that caught in her throat when he nipped on her full lower lip. He dragged her closer, craving more, and had the dizzying delight of feeling every slim curve and line of Megan pressed against his body.

The scent of the ocean through the window had him imagining taking her on some deserted beach, while the surf pounded and the gulls screamed.

She felt herself sinking, and gripped him for balance.

There was too much, much too much, rioting through her system. It would take a great deal more than the little bands around her wrist to level her now.

It would take control, willpower, and, most of all... remembering.

She drew back, would have stumbled if his arms hadn't stayed clamped around her. "No."

He couldn't get his breath. He told himself he would analyze later why one kiss had knocked him flat, like a two-fisted punch. "You'll have to be more specific. No to what?"

"To this. To any of this." Panic kicked in and had her struggling away. "I wasn't thinking."

"Me, neither. It's a good sign you're doing it right, if you stop thinking when you're kissing."

"I don't want you to kiss me."

He slipped his hands into his pockets. Safer there, he decided, since the lady was thinking again. "Sugar, you were doing more than your share."

There was little use in hotly denying the obvious truth. She fell back on cool logic. "You're an attractive man, and I responded in a natural manner."

He had to grin. "Darling, if kissing like that's in your nature, I'm going to die happy."

"I don't intend for it to happen again."

"You know what they say about the road to hell and intentions, don't you?" She was tensed up again. He could see it in the set of her shoulders. He imagined her experience with Dumont had left plenty of scars. "Relax, Meg," he said, more kindly. "I'm not going to jump you. You want to take it slow, we'll take it slow."

The fact that his tone was so reasonable raised her hackles. "We're not going to take it any way at all."

Better, he decided. He didn't mind riling her. In fact, he was looking forward to doing it. Often.

"I'm going to have to say you're wrong. A man and woman set off a fire like that, they're going to keep coming back to the heat."

She was very much afraid he was right. Even now, part of her yearned to fan that blaze again. "I'm not interested in fires or in heat. I'm certainly not interested in an affair with a man I barely know."

"So, we'll get to know each other better before we have one," Nate responded, in an irritatingly reasonable tone.

Megan clamped her teeth together. "I'm not interested in an affair, period. I know that must be a blow to your ego, but you'll just have to deal with it. Now, if you'll excuse me, I'm going to get the children."

He stepped politely out of her way, waited until she'd reached the glass door leading onto the upper deck. "Meg?" It was only partly ego that pushed him to speak. The rest was pure determination. "The first time I make love with you, you won't think about him. You won't even remember his name."

Her eyes sliced at him, twin ice-edged swords. She abandoned dignity and slammed the door.

Chapter 4

"The woman'll be the death of me." Dutch took a bottle of Jamaican rum from his hidey-hole in the back of the pantry. "Mark my words, boy."

Nathaniel kicked back in the kitchen chair, sated and relaxed after the meal he'd enjoyed in the Calhoun dining room. The hotel kitchen was spotless, now that the dinner rush was over. And Coco, Nathaniel knew, was occupied with family. Otherwise, Dutch wouldn't have risked the rum.

"You're not thinking of jumping ship, are you, mate?"

Dutch snorted at the idea. As if he had to take French leave because he couldn't handle a fussy, snooty-nosed female. "I'm sticking." After one wary glance toward the door, he poured them both a healthy portion of rum. "But I'm warning you, boy, sooner or later that woman's going to get her comeuppance. And she's going to get it from yours truly." He stabbed a thick thumb at his wide chest.

Nathaniel downed a swig of rum, hissing through his teeth as it hit. Smooth as silk it wasn't. "Where's that bottle of Cruzan I got you?"

"Used it in a cake. This is plenty good enough for drinking."

"If you don't want a stomach lining," Nathaniel said under his breath. "So, what's the problem with Coco now?"

"Well, if it's not one thing, it's two." Dutch scowled at the kitchen phone when it rang. Room service, he thought with a sneer. Never had any damn room service aboard one of his ships. "Yeah, what?"

Nathaniel grinned into his rum. Tact and diplomacy weren't Dutch's strong points. He imagined that if Coco heard the man growl at guests that way, she'd faint. Or pop Dutch over the head with a skillet.

"I guess you think we've got nothing better to do down here?" he snarled into the phone. "You'll get it when it's ready." He hung up and snagged a plate. "Ordering champagne and fancy cake this time of night. Newlyweds. Ha! Haven't seen hide nor hair of the two in number three all week."

"Where's your romance, Dutch?"

"I leave that to you, lover boy." His ham-size fists delicately cut into the chocolate *gâteau*. "Seen the way you was eyeing that redhead."

"Strawberry blonde," Nathaniel corrected. "More gold than red." Bravely he took another sip of rum. "She's a looker, isn't she?"

"Never seen you go for one that wasn't." With an artist's flair, Dutch ladled vanilla sauce on the side of the twin slices of cake and garnished them with raspberries. "Got a kid, doesn't she?"

"Yeah." Nathaniel studied the cake and decided he

could probably force down a small piece. "Kevin. Dark hair, tall for his age." A smile curved his lips. Damned if the boy hadn't gotten to him. "Big, curious eyes."

"Seen him." Dutch had a weakness for kids that he tried to hide. "Okay-looking boy. Comes around with those other two noisy brats, looking for handouts."

Which, Nathaniel knew, Dutch dispensed with great pleasure behind the mask of a scowl.

"Got herself in trouble pretty young."

Nathaniel frowned at that. It was a phrase, too often used to his way of thinking, that indicated the woman was solely responsible for the pregnancy. "It takes two, Dutch. And the bastard was stringing her along."

"I know. I know. I heard about it. Not much gets past me." It wasn't hard to finesse information out of Coco— if he pushed the right buttons. Though he'd never admit it, that was something he looked forward to doing daily. He buzzed for a waiter, taking delight in holding his thumb down until the kitchen door swung open. "Make up a tray for number three," Dutch ordered. "Two gato's, bottle of house champagne, two flutes, and don't forget the damn napkins."

That done, he tossed back his own rum. "Guess you'll be wanting a piece of this now."

"Wouldn't turn it down."

"Never known you to turn down food—or a female." Dutch cut a slice—a great deal larger than those he'd cut for the newlyweds—and shoved the plate in front of Nathaniel.

"I don't get any raspberries?"

"Eat what's in front of you. How come you ain't out there flirting with that skinny girl?"

"I'm working on it," Nathaniel said with a mouthful of cake. "They're in the dining room, all of them. Family meeting." He rose, poured himself coffee, dumped the rest of his rum in it. "They found some old book. And she's not skinny." He had firsthand knowledge, now that he'd had Megan in his arms. "She's delicate."

"Yeah, right." He thought of Coco, those long, sturdy lines as fine as any well-crafted sloops. And snorted again. "All females are delicate—until they get a ring through your nose."

No one would have called the women in the dining room delicate—not with a typical Calhoun argument in full swing.

"I say we burn it." C.C. folded her arms across her chest and glared. "After everything we learned about Fergus from Bianca's journal, I don't know why we'd consider keeping his lousy account book around."

"We can't burn it," Amanda fired back. "It's part of our history."

"Bad vibes." Lilah narrowed her eyes at the book, now sitting in the center of the table. "Really bad vibes."

"That may be." Max shook his head. "But I can't go along with burning a book. Any kind of book."

"It's not exactly literature," C.C. mumbled.

Trent patted his wife's stiff shoulder. "We can always put it back where it came from—or give Sloan's suggestion some consideration."

"I think a room designed for artifacts, mementos—" Sloan glanced at Amanda "—the pieces of history that go with The Towers, would add something. Not only to the hotel, but for the family."

"I don't know." Suzanna pressed her lips together and tried to be objective. "I feel odd about displaying Fergus's things with Bianca's, or Aunt Colleen's, Uncle Sean's and Ethan's."

"He might have been a creep, but he's still a piece of the whole." Holt toyed with the last of his coffee. "I'm going with Sloan on this one."

That, of course, enticed a small riot of agreements, disagreements, alternate suggestions. Megan could only sit back and watch in amazement.

She hadn't wanted to be there at all. Not at a family meeting. But she'd been summarily outvoted. The Calhouns could unite when they chose.

As the argument swirled around her, she glanced at the object in question. When Amanda left it in her office, she'd eventually given in to temptation. After cleaning off the leather, she'd flipped through pages, idly totaling up columns, clucking her tongue at the occasional mistake in arithmetic. Of course, she'd scanned a few of the marginal notations, as well, and had found Fergus Calhoun a cold, ambitious and self-absorbed man.

But then, a simple account ledger hardly seemed worth this much trouble. Particularly when the last few pages of the books were merely numbers without any rhyme or reason.

She was reminding herself it wasn't her place to comment when she was put directly on the spot.

"What do you think, Megan, dear?" Coco's unexpected question had Megan blinking.

"Excuse me?"

"What do you think? You haven't told us. And you'd be the most qualified, after all."

"Qualified?"

"It's an account book," Coco pointed out. "You're an accountant."

Somehow, the logic in that defeated Megan. "It's really none of my business," she began, and was drowned out by a chorus of reasons why it certainly was. "Well, I…" She looked around the table, where all eyes were focused on her. "I imagine it would be an interesting memento—and it's kind of fascinating to review book-keeping from so long ago. You know, expenses, and wages for the staff. It might be interesting to see how it adds up, what the income and outgo was for your family in 1913."

"Of course!" Coco clapped her hands. "Why, of course it would. I was thinking about you last night, Meg, while I was casting my runes. It kept coming back to me that you were to take on a project—one with numbers."

"Aunt Coco," C.C. said patiently, "Megan is our accountant."

"Well, I know that, darling." With a bright smile, Coco patted her hair. "So at first I didn't think much of it. But then I kept having this feeling that it was more than that. And I'm sure, somehow, that the project is going to lead to something wonderful. Something that will make all of us very happy. I'm so pleased you're going to do it."

"Do it?" Megan looked helplessly at her brother. She got a flash of a grin in return.

"Study Fergus's book. You could even put it all on computer, couldn't you? Sloan's told us how clever you are."

"I could, of course, but—"

She was interrupted by the cry of a baby through the monitor on the sideboard.

"Bianca?" Max said.

"Ethan," C.C. and Lilah said in unison.

And the meeting was adjourned.

* * *

What exactly, Megan wondered later, had she agreed to do? Somehow, though she'd barely said a word, she'd been placed in charge of Fergus's book. Surely that was a family matter.

She sighed as she pushed open the doors to her terrace and stepped outside. If she stated that obvious fact, in the most practical, logical of terms, she would be patted on the head, pinched on the cheek and told that she was family and that was all there was to it.

How could she argue?

She took a deep breath of the scented night air, and all but tasted Suzanna's freesias and roses. She could hear the sea in the distance, and the air she moved through was moist and lightly salty from it. Stars wheeled overhead, highlighted by a three-quarter moon, bright as a beacon.

Her son was dreaming in his bed, content and safe and surrounded by people who loved him.

Dissecting Fergus's book was a small favor that couldn't begin to repay what she'd been given.

Peace of mind. Yes, she thought, the Calhouns had opened the gates to that particular garden.

Too charmed by the night to close it out and sleep, she wandered down the curving stone steps to drift through the moon-kissed roses and star-sprinkled peonies, under an arbor where wisteria twisted triumphantly, raining tiny petals onto the path.

"'She was a phantom of delight when first she gleamed upon my sight.'"

Megan jolted, pressing a hand on her heart when a shadow separated itself from the other shadows.

"Did I startle you?" Nathaniel stepped closer, the

red tip of his cigar glowing. "Wordsworth usually has a different effect."

"I didn't know you were there." And wouldn't have come out had she known. "I thought you'd gone home."

"I was passing a little time with Dutch and a bottle of rum." He stepped fully into the moonlight. "He likes to complain about Coco, and prefers an audience." He drew slowly on his cigar. For a moment, his face was misted by smoke, making it mysterious and beautiful. An angel cast from grace. "Nice night."

"Yes, it is. Well…"

"No need to run off. You wanted to walk in the garden." He smiled, reaching down to snap a pale pink peony from its bush. "Since it's nearly midnight, there's no better time for it."

She accepted the blossom, told herself she wouldn't be charmed. "I was admiring the flowers. I've never had much luck growing them."

"You have to put your heart in it—along with the water and fertilizer."

Her hair was down, waving softly over her shoulders. She still wore the neatly tailored blue jacket and slacks she'd had on at dinner. A pity, he thought. It would have suited the night, and his mood, if she'd drifted outside in a flowing robe. But then, Megan O'Riley wasn't the type of woman to wander midnight gardens in swirling silks.

Wouldn't let herself be.

The only way to combat those intrusive gray eyes, other than to run like a fool, was conversation. "So, do you garden, as well as sail and quote the classics?" she asked him.

"I've an affection for flowers, among other things." Nathaniel put a hand over the peony she held, and lifted it toward him so that he could enjoy its fragrance, and hers. He smiled at her over the feathered petals.

She found herself caught, as if in some slow-motion dream, between the man and the moonlight. The perfume of the garden seemed to rise up and swirl like the breeze, gently invading her senses. Shadows shifted over his face, highlighting all those fascinating clefts and ridges, luring her gaze to his mouth, curved now and inviting.

They seemed so completely alone, so totally cut off from the reality and responsibilities of day-to-day.

Just a man and a woman among star-dappled flowers and moonlit shadows, and the music of the distant sea.

Deliberately she lowered her lashes, as if to break the spell.

"I'm surprised you'd have time for poetry and flowers, with all the traveling."

"You can always make time for what counts."

The fact that the night held magic hadn't escaped him. But then, he was open to such things. There'd been times he'd seen water rise out of itself like a clenched fist, times he'd heard the siren song of mermaids through shifting fog—he believed in magic. Why else had he waited in the garden, knowing, somehow knowing, she would come?

He released the flower, but took her free hand, linking their fingers before she could think of a reason he shouldn't. "Walk with me, Meg. A night like this shouldn't be wasted."

"I'm going back in." She looked back up just as a breeze stirred in the air. Wisteria petals rained down.

"Soon."

So she was walking with him in the fairy-lit garden, with a flower in her hand and fragrant petals in her hair.

"I...really should check on Kevin."

"The boy have trouble sleeping?"

"No, but—"

"Bad dreams?"

"No."

"Well, then." Taking that as an answer, he continued his stroll down the narrow path. "Does having a man flirt with you always make you turn tail and run?"

"I certainly wasn't running. And I'm not interested in flirtations."

"Funny. When you were standing out on the terrace a bit ago, you looked like a woman ready for a little flirting."

She stopped dead. "You were watching me."

"Mmm." Nathaniel crushed his cigar out into the sand of a nearby urn. "I was thinking it was a shame I didn't have a lute."

Annoyance warred with curiosity. "A lute?"

"A pretty woman standing on a balcony in the moonlight—she should be serenaded."

She had to laugh at that. "I suppose you play the lute."

"Nope. Wished I did, though, when I saw you." He began to walk again. The cliff curved downward, toward the seawall. "I used to sail by here when I was a kid and look up at The Towers. I liked to think there was a dragon guarding it, and that I'd scale the cliffs and slay him."

"Kevin still calls it a castle," she murmured, looking back.

"When I got older and took note of the Calhoun sisters, I figured when I killed the dragon, they'd reward me. In the way a sixteen-year-old walking hormone fantasizes."

She laughed again. "Which one of them?"

"Oh, all of them." Grinning, he sat on the low wall, drew her down beside him. "They've always been…remarkable. Holt had this thing for Suzanna, though he wouldn't admit it. Being as he was my friend, I selflessly crossed her off my list. That left three for me after I conquered that dragon."

"But you never did face the dragon?"

A shadow passed over his face. "I had another to deal with. I guess you could say we left it at a draw, and I went to sea." He shook off the mood, and the uncomfortable past. "But I did have a brief and memorable interlude with the lovely Lilah."

Megan's eyes widened. "You and Lilah?"

"Right before I left the island. She set out to drive me crazy. I think she was practicing." He sighed at the memory. "She was damn good at it."

But they were so easy with each other, Megan thought. So relaxed and friendly.

"You're so easy to read, Meg." He chuckled and slipped his arm around her shoulders. "We weren't exactly Romeo and Juliet. I kissed her a few times, did my damnedest to convince her to do more. She didn't. And she didn't break my heart. Well, dented it a little, maybe," he mused.

"And Max isn't bothered?"

"Why would he be? He's got her. If we'd had a flaming affair—which we didn't—it would be a smoldering matchstick compared to what they've got."

He was right there. Each of the Calhoun women had found her match. "Still, it's interesting," she said quietly. "All these connections within connections."

"Are you thinking of me, or yourself?"

She stiffened, abruptly aware that she was sitting

hip-to-hip with him, his arm around her. "That's not something I care to discuss."

"Still raw?" He tightened his arm, comforting. "From what I've heard of Dumont, I wouldn't think he'd be worth it. Settle down," he said when she jerked away. "We'll let it go. Too nice a night to uncover old wounds. Why don't you tell me how they talked you into taking on that old account book?"

"How do you know about that?"

"Holt and Suzanna filled me in." She was still rigid, he noted. But she wasn't running. "I saw them before they left."

She relaxed a little. It was comforting to discuss it with someone else who was just that small step outside the family. "I don't know how they talked me into it. I barely opened my mouth."

"Your first mistake."

She huffed out a breath. "I'd have had to shout to be heard. I don't know why they call it a meeting, when all they do is argue." Her brows knit. "Then they stop arguing and you realize you've been sucked in. If you try to pull yourself out, you find they've united in this solid wall that's impossible to beat."

"I know just what you mean. I still don't know if it was my idea to go into business with Holt. The notion came up, was debated, voted on and approved. The next thing I knew, I was signing papers."

Interesting, she mused, and studied his strong profile. "You don't strike me as someone who could be talked into anything."

"I could say the same."

She considered a moment, then gave up. "You're right. The book's fascinating. I can hardly wait to get at it."

"I hope you're not planning on letting it take up all your free time." He toyed with the ends of her blowing hair. No, not red, he mused. It was gold, enriched by quiet fire. "I want some of it."

Cautiously she inched away. "I explained to you, I'm not interested."

"What you are is worried because you are interested." He cupped a hand under her chin and turned her to face him. "I figure you had a rough time, and maybe it's helped you cope to lump all men in with the bastard who hurt you. That's why I said I'd be patient."

Fury flared in her eyes. "Don't tell me what I am or how I've coped. I'm not asking for your understanding or your patience."

"Okay."

He crushed his mouth to hers, without any patience at all. His lips were demanding, urgent, irresistible, conquering hers before she could draw the breath to deny it.

The embers that had smoldered inside her since the first time he'd kissed her burst into reckless flame. She wanted—craved—this flash point of feeling, this fireball of sensation. Hating herself for the weakness, she let herself burn.

He'd proved his point, Nathaniel thought as he tore his mouth from hers to press it against the thundering pulse in her throat. Proved his point, and wrapped himself up in nasty knots of need.

Needs that would have to wait, because she was far from ready. And because it mattered—she mattered— more than he'd expected.

"Now tell me you're not interested," he muttered against her lips, furious that he was unable to take what was so obviously his. "Tell me you didn't want me to touch you."

"I can't." Her voice broke in despair. She wanted him to touch her, to take her, to throw her on the ground and make wild love to her. And to take the decision, and the responsibility, out of her hands. That made her ashamed. That made her a coward. "But wanting's not enough." Shaken, she pushed away, lurched to her feet. "It's never going to be enough for me. I've wanted before." She stood trembling in the moonlight, her hair blowing free, her eyes fierce and afraid.

Nathaniel cursed himself, then her for good measure. "I'm not Dumont. And you're not a seventeen-year-old girl."

"I know who I am. I don't know who you are."

"You're hedging, Megan. We recognized each other from the first instant."

She stepped back, because she knew he was right. Because it terrified her. "You're talking about chemistry."

"Maybe I'm talking about fate." He said it softly, as he rose. He'd frightened her, and he despised himself for it. Unnerving a woman was one thing, bullying another. "You need time to think about that. So do I. I'll walk you back."

She put out a hand to stop him. "I can find my own way." She whirled and raced up the moonlit path.

Nathaniel swore under his breath. He sat again and took out a fresh cigar, lit it. There wasn't any use heading home yet. He already knew he wouldn't sleep.

Late the following afternoon, Megan roused herself from her ledgers when a knock sounded on her office door.

"Come in."

"Sorry to interrupt." Coco poked her head in the

door—a head, Megan noted with surprise, that was now topped with sleek ebony hair—she apparently was a woman who changed her hair color as often as she changed moods. "You didn't break for lunch," Coco said as she stepped through the door with a large and laden silver tray.

"You didn't have to bother." Megan glanced at her watch and was stunned to see it was after three. "You've got enough to do without waiting on me."

"Just part of the service." After setting the tray on a table, Coco began to arrange a place setting. "We can't have you skipping meals." She glanced over at the computer screen, the open ledgers, the calculator and the neatly stacked files. "My goodness, such a lot of numbers. Numbers have always unsettled me. They're so… unyielding."

"You don't have to let them push you around," Megan said with a laugh. "Once you know that one and one always equals two, you can do anything."

Coco studied the screen doubtfully. "If you say so, dear."

"I've just finished up the first quarter on Shipshape. It was…a challenge."

"It's wonderful that you think so." Coco turned her back on the numbers before they could give her a headache. "But none of us wants you overdoing things. Now, here's some iced tea and a nice club sandwich."

It did look tempting, particularly since she'd had no appetite for breakfast. A residual effect, she knew, of her encounter with Nathaniel.

"Thank you, Coco. I'm sorry I took you away from your work."

"Oh." Coco waved a dismissive hand as Megan rose to pick up her plate. "Don't give it a thought. To be frank, dear, I simply had to get out—away from that man."

"The Dutchman?" Megan smiled over her first bite of sandwich. "I met him this morning, when I was coming down. I made a wrong turn and ended up in the hotel wing."

Restless, Coco began to fiddle with the thick gold links around her throat. "I hope he didn't say anything to offend you. He's a bit…rough."

"No." Megan poured two glasses of tea, offered one to Coco. "He sort of glowered and told me I needed some meat on my bones. I thought he was going to start stuffing me with the Greek omelet he was fixing, but one of the busboys dropped a plate. I escaped while he was swearing at the poor kid."

"His language." Coco seated herself, smoothed down her silk trouser leg. "Deplorable. And he's always contradicting me on recipes." She shut her eyes, shuddered. "I've always considered myself a patient woman—and, if I can be immodest for a moment, a clever one. I had to be both to raise four lively girls." Sighing, she tossed up her hands in a gesture of surrender. "But as far as that man's concerned, I'm at my wits' end."

"I suppose you could let him go," Megan said tentatively.

"Impossible. The man's like a father to Nathaniel, and the children, for reasons that escape me, are terribly fond of him." She opened her eyes again and smiled bravely. "I can cope, dear, and I must admit the man has a way with certain rudimentary dishes." She patted her new hairdo. "And I find little ways to distract myself."

But Megan's attention was stuck back at Coco's first statement. "I suppose Mr. Van Horne has known Nathaniel for some time."

"Oh, more than fifteen years, I believe. They served together, sailed together, whatever you call it. I believe Mr. Van Horn took Nate under his wing. Which is something in his favor, I suppose. God knows the boy needed someone, after the miserable childhood he had."

"Oh?" It wasn't in Megan's nature to probe, but Coco needed little prompting.

"His mother died when he was very young, poor boy. And his father." Her lovely mouth went grim. "Well, the man was little more than a beast really. I barely knew John Fury, but there was always talk in the village. And now and then Nathaniel would come along with Holt when Holt brought us fish. I'd see the bruises for myself."

"Bruises," Megan repeated, horrified. "His father beat him?"

Coco's soft heart had tears swimming in her eyes. "I'm very much afraid so."

"But—didn't anyone do anything about it?"

"Whenever there were questions, the man would claim the boy had fallen, or gotten into a fight with another child. Nathaniel never contradicted him. Sad to say, abuse was something people often overlooked back then. Still is, I'm afraid." Tears threatened her mascara. She dabbed at them with Megan's napkin. "Nathaniel ran off to sea the moment he was of age. His father died a few years back. Nate sent money for the funeral, but didn't come. It was hard to blame him."

Coco sighed, shook herself. "I didn't mean to come in with such a sad story. But it has a good ending. Nate turned out to be a fine man." Coco's damp eyes were deceptively guileless. "All he needs is the right woman. He's terribly handsome, don't you think?"

"Yes," Megan said cautiously. She was still trying to equate the abused child with the confident man.

"And dependable. Romantic, too, with all those tales of the sea, and that air of mystery around him. A woman would be very lucky to catch his eye."

Megan blinked her own eyes as the not-so-subtle hint got through. "I couldn't say. I don't know him very well, and I don't really think about men that way."

"Nonsense." Confident in her own matchmaking skills, Coco patted Megan's knee. "You're young, beautiful, intelligent. Having a man in your life doesn't diminish those things, dear—or a woman's independence. The right man enhances them. And I have a feeling that you'll be finding that out, very soon. Now—" she leaned over and kissed Megan's cheek "—I have to get back to the kitchen, before that man does something horrid to my salmon patties."

She started out the door, then paused—timing it, Coco thought, rather beautifully. "Oh, dear, I'm such a scatterbrain. I was supposed to tell you about Kevin."

"Kevin?" Automatically Megan's gaze shifted to the window. "Isn't he outside with Alex and Jenny?"

"Well, yes, but not here." Coco smiled distractedly—it was a pose she'd practiced for years. "It's Nathaniel's day off, and he was by for lunch. Such a wonderful appetite he has, and never seems to gain an ounce. Of course, he does keep active. That's why he has all those marvelous muscles. They are marvelous, aren't they?"

"Coco, where is Kevin?"

"Oh, there I go, running off again. Kevin's with Nate. All of them are. He took the children with him."

Megan was already on her feet. "With him? Where? On a boat?" Visions of squalls and towering waves of water swam through her head, despite the calm, cloud-less blue of the sky.

"No, no, to his house. He's building a deck or some-thing, and the children were dying to go along and help. It would be such a favor to me if you could go by and pick them up." And, of course, Coco thought cannily, Megan would then see Nate's lovely little home, and his charming way with children. "Suzanna expects the children to be here, you see, but I didn't have the heart to deny them. She won't be back until five, so there's no hurry."

"But, I—"

"You know where Suzanna and Holt's cottage is, don't you, darling? Nathaniel's is only a half a mile past it. Charming place. You can't miss it."

Before Megan could form another word, the door closed gently in her face.

A job, Coco thought as she strode down the corri-dor, very well done.

Chapter 5

Kevin didn't know which was the coolest. It was a very close call between the small fire-breathing dragon on the back of Nathaniel's shoulder and the puckered white scar on the front. The scar was the result of the knife wound, which ought to have put it far ahead in the running. But a tattoo, a tattoo of a *dragon*, was pretty hard to beat.

There was another scar, just above Nathaniel's waistline, near the hip. At Alex's eager questioning, Nathaniel had said it was from a moray eel he'd tangled with in the South Pacific.

Kevin could easily imagine Nathaniel, armed with only a knife clenched between his teeth, fighting to the death with a sea creature on the scale of the Loch Ness monster.

And Nathaniel had a parrot, a big, colorful bird who sat right inside the house on a wooden perch and talked. Kevin's current favorite was "Off with her head."

Kevin figured Nathaniel Fury was about the coolest

man he'd ever met—a man who had traveled the seven seas like Sinbad, and had the scars and stories to prove it. A man who liked puppies and talking birds.

He didn't seem to mind when Kevin hung back while Alex and Jenny raced around the yard with the puppy and killed each other with imaginary laser pistols. It was more fun to crouch close while Nathaniel hammered nails into boards.

It took Kevin about six boards to start asking questions.

"How come you want a deck out here?"

"So I can sit on it." Nathaniel set another board in place.

"But you've already got one in the back."

"I'll still have it." Three strikes of the hammer and the nail was through board and joist. Nathaniel sat back on his haunches. He wore nothing but a bandanna twisted around his head and a pair of ragged cut-off jeans. His skin was bronzed by the sun and coated lightly with sweat. "See how the frame goes?"

Kevin followed the direction of the deck frame as it skirted around the side of the house. "Uh-huh."

"Well, we'll keep going till we meet the other deck."

Kevin's eyes brightened. "So it'll go all around, like a circle."

"You got it." Nathaniel hammered the next nail, and the next, then shifted positions. "How do you like the island?"

He asked the question in such a natural, adult fashion that Kevin first glanced around to see if Nathaniel was speaking to him. "I like it. I like it a lot. We get to live in the castle, and I can play with Alex and Jenny anytime."

"You had friends back in Oklahoma, too, right?"

"Sure. My best friend is John Curtis Silverhorn. He's part Comanche. My mom said he could come visit anytime, and that we can write letters all we want. I already wrote him about the whale." Kevin smiled shyly. "I liked that the best."

"We'll have to go out again."

"Really? When?"

Nathaniel stopped hammering and looked at the boy. He realized he should have remembered from his exposure to Alex and Jenny that when children were raised with love and trust, they believed just about everything you told them.

"You can come out with me whenever you want. 'Long as your mother gives the go-ahead."

His reward for the careless offer was a brilliant smile. "Maybe I can steer the boat again?"

"Yeah." Nathaniel grinned and turned Kevin's baseball cap backward. "You could do that. Want to nail some boards?"

Kevin's eyes widened and glowed. "Okay!"

"Here." Nathaniel scooted back so that Kevin could kneel in front of him. "Hold the nail like this." He wrapped his hands over Kevin's, showing him how to hold both the hammer and the nail to guide the stroke.

"Hey!" Alex rose from the dead on Planet Zero and raced over. "Can I do it?"

"Me too." Jenny leaped on Nathaniel's back, knowing she was always welcome.

"I guess I got me a crew." Nathaniel figured that with all the extra help it would only take about twice as long to finish.

An hour later, Megan pulled up beside the long, classic lines of the T-Bird and stared. The house itself surprised her. The charming two-story cottage, with its neatly painted blue shutters and its window boxes bright with pansies, wasn't exactly the image she had of Nathaniel Fury. Nor was the tidy green lawn, the trimmed hedge, the fat barking puppy.

But it was Nathaniel who surprised her most. She was a bit taken aback by all that exposed golden skin, the lithe, muscled body. She was human, after all. But it was what he was doing that really captured her attention.

He was crouched over her son on the partially finished deck, their heads close, his big hand over Kevin's small one. Jenny was sitting adoringly beside him, and Alex was playing highwire on a joist.

"Hi, Megan! Look, I'm the death-defying Alex." In his excitement, Alex nearly lost his balance and almost plunged a harrowing eight inches to the ground. He pinwheeled his arms and avoided disaster.

"Close call," she said, and grinned at him.

"I'm in the center ring, without a net."

"Mom, we're building a deck." Kevin caught his bottom lip between his teeth and pounded a nail. "See?"

"Yes, I do." Briefcase in tow, Megan stopped to pet the eager puppy, who fell over backward in enthusiasm.

"And it's my turn next." Jenny batted her eyes at Nathaniel. "Isn't it?"

"That's right, sugar. Okay, Captain. Let's drive that baby home."

With a grunt of effort, Kevin sent the nail into the board. "I did it. I did the whole board." Proudly Kevin looked back at his mother. "We each get to do a board. This is my third one."

"It looks like you're doing a good job." To give the

devil his due, she smiled at Nathaniel. "Not everyone could handle it."

"Just takes a steady eye and a sure hand. Hey, mates, where's my timber?"

"We'll get it." Alex and Kevin scrambled together to heave the next plank.

Standing back, Megan watched the routine they'd worked out. Nathaniel took the board, sighted down it, set it in place. He tapped, shifted, using a small block of wood to measure the distance between the last board and the new one. Once he was satisfied, Jenny wriggled in front of him.

She wrapped both little hands around the hammer, and Nathaniel, a braver soul than Megan had imagined, held the nail.

"Keep your eye on the target," Nathaniel warned, then sat patiently while her little strokes gradually anchored the nail. Then, wrapping his hand over hers, he rammed it home. "Thirsty work," he said casually. "Isn't it, mates?"

"Aye, aye." Alex put his hands to his throat and gagged.

Nathaniel held the next nail. "There's some lemonade in the kitchen. If someone was to go fetch the pitcher and a few glasses…"

Four pairs of eyes turned on her, putting Megan firmly in her place. If she wasn't going to be a carpenter, she'd have to be a gofer.

"All right." She set the briefcase down and crossed the finished portion of the deck to the front door.

Nathaniel said nothing, waited.

Seconds later, a shrill wolf whistle sounded from inside, followed by a muffled scream. He was grinning by the time Bird squawked out his invitation: "Hey, sugar, buy you a drink? Here's looking at you, kid." When Bird began to sing a chorus of "There Is Nothing Like a Dame," the children collapsed into fits of laughter.

A few minutes later, Megan carried out a tray of drinks. Bird's voice followed her. "'Give me a kiss, and to that kiss a score!'"

She arched a brow as she set the tray on the deck. "Bogart, show tunes and poetry. That's quite a bird."

"He has an eye for pretty women." Nathaniel picked up a glass and downed half the contents. He scanned Megan, taking in the tidy French twist, the crisp blouse and slacks. "Can't say I blame him."

"Aunt Coco says Nate needs a woman." Alex smacked his lips over the tart lemonade. "I don't know why."

"To sleep with him," Jenny said, and caused both Nathaniel and Megan to gape. "Grown-ups get lonely at night, and they like to have someone to sleep with. Like Mom and Daddy do. I have my bear," she continued, referring to her favorite stuffed animal. "So I don't get lonely."

"Break time." Nathaniel gamely swallowed his choke of laughter. "Why don't you guys take Dog for a walk down by the water?"

The idea met with unanimous approval. With war whoops and slapping feet, they raced off.

"Kid's got a point." Nathaniel rubbed the cold glass over his sweaty brow. "Nights can get lonely."

"I'm sure Jenny will lend you her bear." Megan stepped away from him, as if studying the house. "It's a very nice place, Nathaniel." She flicked a finger over the sassy petals of a pansy. "Homey."

"You were expecting a crow's nest, some oilcloth?"

She had to smile. "Something like that. I want to thank you for letting Kevin spend the day."

"I'd say the three of them are working as a team these days."

Her smile softened. She could hear their laughter from behind the house. "Yes, you're right."

"I like having them around. They're good company." He shifted on the deck, folding his legs under him. "The boy's got your eyes."

Her smile faded. "No, Kevin's are brown." Like his father's.

"No, not the color. The look in them. Goes a lot deeper than brown or blue. How much have you told him?"

"I—" She brought herself back, angled her chin. "I didn't come here to discuss my personal life with you."

"What did you come here to discuss?"

"I came to get the children, and to go over your books."

Nathaniel nodded at her briefcase. "Got them in there?"

"Yes." She retrieved it, then, because she saw little choice, sat on the deck facing him. "I've finished the first quarter—that's January, February, March. Your outlay exceeded your income during that period, though you did have some cash flow through boat repairs. There is an outstanding account payable from February." She took out files, flipped through the neat computer-generated sheets. "A Mr. Jacques LaRue, in the amount of twelve hundred and thirty-two dollars and thirty-six cents."

"LaRue's had a tough year." Nathaniel poured more lemonade. "Holt and I agreed to give him some more time."

"That's your business, of course. Traditionally there would be late charges on any outstanding account after thirty days."

"Traditionally, on the island, we're a little friendlier."

"Your choice." She adjusted her glasses. "Now, as you can see, I've arranged the books into logical columns. Expenses—rent, utilities, office supplies, advertising and so forth. Then we have wages and withholding."

"New perfume."

She glanced over. "What?"

"You're wearing a new perfume. There's a hint of jasmine in it."

Distracted, she stared at him. "Coco gave it to me."

"I like it." He leaned closer. "A lot."

"Well." She cleared her throat, flipped a page. "And here we have income. I've added the weekly ticket sales from the tours to give you a month-by-month total, and a year-to-date. I see that you run a package deal with The Retreat, discounting your tour for hotel guests."

"Seemed friendly—and like good business."

"Yes, it's very smart business. On the average, eighty percent of the hotel guests take advantage of the package. I… Do you have to sit so close?"

"Yeah. Have dinner with me tonight, Meg."

"No."

"Afraid to be alone with me?"

"Yes. Now, as you can see, in March your income began an upswing—"

"Bring the boy."

"What?"

"Am I mumbling?" He smiled at her and slipped her glasses off her nose. "I said bring Kevin along. We'll take a drive out to this place I know. Great lobster rolls."

He gave the word *lobster* a broad New England twist that made her smile. "I can't claim they're up to Coco's standards, but there's plenty of local color."

"We'll see."

"Uh-uh. Parental cop-out."

She sighed, shrugged. "All right. Kevin would enjoy it."

"Good." He handed her glasses back before he rose to heft another board. "Tonight, then."

"Tonight?"

"Why wait? You can call Suzanna, tell her we'll drop the kids off at her house on the way."

"I suppose I could." Now that his back was to her, she had no choice but to watch the ripple of muscles play as he set the board. She ignored the quick tug at her midsection, and reminded herself that her son would be along as chaperon. "I've never had a lobster roll."

"Then you're in for a treat."

He was absolutely right. The long, winding drive in the spectacular T-Bird was joy enough. The little villages they passed through were as scenic as any postcard. The sun dipped down toward the horizon in the west, and the breeze in the open car smelled of fish, then flowers, then sea.

The restaurant was hardly more than a diner, a square of faded gray wood set on stilts in the water, across a rickety gangplank. The interior decoration ran to torn fishnets and battered lobster buoys.

Scarred tables dotted the equally scarred floor. The booths were designed to rip the hell out of panty hose. A dubious effort at romantic atmosphere was added by the painted tuna can and hurricane globe set in the center of each table. The candles globbed in the base of the cans were unlit. Today's menu was scrawled on a chalkboard hanging beside the open kitchen.

"We got lobster rolls, lobster salad and lobster lobster," a waitress explained to an obviously frazzled family of four. "We got beer, we got milk, iced tea and soft drinks. There's French fries and coleslaw, and no ice cream 'cause the machine's not working. What'll you have?"

When she spotted Nathaniel, she abandoned her customers and gave him a hard punch in the chest. "Where you been, Captain?"

"Oh, out and about, Jule. Got me a taste for lobster roll."

"You came to the right place." The waitress, scarecrow-thin with a puff of steel-gray hair, eyed Megan craftily. "So, who's this?"

"Megan O'Riley, her son Kevin. This is Julie Peterson. The best lobster cook on Mount Desert Island."

"The new accountant from The Towers." Julie gave a brisk nod. "Well, sit down, sit down. I'll fix you up when I get a minute." She swiveled back to her other customers. "You make up your mind yet, or are you just going to sit and take the air?"

"The food's better than the service." Nathaniel winked at Kevin as he led them to a booth. "You've just met one of the monuments of the island, Kevin. Mrs. Peterson's family has been trapping lobster and cooking them up for over a hundred years."

"Wow." He eyed the waitress, who, to almost-nine-year-old eyes, seemed old enough to have been handling that job personally for at least a century.

"I worked here some when I was a kid. Swabbing the decks." And she'd been kind to him, Nathaniel remembered. Giving him ice or salve for his bruises, saying nothing.

"I thought you worked with Holt's family—" Megan began, then cursed herself when he lifted a brow at her. "Coco mentioned it."

"I put in some time with the Bradfords."

"Did you know Holt's grandfather?" Kevin wanted to know. "He's one of the ghosts."

"Sure. He used to sit on the porch of the house where Alex and Jenny live now. Sometimes he'd walk up to the cliffs over by The Towers. Looking for Bianca."

"Lilah says they walk there together now. I haven't seen them." And it was a crushing disappointment. "Have you ever seen a ghost?"

"More than once." Nathaniel ignored the stiff kick Megan gave him under the table. "In Cornwall, where the cliffs are deadly and the fogs roll in like something alive, I saw a woman standing, looking out to sea. She wore a cape with a hood, and there were tears in her eyes."

Kevin was leaning forward now, rapt and eager.

"I started toward her, through the mist, and she turned. She was beautiful, and sad. 'Lost,' was what she said to me. 'He's lost. And so am I.' Then she vanished. Like smoke."

"Honest?" Kevin said in an awed whisper.

Honest wasn't the point, Nathaniel knew. The pull of the story was. "They called her the Captain's Lady, and legend is that her husband and his ship went down in a storm in the Irish Sea. Night after night while she lived, and long after, she walked the cliffs weeping for him."

"Maybe you should be writing books, like Max," Megan murmured, surprised and annoyed at the shiver that raced down her spine.

"Oh, he can spin a tale, Nate can." Julie plopped two beers and a soft drink on the table. "Used to badger me about all the places he was going to see. Well, guess you saw them, didn't you, Captain?"

"Guess I did." Nathaniel lifted the bottle to his lips. "But I never forgot you, darling."

Julie gave another cackling laugh, punched his shoulder. "Sweet-talker," she said, and shuffled off.

Megan studied her beer. "She didn't take our order."

"She won't. She'll bring us what she wants us to have." He took another pull of the beer. "Because she likes me. If you're not up for beer, I can charm her into switching it."

"No, it's fine. I suppose you know a lot of people on the island, since you grew up here."

"A few. I was gone a long time."

"Nate sailed around the whole world. Twice." Kevin slurped soda through his straw. "Through hurricanes and typhoons and everything."

"It must have been exciting."

"It had its moments."

"Do you miss it?"

"I sailed on another man's ship for more than fifteen years. Now I sail my own. Things change." Nathaniel draped his arm over the back of the booth. "Like you coming here."

"We like it." Kevin began to stab his straw in the ice. "Mom's boss in Oklahoma was a skinflint."

"Kevin."

"Granddad said so. And he didn't appreciate you. You were hiding your light under a bushel." Kevin didn't know what that meant, but his grandmother had said so.

"Granddad's biased." She smiled and ruffled her son's hair. "But we do like it here."

"Eat hearty," Julie ordered, and dropped three enormous platters on the table.

The long rolls of crusty bread were filled with chunks of lobster and flanked by a mound of coleslaw and a small mountain of French fries.

"Girl needs weight," Julie proclaimed. "Boy, too. Didn't know you liked 'em skinny, Captain."

"I like them any way I can get them," Nathaniel corrected, which sent Julie off into another gale of laughter.

"We'll never eat all of this." Megan stared, daunted, at her plate.

Nathaniel had already dug in. "Sure we will. So, have you looked over Fergus's book yet?"

"Not really." Megan sampled the first bite. Whatever the atmosphere, the food was four-star. "I want to get the backlog caught up first. Since Shipshape's books were the worst, I dealt with them first. I still have to work on your second quarter, and The Retreat's."

"Your mother's a practical woman, Kev."

"Yeah." Kevin managed to swallow a giant bite of lobster roll. "Granddad says she needs to get out more."

"Kevin."

But the warning came too late. Nathaniel was already grinning.

"Does he? What else does Granddad say?"

"She should live a little." Kevin attacked his French fries with the single-minded determination of a child. "'Cause she's too young to hole up like a hermit."

"Your granddad's a smart man."

"Oh, yeah. He knows everything. He's got oil for blood and horses on the brain."

"A quote from my mother," Megan said dryly. "She

knows everything, too. But you were asking about Fergus's book."

"Just wondered if it had scratched your curiosity."

"Some. I thought I might take an hour or so at night to work on it."

"I don't think that's what your daddy meant by living a little, Meg."

"Regardless." She turned back to the safer topic of the account book. "Some of the pages are faded badly, but other than a few minor mistakes, the accounts are very accurate. Except for the last couple of pages, where there are just numbers without any logic."

"Really. They don't add up?"

"They don't seem to, but I need to take a closer look."

"Sometimes you miss more by looking too close." Nathaniel winked at Julie as she set another round of drinks on the table. It was coffee for him this time. She knew that when he was driving he kept it to one beer. "I wouldn't mind taking a look at it."

Megan frowned at her. "Why?"

"I like puzzles."

"I don't think it's much of a puzzle, but if it's all right with the family, I don't have any objection." She leaned back, sighed. "Sorry, I just can't eat any more."

"It's okay." Nathaniel switched his empty plate with hers. "I can."

To Megan's amazement, he could. It wasn't much of a surprise that Kevin had managed to clean his plate. The way he was growing he often seemed in danger of eating china and all when he sat down for a meal. But Nathaniel ate his meal, then half of hers, without a blink.

"Have you always eaten like that?" Megan asked when they were driving away from the restaurant.

"Nope. Always wanted to, though. Never could seem to fill up as a kid." Of course, that might have been because there was little to fill up on. "At sea, you learn to eat anything, and plenty of it, while it's there."

"You should weigh three hundred pounds."

"Some people burn it off." He shifted his eyes to hers. "Like you. All that nervous energy you've got just eats up those calories."

"I'm not skinny," she muttered.

"Nope. Thought you were myself, till I got ahold of you. It's more like willowy—and you've got a real soft feel to you when you're pressed up against a man."

She hissed, started to look over her shoulder.

"He conked out the minute I turned on the engine," Nathaniel told her. And, indeed, she could see Kevin stretched out in the back, his head pillowed on his arms, sleeping soundly. "Though I don't see what harm there is for the boy to know a man's interested in his mother."

"He's a child." She turned back, the gentle look in her eyes gone. "I won't have him think that I'm—"

"Human?"

"It's not your affair. He's my son."

"That he is," Nathaniel agreed easily. "And you've done a hell of a job with him."

She slanted him a cautious look. "Thank you."

"No need to. Just a fact. It's tough raising a kid on your own. You found the way to do it right."

It was impossible to stay irritated with him, especially when she remembered what Coco had told her. "You lost your mother when you were young. Ah… Coco mentioned it."

"Coco's been mentioning a lot of things."

"She didn't mean any harm. You know how she is,

better than I. She cares so much about people, and wants to see them…"

"Lined up two by two? Yeah, I know her. She picked you out for me."

"She—" Words failed her. "That's ridiculous."

"Not to Coco." He steered easily around a curve. "Of course, she doesn't know that I know she's already got me scheduled to go down on one knee."

"It's fortunate, isn't it, that you're forewarned?"

Her indignant tone had a smile twitching at his lips. "Sure is. She's been singing your praises for months. And you almost live up to the advance publicity."

She hissed like a snake and turned to him. His grin, and the absurdity of the situation, changed indignation to amusement. "Thank you." She stretched out her legs, leaned back and decided to enjoy the ride. "I'd hate to have disappointed you."

"Oh, you didn't, sugar."

"I've been told you're mysterious, romantic and charming."

"And?"

"You almost live up to the advance publicity."

"Sugar—" he took her hand and kissed it lavishly "—I can be a lot better."

"I'm sure you can." She drew her hand away, refusing to acknowledge the rippling thrill up her arm. "If I wasn't so fond of her, I'd be annoyed. But she's so kind."

"She has the truest heart of anyone I've ever met. I used to wish she was my mother."

"I'm sorry." Before she could resist the urge, Megan laid a hand on his. "It must have been so hard, losing your mother when you were only a child."

"It's all right. It was a long time ago." Much too long for him to grieve. "I still remember seeing Coco in the village, or when I'd tag along with Holt to take fish up to The Towers. There she'd be, this gorgeous woman—looked like a queen. Never knew what color her hair would be from one week to the next."

"She's a brunette today," Megan said, and made him laugh.

"First woman I ever fell for. She came to the house a couple times, read my old man the riot act about his drinking. Guess she thought if he was sober he wouldn't knock me around so much." He took his eyes off the road again, met hers. "I imagine she mentioned that, too?"

"Yes." Uncomfortable, Megan looked away. "I'm sorry, Nathaniel. I hate when people discuss me, no matter how good their intentions. It's so intrusive."

"I'm not that sensitive, Meg. Everybody knew what my old man was like." He could remember, too well, the pitying looks, the glances that slid uneasily away. "It bothered me back then, but not anymore."

She struggled to find the right words. "Did Coco—did it do any good?"

He was silent a moment, staring out at the lowering sun and the bloodred light it poured into the water. "He was afraid of her, so he beat the hell out of me when she left."

"Oh, God."

"I'd just as soon she didn't know that."

"No." Megan had to swallow the hot tears lodged in her throat. "I won't tell her. That's why you ran away to sea, isn't it? To get away from him."

"That's one of the reasons." He reached over, ran a fingertip down her cheek. "You know, if I'd figured out the way to get to you was to tell you I'd taken a strap a few times, I'd have brought it up sooner."

"It's nothing to joke about." Megan's voice was low and furious. "There's no excuse for treating a child that way."

"Hey, I lived through it."

"Did you?" She shifted back to him, eyes steady. "Did you ever stop hating him?"

"No." He said it quietly. "No, I didn't. But I stopped letting it be important, and maybe that's healthier." He stopped the car in front of The Towers, turned to her. "Someone hurts you, in a permanent way, you don't forget it. But the best revenge is seeing that it doesn't matter."

"You're talking about Kevin's father, and it's not at all the same. I wasn't a helpless child."

"Depends on where you draw the line between helpless and innocent." Nathaniel opened the car door. "I'll carry Kevin in for you."

"You don't have to." She hurried out herself, but Nathaniel already had the boy in his arms.

They stood there for a moment, in the last glow of the day, the boy between them, his head resting securely on Nathaniel's shoulder, dark hair to dark hair, honed muscle to young limbs.

Something locked deep inside her swelled, tried to burst free. She sighed it away, stroked a hand over her son's back and felt the steady rhythm of his breathing.

"He's had a long day."

"So have you, Meg. There are shadows under your eyes. Since that means you didn't sleep any better than I did last night, I can't say I mind seeing them there."

It was hard, she thought, so very hard, to keep pulling away from the current that drew her to him. "I'm not ready for this, Nathaniel."

"Sometimes a wind comes up, blows you off course.

You're not ready for it, but if you're lucky, you end up in a more interesting place than you'd planned."

"I don't like to depend on luck."

"That's okay. I do." He shifted the boy more comfortably, and carried him to the house.

Chapter 6

"Don't see what all the damn to-do's about," Dutch grumbled as he whipped a delicate egg froth for his angel food cake surprise.

"Trenton St. James II is a member of the family." Running on nerves, Coco checked the temperature on her prime rib. She had a dozen things to deal with since the cucumber facial she'd indulged in had thrown off her timetable. "And the president of the St. James hotels." Satisfied that the beef was coming along nicely, she basted her roast duck. "As this is his first visit to The Retreat, it's important that everything run smoothly."

"Some rich bastard coming around to freeload."

"Mr. Van Horne!" Coco's heart lurched. After six months, she knew she shouldn't be shocked by the man. But, *really.* "I've known Mr. St. James for…well, a great number of years. I can assure you he is a successful businessman, an entrepreneur. *Not* a freeloader."

Dutch sniffed, gave Coco the once-over. She'd done herself up good and proper, he noted. The fancy-shmancy dress glittered and flowed down, stopping plenty short to show off her legs. Her cheeks were all pink, too. And he didn't think it was from kitchen heat. His lips curled back in a sneer.

"So what's he, your boyfriend?"

The pink deepened to rose. "Certainly not. A woman of my…experience doesn't have boyfriends." Surreptitiously she checked her face in the stainless-steel exhaust hood on the stove. "Beaux, perhaps."

Beaux. Ha! "I hear he's been married four times and pays enough alimony to balance the national debt. You looking to be number five?"

Speechless, Coco pressed a hand to her heart. "You are—" She stumbled, stuttered, over the words. "Impossibly rude. Impossibly crude."

"Hey, ain't none of my never-mind if you want to land yourself a rich fish."

She squeaked. Though the rolling temper that caused red dots to swim in front of her eyes appalled her—she was, after all, a civilized woman—she surged forward to ram a coral-tipped nail into his massive chest. "I will not tolerate any more of your insults."

"Yeah?" He poked her right back. "Whatcha gonna do about it?"

She leaned forward until they were nose-to-nose. "I will fire you."

"Now that'll break my heart. Go ahead, fancy face, give me the boot. See how you get by with tonight's dinner rush."

"I assure you, I will 'get by' delightfully." Her heart was beating too fast. Coco wondered it didn't soar right out of her breast.

"Like hell." He hated her perfume. Hated that it made

his nostrils twitch and his mouth water. "When I came on board, you were barely treading water."

She couldn't get her breath, simply couldn't. "This kitchen doesn't need you, Mr. Van Horne. And neither do I."

"You need me plenty." How had his hands gotten onto her shoulders? Why were hers pressed to his chest? The hell with how or why, he thought. He'd show her what was what.

Her eyes popped hard when his hard, sneering mouth crushed down on hers in a very thorough kiss. But she didn't see a thing. Her world, so beautifully secure, tilted under her feet. That was why—naturally that was why—she clung to him.

She would slap his face. She certainly would.

In just a few minutes.

Damn women, Dutch thought. Damn them all. Especially tall, curvy, sweet-smelling females with lips like…cooking cherries. He'd always had a weakness for tartness.

He jerked her away, but kept his big hands firm on her shoulders. "Let's get something straight…" he began.

"Now look here…" she said at the same time.

They both leaped apart like guilty children when the kitchen door swung open.

Megan stood frozen in the doorway, her jaw dropping. Surely she hadn't seen what she thought she'd seen. Coco was checking the oven, and Dutch was measuring flour into a bowl. They couldn't have been… embracing. Yet both of them were a rather startling shade of pink.

"Excuse me," she managed. "I'm sorry to, ah…"

"Oh, Megan, dear." Flustered, Coco patted her hair.

She was tingling, she realized. From embarrassment—and annoyance, she assured herself. "What can I do for you?"

"I just wanted to check a couple of the kitchen expenses." She was still goggling, her eyes shifting from Coco to Dutch and back. The tension in the room was thicker than Coco's split-pea soup. "But if you're busy, we can do it later."

"Nonsense." Coco wiped her sweaty palms on her apron. "We're just a little frantic preparing for Trenton's arrival."

"Trenton? Oh, I'd forgotten. Trent's father's expected." She was cautiously backing out of the room. "We don't need to do this now."

"No, no." Oh, Lord, Coco thought, don't leave me. "Now's a perfect time. We're under control here. Let's do it in your office, shall we?" She took Megan firmly by the arm. "Mr. Van Horne can handle things for a few minutes." Without waiting for his assent, she hurried from the room. "Details, details," Coco said gaily, and clung to Megan as though she were a life raft in a churning sea. "It seems the more you handle, the more there are."

"Coco, are you all right?"

"Oh, of course." But she pressed a hand to her heart. "Just a little contretemps with Mr. Van Horne. But that's nothing I can't deal with." She hoped. "How are your accounts coming along, dear? I must say I'd hoped you'd find time to glance at Fergus's book."

"Actually, I have—"

"Not that we want you working too hard." With the buzz going on in Coco's head, she didn't hear a word Megan said. "We want you to feel right at home here, to enjoy yourself. To relax. After all the trouble and excitement last year, we all want to relax. I don't think any of us could stand any more crises."

"I do not have, nor do I require, a reservation."

The crackling, irate voice stopped Coco in her tracks. The becoming flush in her cheeks faded to a dead white.

"Dear God, no. It can't be."

"Coco?" Megan took a firmer grip on Coco's arm. She felt the tremor and wondered if she could hold the woman up if she fainted.

"Young man." The voice rose, echoing off the walls. "Do you know who I am?"

"Aunt Colleen," Coco said in a shaky whisper. She let go one last shuddering moan, drew in a bracing breath, then walked bravely into the lobby. "Aunt Colleen," she said in an entirely different tone. "What a lovely surprise."

"Shock, you mean." Colleen accepted her niece's kiss, then rapped her cane on the floor. She was tall, thin as a rail and formidable as iron in a raw-silk suit and pearls as white as her hair. "I see you've filled the place with strangers. Better to have it burned to the ground. Tell this insolent boy to have my bags taken up."

"Of course." Coco gestured for a bellman herself. "In the family wing, second floor, first room on the right," she instructed.

"And don't toss those bags around, boy." Colleen leaned on her gold-tipped cane and studied Megan. "Who's this?"

"You remember Megan, Aunt Colleen. Sloan's sister? You met at Amanda's wedding."

"Yes, yes." Colleen's eyes narrowed, measured. "Got a son, don't you?" Colleen knew all there was to know about Kevin. Had made it her business to know.

"Yes, I do. It's nice to see you again, Miss Calhoun."

"Ha. You'd be the only one of this lot who thinks so."
Ignoring them both, she walked to Bianca's portrait,
studied it and the emeralds glistening in their case. She
sighed, but so quietly no one could hear.

"I want brandy, Cordelia, before I take a look at what
you've done to this place."

"Of course. We'll just go into the family wing.
Megan, please, join us."

It was impossible to deny the plea in Coco's eyes.

A few moments later, they had settled into the family parlor. Here, the wallpaper was still faded, peeling
in spots. There were scars on the floor in front of the
fireplace where errant embers had seared and burned.

"Nothing's changed here, I see." Colleen sat like a
queen in a wing chair.

"We've concentrated on the hotel wing." Nervous
and babbling, Coco poured brandy. "Now that it's done,
we're beginning renovations. Two of the bedrooms are
finished. And the nursery's lovely."

"Humph." She'd come specifically to see the children—and only secondarily to drive Coco mad. "Where
is everyone? I come to see my family and find nothing
but strangers."

"They'll be along. We're having a dinner party tonight, Aunt Colleen." Coco kept the brilliant smile plas-
tered on her face. "Trent's father's joining us for a few
days."

"Aging playboy," Colleen mumbled into her brandy.
"You." She pointed at Megan. "Accountant, aren't you?"

"Yes, ma'am."

"Megan's a whiz with figures," Coco said desperately. "We're so grateful she's here. And Kevin, too, of
course. He's a darling boy."

"I'm talking to the girl, Cordelia. Go fuss in the kitchen."

"But—"

"Go on, go on."

With an apologetic look for Megan, Coco fled.

"The boy'll be nine soon?"

"Yes, in a couple of months." She was prepared, braced, for a scathing comment on his lineage.

Tapping her fingers on the arm of the chair, Colleen nodded. "Get along with Suzanna's brood, does he?"

"Very well. They've rarely been apart since we arrived." Megan did her best not to squirm. "It's been wonderful for him. And for me."

"Dumont bothering you?"

Megan blinked. "I beg your pardon?"

"Don't be a fool, girl, I asked if that excuse for a human being has been bothering you."

Megan's spine straightened like a steel rod. "No. I haven't seen or heard from Baxter since before Kevin was born."

"You will." Colleen scowled and leaned forward. She wanted to get a handle on this Megan O'Riley. "He's been making inquiries."

Megan's fingers clenched on the snifter of brandy. "I don't understand."

"Poking his nose in, asking questions." Colleen gave her cane an imperious thump.

"How do you know?"

"I keep my ear to the ground when it comes to family." Eyes bright, Colleen waited for a reaction, got none. "You moved here, didn't you? Your son's been accepted as Alex and Jenny—and Christian's—brother."

Ice was forming in Megan's stomach, thin, brittle strips of it. "That has nothing to do with him."

"Don't be a fool. A man like Dumont thinks the world revolves around him. His eye's on politics, girl, and the way that particular circus is running, a few well-chosen words from you to the right reporter…" The idea was pleasant enough to make Colleen smile. "Well, his road to Washington would be a steeper climb."

"I've no intention of going to the press, of exposing Kevin to public attention."

"Wise." Colleen sipped again. "A pity, but wise. You tell me if he tries anything. I'd like to tangle with him again."

"I can handle it myself."

Colleen lifted one snowy brow. "Perhaps you can."

"How come I have to wear a dumb tie?" Kevin squirmed while Megan fumbled with the knot. Her fingers had been stiff and cold ever since her talk with Colleen.

"Because it's a special dinner and you need to look your best."

"Ties are stupid. I bet Alex doesn't have to wear a stupid tie."

"I don't know what Alex is wearing," Megan said, with the last of her patience. "But you're doing as you're told."

The sharp tone, rarely heard, had his bottom lip poking out. "I'd rather have pizza."

"Well, you're not having pizza. Damn it, Kevin, hold still!"

"It's choking me."

"*I'm* going to choke you in a minute." She blew her hair out of her eyes and secured the knot. "There. You look very handsome."

"I look like a dork."

"Fine, you look like a dork. Now put your shoes on."

Kevin scowled at the shiny black loafers. "I hate those shoes. I want to wear my sneakers."

Exasperated, she leaned down until their faces were level. "Young man, you will put your shoes on, and you will watch your tone of voice. Or you'll find yourself in very hot water."

Megan marched out of his room and across the hall to her own. Snatching her brush from the dresser, she began to drag it through her hair. She didn't want to go to the damn dinner party, either. The aspirin she'd downed an hour before hadn't even touched the splitting headache slicing through her skull. But she had to put on her party face and go down, pretend she wasn't terrified and angry and sick with worry over Baxter Dumont.

Colleen might be wrong, she thought. After all, it had been nearly a decade. Why would Baxter bother with her and Kevin now?

Because he wanted to be a United States senator. Megan closed her eyes. She read the paper, didn't she? Baxter had already begun his campaign for the seat. And an illegitimate son, never acknowledged, hardly fit the straight-arrow platform he'd chosen.

"Mom."

She saw Kevin's reflection in the mirror. His shoes were on—and his chin was on his chest. Guilt squeezed its sticky fingers around her heart. "Yes, Kevin."

"How come you're so mad at everything?"

"I'm not." Wearily she sat on the edge of the bed. "I've just got a little headache. I'm sorry I snapped at you." She held out her arms, sighing when he filled them. "You're such a handsome dork, Kev." When he laughed, she kissed the top of his head. "Let's go down. Maybe Alex and Jenny are here."

They were, and Alex was just as disgusted with his tie as Kevin was with his. But there was too much going on for the boys to sulk for long. There were canapés to gobble, babies to play with and adventures to plan.

Everyone, naturally, was talking at once.

The volume in the room cut through Megan's aching head like a rusty saw. She accepted the flute of champagne Trenton II offered her, and did her best to pretend an interest in his flirtation. He was trim and tall and tanned, glossily handsome and charming. And Megan was desperately relieved when he turned his attentions on Coco.

"Make a nice couple, don't they?" Nathaniel murmured in her ear.

"Striking." She took a cube of cheese and forced it down.

"You don't look in the party mood, Meg."

"I'm fine." To distract him, she changed the subject. "You might be interested in what I think I might have walked in on this afternoon."

"Oh?" Taking her arm, he steered her toward the open terrace doors.

"Coco and Dutch."

"Fighting again? Saucepans at twenty paces?"

"Not exactly." She took a deep breath of air, hoping it would clear her head. "They were…at least I think they were…"

Nathaniel's brows shot up. He could fill in the blanks himself. "You're joking."

"No. They were nose-to-nose, with their arms around each other." She managed to smile even as she rubbed at the throbbing in her temple. "At my unexpected and ill-timed entrance, they jumped apart as if they'd been planning murder. And they were blushing. Both of them."

"The Dutchman, blushing?" Nathaniel started to laugh, but it began to sink in. "Good God."

"I think it's sweet."

"Sweet." He looked back inside, where Coco, regally elegant, was laughing over something Trenton had whispered in her ear. "She's out of his league. She'll break his heart."

"What a ridiculous thing to say." Lord, why didn't her head just fall off her shoulders and give her some relief? "Sporting events have leagues, not romances."

"The Dutchman and Coco." It worried him, because they were two of the very few people in the world he could say he loved. "You're the accountant, sugar, and you're going to tell me that adds up?"

"I'm not telling you anything," she shot back. "Except I think they're attracted to each other. And stop calling me 'sugar.'"

"Okay, simmer down." He looked back down at her, focused on her. "What's the matter?"

Guiltily she dropped her hand. She'd been massaging her temple again. "Nothing."

With an impatient oath, he turned her fully to face him, looked into her eyes. "Headache, huh? Bad one?"

"No, it's— Yes," she admitted. "Vicious."

"You're all tensed up." He began to knead her shoulders. "Tight as a spring."

"Don't."

"This is purely therapeutic." He rubbed his thumbs in gentle circles over her collarbone. "Any pleasure either of us gets out of it is incidental. Have you always been prone to headaches?"

His fingers were strong and male and magical. It was impossible not to stretch under them. "I'm not prone to headaches."

"Too much stress." His hands skimmed lightly up to her temples. She closed her eyes with a sigh. "You bottle too much up, Meg. Your body makes you pay for it. Turn around, let me work on those shoulders."

"It's not—" But the protest died away when his hands began to knead at the knots.

"Relax. Pretty night, isn't it? Moon's full, stars are out. Ever walk up on the cliffs in the moonlight, Megan?"

"No."

"Wildflowers growing right out of the rock, the water thundering. You can imagine those ghosts Kevin's so fond of strolling hand in hand. Some people think it's a lonely place, but it's not."

His voice and his hands were so soothing. She could almost believe there was nothing to worry about. "There's a painting at Suzanna's of the cliffs in moonlight," Megan offered, trying to focus on the conversation.

"Christian Bradford's work—I've seen it. He had a feel for that spot. But there's nothing like the real thing. You could walk with me there after dinner. I'll show you."

"This isn't the time to fool around with the girl." Colleen's voice cut through the evening air, and she stamped her cane in the doorway.

Though Megan tensed again, Nathaniel kept his hands where they were and grinned. "Seems like a fine time to me, Miss Colleen."

"Ha! Scoundrel." Colleen's lips twitched. Nothing she liked better than a handsome scoundrel. "Always were. I remember you, running wild through the village. Looks like the sea made a man of you, all right. Stop fidgeting, girl. He's not going to let loose of you. If you're lucky."

Nathaniel kissed the top of Megan's head. "She's shy."

"Well, she'll have to get over it, won't she? Cordelia's finally going to feed us. I want you to sit with me, talk about boats."

"It would be a pleasure."

"Well, come on, bring her. Lived on cruise ships half my life or more," Colleen began. "I'll wager I've seen more of the sea than you, boy."

"I wouldn't doubt it, ma'am." Nathaniel kept one hand on Megan and offered Colleen his arm. "With a trail of broken hearts in your wake."

She gave a hoot of laughter. "Damn right."

The dining room was full of the scents of food and flowers and candle wax. The moment everyone was settled, Trenton II rose, glass in hand.

"I'd like to make a toast." His voice was as cultured as his dinner suit. "To Cordelia, a woman of extraordinary talents and beauty."

Glasses were clinked. From his spy hole at the crack in the doorway, Dutch snorted, scowled, then stomped back to his own kitchen.

"Trent." C.C. leaned toward her husband, her voice low. "You know I love you."

He thought he knew what was coming. "Yes, I do."

"And I adore your father."

"Mmm-hmm…"

"And if he puts the moves on Aunt Coco, I'm going to have to kill him."

"Right." Trent smiled weakly and began on the first course.

At the other end of the table, sublimely ignorant of the threat, Trenton beamed at Colleen. "What do you think of The Retreat, Miss Calhoun?"

"I dislike hotels. Never use them."

"Aunt Colleen." Coco fluttered her hands. "The St. James hotels are world-famous for their luxury and taste."

"Can't stand them," Colleen said complacently as she spooned up soup. "What's this stuff?"

"It's lobster bisque, Aunt Colleen."

"Needs salt," she said, for the devil of it. "You, boy." She jabbed a finger down the table at Kevin. "Don't slouch. You want your bones to grow crooked?"

"No, ma'am."

"Got any ambitions?"

Kevin stared helplessly, and was relieved when his mother's hand closed over his. "I could be a sailor," he blurted out. "I steered the *Mariner*."

"Ha!" Pleased, she picked up her wine. "Good for you. I won't tolerate any idlers in my family. Too thin. Eat your soup, such as it is."

With a quiet moan, Coco rang for the second course.

"She never changes." Lazily content, Lilah rocked while Bianca suckled hungrily at her breast. The nursery was quiet, the lights were low. Megan had headed for it, figuring it would be the perfect escape hatch.

"She's…" Megan searched for a diplomatic phrase. "Quite a lady."

"She's a nosy old nuisance." Lilah laughed lightly. "But we love her."

In the next rocker, Amanda sighed. "As soon as she hears about Fergus's book, she's going to start nagging you."

"And badgering," C.C. put in, cradling Ethan.

"And hounding," Suzanna finished up as she changed Christian's diaper.

"That sounds promising."

"Don't worry." With a laugh, Suzanna slipped Christian into his sleeper. "We're right behind you."

"Notice," Lilah added with a smile, "the direction is *behind.*"

"About the book." Megan flicked a finger over a dancing giraffe on a mobile. "I've made copies of several pages I thought you'd be interested in. He made a lot of notations, about business deals, personal business, purchases. At one point he inventories jewelry— Bianca's, I assume—for insurance purposes."

"The emeralds?" Amanda's brow rose at Megan's nod. "And to think of all the hours we spent going through papers, trying to find proof that they existed."

"There's a number of other pieces—hundreds of thousands of dollars' worth in 1913 dollars."

"He sold nearly everything," C.C. murmured. "We found the documents of sale. He got rid of anything that reminded him of Bianca."

"It still hurts," Lilah admitted. "Not the money, though God knows we could have used it. It's the loss of what was hers, what we won't be able to pass on."

"I'm sorry."

"Don't be." Amanda rose to lay a sleeping Delia in her crib. "We're too sentimental. I suppose we all feel such a close connection with Bianca."

"I know what you mean." It felt odd to admit it, but Megan was compelled. "I feel it, too. I suppose from seeing the references to her in the old book, and having her portrait right there in the lobby." A bit embarrassed, she laughed. "Sometimes, when you walk down the halls at night, it's almost as if you could sense her."

"Of course," Lilah said easily. "She's here."

"Excuse me, ladies." Nathaniel stepped inside, obviously comfortable in a nursery inhabited by babies and nursing mothers.

Lilah smiled slowly. "Well, hello, handsome. What brings you to the maternity wing?"

"Just coming to fetch my date."

When he took Megan's arm, she drew back. "We don't have a date."

"A walk, remember?"

"I never said—"

"It's a lovely night for it." Suzanna lifted Christian into her arms, cooed to him.

"I have to put Kevin to bed."

She was digging in her heels, but it didn't seem to be doing any good.

"I've already tucked him in." Nathaniel propelled her toward the doors.

"You put Kevin to bed?"

"Since he'd fallen asleep in my lap, it seemed the thing to do. Oh, Suzanna, Holt said the kids are ready whenever you are."

"I'm on my way." Suzanna waited until Megan and Nate were out of earshot before she turned to her sisters. "What do you think?"

Amanda smiled smugly. "I think it's working perfectly."

"I have to agree." C.C. settled Ethan comfortably in

his crib. "I thought Lilah had lost her mind when she came up with the idea of getting those two together."

Lilah yawned, sighed. "I'm never wrong." Then her eyes lit. "I bet we can see them from the window."

"*Spy* on them?" Amanda arched her brows. "Good idea," she said, and darted to the window.

They were outlined in the moonlight that sprinkled the lawn.

"You're complicating things, Nathaniel."

"Simplifying," he corrected. "Nothing simpler than a walk in the moonlight."

"That's not where you expect all this to end."

"Nope. But we're still moving at your pace, Meg." He brought her hand to his lips, kissed it absently, when they began the climb. "I seem to have this need to be around you. It's the damnedest thing. Can't shake it. So I figure, why try? Why not just roll with it?"

"I'm not a simple woman." She wished she could be, just for tonight, just for an hour in the starlight. "I have baggage and resentments and insecurities I didn't even realize were there until I met you. I'm not going to let myself be hurt again."

"No one's going to hurt you." In a subtle gesture of protection, he slipped an arm around her and looked up at the sky. "Look how big the moon is tonight. Just hanging there. You can see Venus, and the little star that dogs her. There's Orion." He lifted her hand, tracing the sky with it as he had once traced his charts. "And the Twins. See?"

"Yes." She watched their joined hands connect stars while the breeze lifted lovingly off the water and stirred the flowers that grew wild in the rock.

Romantic, mysterious, Coco had said. Yes, he was,

and Megan realized she was much more susceptible to both than she would have believed.

For she was here, wasn't she, standing on a cliff with a seafaring man whose callused hand held hers, whose voice helped her see the pictures painted by the stars. His body was warm and solid against hers. And her blood was pumping fast and free in her veins.

Alive. The wind and the sea and the man made her feel so alive.

And perhaps there was something more—those ghosts of the Calhouns'. The cliffs seemed to invite spirits to walk, the air filled with contentment. And the glow of love that had outlasted time.

"I shouldn't be here like this." But she didn't move away, not even when his lips brushed over her hair.

"Listen," he murmured. "Close your eyes and listen, and you can hear the stars breathing."

She obeyed, and listened to the whisper and throb of the air. And of her own heart. "Why do you make me feel this way?"

"I don't have an answer. Not everything adds up neat, Meg." Because he had a great need to see her face, he turned her gently. "Not everything has to." And kissed her. His lips skimmed hers, journeyed up to her temple, over her brow and down. "How's the headache?"

"It's gone. Nearly."

"No. Keep your eyes closed." His lips traced over them, soft as air, before trailing slowly over her face. "Kiss me back, will you?"

How could she not, when his mouth was so tempting on hers? With a small sound of surrender, she let her heart lead. Just for tonight, she promised herself. Just for a moment.

That slow, melting change almost undid him. She

went pliant in his arms, those hesitant lips heating, parting, offering. It took all his willpower not to drag her against him and plunder.

She wouldn't resist. Perhaps he'd known that there would be enough magic on those cliffs to bewitch them both, to seduce her into surrender—and to remind him to take care.

"I want you, Megan." He took his lips down her throat, up over her jaw. "I want you so much it's got me tied in knots."

"I know. I wish…" She pressed her face to his shoulder. "I'm not playing games, Nathaniel."

"I know." He stroked a hand down her hair. "It would be easier if you were, because I know all the rules." Cupping her face, he lifted it. "And how to break them." He sighed, kissed her again, lightly. "They make it damn hard for me, those eyes of yours." He stepped back. "I'd better take you in."

"Nathaniel." She laid a hand on his chest. "You're the first man who's made me…who I've wanted to be with since Kevin was born."

Something flashed in his eyes, wild, dangerous, before he banked it. "Do you think it makes it easier on me, knowing that?" He would have laughed, if he hadn't felt so much like exploding. "Megan, you're killing me." But he swung an arm around her shoulders and led her down the cliff path.

"I don't know how to handle this," she said under her breath. "I haven't had to handle anything like this before."

"Keep it up," he warned, "and you're over my shoulder, shanghaied straight to bed. Mine."

The image gave her a quick thrill, and a guilty one. "I'm just trying to be honest."

"Try lying," he said with a grimace. "Make it easier on me."

"I'm a lousy liar." She slanted a look at him. Wasn't it interesting, she mused, that for once he was the one at a disadvantage? "It doesn't seem logical that it would bother you to know what I'm feeling."

"I'm having a lot of trouble dealing with what I'm feeling." He took a long, steadying breath. "And I'm not feeling logical." Nor, he thought ruefully, would he sleep tonight. "'Desire hath no rest.'"

"What?"

"Robert Burton. Nothing."

They walked toward the lights of The Towers. The shouting reached them before they crossed the lawn.

"Coco," Megan said.

"Dutch." Taking firm hold of Megan's hand, Nathaniel quickened his pace.

"You're insulting and obnoxious," Coco snapped at Dutch, her chin up, her hands planted on her hips.

His massive arms were folded across his barrel of a chest. "I saw what I saw, said what I said."

"I was not draped all over Trenton like a…a…"

"Barnacle," Dutch said with relish. "Like a barnacle on the hull of a fancy yacht."

"We happen to have been dancing."

"Ha! That's what you call it. We got another name for it. Where I come from, we call it—"

"Dutch!" Nathaniel cut off the undoubtedly crude description.

"There." Mortified, Coco smoothed down her dress. "You've made a scene."

"You were the one making a scene, with that smooth-skinned rich boy. Flaunting yourself."

"F-f-flaunting." Enraged, she drew herself up to her

full, and considerable, height. "I have never flaunted in my life. You, sir, are despicable."

"I'll show you despicable, lady."

"Cut it out." Prepared for fists to fly, Nathaniel stepped between them. "Dutch, what the hell's wrong with you? Are you drunk?"

"A nip or two of rum never rattled my brain." He glared over Nathaniel's shoulder at Coco. "It's her that's acting snockered. Out of my way, boy, I've got a thing or two left to say."

"You've finished," Nathaniel corrected.

"Out of his way." All eyes turned to Coco. She was flushed, bright-eyed, and regal as a duchess. "I prefer to handle this matter myself."

Megan tugged gently on her arm. "Coco, don't you think you should go inside?"

"I do not." She caught herself and added a friendly pat. "Now, dear, you and Nate run along. Mr. Van Horne and I prefer to handle this privately."

"But—"

"Nathaniel," Coco said, interrupting her, "take Megan inside now."

"Yes, ma'am."

"Are you sure we should leave them alone?"

Nathaniel continued to steer Megan to the terrace doors. "You want to get in the middle of that?"

Megan glanced back over her shoulder. "No." She chuckled, shook her head. "No, I don't think so."

"Well, Mr. Van Horne," Coco began, when she was certain they were alone again. "Do you have something more to say?"

"I got plenty." Prepared for battle, he stepped forward. "You tell that slick-talking rich boy to keep his hands to himself."

She tossed back her head and enjoyed the mad flutter of her heart when her eyes met his. "And if I don't?"

Dutch growled like a wolf—like a wolf, Coco thought, challenging his mate. "I'll break his puny arms like matchsticks."

Oh, my, she thought. Oh, my goodness. "Will you, really?"

"Just you try me." He gave her a jerk, and she let herself tumble into his arms.

This time she was ready for the kiss, and met it head-on. By the time they broke apart, they were both breathless and stunned.

Sometimes, Coco realized, it was up to the woman. She moistened her lips, swallowed hard.

"My room's on the second floor."

"I know where it is." A ghost of a smile flitted around his mouth. "Mine's closer." He swept her into his arms—very much, Coco thought dreamily, like a pirate taking his hostage.

"You're a fine, sturdy woman, Coco."

She pressed a hand on her thundering heart. "Oh, Niels."

Chapter 7

It wasn't like Megan to daydream. Years of discipline had taught her that dreams were for sleeping, not for rainy mornings when the fog was drifting around the house and the windows ran wet, as if with tears. But her computer hummed, unattended, and her chin was on her fist as her mind wandered back, as it had several times over the past few days, toward moonlight and wildflowers and the distant thunder of surf.

Now and again she caught herself and fell back on logic. It wouldn't pay to forget that the only romance in her life had been an illusion, a lie that betrayed her innocence, her emotions and her future. She'd thought herself immune, been content to be immune. Until Nathaniel.

What should she do, now that her life had taken this fast, unexpected swing? After all, she was no longer a child who believed in or needed promises and coaxing words. Now that her needs had been stirred, could she satisfy them without being hurt?

Oh, how she wished her heart wasn't involved. How she wished she could be smart and savvy and sophisticated and indulge in a purely physical affair, without emotion weighing in so heavily.

Why couldn't attraction, leavened with affection and respect, be enough? It should be such a simple equation. Two consenting adults, plus desire, times understanding and passion, equals mutual pleasure.

She just wished she could be sure there wasn't some hidden fraction that would throw off the simple solution.

"Megan?"

"Hmm?" Dreamily she turned toward the sound of the voice. Her imaginings shattered when she saw Suzanna inside the office, smiling at her. "Oh, I didn't hear you come in."

"You were miles away."

Caught drifting, Megan fought back embarrassment and shuffled papers. "I suppose I was. Something about the rain."

"It's lovely—always sets my mind wandering." Suzanna thought she knew just where Megan's mind had wandered. "Though I doubt the tourists or the children think so."

"Kevin thought the fog was great—until I told him he couldn't climb on the cliffs in it."

"And Alex and Jenny's plans for an assault on Fort O'Riley have been postponed. The kids are in Kevin's room, defending the planet against aliens. It's wonderful watching them together."

"I know. They've blended together so well."

"Like a mud ball," Suzanna said with a laugh, and eased a jean-clad hip on the edge of Megan's desk. "How's the work coming?"

"It's moving along. Amanda kept everything in

order, so it's just a matter of shifting it into my own system and computerizing."

"It's a tremendous relief for her, having you take it over. Some days she'd be doing the books with a phone at her ear and Delia at her breast."

The image made Megan grin. "I can see it. She's amazingly organized."

"An expert juggler. Nothing she hates more than to bobble a ball. You'd understand that."

"Yeah, I do." Megan picked up a pencil and ran it between her fingers. "I worried about coming here, Suzanna, bringing Kevin. I was afraid I'd not only bobble a ball, but drop all of them, because I'd be so anxious not to say anything, even think anything, that would make you uncomfortable."

"Aren't we past that, Megan?"

"You were." Sighing, Megan set the pencil down again. "Maybe it's a little harder, being the other woman."

"Were you?" Suzanna said gently. "Or was I?"

Megan could only shake her head. "I can't say I wish I could go back and change things, because if I did I wouldn't have Kevin." She took a long breath, met Suzanna's eyes levelly. "I know you consider Kevin a brother to your children, and that you love him."

"Yes, I do."

"I want you to know that I think of your children as my family and I love them."

Suzanna reached over to lay a hand over Megan's. "I know you do. One of the reasons I dropped in was to ask if you'd mind if Kevin came along with us. I'm going to do some greenhouse work today. Alex and Jenny always enjoy it—especially since it includes pizza for lunch."

"I can't think of anything he'd rather do. And it would make up for having to wear a tie the other night."

Suzanna's eyes lit with humor. "I nearly had to strangle Alex to get him into his. I hope Aunt Coco doesn't plan any more formal dinner parties for some time to come." She tilted her head. "Speaking of Aunt Coco, have you seen her today?"

"Only for a minute, right after breakfast. Why?"

"Was she singing?"

"As a matter of fact, she was." Megan touched her tongue to her top lip. "She's been singing in the morning for several days now."

"She was singing just now, too. And wearing her best perfume." Uneasy, Suzanna nibbled her lip. "I was wondering if Trent's father... Of course, he's gone back to Boston now, so I thought there was nothing to worry about. He's a lovely man, and we're all very fond of him, but, well, he's been married four times, and he doesn't seem able to keep his eye from roving."

"I noticed." After a quick debate on privacy versus disclosure, Megan cleared her throat. "Actually, I don't think Coco's looking in that direction."

"No?"

"Dutch," Megan said, and watched Suzanna's eyes go blank.

"Excuse me?"

"I think she and Dutch are...infatuated."

"Dutch? Our Dutch? But she's always complaining about him, and he's snarling at her every chance he gets. They're always fighting, and..." She trailed off, pressed her hands to her lips. "Oh..." she said, while her eyes danced over them. "Oh, oh, oh..."

They stared at each other, struggled dutifully for perhaps three seconds before bursting into laughter.

Megan fell easily into the sisterly pleasure of discussing a family member. After she told Suzanna about walking in on Coco and Dutch in the kitchen, she followed it up with the scene on the terrace.

"There were sparks flying, Suzanna. At first I thought they were going to come to blows, then I realized it was more of a—well, a mating ritual."

"A mating ritual," Suzanna repeated in a shaky voice. "Do you really think they—?"

"Well." Megan wriggled her eyebrows. "She's been doing a lot of singing lately."

"She certainly has." Suzanna let the idea stew for a moment, found it simmered nicely. "I think I'll drop by the kitchen before I go. Check out the atmosphere."

"I hope I can count on a full report."

"Absolutely." Still chuckling, Suzanna rose to go to the door. "I guess that was some moon the other night."

"It was," Megan murmured. "Some moon."

Suzanna paused with her hand on the knob. "And Nathaniel's some man."

"I thought we were talking about Dutch."

"We were talking about romance," Suzanna corrected. "I'll see you later."

Megan frowned at the closed door. Good Lord, she thought, was she that obvious?

After spending the rest of the morning and the first part of the afternoon on The Retreat's accounts, Megan gave herself the small reward of an hour with Fergus's book. She enjoyed tallying up the costs of stabling horses, maintaining carriages. It was an eye-opener to see how much expense was involved in giving a ball at The Towers in 1913. And, by reading Fergus's margin notes, to come to understand his motives.

Invitations all accepted. No one dare decline.
B. ordered flowers—argued about ostentation.
Told her big display equals success and wife must
never question husband. She will wear emeralds,
not pearl choker as she suggested, show society
my taste and means, remind her of her place.

Her place, Megan thought with pity for Bianca, had
been with Christian. How sad that it had taken death
to unite them.

Wanting to dispel the gloom, she flipped to the back
pages. The numbers simply didn't make sense. Not expenses, she mused. Not dates. Account numbers, perhaps. Stock-market prices, lot numbers?

Perhaps it would be worth a trip to the library to see
if she could unearth any information from 1913 that cor-
related. And on the way she could stop by Shipshape to
drop off the completed spreadsheet for April and pick
up any more receipts.

If she happened to run into Nathaniel, it would be
purely coincidental.

It was a pleasure to drive in the rain. The slow, steady
stream of drops had most of the summer people seeking indoor entertainment. A few pedestrians wandered
the sidewalks, window-shopping under umbrellas. The
water in Frenchman Bay was gray and misted, with the
masts and sails of ships spearing through the heavy air.

She could hear the ring of bell buoys, the drone of
foghorns. It was as if the entire island were tucked under
a blanket, snug and safe and solitary. She was tempted
to keep driving, to take the twisting road to Acadia
National Park, or the meandering one along the shore.

Maybe she would, she thought. After she completed

the day's business, she would take that drive, explore her new home. And maybe she would ask Nathaniel to join her.

But she didn't see his car outside Shipshape. Ridiculous to say it didn't matter whether she saw him or not, she realized. Because it did matter. She wanted to see him, to watch the way his eyes deepened and locked on hers. The way his lips curved.

Maybe he'd parked around the corner, out of sight. Snagging her briefcase, she dashed from her car into the office. It was empty.

The first slap of disappointment was stunning. She hadn't realized just how much she'd counted on him being there until he wasn't. Then she heard, faintly, through the rear wall, the throb of bass from a radio. Someone was in the shop attached to the back of the building, she concluded. Probably working on repairs as the seas were too rough for tours.

She wasn't going to check out who was back there, she told herself firmly. She'd come on legitimate business and she took out the latest spreadsheet and set it on the overburdened desk. But on a purely practical level, she would need to go over, with at least one of them, the second quarter and the projections for the rest of the year. But she supposed it could wait.

A long look around showed her a disorder she couldn't comprehend. How could anyone work, or hope to concentrate, in such a mess?

She was tempted to organize, but turned her back on the chaos and walked to the filing cabinets. She'd take what she needed and leave the rest. Then she would, casually, wander around back, to the shop.

When she heard the door open, she turned, ready

with a smile. It faded a little when she saw a stranger in the doorway. "May I help you?"

The man stepped fully inside and shut the door behind him. When he smiled, something jittered inside Megan's brain. "Hello, Megan."

For an instant, time froze, and then it rewound. Slow motion for five years, six, then back a decade, to a time when she'd been young and careless and ready to believe in love at first sight.

"Baxter," she whispered. How odd, she thought dully, that she hadn't recognized him. He'd hardly changed in ten years. He was as handsome, as smooth and polished, as he'd been when she first saw him. A trim, Savile Row–suited Prince Charming with lies on his lips.

Baxter smiled down at Megan. For days he'd been trying to catch her alone. Frustration had pushed him to approach her here and now. Because he was a man concerned with his image, he'd checked the office thoroughly before he stepped through the door. It was easy to see she was alone in the small space. There were things he intended to settle with her once and for all. Calmly, of course, he thought as she stared at him. Reasonably. Privately.

"Pretty as ever, aren't you?" It pleased him to see her eyes go blank with shock. The advantage was with him, as he preferred it. After all, he'd been planning this reunion for several weeks now. "The years have improved your looks, Megan. You've lost that charming baby fat, and you've become almost elegant. My compliments."

When he stepped closer, she didn't move, couldn't make her legs or her brain respond. Not even when he lifted a finger and trailed it down her cheek, under her chin, to tip it up in an old habit she'd made herself forget.

"You were always a beauty, Megan, with that wide-eyed innocence that makes a man want to corrupt."

She shuddered. He smiled.

"What are you doing here?" *Kevin* was all she could think. Thank God Kevin wasn't with her.

"Funny, I was going to ask you the same. Just what are you doing here, Megan?"

"I live here." She hated hearing the hesitancy in her voice, like the throb of an old scar. "I work here."

"Tired of Oklahoma, were you? Wanted a change of scene?" He leaned closer, until she backed into the filing cabinet. Bribery, he knew, wouldn't work with her. Not with the O'Riley money behind her. Intimidation was the next logical choice. "Don't take me for a fool, Megan. It would be a terrible, costly mistake."

When her back hit the filing cabinet, she realized she was cringing, and her shock melted away, her spine stiffening. She wasn't a child now, she reminded herself, but a woman. Aware, responsible. "It's none of your business why I moved here."

"Oh, but it is." His voice was silky, quiet, reasonable. "I prefer you in Oklahoma, Megan. Working at your nice, steady job, in the midst of your loving family. I really much prefer it."

His eyes were so cold, she thought with dull wonder. Odd, she'd never seen that, didn't remember that. "Your preferences mean nothing to me, Baxter."

"Did you think I wouldn't find out that you'd thrown your lot in with my ex-wife and her family?" he continued, in that same reasonable tone. "That I haven't kept tabs on you over the years?"

With an effort, she steadied her breathing, but when she tried to shift away, he blocked her. She wasn't afraid, yet, but the temper she'd worked so hard to erase from her character was beginning to bubble up toward the surface.

"I never gave a thought to what you'd find out. And no, I wasn't aware you were keeping tabs. Why should you? Neither Kevin nor I ever meant anything to you."

"You've waited a long time to make your move." Baxter paused, struggling to control the fury that had clawed its way into his throat. He'd worked too hard, done too much, to see some old, forgotten mistake rear up and slap him down. "Clever of you, Megan, more clever than I gave you credit for."

"I don't know what you're talking about."

"Do you seriously want me to believe you know nothing about my campaign? I'm not going to tolerate this pathetic stab at revenge."

Her voice was cooler now, despite the fact that she could feel her skin start to tremble with an intense mixture of emotions. "At the risk of repeating myself, I don't know what you're talking about. My life is of no concern to you, Baxter, and yours none of mine. You made that clear a long time ago, when you refused to acknowledge me or Kevin."

"Is that the tack you're going to take?" He'd wanted to be calm, but rage was working through him. Intimidation, he realized, simply wouldn't be enough. "The young, innocent girl, seduced, betrayed, abandoned? Left behind, pregnant and brokenhearted? Please, spare me."

"That's not a tack, it's truth."

"You were young, Megan, but innocent?" His teeth flashed. "Now, that's a different matter. You were willing enough, even eager."

"I believed you!" She shouted it—a mistake, as her own voice tore her composure to pieces. "I believed you loved me, that you wanted to marry me. And you played on that. You never had any intention of making a future with me. You were already engaged. I was just an easy mark."

"You certainly were easy." He pushed her back against the cabinet, kept his hands hard on her shoulders. "And very, very tempting. Sweet, Megan. Very sweet."

"Take your hands off me."

"Not quite yet. You're going to listen to me, carefully. I know why you've come here, linked yourself with the Calhouns. First there'll be whispers, rumors, then a sad story to a sympathetic reporter. The old lady put pressure on me about Suzanna." He thought of Colleen with loathing. "But I've made that work for me. In the interest of the children," he murmured. "Letting Bradford adopt them, selflessly giving up my rights, so the children could be secure in a traditional family."

"You never cared about them, either, did you?" Megan said in a husky voice. "Alex and Jenny never mattered to you, any more than Kevin."

"The point is," he continued, "the old woman has no reason to bother about you. So, Megan, you'd better mind your step and listen to me. Things aren't working out for you here, so you're going to move back to Oklahoma."

"I'm not going anywhere," she began, then gasped when his fingers dug in.

"You're going back to your quiet life, away from here. There will be no rumors, no tearful interviews with reporters. If you try to undermine me, to implicate me in any way, I'll ruin you. When I've finished—and believe me, with the Dumont money I can hire plenty of willing men who'll swear they've enjoyed you—when

I've finished," he repeated, "you'll be nothing more than an opportunistic slut with a bastard son."

Her vision hazed. It wasn't the threat that frightened her, or even infuriated her so very much. It was the term *bastard* in connection with her little boy.

Before she fully realized her intent, her hand was swinging up and slapping hard across his face. "Don't you ever speak about my son that way."

When his hand cracked across her cheek, it wasn't pain she felt, or even shock, but rage.

"Don't push me, Megan," he said, breathing hard. "Don't push me, because you'll be the one to take the fall. You, and the boy."

As crazed as any mother protecting her cub, she lunged at him. The power of the attack rammed them both against the wall. She landed two solid blows before he threw her off.

"You still have that passionate nature, I see." He dragged her against him, infuriated, aroused. "I remember how to channel it."

She struck out again, a glancing blow, before he caught her arms and pinned them against her body. So she used her teeth. Even as Baxter cursed in pain, the door burst in.

Nathaniel plucked him off the floor as he might a flea off a dog. Through the haze of her own vision, Megan saw there was murder in his eye. Hot-blooded. Deadly.

"Nathaniel."

But he didn't look at her. Instead, he rapped Baxter hard against the wall. "Dumont, isn't it?" His voice was viciously quiet, terrifyingly pleasant. "I've heard how you like pushing women around."

Baxter struggled for dignity, though his feet were inches off the ground. "Who the hell are you?"

"Well, now, it seems only fair you should know the name of the man who's going to rip out your damn heart with his bare hands." He had the pleasure of seeing Baxter blanch. "It's Fury, Nathaniel Fury. You won't forget it—" he rammed a fist low, into the kidneys "—will you?"

When Baxter could breathe again, his words struggling out weakly, he wheezed, "You'll be in jail before the night's out."

"I don't think so." His head snapped around when Megan started forward. "Stay back," he said between his teeth. The hot leap of fire in his eyes had her coming to a stop.

"Nathaniel." She swallowed hard. "Don't kill him."

"Any particular reason you want him alive?"

She opened her mouth, shut it again. The answer seemed desperately important, so she offered the truth. "No."

Baxter drew in his breath to scream. Nathaniel cut it off neatly with a hand over the windpipe. "You're a lucky man, Dumont. The lady doesn't want me to kill you, and I don't like to disappoint her. We'll leave it to fate." He dragged Baxter outside, hauling him along as if the man were nothing more than a heavily packed seabag.

Megan raced to the door. "Holt." A shiver of relief worked down her spine when she spotted Suzanna's husband near the pier. "Do something."

Holt merely shrugged. "Fury beat me to it. You should go back in, you're getting wet."

"But—he's not really going to kill him, is he?"

Holt considered a moment, narrowing his eyes against the rain as Nathaniel carted Baxter down the pier. "Probably not."

"I hope to God you can't swim," Nathaniel muttered, then threw Baxter off the pier. He turned away and was striding to Megan before the sound of the splash. "Come on."

"But—"

He simply scooped her up in his arms. "I'm knocking off for the day."

"Fine." Holt stood, his thumbs in his pockets, a look of unholy glee in his eyes. "See you tomorrow."

"Nathaniel, you can't—"

"Shut up, Meg." He dumped her in the car. She craned her neck, and wasn't sure whether she was relieved or disappointed to see Baxter heaving himself back onto the pier.

He needed quiet to pull himself back from violence. He detested the temper that lurked inside him, that made him want to raise his fists and pummel. He could rationalize it, under the circumstances, but it always left him sick inside to know what he was capable of if pushed.

There was no doubt in his mind that he would have come very close to murder if Megan hadn't stopped him.

He'd trained himself to use words and wit to resolve a fight. It usually worked. When it didn't, well, it didn't. But he continued, years after the last blow he'd taken from his father, to remember, and regret.

She was shivering by the time he parked the car in his driveway. It didn't occur to him until that moment that he'd forgotten Dog. Holt would see to him, Nathaniel figured, and plucked Megan from her seat.

"I don't—"

"Just be quiet." He carried her in, past the bird, who squawked greetings, and up the stairs. Megan was ready to babble in shock by the time he dumped her in a chair in the bedroom. Without a word, he turned away to rummage through his dresser drawers. "Get out of those wet clothes," he ordered, tossing her a sweatshirt and sweatpants. "I'm going to go down and make you some tea."

"Nathaniel—"

"Just do it!" he shouted, gritting his teeth. "Just do it," he repeated quietly, and shut the door.

He didn't slam it; nor, when he was down in the kitchen, did he put his fist through a wall. He thought about it. But instead, he put on the kettle, got out the brandy. After a moment's consideration, he took a pull of the fiery liquid, straight from the bottle. It didn't calm him very much, but it took the edge off his sense of self-disgust.

When he heard Bird whistle and invite Megan to come to the Casbah, he set her spiked tea on the table.

She was pale, he noted, and her eyes were too big. So were the sweats. He nearly smiled at the picture she made, hesitating in the doorway, with the shirt drooping off her shoulders and the pants bagging at her ankles.

"Sit down and have something to drink. You'll feel better."

"I'm all right, really." But she sat, and lifted the mug in both hands, because they tended to shake. The first sip had her sucking in her breath. "I thought this was tea."

"It is. I just gave it a little help." He sat across from her, waited until she sipped again. "Did he hurt you?"

She stared down at the table. The wood was polished so brightly she could see her own face in it. "Yes."

She said it calmly. She thought she was calm, until Nathaniel put his hand over hers. Her breath hitched once, twice, and then she put her head on the table and wept.

So much washed out with the tears—the hopes she'd once had, the dreams, the betrayal and the disillusionment, the fears and the bitterness. He didn't try to stop her, only waited it out.

"I'm sorry." She let her cheek rest against the table a moment, comforted by the cool, smooth feel of the wood on her skin and Nathaniel's hand on her hair. "It all seemed to happen so fast, and I wasn't prepared." She straightened, started to wipe the tears away, when a new fear glazed her eyes. "Kevin. Oh, God, if Bax—"

"Holt will take care of Kevin. Dumont won't get near him."

"You're right." She gave a shuddering sigh. "Of course, you're right. Holt would see to Suzanna and all the children right away. And all Baxter wanted to do in any case was frighten me."

"Did he?"

Her eyes were still wet, but they were steady. "No. He hurt me, and he infuriated me, and he made me sick that I'd ever let him touch me. But he didn't frighten me. He can't."

"Attagirl."

She sniffled, smiled weakly. "But I frightened him. That's why he came here today, after all this time. Because he's frightened."

"Of what?"

"Of the past, the consequences." She drew another, deeper breath and smelled Nathaniel—tobacco and salt spray. How oddly comforting it was. "He thinks our coming here is some sort of plot against him. He's been keeping track of me all this time. I didn't know."

"He's never contacted you until today?"

"No, never. I suppose he felt safe when I was in Oklahoma and hadn't any connection with Suzanna. Now, not only is there a connection, but I'm living here. And Kevin and Alex and Jenny... Well, he doesn't seem to understand it has nothing to do with him."

She picked up her tea again. Nathaniel hadn't asked anything, he'd simply sat and held her hand. Perhaps that was why she felt compelled to tell him.

"I met him in New York. I was seventeen, and it was my first real trip away from home. It was during the winter break, and several of us went. One of my friends had relatives there. I guess you've been to New York."

"A time or two."

"I'd never experienced anything like it. The people, the buildings. The city was so exciting, and so unlike the West. Everything crowded in and colorful. I loved it—rushing along Fifth Avenue, having coffee in some hole-in-the-wall in Greenwich Village. Gawking. It sounds silly."

"No, it sounds normal."

"I guess it was," she said with a sigh. "Everything was normal, and simple, before... It was at this party, and he looked so handsome and romantic, I suppose. A young girl's dream, with those movie-star looks and that sheen of sophistication. And he was older—just enough older to be fascinating. He'd been to Europe." She stopped herself, squeezed her eyes shut. "Oh, God, how pathetic."

"You know you don't have to do this now, Meg."

"No, I think I do." Steadying herself, she opened her eyes again. "If you can stand listening to it."

"I'm not going anywhere." He gave her hand a comforting squeeze. "Go ahead, then, get rid of it."

"He said all the right things, made all the right

moves. He sent a dozen roses the next day, and an invitation to dinner."

She paused to choose her words and pushed absently at a pin that had loosened in her hair. It wasn't so horrible, she realized, to look back. It seemed almost like a play, with her as both actor and audience. Vitally involved and breezily detached.

"So I went. There was candlelight, and we danced. I felt so grown-up. I think you only really feel that way when you're seventeen. We went to museums and window-shopping and to shows. He told me he loved me, and he bought me a ring. It had two little diamond hearts, interconnected. It was very romantic. He slipped it on my finger, and I slipped into his bed."

She stopped, waited for Nathaniel to comment. When he didn't, she worked up the courage to continue.

"He said he would come to Oklahoma, and we'd make our plans for the future. But, of course, he didn't come. At first, when I called, he said he'd been delayed. Then he stopped answering my calls altogether. I found out I was pregnant, and I called, I wrote. Then I heard that he was engaged, that he'd been engaged all along. At first I didn't believe it, then I just went numb. It took me a while before I made myself believe it, made myself understand and deal with it. My family was wonderful. I never would have gotten through it without them. When Kevin was born, I realized I couldn't just feel grown-up. I had to *be* grown-up. Later on, I tried to contact Bax one last time. I thought he should know about Kevin, and that Kevin should have some sort of relationship with his father. But…" She trailed off. "When there was absolutely no interest, only anger and hostility, I began to understand that it was best that that didn't happen. Today, maybe for the first time, I was absolutely sure of it."

"He doesn't deserve either of you."

"No, he doesn't." She managed a small smile. Now that she'd said it all, for the first time in so very long, she felt hollowed out. Not limp, she realized. Just free. "I want to thank you for charging to the rescue."

"My pleasure. He won't touch you again, Meg." He took her hand, brought it to his lips. "You or Kevin. Trust me."

"I do." She turned her hand in his, gripped. "I do trust you." Her pulse was starting to skip, but she kept her eyes on his. "I thought, when you carried me in and upstairs… Well, I didn't think you were going to make me tea."

"Neither did I. But you were trembling, and I knew if I touched you before I cooled off, I'd be rough. That it wouldn't be right, for either of us."

Her heart stuttered, then picked up its pace. "Are you cooled off now?"

His eyes darkened. "Mostly." Slowly, he rose, drew her to her feet. "Is that an invitation, Megan?"

"I—" He was waiting, she realized, for her to agree or refuse. No seduction, no pretty promising words. No illusions. "Yes," she said, and met his lips with hers.

When he swept her up this time, she gave a quick, nervous laugh. It slid back down her throat when she met the look in his eyes.

"You won't think of him," Nathaniel said quietly. "You won't think of anything but us."

Chapter 8

She could hear her own heartbeat pounding, pounding, in counterpoint to the rain that pounded against the windows. She wondered whether Nathaniel could hear it, too, and if he did, whether he knew that she was afraid. His arms were so strong, his mouth was so sure each time it swooped down to claim hers again.

He carried her up the stairs as if she weighed no more than the mist that swirled outside the cottage.

She would make a mistake, she would do something foolish, she wouldn't be what either of them wanted. The doubts pinched at her like fingers as he swept her into his bedroom, where the light was dim and the air was sweet with wisteria.

She saw the spear of purple blooms in an old bottle on a scarred wooden chest, the undraped windows that were opened to welcome the moist breeze. And the bed, with its sturdy iron headboard and taut cotton spread.

He set her down beside it, so that she was all too aware of the weakness in her knees. But she kept her eyes on his and waited, terrified and aching, for him to make the first move.

"You're trembling again." His voice was quiet, the fingers he lifted to stroke her cheek were soothing. Did she think he couldn't see all those fears in her eyes? She couldn't know that they stirred his own.

"I don't know what to do." The moment the words were out, she closed her eyes. She'd done it already, she realized. The first mistake. Determined, she dragged his head down to hers for an aggressive kiss.

A fire kindled in his gut, flames leaping and licking at the ready fuel of his need. Muscles tensed in reaction, he fought back the urge to shove her back on the bed and take, take quickly, fiercely. He kept his hands easy, stroking her face, her shoulders, her back, until she quieted.

"Nathaniel."

"Do you know what I want, Meg?"

"Yes— No." She reached for him again, but he caught her hands, kissed them, fingertip by fingertip.

"I want to watch you relax. I want to watch you enjoy." His eyes on hers, he lowered her hands to her sides. "I want to watch you fill up with me." Slowly he began to take the pins from her hair, setting them on the table beside the bed. "I want to hear you say my name when I'm inside you."

He combed his fingers through her hair, contenting himself with the silky texture. "I want you to let me do all the things I've been dreaming of since I first laid eyes on you. Let me show you."

He kissed her first, his mouth soft, smooth, seductive. Endlessly patient, he parted hers with teasing nips and nibbles, with the persuasive caress of his tongue. Degree by torturous degree, he deepened the kiss, until her hands clutched weakly at his waist and her shudders gave way to pliancy.

The lingering taste of brandy, the faint and very male scrape of a day's beard against her cheek, the patter of rain and the drifting scent of flowers. All this whirled in her head like a drug, both potent and possessing.

His lips left hers to journey over her face, to trace the line of her jaw, to nuzzle at her ear, waiting, patiently waiting, until he felt her slip over to the next stage of surrender.

He stepped back, only an inch, and slipped the shirt up her torso, over her head, let it drop to the floor. His muscles coiled like a snake. She thought she saw the lightning flash of desire that darkened his eyes to soot. But he only skimmed a fingertip down her throat, to the aching tip of her breast.

Her breath caught; her head lolled back.

"You're so beautiful, Meg. So soft." He pressed a kiss to her shoulder while his hands gently molded, caressed, aroused. "So sweet."

He was afraid his hands were too big, too rough. As a result, his touch was stunningly tender, humming over her heating skin. They slicked down her sides, leaving tremors in their wake as he eased the loose pants from her hips.

Then those fingertips moved over her, gliding over curves until her shaking breathing turned to unsteady moans.

He undressed, watching her heavy eyes flutter open, seeing the misty blue focus on him, the pupils dilate.

Now, she thought, and her heart stuttered madly in her throat. He would take her now, and ease this glorious ache he'd stirred to life inside her. Sweet and eager, her mouth lifted to his. He gathered her close, laid her on the bed as gently as he might have laid her in a pool of rose petals. She arched to him, accepting, braced for the torrent. He used only his lips, soft as the rain, savoring her flesh as though it were a banquet of the most delicate flavors. Then his hands, big and hard-palmed, skimmed, lingered, discovered.

Nothing could have prepared her. If she'd had a hundred lovers, none could have given more, or taken more. She was lost in a gently rocking sea of sensation, undone by patience, weakened by tenderness.

Her breathing slowed, deepened, even as her heart rate soared. She felt the brush of his hair on her breast before his mouth claimed it, heard his quiet, satisfied groan of pleasure as he suckled. Heard his sigh as he circled and teased with his tongue.

She sank, fathoms deep, in warm, clear waters.

She didn't know when those waters began to churn. The storm gathered so slowly, so subtly. It seemed one moment she was drifting, and the next floundering. She couldn't get her breath, no matter how deeply she gasped for air. Her mind, suddenly reeling, struggled for the surface, even as her body coiled and tensed.

"Nathaniel." She grabbed at him, her fingers digging into his flesh. "I can't—"

But he covered her mouth with his, swallowing her gasps, savoring her moan, as the first dizzy climax racked her.

She reared against his hand, instinctively urging him on as hot red waves of pleasure swept her up. Her neat, rounded nails scored his shoulders before her hands, her body, even her mind, went limp.

"Megan. God." She was so hot, so wet. He pressed his lips to her throat as he fought to level his own breathing. Pleasuring a woman had always pleasured him. But not like this. Never like this. He felt like a king and a beggar all at once.

Her stunned response aroused him unbearably. All he could do was wallow in her, absorbing her shock waves, and his own, feeling each and every nerve in his body sizzle and spark.

He wanted to give her more. Had to give her more. Strapping down his own grinding needs, he slipped inside her, letting himself rock with the pleasure of her quick shudder, her broken sigh.

She was so small. He had to remind himself again and again that she was small, all delicate bones and fragile skin. That she was innocent, and nearly as untouched as a virgin. So while the blood pounded in his head, his heart, his loins, he took her gently, his hands fisted on the bedspread for fear he would touch her and bruise.

He felt her body contract, explode. And then she said his name.

He pressed his lips to hers again, and followed her over.

The rain was still drumming. As she slowly swam back to reality, she heard its steady beat on the roof. She lay still, her hand tangled in Nathaniel's hair, her body glowing. She realized she had a smile on her face.

She began to hum.

Nathaniel stirred himself, pushed back lazily to lean on his elbow. "What are you doing?"

"Singing. Sort of."

He grinned, studying her. "I like your looks, sugar."

"I'm getting used to yours." She traced the cleft in his chin with a fingertip. Her lashes lowered. "It was all right, wasn't it?"

"What?" He waited, wisely holding back a chuckle until she looked at him again. "Oh, that. Sure, it was okay for a start."

She opened her mouth, closed it again with a little humming sound that wasn't at all musical. "You could be a little more…flattering."

"You could be a little less stupid." He kissed her frowning mouth. "Making love isn't a quiz, Meg. You don't get graded."

"What I meant was… Never mind."

"What you meant was…" He hauled her over until she was splayed on top of him. "On a scale of one to ten…"

"Cut it out, Nathaniel." She laid her cheek on his chest. "I hate it when you make me feel ridiculous."

"I don't." Possessively he ran a hand down her back. "I love to make you feel ridiculous. I love to make you feel."

He nearly followed that up with a very simple "I love you." But she wouldn't have accepted it. He'd barely done so himself.

"You did." She kept her head over his heart. "You made me feel things I never have before. I was afraid."

Trouble clouded his eyes. "I don't want you to be afraid of me."

"I was afraid of me," she corrected. "Of us. Of letting this happen. I'm glad it did." It was easier than she'd imagined to shift, to smile, to press her mouth to his. For a moment, she thought he tensed, but she dismissed that as foolish and kissed him again.

His system snapped to full alert. How could he want her again, so desperately, so quickly? he wondered. How could he resist those sweet, tantalizing lips?

"Keep that up," he managed, "and it's going to happen again."

The shiver of excitement was glorious. "Okay." She shared her anticipation in the kiss, torturing his mouth, teasing his tongue. Amazed that there could be more, she gave a low sound of delight when he rolled, shoving her beneath him and crushing her mouth.

For a heady moment, he let those violent needs hold sway, trapping her beneath him, devouring her lips, her skin, dragging a hand through her tousled hair until her throat was exposed to his hungry teeth and tongue.

She moaned, writhed under him. Whimpered.

Rolling away, he lay on his back, cursing himself, while his heart pounded the blood through his veins.

Confused, shivering with needs freshly aroused but unmet, Megan laid a tentative hand on his arm. He jerked away.

"Don't." The order came out harsh. "I need a minute."

Her eyes went dead. "I'm sorry, I did something wrong."

"No, you didn't." He scrubbed his hands over his face and sat up. "I'm just not ready. Look, why don't I go down and rustle us up something to eat?"

He was only inches away. It might as well have been miles, and she felt the sharp sting of rejection. "No, that's all right." Her voice was cool and calm again. "I really should get going. I need to pick up Kevin."

"Kevin's fine."

"Regardless." She brushed at her hair, tried to smooth it. She wished desperately for something to wrap around her nakedness.

"Don't pull that door shut on me now." He battled back fury, and a much more dangerous passion.

"I haven't shut any door. I thought—that is, I assumed you wanted me to stay. Since you don't, I'll—"

"Of course I want you to stay. Damn it, Megan." He whirled on her, and wasn't surprised when she jerked back. "I need a bloody minute. I could eat you alive, I want you so much."

In defense, she crossed an arm over her breasts. "I don't understand you."

"Damn right you don't understand me. You'd run like hell if you did." He fought for control, gained a slippery hold. "We'll be fine, Meg, if you wait until I pull myself together."

"What are you talking about?"

Gripped by frustration, he grabbed her hand, pressed it against his, palm to palm. "I've got big hands, Megan. Got them from my father. I know the right way to use them—and the wrong way."

There was a glint in his eyes, like the honed edge of a sword. It should have frightened her, but it only excited. "You're afraid of me," she said quietly. "Afraid you'll hurt me."

"I won't hurt you." He dropped his hand, left it fisted on the bed.

"No, you won't." She lifted a hand to touch his cheek. His jaw was tight, urging her fingers to stroke and soothe. There was a power here, she realized, a power she'd been unaware of possessing. She wondered what they could make between them if she set it free.

"You want me." Feeling reckless, she edged closer, until her mouth slid over his. "You want to touch me." She lifted his fisted hand to her breast, her heart pounding like a drum as his fingers opened, cupped. "And for me to touch you." Her hands stroked down his chest, felt the quiver of his stomach muscles. So much strength, she thought, so ruthlessly chained. What would it be like if those links snapped free?

She wanted to know.

"Make love with me now, Nathaniel." Eyes half-closed, she linked her arms around his neck, pressed her eager body to his. "Show me how much you want me."

He held himself in check, concentrating on the flavor of her mouth. It would be enough, he told himself, to make her float again.

But she had learned quickly. When he sought to soothe, she enticed. Where he tried to gentle, she enraged.

With an oath, he dragged her up until they were kneeling, body-to-body. And his mouth was wild.

She answered avidly each urgent demand, each desperate moan. His hands were everywhere, hard and possessive, taking more only when she cried out for it. There was no calm water to sink in now, but a violent tempest that spun them both over the bed in a tangle of hot flesh and raging needs.

He couldn't stop, no longer gave a damn about control. She was his, and by God, he would have all of her. With something like a snarl, he clamped her hands above her head and ravished her flesh.

She arched like a bow, twisted, and still he plundered, invading that hot, wet core with probing tongue until she was sobbing his name.

And more, still more, wrestling over the bed with her hands as rough and ready as his, her mouth as bold and ravenous.

He drove himself into her, hard and deep, hissing with triumph, eyes glazed and dark. His hands locked on hers as she rose to meet him.

She would remember the speed, and the wild freedom, of their mindless mating. And she would remember the heady flavor of power as they plunged recklessly off the edge together.

She must have slept. When she woke, she was sprawled on her stomach across the bed. The rain had stopped and night had fallen. When her mind cleared, she became aware of dozens of small aches, and a drugged sense of satisfaction.

She thought of rolling over, but it seemed like too much trouble. Instead, she stretched out her arms, searching the tumbled bed, knowing already that she was alone.

She heard the bird squawk slyly. "You know how to whistle, don't you, Steve?"

She was still chuckling when Nathaniel stepped back into the room.

"What do you do, run old movies for him all day?"

"He's a Bogart fan. What can I tell you?" It amazed him that he felt awkward, holding a dinner tray while a naked woman lolled in his bed. "That's a pretty good scar you've got there, sugar."

She was much too content to be embarrassed when she saw where his eyes had focused. "I earned it. That's a pretty good dragon you've got."

"I was eighteen, stupid, and more than a little buzzed on beer. But I guess I earned it, too."

"Suits you. What have you got there?"

"Thought you might be hungry."

"I'm starving." She braced herself on both elbows and smiled at him. "That smells terrific. I didn't know you cooked."

"I don't. Dutch does. I cadge handouts from the kitchen, then nuke them."

"Nuke them?"

"Zap them in the microwave." He set the tray down on the sea chest at the foot of the bed. "We've got some Cajun chicken, some wine."

"Mmm…" She roused herself enough to lean over and peer at it. "Looks wonderful. But I really need to get Kevin."

"I talked to Suzanna." He wondered if he could talk her into eating dinner just as she was, gloriously naked. "Unless she hears from you, Kevin's set to spend the night with them."

"Oh. Well."

"She says he's already knee-deep in video games with Alex and Jenny."

"And if I called, I'd spoil his party."

"Pretty much." He sat on the edge of the bed, ran a fingertip down her spine. "So, how about it? Sleep with me tonight?"

"I don't even have a toothbrush."

"I can dig up an extra." He broke off a piece of chicken, fed it to her.

"Oh." She swallowed, blew out a breath. "Spicy."

"Yeah." He leaned down to sample her lips, then lifted a glass of wine to them. "Better?"

"It's wonderful."

He tipped the glass so that a few drops of wine spilled on her shoulder. "Oops. Better clean that up." He did so with a lingering lick of his tongue. "What do I have to do to convince you to stay?"

She forgot the food and rolled into his arms. "You just did."

In the morning, the mists had cleared. Nathaniel watched Megan pin up her hair in a beam of sunlight.

It seemed only right that he move behind her and press his lips to the base of her neck.

He thought it was a sweetly ordinary, sweetly intimate gesture that could become a habit.

"I love the way you polish yourself up, sugar."

"Polish myself up?" Her curious eyes met his in the glass. She had on the same tailored suit she'd worn the day before—now slightly wrinkled. Her makeup was sketchy at best, courtesy of the small emergency cosmetic kit she carried in her purse, and her hair was giving her trouble, as she'd lost half of her pins.

"Like you are now. Like some pretty little cupcake behind the bakery window."

"Cupcake." She nearly choked. "I'm certainly not a cupcake."

"I've got a real sweet tooth." To prove it, he nibbled his way to her ear.

"I've noticed." She turned, but put her hands against his chest to hold him off. "I have to go."

"Yeah, me too. I don't suppose I could talk you into coming with me."

"To sight whales?" She cocked her head. "No more than I could talk you into sitting with me in my office all day, running figures."

He winced. "Guess not. How about tonight?"

She yearned, wished, longed. "I have to think of Kevin. I can't spend my nights here with you while he spends them somewhere else."

"I had that figured. I was thinking if you were to leave your terrace doors open…"

"You could come sneaking in?" she asked archly.

"More or less."

"Good thinking." She laughed and drew away. "Now, are you going to drive me back to my car?"

"Looks that way." He took her hand, holding it as they walked downstairs. "Megan…" He hated to bring it up when the sun was shining and his mood was light. "If you hear from Dumont, if he tries to see you or Kevin, if he calls, sends a damn smoke signal, does anything, I want you to tell me."

She gave his hand a reassuring squeeze. "I doubt I will, after the dunking you gave him. But don't worry, Nathaniel, I can handle Baxter."

"Off with his head," Bird suggested, but Nathaniel didn't smile.

"It's not a matter of what you can handle." He pushed the door open, stepped outside. "Maybe you don't figure that last night gives me the right to look out for you and your boy, but I do. I will. So we'll put it this way." He opened the car door for her. "Either you promise me that you'll tell me, or I go after him now."

She started to protest, but the image, absolutely vivid, of the look on Nathaniel's face when he'd rammed Baxter against the wall stopped her. "You would."

"Bank on it."

She tried to separate annoyance from the simple pleasure of being protected. And couldn't. "I want to say I appreciate the concern, but I'm not sure I do. I've been taking care of myself, and of Kevin, for a long time."

"Things change."

"Yes," she said carefully, wondering what was behind those calm, unblinking gray eyes. "I'm more comfortable when they change slowly."

"I'm doing my best to keep at your pace, Meg." Whatever frustrations he had, he told himself, he could handle. "Just a simple yes or no on this'll do."

It wasn't just herself, Megan thought. There was Kevin. And Nathaniel was offering them both a strong, protecting arm. Pride meant nothing when compared to the welfare of her son.

Not at all sure why she was amused, she turned to him once he'd settled into the driver's seat. "You have an uncanny knack for getting your own way. And when you do, you just accept it as inevitable."

"It usually is." He backed out of the drive and headed for Shipshape.

There was a small greeting party waiting for them. Holt and, to Megan's surprise, her brother, Sloan.

"I dropped the kids off at The Towers," Holt told her, before she could ask. "They've got your dog, Nate."

"Thanks." She'd barely stepped from the car when Sloan grabbed her by the shoulders, stared hard into her eyes.

"Are you all right? Why the hell didn't you call me? Did he put his hands on you?"

"I'm fine. Sloan, I'm fine." Instinctively she cupped his face, kissed him. "I didn't call because I already had two white knights charging into battle. And he may have put his hands on me, but I put my fists on him. I think I split his lip."

Sloan said something particularly foul about Dumont and hugged Megan close. "I should have killed him when you first told me about him."

"Stop it." She pressed her cheek to his. "It's over. I want it put aside. Kevin's not to hear about it. Now come on, I'll drive you back to the house."

"I've got some things to do." He gave Nathaniel a steely stare over Megan's shoulder. "You go on up, Meg. I'll be along later."

"All right, then." She kissed him again. "Holt, thanks again for looking after Kevin."

"No problem." Holt tucked his tongue in his cheek

when Nathaniel scooped Megan up for a long, lingering kiss. A glance at Sloan's narrowed eyes had him biting that tongue to keep from grinning.

"See you, sugar."

Megan flushed, cleared her throat. "Yes…well. Bye."

Nathaniel tucked his thumbs in his pockets, waited until she'd driven off before he turned to Sloan. "Guess you want to talk to me."

"Damn right I want to talk to you."

"You'll have to come up to the bridge. We've got a tour going out."

"Want a referee?" Holt offered, and earned two deadly glances. "Too bad. I hate to miss it."

Smoldering, Sloan followed Nathaniel up the gangplank, waited restlessly while he gave orders. Once they were on the bridge, Nathaniel glanced over the charts and dismissed the mate.

"If this is going to take longer than fifteen minutes, you're in for a ride."

"I've got plenty of time." Sloan stepped closer, braced his legs like a gunslinger at high noon. "What the hell were you doing with my sister?"

"I think you have that figured out," Nathaniel said coolly.

Sloan bared his teeth. "If you think I'm going to stand back while you move in on her, you're dead wrong. I wasn't around when she got tangled up with Dumont, but I'm here now."

"I'm not Dumont." Nathaniel's own temper threatened to snap, a dry twig of control. "You want to take out what he did to her on me, that's fine. I've been looking to kick someone's ass ever since I caught that bastard tossing her around. So you want to take me on?" he said invitingly. "Do it."

Though the invitation tempted some elemental male urge, Sloan pulled back. "What do you mean, he was tossing her around?"

"Just what I said. He had her up against the wall." The rage swept back, almost drowning him. "I thought about killing him, but I didn't think she could handle it."

Sloan breathed deep to steady himself. "So you threw him off the pier."

"Well, I punched him a few times first, then I figured there was a chance he couldn't swim."

Calmer, and grateful, Sloan nodded. "Holt had a few words with him when he dragged his sorry butt out. They've tangled before." He'd missed his chance that time, as well, he thought, thoroughly disgusted. "I don't think Dumont'll come back, chance running into any of us again." Sloan knew he should be glad of it, but he regretted, bitterly, not getting his own licks in.

"I appreciate you looking out for her," he said stiffly. "But that doesn't get us past the rest. She'd have been upset, vulnerable. I don't like a man who takes advantage of that."

"I gave her tea and dry clothes," Nathaniel said between his teeth. "It would have stopped right there, if that was what she wanted. Staying with me was her choice."

"I'm not going to see her hurt again. You might look at her and see an available woman, but she's my sister."

"I'm in love with your sister." Nathaniel snapped his head around when the bridge door opened.

"Ready to cast off, Captain."

"Cast off." He cursed under his breath as he stalked to the wheel.

Sloan stood back while he gave orders and piloted the boat into the bay.

"You want to run that by me again?"

"Have you got a problem with plain English?" Nathaniel tossed back. "I'm in love with her. Damn it."

"Well, now." More than a little taken aback, Sloan sat on the bench closest to the helm.

He wanted to think that one through. After all, Megan had barely met the man. Then again, he remembered, he'd fallen for Amanda in little more time than it took her to snap his head off. If he'd been able to choose a man for his sister, it might have been someone very much like Nathaniel Fury.

"Have you told her that?" Sloan asked, his tone considerably less belligerent.

"Go to hell."

"Haven't," he decided, and braced his booted foot on his knee. "Does she feel the same way about you?"

"She will." Nathaniel set his teeth. "She needs time to work it out, that's all."

"Is that what she said?"

"That's what I say." Nathaniel ran a frustrated hand through his hair. "Look, O'Riley, either mind your own damn business or take a punch at me. I've had enough."

Sloan's smile spread slow and easy. "Crazy about her, aren't you?"

Nathaniel merely grunted and started out to sea.

"What about Kevin?" Sloan studied Nathaniel's profile as he probed. "Some might have a problem taking on another man's son."

"Kevin's Megan's son." His eyes flashed to Sloan's, burned. "He'll be mine."

Sloan waited a moment until he was sure. "So, you're going to take on the whole package."

"That's right." Nathaniel pulled out a cigar, lit it. "You got a problem with that?"

"Can't say as I do." Sloan grinned and accepted the cigar Nathaniel belatedly offered him. "You might, though. My sister's a damn stubborn woman. But seeing as you're almost a member of the family, I'll be glad to offer any help."

A smile finally twitched at Nathaniel's mouth. "Thanks, but I'd like to handle it on my own."

"Suit yourself." Sloan settled back to enjoy the ride.

"Are you sure you're all right?"

Megan had no more than stepped in the door of The Towers when she found herself surrounded by concern.

"I'm fine, really." Her protests hadn't prevented the Calhouns from herding her into the family kitchen and plying her with tea and sympathy. "This has gotten blown out of proportion."

"When somebody messes with one of us," C.C. corrected, "he messes with all of us."

She glanced outside, where the children were playing happily in the yard. "I appreciate it. Really. But I don't think there's anything more to worry about."

"There won't be." Colleen stepped into the room, her gaze scanning each face in turn. "What are you all doing in here, smothering the girl? Get out."

"Aunt Colleen..." Coco began.

"Out, I said, all of you. You, go back to your kitchen and flirt with that big Dutchman you've got sneaking into your room at night."

"Why, I—"

"Go. And you." Now her cane gestured threateningly at Amanda. "You've got a hotel to run, don't you? Go weed some flowers," she ordered Suzanna. "And you go tinker with an engine." She flicked her gaze from C.C. to Lilah.

"Tougher with me, isn't it, Auntie?" Lilah said lazily.

"Take a nap," Colleen snapped.

"Got me," Lilah said with a sigh. "Come on, ladies, we've been dismissed."

Satisfied when the door swung shut behind them, Colleen sat heavily at the table. "Get me some of that tea," she ordered Megan. "See that it's hot."

Though she moved to obey, Megan wasn't cowed. "Do you always find rudeness works to your advantage, Miss Calhoun?"

"That, old age, and a hefty portfolio." She took the tea Megan set in front of her, sipped, nodded grudgingly when she found it hot and strong. "Now then, sit down and listen to what I have to say. And don't prim your mouth at me, young lady."

"I'm very fond of Coco," Megan told her. "You embarrassed her."

"Embarrassed her? Ha! She and that tattooed hulk have been mooning around after each other for days. Gave her a prod is what I did." But she eyed Megan craftily. "Loyal when it's deserved, are you?"

"I am."

"And so am I. I made a few calls this morning, to some friends in Boston. Influential friends. Hush," she ordered when Megan started to speak. "Detest politics myself, but it's often necessary to dance with the devil. Dumont should be being made aware, at this moment, that any contact with you, or your son, will fatally jeopardize his ambitions. He will not trouble you again."

Megan pressed her lips together. She wanted her voice to be steady. No matter what she had said, how she had pretended, there had been an icy fear, like a cold ax balanced over her head, of what Baxter might do. In one stroke, Colleen had removed it.

"Why did you do it?"

"I loathe bullies. I particularly loathe bullies who interfere with the contentment of my family."

"I'm not your family," Megan said softly.

"Ha! Think again. You stuck your toe in Calhoun waters, girl. We're like quicksand. You're a Calhoun now, and you're stuck."

Tears rushed into her eyes, blinding her. "Miss Calhoun—" Megan's words were cut off by the impatient rap of Colleen's cane. After a sniffle, Megan began again. "Aunt Colleen," she corrected, understanding. "I'm very grateful."

"So you should be." Colleen coughed to clear her own husky voice. Then she raised it to a shout. "Come back in here, the lot of you! Stop listening at the door!"

It swung open, Coco leading the way. She walked to Colleen, bent, kissed the papery cheek.

"Stop all this nonsense." She waved her grandnieces away. "I want the girl to tell me how that strapping young man tossed that bully in the drink."

Megan laughed, wiped her eyes. "He choked him first."

"Ha!" Colleen rapped her cane in appreciation. "Don't spare the details."

Chapter 9

B. behaving oddly. Since return to island for summer she is absentminded, daydreaming. Arrived late for tea, forgot luncheon appointment. Intolerable. Unrest in Mexico annoying. Dismissed valet. Excess starch in shirts.

Unbelievable, Megan thought, staring at the notes Fergus had written in his crabbed hand beside stock quotations. He could speak of his wife, a potential war and his valet in the same faintly irritated tone. What a miserable life Bianca must have had. How terrible to be trapped in a marriage, ruled by a despot and without any power to captain your own destiny.

How much worse, she thought, if Bianca had loved him.

As she often did in the quiet hours before sleep, Megan flipped through the pages to the series of numbers. She had time now to regret that she'd never made it to the library.

Or perhaps Amanda was a better bet. Amanda might know whether Fergus had had foreign bank accounts, safe-deposit boxes.

Peering down, she wondered whether that was the answer. The man had had homes in Maine and in New York. These could be the numbers of various safe-deposit boxes. Even combinations to safes he'd kept in his homes.

That idea appealed to her, a straightforward answer to a small but nagging puzzle. A man as obsessed with his wealth and the making of money as Fergus Calhoun had been would very likely have kept a few secret stores.

Wouldn't it be fantastic, she thought, if there was some dusty deposit box in an old bank vault? Unopened all these years, she imagined. The key lost or discarded. The contents? Oh…priceless rubies or fat, negotiable bonds. A single faded photograph. A lock of hair wound with a gold ribbon.

She rolled her eyes and laughed at herself. "Imagination's in gear, Megan," she murmured. "Too bad it's so farfetched."

"What is?"

She jumped like a rabbit, her glasses sliding down to her chin. "Damn. Nathaniel."

He was grinning as he closed and locked the terrace doors at his back. "I thought you'd be happy to see me."

"I am. But you didn't have to sneak up on me that way."

"When a man comes through a woman's window at night, he's supposed to sneak."

She shoved her glasses back in place. "They're doors."

"And you're too literal." He leaned over the back of

the chair where she sat and kissed her like a starving man. "I'm glad you talk to yourself."

"I do not."

"You were, just now. That's why I decided to stop watching you and come in." He strolled to the hallway door, locked it. "You looked incredibly sexy sitting there at your neat little desk, your hair scooped up, your glasses sliding down your nose. In that cute, no-nonsense robe."

She wished heartily that the practical terry cloth could transform into silk and lace. But she had nothing seductive to adorn herself in, and had settled for the robe and Coco's perfume.

"I didn't think you were coming after all. It's getting late."

"I figured there'd be some hoopla over yesterday, and that you'd need to settle Kevin for the night. He didn't get wind of it, did he?"

"No." It touched her that he would ask, that it would matter to him. "None of the children know. Everyone else has been wonderful. It's like thinking you're alone in a battle and then finding yourself surrounded by a circle of shields." She smiled, tilted her head. "Are you holding something behind your back?"

His brows rose, as if in surprise. "Apparently I am." He drew out a peony, a twin to the one he'd given her before. "'A rose,'" he said, "'without a thorn.'"

He crossed to her as he spoke, and all she could think for one awed moment was that this man, this fascinating man, wanted her. He started to take its faded twin from the bud vase on her desk.

"Don't." She felt foolish, but stayed his hand. "Don't throw it out."

"Sentimental, Meg?" Moved that she had kept his

token, he slipped the new bud in with the old. "Did you sit here, working late, looking at the flower and thinking of me?"

"I might have." She couldn't fight the smile in his eyes. "Yes, I thought of you. Not always kindly."

"Thinking's enough." He lifted her hand, kissed her palm. "Nearly." To her surprise, he plucked her from the chair, sat himself down and nestled her in his lap. "But this is a whole lot better."

It seemed foolish to disagree, so she rested her head on his shoulder.

"Everyone's getting prepped for the big Fourth of July celebration," she told him idly. "Coco and Dutch are arguing about recipes for barbecue sauce and the kids are bitterly disappointed we won't let them have small, colorful bombs to set off."

"They'll end up making two kinds of sauce and asking everyone to take sides." It was nice sitting like this, he thought, alone and quiet at the end of the day. "And the kids won't be disappointed after they see the fireworks display Trent organized."

Kevin had talked of nothing else all evening, she remembered. "I've heard it's going to be quite a show."

"Count on it. This bunch won't do anything halfway. Like fireworks, do you, sugar?"

"Almost as much as the kids." She laughed and snuggled against him. "I can't believe it's July already. All I have to do is get about two dozen things out of the way so I can compete in the great barbecue showdown, keep the kids from setting themselves on fire and enjoy the show."

"Business first," he murmured. "Working on Fergus's book?"

"Mmm-hmm… I had no idea how much of a fortune

he'd amassed, or how little he considered people. Look here." She tapped her finger to the page. "Whenever he made a note about Bianca, it's as if she were a servant or, worse, a possession. He checked over the household accounts every day, to the penny. There's a notation about how he docked the cook thirty-three cents for a kitchen discrepancy."

"A lot of people think more of money than souls." He flipped idly through the book. "I can be sure you're not sitting on my lap because of my bank balance—since you know it down to the last nickel."

"You're in the black."

"Barely."

"Cash flow is usually thin the first few years in any business—and when you add in the outlay in equipment you've purchased, the down payment for the cottage, insurance premiums and licensing fees—"

"God, I love it when you talk profit and loss." Letting the book close, he nipped playfully at her ear. "Talk to me about checks and balances, or quarterly returns. Quarterly returns make me crazy."

"Then you'll be happy to know you and Holt underestimated your federal payments."

"Mmm…" He stopped, narrowed his eyes. "What do you mean?"

"You owe the government another two hundred and thirty dollars, which can be added to your next quarter due, or, more wisely, I can file an amended return."

He swore halfheartedly. "How come we have to pay them in advance, anyway?"

She gave him a light kiss in sympathy. "Because, Nathaniel, if you don't, the IRS will make your life a living hell. I'm here to save you from them. I'm also, if your system can take the excitement, going to suggest you open a Keogh—a retirement account for the self-employed."

"Retirement? Hell, Meg, I'm thirty-three."

"And not getting a day younger. Do you know what the cost-of-living projections are for your golden years, Mr. Fury?"

"I changed my mind. I don't like it when you talk accountant to me."

"It's also good tax sense," she persisted. "The money you put in won't be taxable until you're of retirement age. When, usually, your bracket is lower. Besides, planning for the future might not be romantic, but it is rewarding."

He slid a hand under the terry cloth. "I'd rather have instant gratification."

Her pulse scrambled. "I have the necessary form."

"Damn right you do."

"For the Keogh. All you need to— Oh." The terry cloth parted like water under his clever hands. She gasped, shuddered, melted. "How did you do that?"

"Come to bed." He lifted her. "I'll show you."

Just past dawn, Nathaniel strolled down the curve of the terrace steps, his hands in his pockets and a whistle on his lips. Dutch, in a similar pose, descended the opposite curve. Both men stopped dead when they met in the center.

They stared, swore.

"What are you doing here at this hour?" Dutch demanded.

"I could ask you the same question."

"I live here, remember?"

Nathaniel inclined his head. "You live down there." He pointed toward the kitchen level.

"I'm taking the air," Dutch said, after a fumble for inspiration.

"Me too."

Dutch flicked a glance toward Megan's terrace. Nathaniel gave Coco's a studying look. Each decided to leave well enough alone.

"Well, then. Suppose you want some breakfast."

Nathaniel ran his tongue around his teeth. "I could do with some."

"Come on, can't dawdle out here all morning."

Relieved with the solution, they walked down together in perfect agreement.

She overslept. It was a breach in character that had her racing out of her room, still buttoning her blouse. She stopped to peek into Kevin's bedroom, spotted the haphazardly made bed and sighed.

Everyone was up and about, it seemed, but her.

She made a dash toward her office, crossing breakfast with her son off her list of small pleasures for the day.

"Oh, dear." Coco fluttered her hands when Megan nearly mowed her down in the lobby. "Is something wrong?"

"No, I'm sorry. I'm just late."

"Did you have an appointment?"

"No." Megan caught her breath. "I meant I was late for work."

"Oh, my, I thought there was a problem. I just this minute left a memo on your desk. Go ahead in, dear, I don't want to hold you up."

"But—" Megan found herself addressing Coco's retreating back, so she turned into her office to read the message.

Coco's idea of an interoffice memo was something less than professional.

Megan, dear, I hope you slept well. There's fresh coffee in your machine, and I've left you a nice basket of muffins. You really shouldn't skip breakfast. Kevin ate like a young wolf. It's so rewarding to see a boy enjoy his food. He and Nate will be back in a few hours. Don't work too hard. Love, Coco

P.S. The cards say you have two important questions to answer. One with your heart, one with your head. Isn't that interesting?

Megan blew out a breath, and was reading the memo again when Amanda popped in. "Got a minute?"

"Sure." She handed over the paper she held. "Do you think you could interpret this for me?"

"Ah, one of Aunt Coco's convoluted messages." Lips pursed, Amanda studied it. "Well, the coffee and muffins are easy."

"I got that part." In fact, Megan helped herself to both. "Want some?"

"No, thanks, she already delivered mine. Kevin ate a good breakfast. I can vouch for that. When I saw him, he was scarfing down French toast, with Nathaniel battling him for the last piece."

Megan bobbled her coffee. "Nathaniel was here for breakfast?"

"Eating and charming Aunt Coco, while telling Kevin some story about a giant squid. They'll be back in a few hours," she continued, tapping the note, "because Kevin talked Nate into taking him out on the tour again. It didn't take much talking," she added with a smile. "And we didn't think you'd mind."

"No, of course not."

"And the bit about the cards defies interpretation. That's pure Aunt Coco." Amanda set the memo down again. "It's spooky, though, just how often she hits the mark. Been asked any questions lately?"

"No, nothing in particular."

Amanda thought of what Sloan had related to her about Nathaniel's feelings. "Are you sure?"

"Hmmm? Yes. I was thinking about Fergus's book. I suppose it could loosely be considered a question. At least there's one I want to ask you."

Amanda made herself comfortable. "Shoot."

"The numbers in the back. I mentioned them before." She opened a file, handing a copy of the list to Amanda. "I was wondering if they might be passbook numbers, or safe-deposit boxes, safe combinations. Lot numbers, maybe, on some real estate deal?" She moved her shoulders. "I know it's silly to get so hung up on them."

"No." Amanda waved the notion away. "I know just what you mean. I hate it when things don't fit into place. We went through most of the papers from this year when we were looking for clues to find the necklace. I don't recall anything that these figures might connect to, but I can look through the material again."

"Let me do it," Megan said quickly. "I feel like it's my baby."

"Glad to. I've got more than enough on my plate, and with the big holiday tomorrow, barely time to clean up. Everything you'd want is in the storeroom under Bianca's tower room. We've got it all boxed according to year and content, but it's still a nasty, time-consuming job."

"I live for nasty, time-consuming jobs."

"Then you'll be in heaven. Megan, I hate to ask, but it's the nanny's day off, and Sloan's up to his ears in plywood or something. We've been playing pass-the-babies this morning, but I've got an appointment in the village this afternoon. I could reschedule."

"You want me to baby-sit."

"I know you're busy, but—"

"Mandy, I thought you'd never ask me." Megan's eyes lit up. "When can I get my hands on her?"

Kevin figured this was the best summer of his life. He missed his grandparents, and the horses, and his best friend, John Silverhorn, but there was too much to do for him to be really homesick.

He got to play with Alex and Jenny every day, had his own fort, and lived in a castle. There were boats to sail, and rocks to climb—and Coco or Mr. Dutch always had a snack waiting in the kitchen. Max told him really neat stories. Sloan and Trent sometimes let him help with the renovations, and Holt had let him drive the little powerboat.

All his new aunts played games with him, and sometimes, if he was really, really careful, they let him hold one of the babies.

It was, to Kevin's thinking, a really good deal.

Then there was Nathaniel. He snuck a look at the man who sat beside him, driving the big convertible up the winding road to The Towers. Kevin had decided that Nathaniel knew something about everything. He had muscles and a tattoo and most always smelled like the sea.

When he stood at the helm of the big tour boat, his eyes narrowed against the sun and his broad hands on the wheel, he was every little boy's idea of a hero.

"Maybe…" Kevin trailed off until Nathaniel glanced down at him.

"Maybe what, mate?"

"Maybe I could go back out with you sometime," Kevin blurted out. "I won't ask so many questions next time, or get in the way."

Was there ever a man, Nathaniel wondered, who could defend himself against the sweetness of a child? He stopped the car at the family entrance. "I'll pipe you aboard my ship anytime." He flicked a finger down the brim of the captain's hat he'd carelessly dropped on Kevin's head. "And you can ask all the questions you want."

"Really?" Kevin pushed the brim back up, so that he could see.

"Really."

"Thanks!" Kevin threw his arms around Nathaniel in a spontaneous hug that had Nathaniel's heart sliding down the slippery chute toward love. "I gotta tell Mom. Are you going to come in?"

"Yeah." He let his hands linger on the boy a moment before they dropped away.

"Come on." Bursting with tidings, Kevin scrambled out of the car and up the steps. He hit the door running. "Mom! I'm back!"

"What a quiet, dignified child," Megan commented as she stepped into the hallway from the parlor. "It must be my Kevin."

With a giggle, Kevin darted to her, rising on his toes to see which baby she was holding. "Is that Bianca?"

"Delia."

Kevin squinted and studied. "How can you tell them apart? They look the same."

"A mother's eyes," she murmured, and bent to kiss him. "Where've you been, sailor?"

"We went way, way out in the ocean and back, twice. We saw nine whales. One was like a baby. When they're all together, they're called a pod. Like what peas grow in."

"Is that so?"

"And Nate let me steer and blow the horn, and I helped chart the course. And this man on the second deck was sick the whole time, but I wasn't 'cause I've got good sea legs. And Nate says I can go with him again, so can I?"

Nearly nine years as a mother had Megan following the stream of information perfectly. "Well, I imagine you can."

"Did you know whales mate for life, and they're not really fish at all, even though they live in the water? They're mammals, just like us and elephants and dogs, and they've got to breathe. That's how come they come up and blow water out of their spouts."

Nathaniel walked in on the lecture. And stopped, and looked. Megan stood, smiling down at her son, his hand in hers and a baby on her hip.

I want. The desire streamed through Nathaniel like sunlight, warm, bright. The woman—there had never been a question of that. But he wanted, as Sloan had said, the whole package. The woman, the boy, the family.

Megan looked over and smiled at him. His heart all but stopped.

She started to speak, but the look in Nathaniel's eyes had her throat closing. Though she took an unconscious step back, he was already there, his hand on her cheek, his lips on hers with a tenderness that turned her to putty.

The baby laughed in delight and reached for a fistful of Nathaniel's hair.

"Here we go." Nathaniel took Delia, hefted her high so that she could squeal and kick her feet. When he settled her on his hip, both Megan and Kevin were still staring at him. He jiggled the baby and cocked his head at the boy. "Do you have a problem with me kissing your mom?"

Megan made a little strangled sound. Kevin's gaze dropped heavily to the floor. "I don't know," he mumbled.

"She sure is pretty, isn't she?"

Kevin shrugged, flushed. "I guess." He wasn't sure how he was supposed to feel. Lots of men kissed his mother. His granddad and Sloan—and Holt and Trent and Max. But this was different. He knew that. After all, he wasn't a baby. He shot a look up, lowered his eyes again. "Are you going to be her boyfriend now?"

"Ah…" Nathaniel glanced at Megan, was met with a look that clearly stated that he was on his own. "That's close enough. Does that bother you?"

Because his stomach was suddenly jittery, Kevin moved his thin shoulders again. "I don't know."

If the boy wasn't going to look up, Nathaniel figured it was time to move down. He crouched, still holding the baby. "You can take plenty of time to think about it, and let me know. I'm not going anywhere."

"Okay." Kevin's eyes slid up toward his mother's, then back to Nathaniel's. He sidled closer and leaned toward Nathaniel's ear. "Does she like it?"

Nathaniel clamped down on a chuckle and answered solemnity with solemnity. "Yeah, she does."

After a long breath, Kevin nodded. "Okay, I guess you can kiss her if you want."

"I appreciate it." He offered Kevin a hand, and the man-to-man shake had the boy's chest swelling like a balloon.

"Thanks for taking me today." Kevin took off the captain's hat. "And for letting me wear this."

Nathaniel dropped the hat back on Kevin's head, pushed up the brim. "Keep it."

The boy's eyes went blank with shocked pleasure. "For real?"

"Yeah."

"Wow. Thanks. Thanks a lot. Look, Mom, I can keep it. I'm going to show Aunt Coco."

He raced upstairs with a clatter of sneakers. When Nathaniel straightened again, Megan was eyeing him narrowly.

"What did he ask you?"

"Man talk. Women don't understand these things."

"Oh, really?" Before she could disabuse him of that notion, Nathaniel hooked his fingers in her waistband and jerked her forward.

"I've got permission to do this now." He kissed her thoroughly, while Delia did her best to snuggle between them.

"Permission," Megan said when she could breathe again. "From whom?"

"From your men." He strolled casually into the parlor, laid Delia on her play rug, where she squealed happily at her favorite stuffed bear. "Except your father, but he's not around."

"My men? You mean Kevin and Sloan." Realization dawned, and had her sinking onto the arm of a chair. "You spoke to Sloan about…this?"

"We were going to beat each other up about it, but it didn't come to that." Very much at home, Nathaniel walked to the side table and poured himself a short whiskey from a decanter. "We straightened it out."

"You did. You and my brother. I suppose it didn't occur to either of you that I might have some say in the matter."

"It didn't come up. He was feeling surly about the fact that you'd spent the night with me."

"It's none of his business," Megan said tightly.

"Maybe it is, maybe it isn't. It's water under the bridge now. Nothing to get riled about."

"I'm not riled. I'm irritated that you took it upon yourself to explain our relationship to my family without discussing it with me." And she was unnerved, more than a little, by the worshipful look she'd seen in Kevin's eyes.

Women, Nathaniel thought, and tossed back his whiskey. "I was either going to explain it to Sloan or take a fist in the face."

"That's ridiculous."

"You weren't there, sugar."

"Exactly." She tossed back her head. "I don't like to be discussed. I've had my fill of that over the years."

Very carefully, Nathaniel set his glass down. "Megan, if you're going to circle back around to Dumont, you're just going to get me mad."

"I'm not doing that. I'm simply stating a fact."

"And I stated a fact of my own. I told your brother I was in love with you, and that settled it."

"You should have…" She trailed off, gasped for air that had suddenly gone too thin. "You told Sloan you were in *love* with me?"

"That's right. Now you're going to say I should have told you first."

"I… I don't know what I'm going to say." But she was glad, very glad, that she was already sitting down.

"The preferred response is 'I love you, too.'" He waited, ignored the slow stroke of pain. "Can't get your tongue around that."

"Nathaniel." Be calm, she warned herself. Reasonable. Logical. "This is all moving so fast. A few weeks ago, I didn't even know you. I never expected what's happened between us. And I'm still baffled by it. I have very strong, very real feelings for you, otherwise I couldn't have stayed with you that first night."

She was killing him, bloodlessly. "But?"

"Love isn't something I'll ever be frivolous about again. I don't want to hurt you, or be hurt, or risk a misstep that could hurt Kevin."

"You really think time's the answer, don't you? That no matter what's going on inside you, if you just wait a reasonable period, study all the data, balance all the figures, the right answer comes up."

Her shoulders stiffened. "If you're saying do I need time, then yes, I do."

"Fine, take your time, but add this into your equation." In two strides he was in front of her, dragging her up, crushing her mouth with his. "You feel just what I feel."

She did—she was very much afraid she did. "That's not the answer."

"It's the only answer." His eyes burned into hers. "I wasn't looking for you, either, Megan. My own course was plotted out just fine. You changed everything for me. So you're going to have to adjust your nice neat columns and make room for me. Because I love you, and I'm going to have you. You and Kevin are going to belong to me." He released her. "Think about it," he said, and walked out.

Idiot. Nathaniel continued to curse himself as he spun his wheels pulling up in front of Shipshape. Obviously he'd found a new way to court a woman: Yell and offer ultimatums. Clearly the perfect way to win a heart.

He snatched Dog out of the back seat and received a sympathetic face bath. "Want to get drunk?" he asked the wriggling ball of fur. "Nope, you're right, bad choice." He stepped inside the building, set the dog down and wondered where he might find an alternative.

Work, he decided, was a wiser option than a bottle.

He busied himself with an engine until he heard the familiar blat of a horn. That would be Holt, bringing in the last tour of the day.

His mood still sour, Nathaniel went out and down to the pier to help secure lines.

"The holiday's bringing in a lot of tourists," Holt commented when the lines were secured. "Good runs today."

"Yeah." Nathaniel scowled at the throng of people still lingering on the docks. "I hate crowds."

Holt's brow lifted. "You were the one who came up with the Fourth of July special to lure them in."

"We need the money." Nathaniel stomped back into the shop. "Doesn't mean I have to like it."

"Who's ticked you off?"

"Nobody." Nathaniel took out a cigar, lit it defiantly. "I'm not used to being landlocked, that's all."

Holt very much doubted that was all, but, in the way of men, shrugged his acceptance and picked up a wrench. "This engine's coming along."

"I can pick up and go anytime." Nathaniel clamped the cigar between his teeth. "Nothing holding me. All I got to do is pack a bag, hop a freighter."

Holt sighed, accepted his lot as a sounding board. "Megan, is it?"

"I didn't ask for her to drop in my lap, did I?"

"Well…"

"I was here first." Even when he heard how ridiculous that sounded, Nathaniel couldn't stop. "Woman's got a computer chip in her head. She's not even my type, with those neat little suits and that glossy briefcase. Who ever said I was going to settle down here, lock myself in for life? I've never stayed put anywhere longer than a month since I was eighteen."

Holt pretended to work on the engine. "You started a business, took out a mortgage. And it seems to me you've been here better than six months now."

"Doesn't mean anything."

"Is Megan dropping hints about wedding bells?"

"No." Nathaniel scowled around his cigar and snarled. "I am."

Holt dropped his wrench. "Hold on a minute. Let me get this straight. You're thinking of getting married, and you're kicking around here muttering about hopping a freighter and not being tied down?"

"I didn't ask to be tied down, it just happened." Nathaniel took a deliberate puff, then swore. "Damn it, Holt, I made a fool of myself."

"Funny how we do that around women, isn't it? Did you have a fight with her?"

"I told her I loved her. She started the fight." He paced the shop, nearly gave in to the urge to kick the tool bench. "What happened to the days when women wanted to get married, when that was their Holy Grail, when they set hooks for men to lure them in?"

"What century are we in?"

The fact that Nathaniel could laugh was a hopeful sign. "She thinks I'm moving too fast."

"I'd tell you to slow down, but I've known you too long."

Calmer, he took up a ratchet, considered it, then set it down again. "Suzanna took her lumps from Dumont. How'd you get past it?"

"I yelled at her a lot," Holt said, reminiscing.

"I've tried that."

"Brought her flowers. She's got a real weakness for flowers." Which made him think that perhaps he'd stop on the way home and pick some up.

"I've done that, too."

"Have you tried begging?"

Nathaniel winced. "I'd rather not." His eyes narrowed curiously. "Did you?"

Holt took a sudden, intense interest in the engine. "We're talking about you. Hell, Nate, quote her some of that damn poetry you're so fond of. I don't know. I'm not good at this romance stuff."

"You got Suzanna."

"Yeah." Holt's smile spread. "So get your own woman."

Nathaniel nodded, crushed out his cigar. "I intend to."

Chapter 10

The sun had set by the time Nathaniel returned home. He'd overhauled an engine and repaired a hull, and he still hadn't worked off his foul mood.

He remembered a quote—Horace, he thought—about anger being momentary insanity. If you didn't figure out a way to deal with momentary insanity, you ended up in a padded room. Not a cheerful image.

The only way to deal with it, as far as he could see, was to face it. And Megan. He was going to do both as soon as he'd cleaned up.

"And she'll have to deal with me, won't she?" he said to Dog as the pup scrambled out of the car behind him. "Do yourself a favor, Dog, and stay away from smart women who have more brains than sense."

Dog wagged his tail in agreement or sympathy, then toddled away to water the hedges.

Nathaniel slammed the car door and started across the yard.

"Fury?"

He stopped, squinted into the shadows of dusk, toward the side of the cottage. "Yeah?"

"Nathaniel Fury?"

He watched the man approach, a squat, muscled tank in faded denim. Creased face, strutting walk, a grease-smeared cap pulled low over the brow.

Nathaniel recognized the type. He'd seen the man, and the trouble he carried with him like a badge, in dives and on docks the world over. Instinctively he shifted his weight.

"That's right. Something I can do for you?"

"Nope." The man smiled. "Something *I* can do for *you*."

Even as the first flash of warning lit in Nathaniel's brain, he was grabbed from behind, his arms viciously twisted and pinned. He saw the first blow coming, braced, and took a heavy fist low in the gut. The pain was incredible, making his vision double and waver before the second blow smashed into his jaw.

He grunted, went limp.

"Folded like a girl. Thought he was supposed to be tough." The voice behind him sneered, giving him the height and the distance. In a fast, fluid movement, Nathaniel snapped his head back, rapping his skull hard against the soft tissue of a nose. Using the rear assailant for balance, he kicked up both feet and slammed them into a barrel chest.

The man behind him cursed, loosened his grip enough for Nathaniel to wrest himself away. There were only seconds to judge his opponents and the odds.

He saw that both men were husky, one bleeding profusely now from his broken nose, the other snarling as he wheezed, trying to get back his breath after the double kick to his chest. Nate snapped his elbow back, had the momentary pleasure of hearing the sound of bone against bone.

They came at him like dogs.

He'd been fighting all his life, knew how to mentally go around the pain and plow in. He tasted his own blood, felt the power sing up his arm as his fist connected. His head rang like church bells when he caught a blow to the temple. His breath burned from another in the ribs.

But he kept moving in as they circled him, lashing out, dripping sweat and blood. Avoiding a leap at his throat with a quick pivot, he followed through with a snapping, backhanded blow. The flesh on his knuckles ripped, but the pain was sweet.

He caught the quick move out of the corner of his eye and turned into it. The blow skimmed off his shoulder, and he answered it with two stinging jabs to the throat that had one of the men sinking bonelessly to his knees.

"Just you and me now." Nathaniel wiped the blood from his mouth and measured his foe. "Come on."

The loss of his advantage had his opponent taking a step in retreat. Facing Nathaniel now was like facing a wolf with fangs sharp and exposed. His partner was useless, and the man shifted his eyes for the best route of escape.

Then his eyes lit up.

Lunging, he grabbed one of the boards waiting to be nailed to the deck. He was grinning now, advancing and swinging the board like a bat. Nathaniel felt the wind whistle by his ear as he feinted left, then the wood slapping on his shoulder on the return swing.

He went in low. The rushing power took them both over the deck and smashing through the front door.

"Fire in the hole!" Bird shouted out. "All hands on

deck!" His wings flapped frantically as the two men hurtled across the room.

A small table splintered like toothpicks under their combined weight. The wrestling wasn't pretty, nor was there any grace in the short body punches or the gouging fingers. The cottage rang with smashing furniture and harsh breathing.

Something new crept into the jungle scent of sweat and blood. When he recognized fear, Nathaniel's adrenaline pumped faster, and he used the new weapon as ruthlessly as his fists.

He closed his hand around the thick throat, thumb crushing down on the windpipe. The fight had gone out of his opponent. The man was flailing now, gagging.

"Who sent you?" Nathaniel's teeth were bared in a snarl as he grabbed the man by the hair and rapped his head hard on the floor.

"Nobody."

Breathing through his teeth, Nathaniel hauled him over, twisted his arm and jerked it viciously up his back. "I'll snap it like a twig. Then I'll break the other one, before I start on your legs. Who sent you?"

"Nobody," the man repeated, then screamed thinly when Nathaniel increased the pressure. "I don't know his name. I don't!" He screamed again, almost weeping now. "Some dude outa Boston. Paid us five hundred apiece to teach you a lesson."

Nathaniel kept the arm twisted awkwardly, his knee on the man's spine. "Draw me a picture."

"Tall guy, dark hair, fancy suit." The squat man babbled out curses, unable to move without increasing his own agony. "Name of God, you're breaking my arm."

"Keep talking and it's all I'll break."

"Pretty face—like a movie star. Said we was to come

here and look you up. We'd get double if we put you in the hospital."

"Looks like you're not going to collect that bonus." After releasing his arm, Nathaniel dragged the man up by the scruff of his neck. "Here's what you're going to do. You're going to go back to Boston and tell your pretty-faced pal that I know who he is and I know where to find him." For the hell of it, Nathaniel rammed the man against the wall on the way out the door. "Tell him not to bother looking over his shoulder, because if I decide he's worth going after, he won't see me coming. You got that?"

"Yeah, yeah, I got it."

"Now pick up your partner." The other man was struggling onto his hands and knees. "And start running."

They didn't need any more urging. Pressing a hand to his ribs, Nathaniel watched until they'd completed their limping race out of sight.

He gave in to a groan then, hobbling painfully through the broken door and into the house.

"I have not yet begun to fight," Bird claimed.

"A lot of help you were," Nathaniel muttered. He needed ice, he thought, a bottle of aspirin and a shot of whiskey.

He took another step, stopping, then swearing, when his vision blurred and his legs wobbled like jelly. Dog came out of the corner where he'd huddled, whimpering, and whined at Nate's feet.

"Just need a minute," he said to no one in particular, and then the room tilted nastily on its side. "Oh, hell," he murmured, and passed out cold.

Dog licked at him, tried to nuzzle his nose, then sat,

thumped his tail and waited. But the smell of blood made him skittish. After a few moments, he waddled out the door.

Nathaniel was just coming to when he heard the footsteps approaching. He struggled to sit up, wincing at every blow that had gone unfelt during the heat of battle. He knew that if they'd come back for him, they could tap-dance on his face without any resistance from him.

"Man overboard," Bird announced, and earned a hissing snarl from Nathaniel.

Holt stopped in the doorway and swore ripely. "What the hell happened?" Then he was at Nathaniel's side, helping him to stand.

"Couple of guys." Too weak to be ashamed of it, Nathaniel leaned heavily on Holt. It began to occur to him that he might need more than aspirin.

"Did you walk into a robbery?"

"No. They just stopped by to beat me to a pulp."

"Looks like they did a good job of it." Holt waited for Nathaniel to catch his breath and his balance. "Did they mention why?"

"Yeah." He wiggled his aching jaw and saw stars. "They were paid to. Courtesy of Dumont."

Holt swore again. His friend was a mess, bruised, bloodied and torn. And it looked as though he were too late to do anything other than mop up the spills.

"Did you get a good look at them?"

"Yeah, good enough. I kicked their butts back to Boston to deliver a little message to Dumont."

Half carrying Nathaniel to the door, Holt stopped, took another survey. "You look like this, and you won?"

Nathaniel merely grunted.

"Should have known." The news made Holt marginally more cheerful. "Well, we'll get you to the hospital."

"No." Damned if he'd give Dumont the satisfaction. "Son of a bitch told them they'd get a bonus if they put me in the hospital."

"Then that's out," Holt said with perfect understanding. "Just a doctor then."

"It's not that bad. Nothing's broke." He checked his tender ribs. "I don't think. Just need some ice."

"Yeah, right." But, being a man, Holt was in perfect sympathy with the reluctance to be bundled off to a doctor. "Okay, we're going to the next-best place." He eased Nathaniel into the car. "Take it slow, ace."

"I can't take it otherwise."

With a snap of his fingers, Holt ordered Dog into the car. "Hold on a minute while I phone Suzanna, let her know what's going on."

"Feed the bird, will you?"

Nathaniel drifted between pain and numbness until Holt returned.

"How'd you know to come by?"

"Your dog." Holt started the car and eased it as gently as possible out of the drive. "He played Lassie."

"No fooling?" Impressed, Nathaniel made the effort to reach back and pat Dog on the head. "Some dog, huh?"

"It's all in the bloodlines."

Nathaniel roused himself enough to probe his face with cautious fingers. "Where are we going?"

"Where else?" Holt headed for The Towers.

Coco squealed at the sight of him, pressing both hands to her cheeks, as Nathaniel hobbled into the family kitchen with one arm slung over Holt's supporting shoulders.

"Oh, you poor *darling*! What happened? Was there an accident?"

"Ran into something." Nathaniel dropped heavily into a chair. "Coco, I'll trade you everything I own, plus my immortal soul, for a bag of ice."

"Goodness."

Brushing Holt away, she took Nathaniel's battered face in her hands. In addition to bruises and scrapes, there was a jagged cut under one eye. The other was bloodshot and swelling badly. It didn't take her longer than a moment to see that the something he'd run into was fists.

"Don't you worry, sweetheart, we'll take care of you. Holt, run up to my room. There's a bottle of painkillers in the medicine chest, from when I had that nasty root canal."

"Bless you," Nathaniel managed. He closed his eyes, listening to her bustling around the kitchen. Moments later he hissed and jerked when a cool cloth dabbed the cut under his eye.

"There, there, dear," she cooed. "I know it hurts, but we have to get it clean so there's no infection. I'm going to put a little peroxide on it now, so you just be brave."

He smiled, but found that did nothing to help his torn lip. "I love you, Coco."

"I love you, too, sweetie."

"Let's elope. Tonight."

Her answer was to lay her lips gently on his brow. "You shouldn't fight, Nathaniel. It doesn't solve anything."

"I know."

Breathless from the run, Megan burst into the

kitchen. "Holt said— Oh, God." She streaked to Nathaniel's side, grabbed his sore hand so tightly he had to bite down to suppress a yelp. There was blood drying on his face, and there were bruises blooming. "How bad are you hurt? You should be in the hospital."

"I've had worse."

"Holt said two men came after you."

"Two?" Coco's hand paused. "*Two* men attacked you?" All the softness fled from her eyes, hardening them to tough blue steel. "Why, that's reprehensible. Someone should teach them how to fight fair."

Despite his lip, Nathaniel grinned. "Thanks, beautiful, but I already did."

"I hope you knocked their heads together." After a huffing breath, Coco went back to work on his face. "Megan, dear, fix Nate an ice bag for his eye. It's going to swell."

Megan obeyed, torn into dozens of pieces, by the damage to his face, by the fact that he hadn't even looked at her.

"Here." She laid the cool bag against his eye while Coco cleaned his torn knuckles.

"I can hold it. Thanks." He took it from her, let the ice numb the pain.

"There's antiseptic in the left-hand cupboard, second shelf," Coco said.

Megan, feeling weepy, turned to get it.

The door opened again, this time letting in a crowd. Nathaniel's initial discomfort with the audience turned to reluctant amusement as the Calhouns fired questions and indignation. Plans for revenge were plotted and discarded while Nathaniel suffered the sting of iodine.

"Give the boy air!" Colleen commanded, parting her angry grandnieces and nephews like a queen moving through her court. She eyed Nathaniel. "Banged you up pretty good, did they?"

"Yes, ma'am."

Her eyes were shrewd. "Dumont," she murmured, so that only he could hear.

Nathaniel winced. "Right the first time."

She glanced at Coco. "You seem to be in able hands, here. I have a call to make." She smiled thinly. It helped to have connections, she thought as she tapped out of the room with her cane. And through them she would see that Baxter Dumont knew he had put a noose around his own neck, and that one false move would mean his career would come to an abrupt and unpleasant stop.

Nobody trifled with Colleen Calhoun's family.

Nathaniel watched Colleen go, then took the pill Coco held out to him and gulped it down. The movement sent fresh pain radiating up his side.

"Let's get that shirt off." Trying to sound cheerful, Coco attacked the torn T-shirt with kitchen shears. The angry mutters died away as Nathaniel's bruised torso was exposed.

"Oh." Tears stung Coco's eyes. "Oh, baby."

"Don't pamper the boy." Dutch came in holding two bottles. Witch hazel and whiskey. One look at Nathaniel had him gritting his teeth together so hard they ached, but he kept his voice careless. "He ain't no baby. Take a shot of this, Captain."

"He's just taken a pill," Coco began.

"Take a shot," Dutch repeated.

Nathaniel winced once as the whiskey stung his lip. But it took the edge off a great many other aches. "Thanks."

"Look at ya." Dutch snorted and dumped the witch

hazel onto a cloth. "Let 'em pound all over you, like some city boy with sponges where his fists should be."

"There were two of them," Nathaniel muttered.

"So?" Dutch gently swabbed the bruises. "You getting so outa shape you can't take two?"

"I kicked their butts." Experimentally Nathaniel probed a tooth with his tongue. It hurt, but at least it wasn't loose.

"Better had," Dutch returned, with a flash of pride. "Tried to rob you, did they?"

Nathaniel's gaze flashed to Megan. "No."

"Ribs're bruised." Ignoring Nathaniel's curse, Dutch prodded and poked until he was satisfied. "Not cracked though." He crouched, peered into Nathaniel's eyes. "D'ya pass out?"

"Maybe." It was almost as bad as another thumping to admit it. "For a minute."

"Vision blurred?"

"No, Doc. Not now."

"Don't get smart. How many?" He held up two thick fingers.

"Eighty-seven." Nathaniel would have reached for the whiskey again, but Coco shoved it aside.

"He's not drinking any more on top of the pill I gave him."

"Women think they know every damn thing." But Dutch sent her a look, reassuring her that their charge would be all right. "Bed's what you need now. A hot soak and cool sheets. Want I should carry you?"

"Hell, no." That was one humiliation he could do without. He took Coco's hand, kissed it. "Thanks, darling. I'd do it all again if I knew you'd be my nurse." He looked back at Holt. "I could use a ride home."

"Nonsense." Coco disposed of that idea instantly.

"You'll stay here, where we can look after you. You may very well have a concussion, so we'll take shifts waking you up through the night to be sure you don't slip into a coma."

"Wives' tales," Dutch grunted, but nodded at her behind Nathaniel's back.

"I'll turn down the bed in the rose guest room," Amanda stated. "C.C., why don't you run our hero a nice hot bath? Lilah, bring that ice along."

He didn't have the energy to fight the lot of them, so he sat back as Lilah walked over and touched her lips gently to his. "Come on, tough guy."

Sloan moved over to help him to his feet. "Two of them, huh? Puny guys?"

"Bigger than you, pal." He was floating just a little as he hobbled up the stairs between Sloan and Max.

"Let's get those pants off," Lilah said, when they'd eased him down to sit on the side of the bed.

He still had the wit to arch a brow at her. "You never said that when it counted. No offense," he added to Max.

"None taken." With a chuckle, Max bent down to pull off Nathaniel's shoes. He knew what it was to be nursed back to health by the Calhoun women, and he figured that once Nathaniel got past the worst of the pain, he'd realize he'd landed in heaven. "Need some help getting in the tub?"

"I can handle it, thanks."

"Give a call if you run into trouble." Sloan held the door open, waiting until the room cleared. "And, when you're more up to it, I'd like the whole story."

Alone, Nathaniel managed to ease himself into the hot water. The first flash of agony passed, transforming gradually into something closer to comfort. By the time he'd climbed out again, the worst seemed to be over.

Until he looked in the mirror.

There was a bandage under his left eye, another on his temple. His right eye looked like a rotting tomato. That left the bruises, the swollen lip, the nasty scrape on his jaw. All in all, he thought, he looked like hell.

With a towel slung around his waist, he stepped back into the bedroom, just as Megan came in the hallway door.

"I'm sorry." She pressed her lips together to keep herself from saying all manner of foolish things. "Amanda thought you might want another pillow, some more towels."

"Thanks." He made it to the bed and lay back with a sigh of relief.

Grateful for something practical to do, she hurried to the bed, plumped and arranged pillows for him, smoothed the sheets. "Is there anything I can get you? More ice? Some soup?"

"No, this is fine."

"Please, I want to help. I need to help." She couldn't bear it any longer, and she laid a hand to his cheek. "They hurt you. I'm so sorry they hurt you."

"Just bruises."

"Damn it, don't be so stupid—not when I'm looking right at you, not when I can see what they did." She pulled back on the need to rage and looked helplessly into his eyes. "I know you're angry with me, but can't you let me do something?"

"Maybe you'd better sit down." When she did, he took her hand in his. He needed the contact every bit as much as she did. "You've been crying."

"A little." She looked down at his damaged knuckles. "I felt so helpless downstairs, seeing you like this. You let Coco tend you, and you wouldn't even look at me."

Drenched with emotion, her eyes came back to his. "I don't want to lose you, Nathaniel. It's only that I've just found you, and I don't want to make another mistake."

"It always comes back to him, doesn't it?"

"No, no. It comes back to me."

"What he did to you," Nathaniel corrected grimly.

"All right, yes." She brought his hand to her cheek. "Please, don't walk away from me. I don't have all the answers yet, but I know when Holt said you'd been hurt—my heart just stopped. I've never been so frightened. You mean so much to me, Nathaniel. Let me just take care of you until you're better."

"Well." He was softening, and he reached out to stroke her hair. "Maybe Dumont did me a favor this time."

"What do you mean?"

He shook his head. Maybe his brain was a little addled by the drug and the pain. He hadn't meant to tell her, at least not yet. But he thought she had the right to know.

"The two guys that jumped me tonight. Dumont hired them."

Every ounce of color faded from her cheeks. "What are you saying? You're saying that Baxter paid them to attack you? To—"

"Rough me up, that's all. I'd say he was sore about me tossing him in the water and was looking for some payback." He shifted, winced. "He'd have been smarter to put his money on a couple of pros. These two were real amateurs."

"*Baxter* did this." Megan's vision hazed. She shut her eyes until she was sure it had cleared again. "My fault."

"Like hell. None of it's been yours, not from the start. He did what he did to you, Suzanna, the kids. Chicken-hearted bastard couldn't even fight for himself. Hey." He tugged on her hair. "I won, remember. He didn't get what he'd paid for."

"Do you think that matters?"

"It does to me. If you want to do something for me, Megan, really want to do something for me, you'll push him right out of your head."

"He's Kevin's father," she whispered. "It makes me sick to think it."

"He's nothing. Lie down here with me, will you?"

Because she could see that he was fighting off the drug, she did as he asked. Gently she shifted his head so that it rested on her breast.

"Sleep for a while," she murmured. "We won't think of it now. We won't think of anything."

He sighed, let himself drift. "I love you, Megan."

"I know." She stroked his hair and lay wakeful while he slept.

Neither of them saw the little boy with shattered eyes and pale cheeks in the open doorway.

Nathaniel woke to the rhythm of his own pain. There was a bass drum in his head, pounding low in the skull, with a few more enthusiastic riffs at the left temple. It was more of a snare along his ribs, a solid rat-a-tat that promised to remain steady and persistent. His shoulder sang along in a droning hum.

Experimentally, he sat up. Stiff as a week-old corpse, he thought in disgust. With slow, awkward movements, he eased out of the bed. Except for the pounding in his head, it was clear. Maybe too clear, he thought with a wince as he limped into the shower. His one pleasure was that he knew his two unexpected visitors would be suffering more than he was at the moment.

Even the soft needles of spray brought a bright bloom of pain to the worst of his bruises. Teeth clenched, he waited out the pain until it mellowed to discomfort.

He'd live.

Naked and dripping, he stepped out of the shower, then filled the basin with icy water. Taking one bracing breath, he lowered his face into it until the shocking cold brought on a blessed numbness.

Steadier, he went back into the bedroom, where fresh clothes had been left folded on a chair. With a great deal of swearing, he managed to dress. He was thinking of coffee, aspirin and a full plate when the door creaked open.

"You shouldn't be up." Coco, a tray balanced in both hands, clucked her tongue. "Now get that shirt off and get back into bed."

"Darling, I've been waiting all my life to hear you say that."

"You must be feeling a little better," Coco said, and laughed, then set the tray on the bedside table and fluffed at her hair. It occurred to Nathaniel as he followed the familiar gesture that her hair hadn't changed color in a couple weeks, maybe more. Must be some mood she was in, he decided.

"I'll do."

"Poor dear." She lifted a hand to gently touch the bruises on his face. He looked even worse this morning, but she didn't have the heart to say so. "At least sit down and eat."

"You read my mind." More than willing, he eased himself into a chair. "I appreciate the service."

"It's the least we can do." Coco fit the legs of the bedside table over the chair and unfolded his napkin. Nathaniel thought she would have tucked it into his collar if he hadn't taken it himself. "Megan told me what happened. That Baxter hired those—those thugs. I've a mind to go to Boston myself and deal with that man."

The fierce look in her eyes warmed Nathaniel's heart. She was like some fiery Celtic goddess. "Sugar, he wouldn't have a chance against you." He sampled his eggs, closed his eyes on the simple pleasure of hot, delicious food. "We'll let it go, darling."

"Let it go! You can't. You have to contact the police. Of course, I'd prefer if all you boys got together and took a trip down to blacken that man's eyes…" She pressed a hand to her heart as the image caused it to beat fast. "But," she continued with some regret, "the proper thing to do is contact the authorities and have them handle it."

"No cops." He scooped up delicately fried hash-brown potatoes. "Dumont's going to suffer a lot more, not knowing what I'll do or when I'll do it."

"Well…" Considering that, Coco began to smile. "I suppose he would. Like waiting for the other shoe to drop."

"Yeah. And bringing the police in would make it tough for Megan and the boy."

"You're right, of course." Gently she brushed a hand over his hair. "I'm so glad they have you."

"I wish she felt the same way."

"She does. She's just afraid. Megan's had so much to handle in her life. And you—well, Nathaniel, you're a man who'd leave any woman a bit addled."

"You think so, huh?"

"I know so. Are you having much pain this morning, dear? You can take another pill."

"I'll settle for aspirin."

"I thought you might." Coco took a bottle out of her apron pocket. "Take these with your juice."

"Yes, ma'am." He obeyed, then went back to his eggs. "So, you've seen Megan this morning?"

"It was nearly dawn before I could convince her to leave you and get some sleep."

That information went down even better than the food. "Yeah?"

"And the way she looked at you…" Coco patted his hand. "Well, a woman knows these things. Especially when she's in love herself." A becoming blush bloomed on her cheeks. "I suppose you know that Niels and I— that we're…involved."

He made some sound. He didn't want the image in his brain of them together in the dark. Coco and Dutch were as close to parents as he'd ever had, and no child, even at thirty-three, wanted to think about that side of a parental relationship.

"These past few weeks have been wonderful. I had a lovely marriage, and there are memories I've cherished and will cherish all of my life. And over the years, I've had some nice, compatible relationships. But with Niels…" The dreamy look came into her eyes. "He makes me feel young and vital, and almost delicate. It's not just the sex," she added, and had Nathaniel wincing.

"Aw, jeez, Coco." He took a sip of coffee, as he was rapidly losing his appetite. "I don't want to know about that."

She chuckled, adoring him. "I know how close you are to Niels."

"Well, sure." He was beginning to feel trapped in the chair, barred by the tray. "We sailed together a long time, and he's…"

"Like a father to you," she said gently. "I know. I

just wanted you to know I love him, too. We're going to be married."

"What?" His fork clattered against china. "*Married? You and the Dutchman?*"

"Yes." Nervous now, because she couldn't tell whether his expression was horrified or simply shocked, Coco fiddled with the jet beads at her throat. "I hope you don't mind."

"Mind?" His brain had gone blank. Now it began to fill again—the restless movements of her hands, the tone of her voice, the anxious look in her eyes. Nathaniel shifted the table away from his chair and rose. "Imagine a classy woman like you falling for that old tar. Are you sure he hadn't been slipping something into your soup?"

Relieved, she smiled. "If he has, I like it. Do we have your blessing?"

He took her hands, looked down at them. "You know, for nearly as far back as I can remember, I wanted you to be my mother."

"Oh." Her eyes filled, overflowed. "Nathaniel."

"Now I guess you will be." His gaze lifted to hers again before he kissed her, one cheek, the other, then her lips. "He'd better be good to you, or he'll answer to me."

"I'm so happy." Coco sank, weeping, into his arms. "I'm so very happy, Nate. I didn't even see it coming in the cards." Her breath hitched as she pressed her wet face to his throat. "Or the tea leaves, even the crystal. It just happened."

"The best things usually do."

"I want you to be happy." Drawing back, she fumbled in her pocket for one of her lace-trimmed hankies. "I want you to believe in what you have with

Megan, and not let it slip away. She needs you, Nate. So does Kevin."

"That's what I told her." He smiled a little as he took the hankie and dried Coco's tears himself. "I don't guess she was ready to hear it."

"You just keep saying it." Her voice became firm. "Keep right on saying it until she is." And if Megan needed an extra push, Coco thought, she'd be happy to supply it herself. "Now, then." She smoothed down her hair, her slacks. "I have a million things to do. I want you to rest, so you'll be up to the picnic and the fireworks."

"I feel okay."

"You feel as if you've been run over by a truck." She marched to the bed, busying herself with smoothing sheets and fluffing pillows. "You can lie down for another hour or two, or you can sit out on the terrace in the sun. It's a lovely day, and we can fix you up a nice chaise. When Megan wakes up, I'll have her come give you a rubdown."

"Now that sounds promising. I'll take the sun." He started toward the terrace doors, but then he heard footsteps hurrying down the hall.

Megan rushed in. "I can't find Kevin," she blurted out. "No one's seen him all morning."

Chapter 11

She was pale as ice, and struggling to be calm. The idea of her little boy running away was so absurd that she continued to tell herself it was a mistake, a prank. Maybe a dream.

"No one's seen him," she repeated, bracing a hand on the doorknob to stay upright. "Some—some of his clothes are gone, and his knapsack."

"Call Suzanna," Nathaniel said quickly. "He's probably with Alex and Jenny."

"No." She shook her head slowly, side to side. Her body felt like glass, as though it would shatter if she moved too quickly. "They're here. They're all here. They haven't seen him. I was sleeping." She said each word deliberately, as if she were having trouble understanding her own voice. "I slept late, then I checked his room, like I always do. He wasn't there, but I thought he'd be downstairs, or outside. But when I went down, Alex was looking for him." The fear began to claw at her, little cat feet up and down her spine. "We hunted around, then I came back up. That's when I saw that some of his things…some of his things…"

"All right, dear, now don't you worry." Coco hurried over to slip a supporting arm around Megan's waist. "I'm sure he's just playing a game. There are so many places to hide in the house, on the grounds."

"He was so excited about today. It's all he could talk about. He's supposed to be playing Revolutionary War with Alex and Jenny. He—he was going to be Daniel Boone."

"We'll find him," Nathaniel told her.

"Of course we will." Gently Coco began to ease Megan along. "We'll organize a search party. Won't he be excited when he finds out?"

An hour later, they were spread throughout the house, searching corners and hidey-holes, retracing and backtracking. Megan kept a steel grip on her composure and covered every inch, starting in the tower and working her way down.

He had to be here, she reassured herself. Of course, she would find him any minute. It didn't make sense otherwise.

Bubbles of hysteria rose in her throat and had to be choked down.

He was just playing a game. He'd gone exploring. He loved the house so much. He'd drawn dozens of pictures of it to send back to Oklahoma so that everyone could see that he lived in a castle.

She would find him behind the next door she opened.

Megan told herself that, repeating it like a litany, as she worked her way from room to room.

She ran into Suzanna in one of the snaking hallways. She felt cold, so cold, though the sun beat hot against the windows. "He doesn't answer me," she said faintly. "I keep calling him, but he doesn't answer."

"It's such a big house." Suzanna took Megan's hands, gripped hard. "Once when we were kids we played hide-and-seek and didn't find Lilah for three hours. She'd crawled into a cabinet on the third floor and had a nap."

"Suzanna." Megan pressed her lips together. She had to face it, and quickly. "His two favorite shirts are missing, and both pairs of his sneakers. His baseball caps. The money he'd been saving in his jar is gone. He's not in the house. He's run away."

"You need to sit down."

"No, I—I need to do something. Call the police. Oh, God—" Breaking, Megan pressed her hands to her face. "Anything could have happened to him. He's just a little boy. I don't even know how long he's been gone. I don't even know." Her eyes, swimming with fear, locked on Suzanna's. "Did you ask Alex, Jenny? Maybe he said something to them. Maybe—"

"Of course I asked them, Megan," Suzanna said gently. "Kevin didn't say anything to them about leaving."

"Where would he go? Why? Back to Oklahoma," she said on a wild, hopeful thought. "Maybe he's trying to get back to Oklahoma. Maybe he's been unhappy, just pretending to like it here."

"He's been happy. But we'll check it out. Come on, let's go down."

"Been over every bit of this section," Dutch told Nathaniel. "The pantries, the storerooms, even the meat locker. Trent and Sloan are going over the renovation areas, and Max and Holt are beating the bushes all over the grounds."

There was worry in his eyes, but he was brewing a pot of fresh coffee with steady hands.

"Seems to me if the kid was just playing and heard all this shouting and calling, he'd come out to see what the excitement was all about."

"We've been over the house twice." Nathaniel stared grimly out the window. "Amanda and Lilah have combed every inch of The Retreat. He's not in here."

"Don't make a lick of sense to me. Kevin's been happy as a clam. He's in here every blessed day, getting under my feet and begging for sea stories."

"Something's got him running." There was a prickle at the back of his neck. Rubbing it absently, Nathaniel looked out toward the cliffs. "Why does a kid run? Because he's scared, or he's hurt, or he's unhappy."

"That boy ain't none of those things," Dutch said staunchly.

"I wouldn't have thought so." Nathaniel had been all three at that age, and he believed he would have recognized the signs. There had been times he ran, too. But he'd had nowhere to go.

The tickle at the back of his neck persisted. Again, he found his gaze wandering toward the cliffs. "I've got a feeling," he said almost to himself.

"What?"

"No, just a feeling." The prickle was in his gut now. "I'm going to check it out."

It was as though he were being pulled to the cliffs. Nathaniel didn't fight it, though the rocky ground jarred the pain back into his bones and the steep climb stole his breath. With one hand pressed to his aching ribs, he continued, his gaze sweeping the rocks and the high wild grass.

It was, he knew, a place that would draw a child. It had drawn him as a boy. And as a man.

The sun was high and white, the sea sapphire blue, then frothy where it lashed and foamed on the rocks. Beautiful and deadly. He thought of a young boy stumbling along the path, missing a step, slipping. The nausea churned so violently he had to stop and choke it back.

Nothing had happened to Kevin, he assured himself. He wouldn't let anything happen to Kevin.

He turned, started to climb higher, calling the boy's name as he searched.

It was the bird that caught his eye. A pure white gull, graceful as a dancer, swooped over the grass and rock, circled back with a musical call that was almost human, eerily feminine. He stood, staring at it. For one sun-struck second, Nathaniel would have sworn the gull's eyes were green, green as emeralds.

It glided down, perched on the ledge below and looked up, as if waiting for him.

Nathaniel found himself clambering down, ignoring the jolts to his abused body. The thunder of the surf seemed to fill his head. He thought he smelled a woman, sweet, soft, soothing, but then it was only the sea.

The bird wheeled away, skyward, joined its mate—another gull, blindingly white. For a moment they circled, calling together in something like joy. Then they winged out to sea.

Wheezing a bit, Nathaniel gained the ledge, and saw the shallow crevice in the rock where the boy was huddled.

His first instinct was to scoop the child up, hold him. But he checked it. He wasn't altogether certain he wasn't the reason Kevin had run.

Instead, he sat down on the ledge and spoke quietly. "Nice view from here."

Kevin kept his face pressed to his knees. "I'm going back to Oklahoma." It was an attempt at defiance that merely sounded weary. "I can take a bus."

"I guess so. You'd see a lot of the country that way. But I thought you liked it here."

His answer was a shrug. "It's okay."

"Somebody give you a hard time, mate?"

"No."

"Did you have a fight with Alex?"

"No, it's nothing like that. I'm just going back to Oklahoma. It was too late to take the bus last night, so I came up here to wait. I guess maybe I fell asleep." He hunched his shoulder, kept his face averted. "You can't make me go back."

"Well, I'm bigger than you, so I could." He said it gently, touched a hand to Kevin's hair. But the boy jerked away. "I'd rather not make you do anything until I understand what's on your mind."

He let some time pass, watching the sea, listening to the wind, until he sensed Kevin relaxing a little beside him.

"Your mother's kind of worried about you. Everybody else is, too. Maybe you ought to go back and tell them goodbye before you leave."

"She won't let me go."

"She loves you a lot."

"She should never have had me." There was bitterness in the words, words that were much too sharp for a little boy.

"That's a stupid thing to say. I figure you've got a right to get mad if you want but there's not much point in just being stupid."

Kevin's head shot up. His face was streaked with tears and dirt, and it sliced through Nathaniel's heart.

"If she hadn't had me, things would be different. She always pretends it doesn't matter. But I know."

"What do you know?"

"I'm not a baby anymore. I know what he did. He made her pregnant, then he went away. He went away, and he never cared. He went away and married Suzanna, and then he left her, too. And Alex and Jenny. That's how come I'm their brother."

Those were stormy seas, Nathaniel thought, that needed to be navigated with care. The boy's eyes, hurt and angry, latched onto his.

"Your mother's the one who has to explain that to you, Kevin."

"She told me that sometimes people can't get married and be together, even when they have kids. But he didn't want me. He never wanted me, and I hate him."

"I'm not going to argue with you about that," Nathaniel said carefully. "But your mother loves you, and that counts for a lot more. If you take off, it's going to hurt her, bad."

Kevin's lips trembled. "She could have you if I was gone. You'd stay with her if it wasn't for me."

"I'm afraid I'm not following you, Kevin."

"He—he had you beaten up." Kevin's voice hitched as he fought to get the words out. "I heard last night. I heard you and Mom, and she said it was her fault, but it's mine. 'Cause he's my father and he did it and now you hate me, too, and you'll go away."

"Little jerk." On a flood of emotion, Nathaniel yanked the boy to his knees and shook him. "You pulled this stunt because I got a few bruises? Do I look like I can't take care of myself? Those other two wimps had to crawl away."

"Really?" Kevin sniffed and rubbed at his eyes. "But still—"

"Still, hell. You didn't have anything to do with it, and I ought to shake you until your teeth fall out for worrying us all this way."

"He's my father," Kevin said, tilting his chin up. "So that means—"

"That means nothing. My father was a drunk who used to kick my butt for the pleasure of it, six days out of seven. Does that make me like him?"

"No." Tears began to roll more freely now. "But I thought you wouldn't like me anymore, and you'd never stay and be my father now, like Holt is with Alex and Jenny."

Nathaniel's hands gentled as he drew the sobbing boy into his arms. "You thought wrong." He rubbed his lips over Kevin's hair, absorbed the jolt of love. "I ought to hang you from the yardarm, sailor."

"What's that?"

"I'll show you later." He tightened his grip. "Did you stop and think that I might be hoping you'd be my son? That I want you and your mom to be mine?"

"Honest?" Kevin's voice was muffled against Nathaniel's chest.

"Do you figure I've been training you to take the helm just to have you walk off?"

"I don't know. I guess not."

"I've been looking for you, Kevin, longer than just today."

With a sigh, Kevin let his head rest in the curve of Nathaniel's shoulder. "I was awful scared. But then the bird came."

"Bird?" Remembering, Nathaniel glanced around. But the rocks were empty.

"Then I wasn't so scared. She stayed all night. She was there whenever I woke up. She flew away with the other one, but then you came. Is Mom mad at me?"

"Probably."

Kevin sighed again—a long-suffering sound that made Nathaniel smile. "I guess I'm in trouble."

"Well, let's get your things and go back and face the music."

Kevin picked up his knapsack and put his hand trustingly in Nathaniel's. "Does it hurt?" he asked, studying Nathaniel's face.

"You bet."

"Later, can I see all your bruises?"

"Sure. I've got some beauts."

Nathaniel felt every one of them as they climbed back up to the cliff path and started down the rocky slope toward home. It was worth it, worth every jar and wince, to see the look on Megan's face.

"Kevin!" She flew across the lawn, hair blowing, cheeks tracked with tears.

"Go on," Nathaniel murmured to the boy. "She'll want to hug you first."

With a nod, Kevin dropped his knapsack and raced into his mother's arms.

"Oh, Kevin…" She couldn't hold him tight enough, even kneeling on the grass, pressing him close, rocking and weeping in terrible relief.

"Where'd you find him?" Trent asked Nathaniel quietly.

"Up on the cliffs, holed up in a crevice in the rocks."

"Good God." C.C. shuddered. "Did he spend the night up there?"

"Looked that way. I had this feeling, I can't explain it. And there he was."

"A feeling?" Trent exchanged a look with his wife. "Remind me to tell you sometime how I found Fred when he was a puppy."

Max gave Nathaniel a pat on the back. "I'll go call the police, let them know we've found him."

"He'll be hungry." Coco swallowed fresh tears and burrowed closer to Dutch. "We'll go fix him something to eat."

"You bring 'em in when she's finished slobbering over him—" Dutch camouflaged the break in his voice with a cough. "Women. Always making a fuss."

"Come on, let's go in." Suzanna tugged on Alex and Jenny's hands.

"But I want to ask if he saw the ghosts," Alex complained.

"Later." Holt solved the problem by hoisting Alex onto his shoulders.

With a shuddering sigh, Megan drew back, ran her hands over Kevin's face. "You're all right? You're not hurt?"

"Nuh-uh." It embarrassed him that he'd cried in front of his brother and sister. After all, he was nearly nine. "I'm okay."

"Don't you *ever* do that again." The swift change from weeping mother to fierce parent had Nathaniel's brows rising. "You had us all worried sick, young man. We've been looking for you for hours, even Aunt Colleen. We've called the police."

"I'm sorry." But the thrill of knowing the police had been alerted overpowered the guilt.

"Sorry isn't enough, Kevin Michael O'Riley."

Kevin's gaze hit the ground. It was big-time trouble when she used all his names. "I won't ever do it again. I promise."

"You had no business doing it this time. I'm supposed to be able to trust you, and now— Oh." On another hitching sob, she pressed his head to her breast. "I was so scared, baby. I love you so much. Where were you going?"

"I don't know. Maybe Grandma's."

"Grandma's." She sat back on her heels and sighed. "Don't you like it here?"

"I like it best of anything."

"Then why did you run away, Kevin? Are you mad at me?"

He shook his head, then dropped his chin on his chest. "I thought you and Nate were mad at me because he got beaten up. But Nate says it's not my fault and you're not mad. He says it doesn't matter about *him*. You're not mad at me, are you?"

Her horrified eyes flew to Nate's, held there as she drew Kevin close again. "Oh, no, baby, I'm not. No one is." She looked at her son again, cupping his face in her hands. "Remember when I told you that sometimes people can't be together? I should explain that sometimes they shouldn't be together. That's the way it was with me and—" She couldn't refer to him as Kevin's father. "With me and Baxter."

"But I was an accident."

"Oh, no." She smiled then, kissed his cheeks. "An accident's something you wish hadn't happened. You were a gift. The best one I ever had in my life. If you ever think I don't want you again, I guess I'll have to stuff you into a box and tie it up with a bow so you'll get the point."

He giggled. "I'm sorry."

"Me too. Now let's go get you cleaned up." She rose, gripped her son's hand in hers and looked at Nathaniel. "Thank you."

In the way of children, Kevin bounced back from his night on the cliffs and threw himself into the holiday. He was, for the moment, a hero, desperately impressing his siblings with his tales of the dark and the sea and a white bird with green eyes.

In keeping with the family gathering, all the dogs attended, so Sadie and Fred raced with their puppies and the children over the rolling lawn. Babies napped in playpens or rocked in swings or charmed their way into willing arms. A few hotel guests wandered over from their own feast provided by The Retreat, drawn by the laughter and raised voices.

Nathaniel passed, reluctantly, on the impromptu softball game, figuring one slide into third would have him down for the count. Instead, he designated himself umpire and had the pleasure of arguing with every batter he called out.

"Are you blind or just stupid?" C.C. tossed down her bat in disgust. "A sock in the eye's no excuse for missing that call. That ball was outside a half a mile."

Nathaniel clamped his cigar in his teeth. "Not from where I'm standing, sugar."

She slapped her hands on her hips. "Then you're standing in the wrong spot." Jenny took the opportunity to attempt a cartwheel over home plate, and earned some applause from the infield.

"C.C., you've got one of the best-looking strike zones

I've ever had the pleasure of seeing. And that was strike three. You're out."

"If you weren't already black-and-blue..." She swallowed a laugh, and sneered instead. "You're up, Lilah."

"Already?" In a lazy gesture, Lilah brushed her hair away from her face and stepped into the box.

From her position at short, Megan glanced at her second baseman. "She won't run even if she connects."

Suzanna sighed, shook her head. "She won't have to. Just watch."

Lilah skimmed a hand down her hip, cast a sultry look back at Nathaniel, then faced the pitcher. Sloan went through an elaborate windup that had the children cheering. Lilah took the first strike with the bat still on her shoulder. Yawned.

"We keeping you up?" Nathaniel asked her.

"I like to wait for my pitch."

Apparently the second one wasn't the one she was waiting for. She let it breeze by, and earned catcalls from the opposing team.

She stepped out of the box, stretched, smiled at Sloan. "Okay, big guy," she said as she took her stance again. She cracked the low curveball and sent it soaring for a home run. Amid the cheers, she turned and handed her bat to Nathaniel. "I always recognize the right pitch," she told him, and sauntered around the bases.

When the game broke for the feast, Nathaniel eased down beside Megan. "You've got a pretty good arm there, sugar."

"I coached Kevin's Little League team back in Oklahoma." Her gaze wandered to her son, as it had dozens of times during the afternoon. "He doesn't seem any the worse for wear, does he?"

"Nope. How about you?"

"The bats in my stomach have mellowed out to butterflies." She pressed a hand to them now, lowered her voice. "I never knew he thought about Baxter. About... any of it. I should have."

"A boy's got to have some secrets, even from his mother."

"I suppose." It was too beautiful a day, she decided, too precious a day, to waste on worry. "Whatever you said to him up there, however you said it, was exactly right. It means a lot to me." She looked over at him. "You mean a lot to me."

Nathaniel sipped his beer, studied her. "You're working up to something, Meg. Why don't you just say it?"

"All right. After you left yesterday, I spent a lot of time thinking. About how I'd feel if you didn't come back. I knew there'd be a hole in my life. Maybe I'd be able to fill it again, part of the way, but something would always be missing. When I asked myself what that would be, I kept coming up with the same answer. No matter how many ways I looked at it or juggled it around, the answer never changed."

"So what's the answer, Meg?"

"You, Nathaniel." She leaned over and kissed him. "Just you."

Later, when the sky was dark and the moon floated over the water, she watched the fireworks explode. . Color bloomed into color. Waterfalls of glowing sparks rained from sky to water in a celebration of freedom, new beginnings and, Megan thought, hope.

It was a dazzling display that had the children staring upward, wide-eyed and openmouthed. The echoing booms shivered the air until, with a machine-gun crescendo, color and light spewed high in the finale. For a heart-pounding interlude, the sky was bright with golds and reds, blues and blinding whites, circles and spirals, cascades and towers, that shattered into individual stars over the sea.

Long after it was over, the dregs of the party cleared away, the children tucked into bed, she felt the power of the celebration running through her blood. In her own room, she brushed her hair until it flowed over her shoulders. Anticipation vibrating inside her, she belted her borrowed robe loosely at her waist. Quietly she slipped out the terrace doors and walked to Nathaniel's room.

It hadn't taken much pressure to persuade him to stay another night. He'd been tired and aching, and he hadn't relished even the short drive home. But the long soak in the tub hadn't relaxed him, as he hoped. He was still filled with restless urges, and with flashing images of Megan's face, lit with the glow of rockets.

Then he stepped into the bedroom and saw her.

She wore a silky robe of deep blue that flowed down her body and clung to her curves. Her hair glinted, golden fire, and her eyes were as dark and mysterious as sapphires.

"I thought you could use a rubdown." She smiled hesitantly. "I've had a lot of experience loosening stiff muscles. With horses, anyway."

He was almost afraid to breathe. "Where did you get that?"

"Oh." Self-consciously she ran a hand down the robe. "I borrowed it from Lilah. I thought you'd like it better than terry cloth." When he said nothing, her nerve began to slip. "If you'd rather I go, I understand. I don't expect that you'd feel well enough to— We don't have to make love, Nathaniel. I just want to help."

"I don't want you to go."

Her smile bloomed again. "Why don't you lie down, then? I'll start on your back. Really, I'm good at this." She laughed a little. "The horses loved me."

He crossed to the bed, touched her hair, her cheek. "Did you wear silk robes to work the stock?"

"Always." She eased him down. "Roll onto your stomach," she said briskly. Pleased with the task, she poured liniment into her hands, then rubbed her palms together to warm it. Carefully, so that the movement of the mattress didn't jar him, she knelt over him. "Tell me if I hurt you."

She started on his shoulders, gently over the bruises, more firmly over knotted muscles. He had a warrior's body, she thought, tough and tight, and carrying all the marks of battle.

"You overdid it today."

He only grunted, closing his eyes and letting his body reap the pleasure of her stroking hands. He felt the brush of silk against his skin when she shifted. Drifting through the sharp scent of liniment was her subtle perfume, another balm to the senses.

The aches began to fade, then shifted into a deeper, more primal pain that coursed smoothly through his blood when she lowered her lips to his shoulder.

"Better?" she murmured.

"No. You're killing me. Don't stop."

Her laugh was low and soft as she eased the towel from his hips, and pressed competent fingers low on his spine. "I'm here to make you feel better, Nathaniel. You have to relax for me to do this right."

"You're doing just fine." He moaned as her hands

moved lower, circling, kneading. Then her lips, skimming, whisper-soft.

"You have such a beautiful body." Her own breathing grew heavy as she stroked and explored. "I love looking at it, touching it." Slowly she took her lips up his spine, over his shoulder again, to nuzzle at his ear. "Turn over," she whispered. "I'll do the rest."

Her lips were there to meet his when he shifted, to linger, to heat. But when he reached up, groaning, to cup her breasts, she drew back.

"Wait." Though her hands trembled, she freshened the liniment. With her eyes on his, she spread her fingers over his chest. "They put marks on you," she murmured.

"I put more on them."

"Nathaniel the dragon-slayer. Lie still," she whispered, and bent close to kiss the scrapes and bruises on his face. "I'll make it all go away."

His heart was pounding. She could feel it rocket against her palm. In the lamplight, his eyes were dark as smoke. The robe pooled around her knees when she straddled him. She massaged his shoulders, his arms, his hands, kissing the scraped knuckles, laving them with her tongue.

The air was like syrup, thick and sweet. It caught in his lungs with each labored breath. No other woman had ever made him feel helpless, drained and sated, all at once.

"Megan, I need to touch you."

Watching him, she reached for the belt of the robe, loosened it. In one fluid movement, the silk slid from her shoulders. Beneath she wore a short slip of the same color and texture. As he reached up, one thin strap spilled off her shoulder.

She closed her eyes, let her head fall back, as his hands stroked over the silk, then beneath. The colors were back, all those flashing, dazzling lights that had erupted in the sky. Stars wheeled inside her head, beautifully hot. Craving more, she rose over him, took him into her with a delicious slowness that had them both gasping.

She shuddered when he arched up, gripping her hips in his hands. Now the colors seemed to shoot into her blood, white-hot, and her skin grew damp and slick. Suddenly greedy, she swooped down, devouring his lips, fingers clutching the bruised flesh she'd sought to soothe.

"Let me." She moaned and pressed his hands against her breasts. "Let me."

With a wildness that staggered him, she drove him hard, riding him like lightning. He called out her name as his vision dimmed, as the frantic need convulsed like pain inside him. Release was like a whiplash that stung with velvet.

She tightened around him like a fist and shattered him.

Weak as water, she flowed down, rested her head on his chest. "Did I hurt you?"

He couldn't find the strength to wrap his arms around her and let them lie limp on the bed. "I can't feel anything but you."

"Nathaniel." She lifted her head to press a kiss to his thundering heart. "There's something I forgot to tell you yesterday."

"Hmm… What's that?"

"I love you, too." She watched his eyes open, saw the swirl of emotion darken them.

"That's good." His arms, no longer weak, circled her, cradled her.

"I don't know if it's enough, but—"

He turned his lips to hers to quiet her. "Don't mess it up. 'For love's sake only,' Megan. That's enough for tonight." He kissed her again. "Stay with me."

"Yes."

Chapter 12

Fireworks were one thing, but when the Calhouns put their heads together planning Coco's engagement party, there promised to be plenty of skyrockets.

Everything from a masked ball to a moonlight cruise had been considered, with the final vote going to dinner and dancing under the stars. With only a week to complete arrangements, assignments were handed out.

Megan squeezed time out of each day to polish silver, wash crystal and inventory linens.

"All this fuss." Colleen thumped her way to the closet where Megan was counting napkins. "When a woman her age straps herself down to a man, she should have the sense to do it quietly."

Megan lost count and patiently began again. "Don't you like parties, Aunt Colleen?"

"When there's a reason for them. Never considered putting yourself under a man's thumb reason to celebrate."

"Coco's not doing that. Dutch adores her."

"Humph. Time will tell. Once a man's got a ring on your finger, he doesn't have to be so sweet and obliging." Her crafty eyes studied Megan's face. "Isn't that why you're putting off that big-shouldered sailor? Afraid of what happens after the 'I-dos'?"

"Of course not." Megan laid a stack of linens aside before she lost count again. "And we're talking about Coco and Dutch, not me. She deserves to be happy."

"Not everybody gets what they deserve," Colleen shot back. "You'd know that well, wouldn't you?"

Exasperated, Megan whirled around. "I don't know why you're trying to spoil this. Coco's happy, I'm happy. I'm doing my best to make Nathaniel happy."

"I don't see you out buying any orange blossoms for yourself, girl."

"Marriage isn't the answer for everyone. It wasn't for you."

"No, I'm too smart to fall into that trap. Maybe you're like me. Men come and go. Maybe the right one goes with the rest, but we get by, don't we? Because we know what they're like, deep down." Colleen eased closer, her dark eyes fixed on Megan's face. "We've known the worst of them. The selfishness, the cruelty, the lack of honor and ethics. Maybe one steps into our lives for a moment, one who seems different. But we're too wise, too careful, to take that shaky step. If we live our lives alone, at least we know no man will ever have the power to hurt us."

"I'm not alone," Megan said in an unsteady voice.

"No, you have a son. One day he'll be grown, and if you've done a good job, he'll leave your nest and fly off to make his own."

Colleen shook her head, and for one moment she

looked so unbearably sad that Megan reached out. But the old woman held herself stiff, her head high.

"You'll have the satisfaction of knowing you escaped the trap of marriage, just as I did. Do you think no one ever asked me? There was one," Colleen went on, before Megan could speak. "One who nearly lulled me in before I remembered, before I turned him away, before I risked the hell my mother had known."

Colleen's mouth thinned at the memory. "He tried to break her in every way, with his rules, his money, his need to own. In the end, he killed her, then he slowly, slowly, went mad. But not with guilt. What ate at him, I think, was the loss of something he'd never been able to fully own. That was why he rid the house of every piece of her, and locked himself in his own private purgatory."

"I'm sorry," Megan murmured. "I'm so sorry."

"For me? I'm old, and long past the time to grieve. I learned from my experience, as you learned from yours. Not to trust, never to risk. Let Coco have her orange blossoms, we have our freedom."

She walked away stiffly, leaving Megan to flounder in a sea of emotion.

Colleen was wrong, she told herself, and began to fuss with napkins again. She wasn't cold and aloof and blocked off from love. Just days ago she'd declared her love. She wasn't letting Baxter's shadow darken what she had with Nathaniel.

Oh, but she was. Wearily she leaned against the doorjamb. She was, and she wasn't sure she could change it. Love and lovemaking didn't equal commitment. No one knew that better than she. She had loved Baxter fully, vitally. And that was the shadow. Even knowing that what she felt for Nathaniel was fuller, richer, and much, much truer, she couldn't dispel that doubt.

She would have to think it through, calmly, as soon as she had time. The answer was always there, she assured herself, if you looked for it long enough, carefully enough. All she had to do was process the data.

She tossed down her neatly counted napkins in disgust. What kind of woman was she? she wondered. She was trying to turn emotions into equations, as if they were some sort of code she had to decipher before she could know her own heart.

That was going to stop. She was going to stop. If she couldn't look into her own heart, it was time to…

Her thoughts trailed off, circled back, swooping down on one errant idea like a hawk on a rabbit.

Oh, God, a code. Leaving the linens in disarray, she flew down the hall to her own bedroom.

Fergus's book was where she'd left it, lying neatly on the corner of her desk. She snatched it up and began flipping frantically through pages.

It didn't have to be stock quotations or account numbers, she realized. It didn't have to be anything as logical as that. The numbers were listed in the back of the book, after dozens of blank sheets—after the final entry Fergus had written. On the day before Bianca died.

Why hadn't she seen it before? There were no journal entries, no careful checks and balances after that date. Only sheet after blank sheet. Then the numbers, formed in a careful hand.

A message, Megan wondered, something he'd been compelled to write down but hadn't wanted prying eyes to read. A confession of guilt, perhaps? Or a plea for understanding?

She sat and took several clearing breaths. They were numbers, after all, she reminded herself. There was nothing she couldn't do with numbers.

An hour passed, then two. As she worked, the desk became littered with discarded slips of paper. Each time she stopped to rest her eyes or her tired brain, she wondered whether she had tumbled into lunacy even thinking she'd found some mysterious code in the back of an old book.

But the idea hooked her, kept her chained to the desk. She heard the blast of a horn as a tour boat passed. The shadows lengthened from afternoon toward evening.

She grew only more determined as each of her efforts failed. She would find the key. However long it took, she would find it.

Something clicked, causing her to stop, sit back and study anew. As if tumblers had fallen into place, she had it. Slowly, painstakingly, she transcribed numbers into letters and let the cryptogram take shape.

The first word to form was *Bianca*.

"Oh, God." Megan pressed her hand to her lips. "It's real."

Step by step she continued, crossing out, changing, advancing letter by letter, word by word. When the excitement began to build in her, she pushed it back. This was an answer she would find only with her mind. Emotions would hurry her, cause mistakes. So she thought of nothing but the logic of the code.

The figures started to blur in front of her eyes. She forced herself to close them, to sit back and relax until her mind was clear again. Then she opened them again, and read.

Bianca haunts me. I have no peace. All that was hers must be put away, sold, destroyed. Do spirits walk? It is nonsense, a lie. But I see her eyes, staring at me as she fell. Green as her emeralds. I

will leave her a token to satisfy her. And that will
be the end of it. Tonight I will sleep.

Breathless, Megan read on. The directions were very
simple, very precise. For a man going mad with the
enormity of his own actions, Fergus Calhoun had re-
tained his conciseness.

Tucking the paper in her pocket, Megan hurried out.
She didn't consider alerting the Calhouns. Something
was driving her to finish this herself. She found what
she needed in the renovation area in the family wing.
Hefting a crowbar, a chisel, a tape measure, she climbed
the winding iron steps to Bianca's tower.

She had been here before, knew that Bianca had
stood by the windows and watched the cliffs for Christian. That she had wept here, dreamed here, died here.

The Calhouns had made it charming again, with
plump, colorful pillows on the window seat, delicate
tables and china vases. A velvet chaise, a crystal lamp.

Bianca would have been pleased.

Megan closed the heavy door at her back. Using the
tape measure, she followed Fergus's directions. Six feet
in from the door, eight from the north wall.

Without a thought to the destruction she was about
to cause, Megan rolled up the softly faded floral carpet, then shoved the chisel between the slats of wood.

It was hard, backbreaking work. The wood was old,
but thick and strong. Someone had polished it to a fine
gleam. She pried and pulled, stopping only to flex her
straining muscles and, when the light began to fail, to
switch on the lamps.

The first board gave with a protesting screech. If
she'd been fanciful, she might have thought it sounded
like a woman. Sweat dripped down her sides, and she

cursed herself for forgetting a flashlight. Refusing to think of spiders, or worse, she thrust her hand into the gap.

She thought she felt the edge of something, but no matter how she stretched and strained, she couldn't get a grip. Grimly resigned, she set to work on the next board.

Swearing at splinters and her own untried muscles, she fought it loose. With a grunt, she tossed the board aside, and panting, stretched out on her stomach to grope into the hole.

Her fingertip rang against metal. She nearly wept. The handle almost slipped out of her sweaty hand, but she pulled the box up and free and set it on her lap.

It was no more than a foot long, a foot wide and a few pounds in weight, and it was grimy from the years it had spent in the darkness. Almost tenderly, she brushed away the worst of the dust. Her fingers hovered at the latch, itching to release it, then dropped away.

It wasn't hers to open.

"I don't know where she could be." Amanda strode back into the parlor, tossing up her hands. "She's not in her office, or her room."

"She was fussing in a closet when I saw her last." Colleen tipped back her glass. "She's a grown woman. Might be taking a walk."

"Yes, but…" Suzanna trailed off with a glance at Kevin. There was no point in worrying the child, she reminded herself. Just because Megan was never late, that was no reason to assume something was wrong. "Maybe she's in the garden." She smiled and handed the baby to Holt. "I can go look."

"I'll do it." Nathaniel stood up. He didn't really believe Megan had forgotten their date for dinner and gone walking in the garden, but looking was better than worrying. "If she comes in while I'm gone—" But then he heard her footsteps and glanced toward the doorway.

Her hair was wild, her eyes were wide. Her face and clothes were smeared with dirt. And she was smiling, brilliantly. "I'm sorry I'm late."

"Megan, what on earth?" Dumbfounded, Sloan stared at her. "You look as if you've been crawling in a ditch."

"Not quite." She laughed and pushed a hand through her disordered hair. "I got a little involved, lost track of the time. Sloan, I borrowed some of your tools. They're in the tower."

"In the—"

But she was crossing the room, her eyes on Colleen. She knelt at the old woman's feet, set the box in her lap. "I found something that belongs to you."

Colleen scowled down at the box, but her heart was thrumming in her ears. "Why would you think it belongs to me?"

Gently Megan took Colleen's hand, laid it on the dusty metal. "He hid it under the floor of the tower, her tower, after she died." Her quiet voice silenced the room like a bomb. "He said she haunted him." Megan pulled the transcribed code out of her pocket, set it on top of the box.

"I can't read it," Colleen said impatiently.

"I'll read it for you." But when Megan took the sheet again, Colleen grabbed her wrist.

"Wait. Have Coco come in. I want her here."

While they waited, Megan got up and went to Nathaniel. "It was a code," she told him, before turning to face the room. "The numbers in the back of the book. I don't know why I didn't see it…" Then she smiled. "I was looking too hard, too closely. And today I knew. I just knew." She stopped, lifted her hands, let them fall. "I'm sorry. I should have told you as soon as I'd solved it. I wasn't thinking."

"You did what you were meant to do," Lilah corrected. "If one of us was supposed to find it, we would have."

"Is it like a treasure hunt?" Kevin wanted to know.

"Yes." Megan drew him close to ruffle his hair.

"I really don't have time right now, dear." Coco was arguing as Amanda dragged her into the room. "It's the middle of the dinner rush."

"Sit and be quiet," Colleen ordered. "The girl has something to read. Get your aunt a drink," she said to C.C. "She may need it. And freshen mine, while you're at it." She lifted her eyes, bird-bright, to Megan's. "Well, go on. Read it."

As she did, Megan slipped her hand into Nathaniel's. She heard Coco's quick gasp and sigh. Her own throat was raw with unshed tears when she lowered the page again.

"So… I went up and I pried up some floorboards. And I found it."

Even the children were silent when Colleen placed her thin hands on the box. They trembled once, then steadied as she worked the latch free, and opened the lid. Now it was her lips that trembled, and her eyes filled. She drew out a small oval frame, tarnished black with age.

"A photograph," she said in a thick voice. "Of my mother with me and Sean and Ethan. It was taken the year before she died. We sat for it in the garden in New York." She stroked it once, then offered it to Coco.

"Oh, Aunt Colleen. It's the only picture we have of all of you."

"She kept it on her dressing table, so that she could look at it every day. A book of poetry." Colleen drew out the slim volume, caressed it. "She loved to read poetry. It's Yeats. She would read it to me sometimes, and tell me it reminded her of Ireland. This brooch." She took out a small, simple enamel pin decorated with violets. "Sean and I gave it to her for Christmas. Nanny helped us buy it, of course. We were too young. She often wore it."

She caressed a marcasite watch, its pin shaped like a bow, and a carved jade dog hardly bigger than her thumb.

There were other small treasures—a smooth white stone, a pair of tin soldiers, the dust of an ancient flower. Then the pearls, an elegant choker of four delicate strands that had slept the decades away in a black velvet pouch.

"My grandparents gave her these as a bridal gift." Colleen ran a fingertip over the smooth orbs. "She told me it would be mine on my wedding day. He didn't like her to wear it. Too plain, he said. Too ordinary. She kept them in the pouch, in her jewel case. She would often take them out and show them to me. She said that pearls given with love were more precious than diamonds given for show. She told me to treasure them as she did, and to wear them often, because—" Her voice broke, and she reached for her glass, sipped to clear her throat. "Because pearls needed warmth."

She closed her eyes and sat back. "I thought he'd sold them, disposed of them with the rest."

"You're tired, Aunt Colleen." Suzanna went quietly

to her side. "Why don't I take you upstairs? I can bring you a dinner tray."

"I'm not an invalid." Colleen snapped the words out, but her hand covered Suzanna's and squeezed. "I'm old, but I'm not feeble. I've wit enough to make some bequests. You." She pressed the brooch into Suzanna's hand. "This is yours. I want to see you wear it."

"Aunt Colleen—"

"Put it on now. Put it on." She brushed Suzanna away and picked up the book of poetry. "You spend half your time dreaming," she said to Lilah. "Dream with this."

"Thank you." Lilah bent down, kissed her.

"You'll have the watch," she said to Amanda. "You're the one who's always worrying about what time it is. And you," she continued, looking at C.C. and waving Amanda's thanks away, "take the jade. You like to set things around that gather dust."

Her eyebrow cocked at Jenny.

"Waiting for your turn, are you?"

Jenny smiled guilelessly. "No, ma'am."

"You'll have this." She offered Jenny the stone. "I was younger than you when I gave this to my mother. I thought it was magic. Maybe it is."

"It's pretty." Delighted with her new treasure, Jenny rubbed it against her cheek. "I can put it on my windowsill."

"She'd have been pleased," Colleen said softly. "She kept it on hers." With a harsh cough, she cleared her voice to briskness again. "You boys, take these, and don't lose them. They were my brother's."

"Neat," Alex whispered, reverently holding a perfectly detailed soldier. "Thanks."

"Thanks," Kevin echoed. "It's just like a treasure

box," he said, grinning at her. "Aren't you going to give anything to Aunt Coco?"

"She'll have the photograph."

"Aunt Colleen." Overcome, Coco reached for her hankie. "Really, you mustn't."

"You'll take it as a wedding gift, and be grateful."

"I am grateful. I don't know what to say."

"See that you clean that tarnish off the frame." Bracing her weight on the cane, Colleen rose and turned to Megan. "You look pleased with yourself."

Megan's heart was too full for pretense. "I am."

For a moment, Colleen's damp eyes twinkled back. "You should be. You're a bright girl, Megan. And a resourceful one. You remind me of myself, a very long time ago." Gently she picked up the pearls, letting the glowing strands run through her bent fingers.

"Here." Megan stepped toward her. "Let me help you put them on."

Colleen shook her head. "Pearls need youth. They're for you."

Stunned, Megan dropped her hands again. "No, you can't give them away like that. Bianca meant them for you."

"She meant them to be passed on."

"Within the family. They…they should go to Coco, or—"

"They go where I say they go," Colleen said imperiously.

"It isn't right." Megan searched the room for help, but found only satisfied smiles.

"It seems perfectly right to me," Suzanna murmured. "Amanda?"

Amanda touched a hand to the watch she'd pinned to her lapel. "Completely."

"Lovely." Coco wept into her hankie. "Just lovely."

"Fits like a glove," C.C. agreed, and glanced at Lilah.

"Destined." She tilted her face up to Max. "Only a fool fights destiny."

"Then we're agreed?" Suzanna took a quick survey and received nods from the men. "The vote's in."

"Ha!" Though she was enormously proud, Colleen scowled. "As if I needed approval to dispose of what's mine. Take them." She thrust them into Megan's hands. "Go upstairs and clean yourself up. You look like a chimney sweep. I want to see you wearing them when you come down."

"Aunt Colleen..."

"No blubbering. Do as you're told."

"Come on." Suzanna took Megan's arm to lead her from the room. "I'll give you a hand."

Satisfied, Colleen sat again, thumped her cane. "Well, where's my drink?"

Later, when the waning moon had tipped over the edge of the sea, Megan walked with Nathaniel to the cliffs. The breeze whispered secrets in the grass and teased the wildflowers.

She wore blue, a simple summer dress with a full skirt that swirled in the wind. The pearls, glowing like small, perfect moons, circled her throat.

"You've had quite a day, Megan."

"My head's still spinning. She gave it all away, Nathaniel. I can't understand how she could give away all the things that mattered so much."

"She's a hell of a woman. It takes a special one to recognize magic."

"Magic?"

"My practical, down-to-earth Megan." He tugged

on her hand until they sat on a rock together, looking out over the churning water. "Didn't you wonder, even for a moment, why each gift was so perfectly suitable? Why eighty years ago Fergus Calhoun would have been compelled to select just those things to hide away? The flower brooch for Suzanna, the watch for Amanda, Yeats for Lilah and the jade for C.C.? The portrait for Coco?"

"Coincidence," Megan murmured, but there was doubt in her voice.

He only laughed and kissed her. "Fate thrives on coincidence."

"And the pearls?"

"These." He lifted a finger to trace them. "A symbol of family, endurance, innocence. They suit you very well."

"They— I know I should have found a way not to accept them, but when Suzanna put them on me upstairs, they felt as though they were mine."

"They are. Ask yourself why you found them, why, with all the months the Calhouns searched for the emeralds, they never came across a hint of the strongbox. Fergus's book turns up after you move into The Towers. There's a numbered code. Who better to solve it than our logical CPA?"

Megan shook her head and blew out a laughing breath. "I can't explain it."

"Then just accept it."

"A magic rock for Jenny, soldiers for the boys." She rested her head against Nathaniel's shoulder. "I suppose I can't argue with that kind of coincidence. Or fate." Content, she closed her eyes and let the air caress her cheeks. "It's hard to believe that just a few days ago I was frantic with worry. You found him near here, didn't you?"

"Yes." He thought it best for her peace of mind not to mention the dicey climb down to the ledge. "I followed the bird."

"The bird?" Puzzled, she drew back. "That's odd. Kevin told me about a bird. A white one with green eyes that stayed with him that night. He's got a good imagination."

"There was a bird," Nathaniel told her. "A white gull with emerald eyes. Bianca's eyes."

"But—"

"Take magic where you find it." He slipped an arm around her shoulders so that they both could enjoy the sounds of the surf. "I have something for you, Megan."

"Mmm?" She was comfortable, almost sleepy, and she moaned in protest when he shifted away.

Nathaniel reached inside his jacket and drew out a sheaf of papers. "You might have a hard time reading them in this light."

"What's this?" Amused, she took them. "More receipts?"

"Nope. It's a life insurance policy."

"A— For heaven's sake. You shouldn't be carrying this around. You need to put it in a safe-deposit box, or a safe. Fireproof."

"Shut up." His nerves were beginning to stretch, so he stood, then paced to the edge of the cliff and back. "There's a hospitalization policy, too, my mortgage, a couple of bonds. And a damn Keogh."

"A Keogh." Megan held the papers as if they were diamonds. "You filled out the form."

"I can be practical, if that's what it takes. You want

security, I'll give you security. There are plenty of figures there for you to tally."

She pressed her lips together. "You did this for me."

"I'd do anything for you. You'd rather I invest in municipal bonds than slay dragons? Fine."

She stared at him as he stood with the sea and sky at his back, his feet braced as if he were riding the deck of a ship, his eyes lit with a power that defeated the dark. And with bruises fading on his face.

"You faced your dragon years ago, Nathaniel." To keep her hands occupied, she smoothed the papers. "I've had trouble facing my own." Rising, she walked to him, slipped the papers back into his pocket. "Aunt Colleen cornered me today. She said a lot of things, how I was too smart to take risks. How I'd never make the mistake of letting a man be too important. That I'd be better off alone than giving someone my trust, my heart. It upset me, and it frightened me. It took me a while to realize that's just what she'd meant to do. She was daring me to face myself."

"Have you?"

"It's not easy for me. I didn't like everything I saw, Nathaniel. All these years I've convinced myself that I was strong and self-reliant. But I'd let someone so unimportant shadow my life, and Kevin's. I thought I was protecting my son, and myself."

"You did a hell of a good job, from where I'm standing."

"Too good, in some ways. I closed myself off because it was safer. Then there was you." She reached up to lay a hand on his cheek. "I've been so afraid of what I feel for you. But that's over. I love you, Nathaniel. It doesn't matter if it was magic or fate, coincidence or sheer luck. I'm just glad I found you."

She lifted her face to his, reveled in the freedom of the kiss, the scent of the sea, the promise of his arms.

"I don't need retirement plans and insurance policies, Nathaniel," she murmured. "Not that you don't. It's very important that you... Stop laughing."

"I'm crazy about you." Still laughing, Nathaniel scooped her off her feet and swung her in dizzying circles.

"Crazy period." She struggled to catch her breath and clung to him. "We're going to fall off the cliff."

"Not tonight we're not. Nothing can happen to us tonight. Can't you feel it? We're the magic now." He set her on her feet again and held her close, so that even the air couldn't come between them. "I love you, Meg, but damned if I'm going to get down on one knee."

She went very still. "Nathaniel, I don't think—"

"Good. Don't think. Just listen. I've sailed around the world more than once, and seen in a decade more than most people see in their lifetimes. But I had to come home to find you. Don't say anything," he murmured. "Sit."

He led her back to the rock and sat with her. "I have something more for you than paperwork. That was just to smooth the path. Take a look at it," he said as he drew a box from his pocket. "Then tell me it wasn't meant."

With trembling fingers, she opened the box. With a sound of wonder, she lifted her eyes to his. "It's a pearl," she whispered.

"I was going to go for the traditional diamond. Seemed like the right thing. But when I saw this, I knew." He took it out of the box. "Coincidence?"

"I don't know. When did you buy this?"

"Last week. I thought about walking here with you, that first time. The moon and the stars." He studied the ring, the single glowing pearl surrounded by small, bright diamonds. "The moon and the stars," he said again, taking her hands. "That's what I want to give you, Megan."

"Nathaniel." She tried to tell herself it was too fast, too foolish, but the thought wouldn't lodge. "It's lovely."

"It's meant." He touched his lips to hers. "Just as we're meant. Marry me, Megan. Start a life with me. Let me be Kevin's father and make more children with you. Let me grow old loving you."

She couldn't find the logic, or think of all the reasons they should wait. So she answered with her heart. "Yes. Yes to everything." Laughing, she threw her arms around him. "Oh, Nathaniel. Yes, yes, yes…"

He squeezed his eyes tight on relief and joy. "You sure you don't want to qualify that?"

"I'm sure. I'm so sure." Drawing back, she held out her left hand. "Please. I want the moon and the stars. I want you."

He slipped the ring on her finger. "You've got me, sugar."

When he drew her close again, he thought he heard the air sigh, like a woman.

Epilogue

"**M**om! We're here!"

Megan glanced up from her desk just as Kevin flew in the office door. She lifted her brow at the suit jacket and tie he wore.

"My, my, don't you look handsome!"

"You said I had to dress up 'cause it's Aunt Colleen's birthday dinner. I guess it's okay." He stretched his neck. "Dad showed me how to tie the tie by myself."

"And you did a fine job." She restrained herself from smoothing and straightening the knot. "How was the tour business today?"

"It was great. Calm seas and a freshening breeze. We sighted the first whale off the port bow."

"Oh, I love that nautical talk." She kissed his nose.

"If I didn't have to go to school, I could work with Dad and Holt every day, and not just on Saturday."

"And if you didn't go to school, you'd never know much more than you do today. Saturdays will have to do." She gave his hair a tug. "Mate."

He'd expected as much. And, really, he didn't mind school. After all, he was a whole year in front of Alex. He grinned at his mother. "Everybody's here. When are the new babies coming?"

"Mmm…" With the Calhoun sisters in varying stages of pregnancy, it was an interesting question. "I'd say on and off starting next month and through the New Year."

He ran a fingertip over the corner of her desk. "Who do you think's going to be first? C.C. or Suzanna?"

"Why?" She glanced up from the ledger, and her eyes narrowed. "Kevin, you are not betting on who has the next baby."

"But, Mom—"

"No betting," she repeated, and smothered a laugh. "Give me just a minute to finish up here, and I'll be along."

"Hurry up." Kevin was bouncing. "The party's already started."

"All right, I'll just—" Just nothing, she thought, and closed the ledger with a snap. "Office hours are over. Let's go party."

"All right!" Grabbing her hand, Kevin hauled her out of the room. "Alex said Dutch made this really big cake and it's going to have about a hundred candles on it."

"Not quite a hundred," Megan said with a laugh. When they neared the family wing, she glanced toward the ceiling. "Honey, I'd better check upstairs first."

"Looking for someone?" Nathaniel came down the steps. There was a twinkle in his eye and a tiny pink bundle in his arms.

"I should have known you'd wake her up."

"She was awake. Weren't you, sugar?" He bent his

head to kiss his daughter's cheek. "She was asking for me."

"Really."

"She can't talk yet," Kevin informed his father. "She's only six weeks old."

"She's very advanced for her age. Smart, like her mama."

"Smart enough to know a sucker when she sees one." They made such a picture, she thought, the big man with a boy at his side and a baby in his arms. Her picture, she thought, and smiled. "Come here, Luna."

"She wants to go to the party, too," Kevin declared, reaching up to stroke a finger over his sister's cheek.

"Sure she does. That's what she told me."

"Oh, Dad."

Grinning, Nathaniel ruffled Kevin's hair. "I could eat a pod of whales, mate. How about you?"

"Aye, aye." Kevin made a dash for the parlor. "Come on, come on, everybody's waiting."

"I've got to do this first." Nathaniel leaned over his daughter to kiss Megan.

"Jeez." With a roll of his eyes, Kevin headed for the noise, and the real fun.

"You're looking awfully pleased with yourself," Megan murmured.

"Why shouldn't I? I've got a beautiful wife, a terrific son, an incredible daughter." He ran his knuckles over Megan's pearl choker. "What else could I ask for? How about you?"

Megan lifted her hand to pull his mouth back to hers. "I've got the moon and the stars."

* * * * *

BEST LAID PLANS

For Bruce,
who knows how to build and make it last

Chapter 1

She was definitely worth a second look.

There were more reasons—more basic reasons—than the fact that she was one of the few women on the building site. It was human nature for a man's eyes to be lured by the female form, especially when it was found in what was still predominantly a man's domain. True, a good many women donned hard hats to work construction, and as long as they could hammer a nail or lay a brick it didn't matter to Cody how they buttoned their shirts. But there was something about this particular woman that pulled his gaze back.

Style. Though she wore work clothes and stood on a mound of debris, she had it. Confidence, he mused as he rocked back on the worn heels of his boots. He supposed confidence was its own brand of style. It appealed to him as much—well, nearly as much—as black lace or white silk.

He didn't have the time to sit and speculate, though. He'd been almost a week late making the trip from Florida to Arizona to take over this project, and there was a lot of catching up to do. The morning was a busy one, with plenty of distractions: the noise of men and machines; orders being shouted and followed; cranes lifting heavy metal beams to form the skeleton of a building where there had been only rock and dirt; the vivid color of that rock and dirt under the white sun; even his own growing thirst. But he didn't mind distractions.

Cody had spent enough time on building sites to be able to look beyond the rubble, through what to the uninitiated might seem like confusion or even destruction. He saw instead the sweat, the strain, the thought and the possibilities.

But just now he found himself watching the woman. There were possibilities there, as well.

She was tall, he noted, five-nine or five-ten in her work boots, and lean rather than slender. Her shoulders looked strong under a dandelion-yellow T-shirt that was dark with sweat down the back. As an architect, he appreciated clean, economical lines. As a man, he appreciated the way her worn jeans fit snugly over her hips. Beneath a hard hat as bright as her shirt was a thick short braid the color of polished mahogany—one of his favorite woods to work with because of its beauty and richness.

He pushed his sunglasses farther up on his nose as the eyes behind them scanned her from hard hat to boot tip. Definitely worth a second look, he thought again, admiring the way she moved, with no wasted gestures as she leaned over to look through a surveyor's transit. There was a faint white outline worn into her back pocket, where he imagined she tucked her wallet. A practical woman, he decided. A purse would get in the way on the site.

She didn't have a redhead's pale, fragile complexion, but a warm, golden tan that probably came from the blistering Arizona sun. Wherever it came from, he approved, just as he approved of the long, somewhat sharp angles of her face. Her tough-looking chin was offset by elegant cheekbones, and both were balanced by a soft, unpainted mouth that was even now turning down.

He couldn't see her eyes because of the distance and the shade from the brim of her hat, but her voice as she called out an order was clear enough. It sounded more appropriate for quiet, misty nights than for sweaty afternoons.

Tucking his thumbs in the pockets of his jeans, he grinned. Yes, indeed, there were endless possibilities.

Unaware of his study, Abra continued to frown as she swiped an arm over her damp brow. The sun was merciless today. At 8:00 a.m., it was already blistering. Sweat rolled down her back, evaporated, then rolled again in a cycle she had learned to live with.

You could only move so fast in this heat, she thought. You could only haul so much metal and chip so much rock when the temperature hovered in the nineties. Even with water barrels filled and salt tablets dispensed, every day was a struggle to stay ahead of the clock. So far they were pulling it off, but... There couldn't be any buts, she reminded herself. The construction of this resort was the biggest thing she'd been involved with in her career, and she wasn't going to mess it up. It was her springboard.

Though she could have murdered Tim Thornway for tying Thornway Construction, and her, to such a tightly scheduled project. The penalty clauses were outrageous, and in the way Tim had of delegating he'd put the responsibility for avoiding them squarely on her shoulders.

Abra straightened as if she could actually feel the

weight. It would take a miracle to bring the project in on time and under budget. Since she didn't believe in miracles, she accepted the long hours and hard days ahead. The resort would be built, and built on time, if she had to pick up hammer and saw herself. But this was the last time, she promised herself as she watched a steel girder rise majestically into place. After this project she was cutting her ties with Thornway and striking out on her own.

She owed them for giving her a shot, for having enough faith in her to let her fight her way up from assistant to structural engineer. It wasn't something she'd forget—not now, not ever. But her loyalty had been to Thomas Thornway. Now that he was gone, she was doing her best to see that Tim didn't run the business into the ground. But she'd be damned if she was going to babysit him for the rest of her career.

She took a moment to wish for one of the cold drinks stashed in the cooler, then picked her way around and over the rubble of construction to supervise the placing of the beams.

Charlie Gray, the ever-eager assistant Cody had found himself stuck with, all but tugged at his shirt. "Want me to tell Ms. Wilson you're here?" Cody tried to remember that he, too, had once been twenty-two and annoying.

"Got her hands full at the moment." Cody pulled out his cigarettes, then searched through two pockets before he found some matches. They were from some little hotel in Natchez and were damp with his own sweat.

"Mr. Thornway wanted you to get together."

Cody's lips curved a little. He'd just been thinking that it wouldn't be such a hardship to get together with Abra Wilson. "We'll get around to it." He struck a match, automatically curling his fingers around the flame, though there wasn't a breath of wind.

"You missed yesterday's meeting, so—"

"Yeah." The fact that he'd missed the meeting wouldn't cause him to lose any sleep. The design for the resort was Cody's, but when family problems had cropped up his partner had handled most of the preliminary work. Looking back at Abra, Cody began to think that was a shame.

There was a trailer parked a few yards away. Cody headed for it, with Charlie scrambling to keep up with him. He pulled a beer from a cooler, then pried the top off as he walked inside, where portable fans battled the heat. The temperature dropped a few precious degrees.

"I want to take a look at the plans for the main building again."

"Yes, sir, I have them right here." Like a good soldier, Charlie produced the tube of blueprints, then practically stood at attention. "At the meeting—" he cleared his throat "—Ms. Wilson pointed out a few changes she wanted made. From an engineering standpoint."

"Did she now?" Unconcerned, Cody propped himself on the thin, narrow cushions of the convertible couch. The sun had mercifully faded the vivid orange-and-green upholstery to a nearly inoffensive blur. He glanced around for an ashtray and settled on an empty cup, then unrolled the blueprints.

He liked the look of it, the feel of it. The building would be dome-shaped, topped by stained glass at the apex. Floors of offices would circle a center atrium, giving a sense of open, unstructured space. Breathing room, he thought. What was the use of coming west if you didn't have room to take a breath? Each office would have thick tinted glass to hold out the brilliance of the sun while affording an unhampered view of the resort and the mountains.

On the ground level the lobby would curve in a half circle, making it easily accessible from the entrance, from the double-level bar and the glassed-in coffee shop.

Patrons could take the glass elevators or the winding staircase up a floor to dine in one of three restaurants, or they could venture a bit higher and explore one of the lounges.

Cody took a long swallow of his beer as he looked it over. He saw in it a sense of fantasy, even of humor, and more basically a marriage of the modern with the ancient. No, he couldn't see anything in his basic design that needed changing, or that he'd allow to be changed.

Abra Wilson, he thought, was going to have to grin and bear it.

When he heard the door of the trailer open, he glanced over. She was even better close up, Cody decided as Abra stepped inside. A little sweaty, a little dusty and, from the looks of her, a lot mad.

He was right about the mad. Abra had enough to do without having to chase down errant laborers taking unscheduled breaks. "What the hell are you doing in here?" she demanded as Cody lifted the can to his lips again. "We need everyone out there." She snatched the beer away before Cody could swallow. "Thornway isn't paying you to sit on your butt, and nobody on this project drinks on the job." She set the beer on the counter before she could be tempted to soothe her own dry throat with it.

"Ms. Wilson—"

"What?" Her patience in tatters, she turned on Charlie. "Oh, it's Mr. Gray, right? Hold on a minute." First things first, she thought as she rubbed her damp cheek against the sticky sleeve of her shirt. "Listen, pal," she said to Cody, "unless you want your walking papers, get yourself up and report to your foreman."

He grinned insolently at her. Abra felt reckless, un-professional words bubble to her lips and battled them back with what control she had left. Just as she battled back the urge to jam her fist into his cocky chin.

A good-looking sonofa— She cau_ .it herself there, as well. Men with those kind of rough-and-ready looks al-ways thought they could smile their way out of trouble— and they usually could. Not with her, though, Abra reminded herself. Still, it wouldn't do any good to threaten a union employee.

"You're not allowed in here." Frustrated, she bit the words off and snatched up the blueprints. Maybe if the morning had gone more smoothly she wouldn't have been ready to bite someone's—anyone's—head off. But he was in the wrong place at the wrong time. "And you certainly have no business poking around in these." She wondered what color his eyes were behind his dark glasses. If for no other reason than his continued grin, she would have been delighted to blacken them.

"Ms. Wilson..." Charlie said again, desperately.

"What, damn it?" She shook off his hand even as she reminded herself to be polite. The devil with polite, she thought. She was hot, tired, frustrated and delighted to have a target. "Have you got that illustrious architect of yours out of his hot tub yet, Gray? Thornway's interested in seeing this project move on schedule."

"Yes, you see—"

"Just a minute." Cutting him off again, she turned to Cody again. "Look, I told you to move. You speak English, don't you?"

"Yes, ma'am."

"Then move."

He did, but not as she'd expected. Lazily, like a cat stretching before it jumps off a windowsill, he unfolded his body. It appeared that most of him was leg. He didn't look like a man afraid of losing his job as he sidled between the table and the sofa, plucking his beer from the counter. He took a long, easy sip, leaned against the compact refrigerator and grinned at her again.

"You're a tall one, aren't you, Red?"

Barely, just barely, she caught herself before her mouth fell open. Building might still be primarily a man's trade, but no one Abra worked with had the nerve to be condescending. At least not to her face. He was out, she told herself. Schedule or no schedule, union or no union, she was going to issue him his walking papers personally.

"Find your lunch bucket, get in your pickup and make tracks, jerk." She snatched his beer again, and this time she poured the contents on his head. Fortunately for Cody, there was only a swallow left. "File that with your union representative."

"Ms. Wilson…" Charlie's face had gone bone white, and his voice was shaking. "You don't understand."

"Take a walk, Charlie." Cody's voice was mild as he lifted a hand to tunnel his fingers through his damp hair.

"But…but…"

"Out."

"Yes, sir." More than willing to desert a sinking ship, Charlie fled. Because he did, and because he'd called the lanky, pretty-faced cowboy "sir," Abra began to suspect that she'd taken a wrong turn down a blind alley. Automatically her eyes narrowed and her shoulders tensed.

"I don't guess we've been introduced." Cody drew his shaded glasses off. She saw that his eyes were brown, a soft, golden brown. They weren't lit with anger or embarrassment. Rather, they assessed her with a flat neutrality. "I'm Cody Johnson. Your architect."

She could have babbled. She could have apologized. She could have laughed off the incident and offered him another beer. All three options occurred to her but, because of his calm, unblinking stare, were rejected. "Nice of you to stop by," she said instead.

A tough one, he decided, despite the hazel eyes and the sultry mouth. Well, he'd cracked tough ones before. "If I'd known what a warm reception I'd get, I'd have been here sooner."

"Sorry, we had to let the brass band go." Because she wanted to salvage her pride, she started to move past him, and discovered quickly that if she wanted to get to the door, the sofa or anywhere else she'd have to move through him. She didn't question why the prospect appealed to her. He was an obstacle, and obstacles were meant to be knocked down. An angling of her chin, very slight, was all she needed to keep her eyes level with his.

"Questions?" she asked him.

"Oh, a few." Like who do I have to kill to have you? Does your chin really take a punch as well as you think? And since when is a hard hat sexy? "Do you always pour beer on your men?"

"Depends on the man." Leaving it at that, she started by him again—and found herself lodged between him and the refrigerator. He'd only had to turn to accomplish it. He took a moment, keeping his eyes on hers. He didn't see fear or discomfort in them, only a spitting fury that made him want to grin again. So he did.

"Close quarters in here… *Ms.* Wilson."

She might be an engineer, she might be a professional who had come up the hard way and knew the ropes, but she was still a woman, and very much aware of the press of his body against hers, the hard line of hip, the solid length of thigh. Whatever her reaction might have been, the glint of amusement in his eyes erased it.

"Are those teeth yours?" she asked calmly.

He lifted a brow. "Last time I checked."

"If you want to keep it that way, back off."

He would have liked to kiss her then, as much in appreciation for her guts as in desire for her taste. Though he was often impulsive, he also knew when to change tactics and take the long route. "Yes, ma'am."

When he moved aside, she slipped past him. She would have preferred to walk through the door and keep going, but she sat on the sofa and spread the prints out again. "I assume that Gray filled you in on the meeting you missed?"

"Yeah." He slid behind the table and sat down. As he'd said, the quarters were close. For the second time, their thighs brushed, denim against denim, muscle against muscle. "You wanted some changes."

She shouldn't be defensive. It did no good to be defensive. She couldn't help it. "I've had a problem with the basic design from the beginning, Mr. Johnson. I made no secret of it."

"I've seen the correspondence." Stretching out his legs was a bit of a trick in such cramped quarters, but he managed it. "You wanted standard desert architecture."

Her eyes narrowed fractionally, and he caught the glint. "I don't recall the word *standard* coming up, but there are good reasons for the style of architecture in this region."

"There are also good reasons for trying something new, don't you think?" He said it easily as he lit another cigarette. "Barlow and Barlow want the ultimate resort," he continued before she could comment. "Totally self-contained, and exclusive enough to draw in big bucks from the clientele. They wanted a different look, a different mood, from what can be found in the resorts sprinkled around Phoenix. That's what I'm giving them."

"With a few modifications—"

"No changes, *Ms.* Wilson."

She nearly ground her teeth. Not only was he being pigheaded—a typical architect—but it infuriated her the way he drew out "Ms." in that sarcastic drawl. "For some reason," she began calmly, "we've been unfortunate enough to have been chosen to work together on this."

"Must have been fate," he murmured.

She let that pass. "I'm going to tell you up front, Mr. Johnson, that from an engineering standpoint your design stinks."

He dragged on his cigarette, letting the smoke escape in a slow stream. She had amber flecks in her eyes, he noted. Eyes that couldn't make up their mind whether they wanted to be gray or green. Moody eyes. He smiled into them. "That's your problem. If you're not good enough, Thornway can assign someone else."

Her fingers curled into her palms. The idea of stuffing the plans down his throat had a certain appeal, but she reminded herself that she was committed to this project. "I'm good enough, Mr. Johnson."

"Then we shouldn't have any problems." He crossed his booted ankles. The noise from the site was steady. A productive sound, Cody had always thought. He didn't find it intrusive as he studied the woman across from him. It helped remind him that there was a time for business and a time for... pleasure.

"Why don't you fill me in on the progress?"

It wasn't her job. She almost snapped that at him. But she was tied to a contract, one that didn't leave much margin for error. By God, she'd pay her debt to Thornway, even if it meant working hand in glove with some overconfident, high-flying East Coast architect. She pushed the hard hat back on her head but didn't relax.

"As you've probably seen, the blasting went on schedule. Fortunately, we were able to keep it to a minimum and preserve the integrity of the landscape."

"That was the idea."

"Was it?" She glanced at the prints, then back at him. "In any case, we'll have the frame of the main building completed by the end of the week. If no changes are made—"

"None will be."

"If no changes are made," she repeated between clenched teeth, "we'll meet the first contract deadline. Work on the individual cabanas won't begin until the main building and the health center are under roof. The golf course and tennis courts aren't my province, so you'll have to discuss them with Kendall. That also goes for the landscaping."

"Fine. Do you know if the tiles for the lobby have been ordered?"

"I'm an engineer, not a purchaser. Marie Lopez handles supplies."

"I'll keep that in mind. Question."

Rather than give him a go-ahead nod, she rose and opened the refrigerator. It was stockpiled with sodas, juices and bottled water. Taking her time with her selection, she opted for the water. She was thirsty, she told herself. The move didn't have anything to do with wanting to put some distance between them. That was just a side benefit. Though she knew it was nasty, she screwed the top off the bottle and drank without offering him any.

"What?"

"Is it because I'm a man, an architect or an Easterner?"

Abra took another long sip. It only took a day in the sun to make you realize that paradise could be found in a bottle of water. "You'll have to clarify that."

"Is it because I'm a man, an architect or an Easterner that makes you want to spit in my eye?"

She wouldn't have been annoyed by the question itself, not in the least. But he grinned while he asked. After less than an hour's acquaintance, she'd already damned him a half-dozen times for that smile. Still, she leaned back against the counter, crossed her own ankles and considered him.

"I don't give a damn about your sex."

He continued to grin, but something quick and dangerous came into his eyes. "You like waving red flags at bulls, Wilson?"

"Yes." It was her turn to smile. Though the curving of her lips softened her mouth, it did nothing to dim the flash of challenge in her eyes. "But to finish my answer—architects are often pompous, temperamental artists who put their egos on paper and expect engineers and builders to preserve it for posterity. I can live with that. I can even respect it—when the architect takes a good, hard look at the environment and creates with it rather than for himself. As for you being an Easterner, that might be the biggest problem. You don't understand the desert, the mountains, the heritage of this land. I don't like the idea of you sitting under an orange tree two thousand miles away and deciding what people here are going to live with."

Because he was more interested in her than in defending himself, he didn't mention that he had made three trips to the site months before. Most of the design work had been done almost where he was sitting now, rather than back at his home base. He had a vision, but he was a man who drew and built his visions more than a man who spoke of them.

"If you don't want to build, why do you?"

"I didn't say I didn't want to build," she said. "I've never thought it necessary to destroy in order to do so."

"Every time you put a shovel in the ground you take away some land. That's life."

"Every time you take away some land you should think hard about what you're going to give back. That's morality."

"An engineer *and* a philosopher." He was baiting her, and he knew it. Even as he watched, angry color rose to her cheeks. "Before you pour that over my head, let's say I agree with you—to a point. But we're not putting up neon and plastic here. Whether you agree with my design or not, it is my design. It's your job to put it together."

"I know what my job is."

"Well, then." As if dismissing the disagreement, Cody began to roll up the plans. "How about dinner?"

"I beg your pardon?"

"Dinner," he repeated. When the prints were rolled up, he slid them into their cylinder and rose. "I'd like to have dinner with you."

Abra wasn't sure it was the most ridiculous statement she'd ever heard, but it certainly ranked in the top ten. "No thanks."

"You're not married?" That would have mattered.

"No."

"Involved?" That wouldn't have.

Patience wasn't her strong suit. Abra didn't bother to dig for it. "None of your business."

"You've got a quick trigger, Red." He picked up his hard hat but didn't put it on. "I like that."

"You've got nerve, Johnson. I don't like that." She moved to the door, pausing just a moment with her hand on the knob. "If you have any questions that deal with the construction, I'll be around."

He didn't have to move much to put a hand on her shoulder. Under his palm he felt her coil up like a cat ready to spring. "So will I," he reminded her. "We'll have dinner some other time. I figure you owe me a beer."

After one self-satisfied glance at the top of his head, Abra stepped out into the sun.

He certainly wasn't what she'd been expecting. He was attractive, but she could handle that. When a woman took root in male territory, she was bound to come into contact with an attractive man from time to time. Still, he looked more like one of her crew than a partner in one of the country's top architectural firms. His dark blond hair, with its sun-bleached tips, was worn too long for the nine-to-five set, and his rangy build held ripples of muscle under the taut, tanned skin. His broad, callused hands were those of a workingman. She moved her shoulders as if shrugging off the memory of his touch. She'd felt the strength, the roughness and the appeal of those hands. Then there was that voice, that slow take-your-time drawl.

She settled the hard hat more securely as she approached the steel skeleton of the building. Some women would have found that voice appealing. She didn't have time to be charmed by a southern drawl or a cocky grin.

She didn't, when it came right down to it, have much time to think of herself as a woman.

He'd made her feel like one.

Scowling against the sun, she watched beams being riveted into place. She didn't care for Cody Johnson's ability to make her feel feminine. "Feminine" too often meant "defenseless" and "dependent." Abra had no intention of being either of those. She'd worked too hard and too long at self-sufficiency. A couple of…flutters, she decided, just flutters…weren't going to affect her.

She wished the can of beer had been full.

With a grim smile she watched the next beam swing into place. There was something beautiful about watching a building grow. Piece by piece, level by level. It had always fascinated her to watch something strong and useful take shape—just as it had always disturbed her to see the land marred by progress. She'd never been able to resolve that mixture of feelings, and it was because of that that she'd chosen a field that allowed her to have a part in seeing that progress was made with integrity.

But this one… She shook her head as the sound of riveting guns split the air. This one struck her as an outsider's fantasy, the domed shape, the curves and spirals. She'd spent countless nights at her drawing board with slide rule and calculator, struggling to come up with a satisfactory support system. Architects didn't worry about mundane matters like that, she thought. It was all aesthetics with them. All ego. She'd build the damn thing, she thought, kicking some debris out of her way. She'd build it and build it well. But she didn't have to like it.

With the sun baking her back, she bent over the transit. They'd had the mountain to deal with, and an uneven bed of rock and sand, but the measurements and placement were right on. She felt a tug of pride as she checked angles and degrees. Inappropriate or not, the structure was going to be perfectly engineered.

That was important—being perfect. Most of her life she'd had to deal with second best. Her education, her training and her skill had lifted her beyond that. She had no intention of ever settling for second best again, not for herself, and not in her work.

She caught his scent and felt the light tickle of awareness at the back of her neck. Soap and sweat, she thought, and had to fight not to shift uncomfortably. Everybody on the site smelled of soap and sweat, so why was she certain Cody was behind her? She only knew she was certain, and she determinedly remained bent over the eyepiece.

"Problem?" she said, pleased with the disdain she was able to put into the single word.

"I don't know until I look. Do you mind?"

She took her time before stepping back. "Be my guest."

When he moved forward, she hooked her thumbs in her back pockets and waited. He'd find no discrepancies—even if he knew enough to recognize one. Hearing a shout, she glanced over to see two members of the crew arguing. The heat, she knew, had a nasty way of bringing tempers to a boil. Leaving Cody to his survey, she strode across the broken ground.

"It's a little early for a break," she said calmly as one crewman grabbed the other by the shirtfront.

"This sonofabitch nearly took my fingers off with that beam."

"If this idiot doesn't know when to get out of the way, he deserves to lose a few fingers."

Neither man had much on her in height, but they were

burly, sweaty and on the edge. Without thinking twice, she stepped between them as fists were raised. "Cool off," she ordered.

"I don't have to take that sh—"

"You may not have to take his," Abra said levelly, "but you have to take mine. Now cool off or take a walk." She looked from one angry face to the other. "If you two want to beat each other senseless when you're off the clock, be my guest, but either of you takes a swing on my time, you're unemployed. You." She pointed to the man she judged the more volatile of the two. "What's your name?"

The dark-haired man hesitated briefly, then spit out, "Rodriguez."

"Well, Rodriguez, go take a break and pour some water over your head." She turned away as if she had no doubts about his immediate obedience. "And you?"

The second man was ruddy and full-faced and was smirking. "Swaggart."

"Okay, Swaggart, get back to work. And I'd have a little more respect for my partner's hands if I were you, unless you want to count your own fingers and come up short."

Rodriguez snorted at that but did as he was told and moved away toward the water barrels. Satisfied, Abra signaled to the foreman and advised him to keep the men apart for a few days.

She'd nearly forgotten about Cody by the time she turned and saw him. He was still standing by the transit, but he wasn't looking through it. Legs spread, hands resting lightly on his hips, he was watching her. When she didn't make a move toward him, he made one toward her.

"You always step into the middle of a brawl?"

"When it's necessary."

He tipped his shaded glasses down to study her, then scooted them up again. "Ever get that chip knocked off your shoulder?"

She couldn't have said why she had to fight back a grin, but she managed to. "Not yet."

"Good. Maybe I'll be the first."

"You can try, but you'd be better off concentrating on this project. More productive."

He smiled slowly, and the angles of his face shifted with the movement. "I can concentrate on more than one thing at a time. How about you?"

Instead of answering, she took out a bandanna and wiped the back of her neck. "You know, Johnson, your partner seemed like a sensible man."

"Nathan *is* sensible." Before she could stop him, he took the bandanna from her and dabbed at her temples. "He saw you as a perfectionist."

"And what are you?" She had to resist the urge to grab the cloth back. There was something soothing, a little too soothing, in his touch.

"You'll have to judge that for yourself." He glanced back at the building. The foundation was strong, the angles were clear, but it was just the beginning. "We're going to be working together for some time yet."

She, too, glanced toward the building. "I can take it if you can." Now she did take the bandanna back, stuffing it casually in her back pocket.

"Abra." He said her name as if he were experimenting with a taste. "I'm looking forward to it." She jolted involuntarily when he brushed a thumb down her cheek. Pleased with the reaction, he grinned. "See you around."

Jerk, she thought again as she stomped across the rubble and tried to ignore the tingling along her skin.

Chapter 2

If there was one thing she didn't need, Abra thought a few days later, it was to be pulled off the job and into a meeting. She had mechanics working on the main building, riveters working on the health club, and a running feud between Rodriguez and Swaggart to deal with. It wasn't as though those things couldn't be handled without her—it was simply that they could be handled better with her. And here she was cooling her heels in Tim's office waiting for him to show up.

She didn't have to be told how tight the schedule was. Damn it, she knew what she had to do to see that the contract was brought in on time. She knew all about time.

Her every waking moment was devoted to this job. Each day was spent sweating out on the site with the crews and the supervisors, dealing with details as small as the delivery of rivets. At night she either tumbled into bed at sundown or worked until three, fueled by coffee and ambition, over her drawing board. The project was hers, hers more than it could ever be Tim Thornway's. It had become personal, in a way she could never have explained. For her, it was a tribute to the man who had had enough faith in her to push her to try for more than second best. In a way, it was her last job for Thomas Thornway, and she wanted it to be perfect.

It didn't help to have an architect who demanded materials that made cost overruns and shipping delays inevitable. Despite him and his marble sinks and his oversize ceramic tiles, she was going to pull it off. If she wasn't constantly being dragged into the office for endless meetings.

Impatient, she paced to the window and back again. Time was wasting, and there were few things that annoyed her more than waste of any kind. If she hadn't had a specific point to bring up to Tim, she would have found a way to avoid the meeting altogether. The one good thing about Tim, she thought with a humorless smile, was that he wasn't really bright enough to recognize double-talk. In this case, she wanted to make the pitch herself, so she'd come. But—she glanced at her watch—she wasn't going to twiddle her thumbs much longer.

This had been Thornway's office. She'd always liked the cool, authoritative colors and the lack of frills. Since Tim had taken over, he'd made some changes. Plants, she thought, scowling at a ficus. It wasn't that she disliked plants and thick, splashy pillows, but it annoyed her to find them here.

Then there were the paintings. Thornway had preferred Indian paintings and landscapes. Tim had replaced them with abstracts that tended to jar Abra's nerves. The new carpet seemed three inches thick and was salmon-colored. The elder Thornway had used a

short-napped buff so that the dust and dirt wouldn't
show. But then, Tim didn't often visit the sites or ask his
foremen to join him for an after-hours drink.

Stop it, Abra ordered herself. Tim ran things differently, and that was his privilege. It was his business in
every way. The fact that she had loved and admired the
father so much didn't mean she had to find fault with
the son.

But she did find fault with him, she thought as she
studied the tidy, polished surface of his desk. He lacked
both the drive and the compassion that had been so much
a part of his father. Thornway had wanted to build first
for the love of building. With Tim, the profit margin
was the bottom line.

If Thomas Thornway had still been alive, she
wouldn't have been preparing to make a break. There
was a certain freedom in that, in knowing that this current project would be her last for the company. There
would be no regrets in leaving, as there might once have
been. Instead, there was excitement, anticipation. Whatever happened next, she would be doing it for herself.

Terrifying, she thought, closing her eyes. The idea
was as terrifying as it was compelling. All unknowns
were. Like Cody Johnson.

Catching herself, she walked back to the window.
That was ridiculous. He was neither terrifying nor compelling. Nor was he an unknown. He was just a man—a
bit of a pest, with the way he kept popping up on the site.
He was the kind of man who knew he was a pleasure
to look at and exploited it. The kind who always had a
line, an angle and an escape route.

She'd seen men like Cody operate before. Looking
back, Abra considered herself lucky that she'd only
fallen for a pretty face and a smooth line once. Some

women never learned and kept walking blindly into the trap again and again. Her mother was one, Abra thought with a shake of her head. Jessie Wilson would have taken one look at a man like Cody and taken the plunge. Thank God, in this way it was not "like mother like daughter."

As for herself, Abra wasn't interested in Cody Johnson personally and could barely tolerate him professionally.

When he walked in seconds later, she wondered why her thoughts and her feelings didn't seem to jibe.

"Abra, sorry to keep you waiting." Tim, trim in a three-piece suit, offered her a hearty smile. "Lunch ran a bit over."

She only lifted a brow. This meeting in the middle of the day had caused her to miss her lunch altogether. "I'm more interested in why you called me in from the field."

"Thought we needed a little one-on-one." He settled comfortably behind his desk and gestured for both her and Cody to sit.

"You've seen the reports."

"Absolutely." He tapped a finger on a file. He had a nice, engaging grin that suited his round face. More than once Abra had thought he'd have done well in politics. If anyone knew how to answer a question without committing himself, it was Tim Thornway. "Efficient, as always. I'm having a dinner meeting with Barlow senior this evening. I'd like to give him something more than facts and figures."

"You can give him my objections to the interior layout of the main building." She crossed her ankles and spared Cody the briefest glance. Tim began to fiddle with one of his monogrammed pens.

"I thought we'd settled all that."

Abra merely shrugged. "You asked. You can tell him

that the wiring should be completed on the main structure by the end of the week. It's a tricky process, given the size and shape of the building. And it's going to cost his company a fortune to cool."

"He has a fortune," Cody commented. "I believe they're more interested in style than saving on the electric bill."

"Indeed." Tim cleared his throat. The way things stood, the Barlow project was going to bring him a tidy profit. He wanted to keep it that way. "Of course, I've looked over the specs and can assure our client that he's receiving only the best in materials and in brainpower."

"I'd suggest you tell him to come see for himself," Abra said.

"Well, I don't think—"

Cody cut in. "I agree with Ms. Wilson. Better he should buck now about something that doesn't suit him than buck later, after it's in concrete."

Tim frowned and backpedaled. "The plans have been approved."

"Things look different on paper," Cody said, looking at Abra. "Sometimes people are surprised by the finished product."

"Naturally, I'll suggest it." Tim tapped his pen on his spotless blotter. "Abra, you have a suggestion in your report about extending the lunch break to an hour."

"Yes, I wanted to talk with you about that. After a few weeks on the site I've seen that until and unless we get some relief in the weather the men are going to need a longer break at midday."

Tim set down the pen and folded his hands. "You have to understand what a thirty-minute extension means in terms of overall time and money."

"You have to understand that men can't work in that

sun without a reasonable reprieve. Chugging salt tablets isn't enough. It may be March, and it may be cool inside when you're having your second martini, but out there it's a killer."

"These men get paid to sweat," Tim reminded her. "And I think you can only agree that they'll be better off to have the buildings under roof by summer."

"They can't build if they drop from heat exhaustion or sunstroke."

"I don't believe I've had any reports of that happening."

"Not yet." It would be a miracle if she held on to her temper. He'd always been pompous, she thought. When he'd been a junior executive she'd been able to skirt him and go straight to the top. Now he *was* the top. Abra gritted her teeth and tried again. "Tim, they need the extra time off. Working out in that sun drains you. You get weak, you get sloppy, then you make mistakes— dangerous mistakes."

"I pay a foreman to see that no one makes mistakes."

Abra was on her feet and ready to explode when Cody's calm voice cut in. "You know, Tim, men tend to stretch out breaks in the heat in any case. You give them an extra thirty minutes, makes them feel good—obliged, even. Most of them won't be as liable to take more. You end up getting the same amount of work and good PR."

Tim ran his pen through his fingers. "Makes sense. I'll keep it in mind."

"You do that." With an easy smile, he rose. "I'm going to hitch a ride back to the site with Ms. Wilson. Then we can discuss that idea about our working more closely together. Thanks for lunch, Tim."

"Any time, any time."

Before Abra could speak, Cody had her by the elbow

and was leading her out. They were in front of the elevators before she managed to jerk away. "I don't need to be shown the way," she said through clenched teeth.

"Well, *Ms.* Wilson, looks like we disagree again." He strolled into the elevator with her, then punched the button for the parking garage. "In my opinion, you could definitely use some guidance—in how to handle birdbrains."

"I don't need you to…" She let her words trail off, glancing over at his face. The hint of amusement in his eyes matched the reluctant smile in hers. "I assume you're referring to Tim."

"Did I say that?"

"I have to assume you were—unless you were talking about yourself."

"Take your choice."

"That leaves me with a tough decision." The elevator shuddered slightly when it reached the parking level. Abra put her hand out to keep the door from sliding shut again as she studied him. There was a sharp intelligence in his eyes, and an easy confidence around his mouth. Abra nearly sighed as she moved through the doors and into the garage.

"Made up your mind?" he asked as he fell into step beside her.

"Let's just say I've already made up my mind how to handle you."

The slap of their boots echoed as they walked between the lines of cars. "How's that?"

"You've heard of ten-foot poles?"

His mouth quirked at the corners. She was wearing a braid again. It gave him the urge to loosen it, strand by strand. "That's downright unfriendly."

"Yeah." She stopped in front of a compact station

wagon. Its white paint was scarred and dusty, and its windows were tinted violet to combat the merciless sun. Thoughtfully she dug out her keys. "Are you sure you want to go to the site? I could drop you by your hotel."

"I do have a mild interest in this project."

She moved her shoulders in a quick, restless gesture. "Suit yourself."

"Usually do."

Once in he cocked his seat back and nearly managed to stretch out his legs. When she turned the key, the engine coughed, objected, then caught. The radio and air conditioner sprang to life. Music jangled out, but she didn't bother to turn it down. Scattered across the dashboard were a family of decorative magnets— a banana, an ostrich, a map of Arizona, a grinning cat and a lady's hand with pink fingernails. Scribbled notes were held in place by them. As far as Cody could make out, she had to pick up milk and bread and check on fifty tons of concrete. And call Mongo? He narrowed his eyes and tried again. Her mother. She was supposed to call her mother.

"Nice car," he commented when it shuddered and bucked to a stop at a light.

"Needs a tune-up." She shifted into neutral to let the engine idle. "I haven't gotten around to it."

He studied her hand as she jammed the car into first and accelerated. It was long and lean and suited her build. She wore her nails short and, unlike the plastic depiction of a lady's hand, unpainted. No jewelry. He could imagine those hands serving delicate cups of tea—just as he could imagine them changing spark plugs.

"So how would you handle Tim?"

"What?" He'd been lost in a quiet little fantasy about

how those narrow, competent hands would feel stroking along his skin.

"Tim," she repeated. She gave the car more gas as
they headed south out of Phoenix. "How would you
handle him?"

At the moment he was more interested in how he was
going to handle her. "I take it you two don't always see
things the same way."

"You're the observant type, Johnson."

"Sarcasm, Red." He didn't ask permission to smoke,
just rolled the window down an inch and began to search
through his pockets for matches. "Personally, I don't
mind it a bit, but when you're dealing with Thornway
you'll find oil does better than vinegar."

It was true, absolutely true. It annoyed her that she'd
put herself in a position where she'd had to be reminded
of that. "He doesn't recognize sarcasm if you pour it
over his head." She punched in the car lighter for him.

"Not nine times out of ten, maybe." He touched the
tip of the lighter against his cigarette. "It's that tenth
time that could get you in trouble. Before you say it, I
already know you don't mind a little trouble."

Despite herself, she smiled, and she didn't object
when he turned the radio down. "You know those
horses, the parade horses that wear blinders so they'll
follow the route and not look around and get spooked
by crowds?"

"Yeah, and I've already seen that Thornway wears
blinders so that he can follow the route to profit without being distracted. You want better working condi-
tions for the men, a higher grade of material, whatever,
you've got to learn how to be subtle."

She made that quick, restless movement with her
shoulders again. "I can't."

"Sure you can. You're smarter than Thornway, Red, so you sure as hell ought to be able to outwit him."

"He makes me mad. When I think about—" She shrugged again, but this time there was sorrow in the movement. "He just makes me mad. When I get mad, whatever I think comes out."

That was something he'd already figured out for himself. "All you have to do is use the common denominator. With Thornway, that's profit. You want the men to have an hour lunch break in the heat of the day, you don't tell him it's for their benefit, you tell him he'll get higher efficiency and therefore higher profits."

She scowled for a minute, then let out a long breath. "I suppose I'll have to thank you for talking him into it."

"Okay. How about dinner?"

She cast him a short, level look. "No."

"Why not?"

"Because you've got a pretty face." When he grinned, she granted him the briefest of smiles. "I don't trust men with pretty faces."

"You've got a pretty face. I don't hold it against you."

Her smile widened for a moment, but she kept staring at the long road ahead. "There's the difference between you and me, Johnson."

"If we had dinner, we could find others."

It was tempting. And it shouldn't have been. "Why should we want to find others?"

"Passes the time. Why don't we—" He broke off when the car swerved. Abra swore and wrestled the car to the shoulder of the road.

"A flat," she said in disgust. "A lousy flat, and I'm already late getting back." With that, she slammed out of the car and stomped around to the back, swearing with admirable expertise. By the time Cody joined her, she'd already rolled out her spare.

"That one doesn't seem to be in much better shape," he commented, eyeing the tread.

"I need new ones all around, but this one should hold awhile." She hauled out the jack and, still muttering curses, hooked it under the bumper. It was on the tip of Cody's tongue to offer to change it himself. Then he remembered how much he enjoyed watching her work. He hooked his thumbs in his belt loops and stayed out of her way.

"Where I come from, engineers do pretty well for themselves. Ever think about a new car?"

"This one does the job." She spun the lug nuts off. With easy efficiency she pulled off the flat and rolled the spare into place. The breeze from a passing car fluttered through her hair.

"This is bald," Cody said when he took a look at the flat.

"Probably."

"Probably, hell. I've got more tread on my sneakers. Haven't you got more sense than to drive around on bald tires?" Even as he asked he started around the car to examine the tread on the remaining three. "These aren't much better."

"I said I needed new ones." She brushed the hair out of her eyes. "I haven't had the time to take it in and deal with it."

"Make time."

He was standing behind her now. From her crouched position, she aimed a look over her shoulder. "Back off."

"When I work with someone who's this careless personally, I have to wonder how careless they might be professionally."

"I don't make mistakes on the job." She went back to tightening the lug nuts. He was right. Because it embarrassed her, she refused to admit it out loud. "Check the records."

She stood, and was more annoyed than surprised when he turned her around to face him. It didn't bother her to be close. It bothered her to *feel* close. "How many do you make off the job?"

"Not many." She should move away. The warning flashed in and out of her mind as her throat went dry. They were standing toe-to-toe. She could see the light sheen of dampness on his face and throat, just as she could see, whether she wanted to or not, the flicker of desire in his eyes.

"I don't like to argue with a woman who's holding a tire iron." He took it from her and leaned it against the bumper. Her hands curled into fists at her sides, but it was nerves, pure nerves, and had nothing to do with anger.

"I've got an inspector coming this afternoon."

"At two-thirty." He took her hand, turning the wrist up to glance at her watch. "You've got some time."

"Not my own," she said evenly. "I'm on Thornway's clock."

"Conscientious." He looked down at the bald tire. "Mostly."

It was uncomfortable and unnerving to feel her heart thud against her ribs. As if she'd been running, Abra thought. She didn't want to admit that she'd been running since she'd first laid eyes on him.

"If you've got something you want to say, say it. I've got work to do."

"Can't think of a thing at the moment." But he still held her hand. His thumb lightly grazed the underside of her wrist, where her pulse beat hard and steady. "Can you?"

"No." She started to move past him and found herself brought up firmly against his chest. She'd always been lousy at chess, she thought, flustered. Never looking past the immediate move to the future consequences. It took more effort than it should have to keep her voice steady. "What's your problem, Cody?"

"I don't know." He was every bit as intrigued as she. "There's one way to find out." His free hand was on her face now, not resting there but holding her still. "Do you mind?" Even as he spoke, his lips lowered toward hers.

She wasn't sure what made her pull back at the last moment—or what made her able to pull back. She lifted a hand to his chest and pressed firmly, even as she tasted the warmth of his breath on her lips. "Yes," she said, and was amazed to realize that it was a lie. She wouldn't have minded. In fact, she'd wanted the feel and taste of his mouth on hers.

There was only an inch separating them, perhaps less. He felt, unexpectedly, a churning, a tug, a heat that drew together and centered in his gut. It was more than curiosity, he realized, and he found himself not entirely comfortable with the knowledge. When he stepped back, it was as much for his own sake as anything.

"I shouldn't have asked," he said easily. "Next time I won't."

She'd start trembling in a moment. It stunned her to realize that any second her system was going to betray her and shudder and quake. Again, not from anger. She held it off through sheer will and bent to the ruined tire. "Go find someone else to play with, Cody."

"I don't think so." He took the tire from her and

stored it in the rear of the car. Before she could see to it herself, he had lowered the jack and stored that, as well.

Taking slow, steadying breaths, she walked around to her door. A tractor-trailer rattled by, and the force of the air it displaced hit her like a wall. She braced herself against it, as she had braced herself against him. Her palms were sweaty. Carefully she rubbed them against the thighs of her jeans before settling inside and turning the key.

"You don't strike me as the kind of man who keeps knocking at a door when no one answers."

"You're right." He leaned back again as she pulled onto the road. "After a while I just open it myself." With a friendly grin, he turned the radio up again.

The inspector had come early. Abra swore about it but couldn't do much else, since the wiring passed. She walked through the building, which was already taking shape, and climbed to the second and third floors to supervise the insulating and the first delivery of drywall. It was moving like clockwork, and she should have been more than satisfied.

All she could think of was how she had felt standing on the shoulder of the road with Cody's lips an inch from hers.

She was an engineer, not a romantic, she reminded herself as she stood on a platform twenty feet up and unrolled a drawing. The cooling system, she thought as she went over the specs again. That was going to take enough of her time and energy over the next few days. She didn't have the time or the inclination to stand around and wonder what it would have been like to kiss Cody Johnson.

Hot. Hot and exciting. No woman could look at that

mouth and not see the kind of damage it could do to the
nervous system. It had already jangled hers, and without even making contact. He probably knew it. Men
like him always knew what kind of effect they had on
a woman. They could hardly be blamed for it, but they
could—and should—be avoided.

With another oath, she rolled up the drawings. She
wouldn't think about him or what would have happened
if she'd said yes instead of no. Or if she'd said nothing
at all and had moved on instinct rather than brainpower.

There were the elevators to consider. It wouldn't be
long before they'd be going in. She'd worked hard and
long with another engineer on the design. What was
now on paper would be reality soon enough, running
up and down the walls, glass glittering as they rose and
fell without a sound.

Some men could do that—make your heart rise
and fall, make your pulse hammer though it couldn't
be heard by anyone but you. No matter how you tried,
how you pretended it wasn't happening, inside you'd be
shooting up and shooting down so fast that a crash was
inevitable. No matter how clever you were with a calculator, you could never quite fix the kinks in the system.

Damn him. Damn him for that—for taking that one
step beyond and making her vulnerable. She couldn't
forget the way her hand had felt in his, the way his eyes
had looked when his face had been that close. So now
she would wonder. The blame for that was his. She'd do
well to remember that.

Glancing down, she saw him on the first floor, talking with Charlie Gray. Cody was gesturing toward the
rear wall, where the side of the mountain sloped in to
become part of the building—or the building to become
part of the mountain. There would be long panes of glass

there to form the ceiling, curved glass that would blend the line from the rock to the dome. She'd already decided it would be ostentatious and impractical, but as she'd been told, it was her job to make it work, not to approve.

Cody shook his head at something Gray told him, and his voice rose a little, enough to carry but not enough to make the words clear. Annoyance was there. It pleased her.

Let him be annoyed, she thought. Let him go back east and be annoyed where he would be out of her way.

She started down, using the temporary stairs. She had the progress on the health club to check out, and the excavation work on the first set of cabanas. As long as they could keep one job overlapping the next, they'd be all right. Tim should have been there, overseeing the scheduling. Abra moved a shoulder to work out a kink. It was better that he wasn't, that he had left the responsibility to her. He had a way of irritating the men when he showed up on the site in his expensive suits.

Just as she checked her watch, she heard a shout from above. She had enough time to see the metal stud falling toward her before she was grabbed by the waist and dragged aside.

The stud landed inches from her feet, spewing up dust and clattering. Hard hat or no, she'd have been taking a trip to the hospital now if she'd been under it.

"You all right? Hey." Arms were still around her waist, but now she was turned and pressed against a hard male body. She didn't have to see to know who was holding her.

"Yes." But her voice wasn't steady. Neither were her hands. "I'm okay. Let me—"

"Who the hell's responsible for this?" Cody shouted up, still holding Abra against him. He knew now what it meant to be sick with fear. He'd moved instinctively, but the moment the stud had hit harmlessly his stomach had heaved. Looking at it, he could envision her lying there, bleeding. Two men were already scurrying down the ladder, their faces as white as his.

"It got away from us. God, Ms. Wilson, are you okay? There was an electric box on the floor. It tripped me up, and the stud just went."

"It didn't hit me." She tried to move away from Cody but didn't have the strength.

"Get up there and make sure those floors and platforms are clear. If there's any more carelessness, people are going to be out of a job."

"Yes, sir."

The hammering, which had stopped dead, resumed hesitantly, then with more vigor.

"Look, I'm all right." She had to be. Even if her hands were clammy, she had to be all right. "I can handle the men."

"Just shut up." He fought back the urge to pick her up, and pulled her along instead. "You're white as a sheet." He shoved her down on a crate. "Sit."

Because her legs felt like rubber, she didn't argue. A few deep breaths, she told herself, and she'd be fine.

"Here." Cody pushed a cup of water into her hand.

"Thanks." She drank, forcing herself to take it slow. "You don't have to bother."

"No, I could just leave you in a puddle on the ground." It hadn't come out the way he'd intended, but he was angry, as sick with anger as he'd been with fear. It had been too close, way too close. If he hadn't glanced over at her... "I could've stood there and watched you get smashed, but it seemed a shame to get blood all over the fresh concrete."

"That's not what I meant." She swallowed the last of the water and balled up the paper cup in her hand. He'd saved her from a major injury. She'd wanted to thank him, nicely. And she would have, too, Abra thought, if he hadn't been scowling at her. "I would have gotten out of the way myself, in any case."

"Fine. Next time I'll just go about my business."

"Do that." Biting off the words, she tossed the paper cup aside. She rose and fought back a wave of giddiness. Hammers were still pounding, but more than one man was watching out of the corner of an eye. "There's no need to cause a scene."

"You've no idea the kind of scene I can cause, Wilson." He was tempted to show her, to release some of the fury that had boiled together with the fear and let her have a good long look at what he could throw. But her face was chalk white, and whether she knew it or not her hands were shaking. "If I were you, I'd have your foreman drill some safety rules into these men."

"I'll take that under advisement. Now, if you'll excuse me, I have to get back to work."

When his fingers curled around her arm, she felt the temper in them. She was grateful for it. It made her stronger. Very slowly she turned her head so that she could look at him again. Fury, she thought with a kind of edgy curiosity. The man was absolutely furious— more than a few cross words warranted. His problem, Abra told herself.

"I'm not going to keep telling you to back off, Johnson."

He waited a moment until he was sure he could speak calmly. In his mind he could still hear the sickening crack of metal hitting concrete. "That's something we can agree on, Red. You won't keep telling me to back off."

He let her go. After the briefest hesitation, she strode away.

She wouldn't keep telling him, Cody thought as he watched her disappear outside. And even if she did, it wasn't going to do her any good.

Chapter 3

He had other things to think about. Cody let the hot spray of the shower beat over his head and reminded himself that Abra Wilson wasn't his problem. A problem she undoubtedly was, but not his.

Women that skittish were best avoided, particularly when they had those pretty feminine looks that contrasted with a mean temper. The Barlow project was giving him enough headaches. He didn't need to add her to the list.

But then, she was mighty easy to look at. Cody smiled to himself as he turned off the shower. Easy to look at didn't mean easy to handle. Usually he appreciated challenges, but just now he had enough on his plate. Now that his partner was married and expecting his first baby, Cody was doing what he could to shoulder the excess. With business booming, the excess meant twelve-hour days. In addition to overseeing the construction of the resort, there were innumerable phone calls to make and take, telegrams to send and receive, decisions, approvals and rejections.

He didn't mind the responsibility or the long hours. He was grateful for them. It didn't take much prodding for him to remember the boy who had grown up on a muddy farm on the Georgia-Florida border. The boy had wanted more, and the man had worked to get it.

Come a long way, Cody thought as he knotted the towel at his waist. His body was lean, the torso tanned. He still worked outdoors, though that was from choice now, rather than necessity. It wasn't only drawing boards and dreams with Cody. There was a house on a lake in Florida that was half-built. He was determined to finish it himself. A matter of pride now, rather than lack of funds.

The money was there, and he'd never deny he enjoyed its benefits. Still, he'd grown up working with his hands, and he couldn't seem to break the habit. He corrected himself. He didn't want to break the habit. There were times when he enjoyed nothing more than the feel of a hammer or a piece of wood in his hand.

He dragged his fingers through his wet hair. They were calloused, as they'd been since childhood. He could run a tractor even now, but he preferred a slide rule or a power saw.

He strode into the bedroom of his hotel suite. The suite was nearly as big as the home he'd grown up in. He'd gotten used to the space, to the small luxuries, but he didn't take them for granted. Because he'd grown up skirting poverty he'd learned to appreciate good material, good food, good wine. Perhaps he appreciated them with a more discerning eye than someone who had been born to the good life. But he didn't think about that.

Work, talent and ambition were the keys, with a bit

of luck thrown in. Cody remembered that luck could change, so he never avoided work.

He had come a long way from digging in the mud to make a living. Now he could dream, imagine and create—as long as he didn't forget that making dreams reality meant getting your hands dirty. He could lay a score of brick if it was required, mix mortar, pound in a stud or drive a rivet. He'd worked his way through college as a laborer. Those years had given him not only a practical bent toward building but a respect for the men who sweated to create them.

Which brought him back to Abra. She understood construction workers. He knew firsthand that many of the people who worked at drawing boards forgot the men who hammered the nails and hauled the bricks. But not Abra. Thoughtfully he slipped into a white terry-cloth robe with the vague notion of calling room service and eating in. Abra Wilson, he mused. She would have gone to the wall to get an extra thirty minutes' break for the men. She was a fiend about checking the water supply and the salt tablets.

She was also a woman who would step in between two angry construction workers to break up a fight. Or pour beer over the head of an insubordinate employee. The memory made him grin. No drinking on the job. And she'd meant what she'd said.

He appreciated that. He was a man who preferred frankness to subtleties in both his business and his personal life. She wasn't a woman who would play flirting games or give teasing hints. She would say yes or she would say no.

As she had on the side of the road, he remembered. She'd said no, Cody mused, and she'd wanted to say yes. Discovering the reasons for the contradiction would be interesting work. It was a pity he could only fit Abra into the business slot. They might have had some fun together, he thought, dragging a hand through his still-damp hair. The trouble was, she was too uptight to settle back and have a good time. Perhaps it would be fair to say that she was too honest to take intimacy on a casual level. He couldn't fault her for that, which made one more reason to keep things on a business plane.

And there was too much friction. Friction usually led to a spark, and a spark to a blaze. He didn't have the time to fight fires just now.

With a glance at the clock on the bedside table he calculated the time back east. It was far too late to make any calls to the East Coast. That meant he'd have to get up at five, pull himself together and make all the necessary calls and connections between 6:00 and 7:00 a.m.

With a shrug, he decided that what was called for was a quick room-service meal and an early night. Just as he picked up the phone, the buzzer sounded at his door.

If there was one person he hadn't been expecting, it was Abra.

She stood there, balancing a brown grocery bag on one hip. Her hair was loose—it was the first time he'd seen it unbraided or unpinned—and curled wildly to her shoulders. She still wore jeans and a T-shirt, but she'd changed from work boots to sneakers. The next surprise was that she was almost smiling.

"Hi," she managed. It was ridiculous, but she'd never been so nervous in her life.

"Hi." He leaned against the doorframe and took a long, lazy scan. "Passing by?"

"Not exactly." Her fingers dug into the stiff brown paper bag. The telltale rattle made her relax them again. "Can I come in?"

"Sure." He stepped back, and she stepped through. From behind her, she heard the door click closed. Her heart jerked with it. "This is nice."

The living room of the suite was done in desert colors, mauves and umbers and creams. There were sketches on the walls and narrow louvered blinds at the windows. The room smelled of soap. He smelled of soap. Abra braced herself to turn.

"I wanted to apologize."

His brow lifted in an unconscious gesture as he studied her. She was doing her best, Cody realized, and hating every minute of it. Amused, he decided to draw the scene out.

"For what?"

She nearly ground her teeth. On the trip over she had prepared herself for the likelihood that he wouldn't make it easy. "For being rude and ungrateful this afternoon."

Cody slipped his hands into the pockets of his robe. "Just this afternoon?"

Venom nearly poured out, and it was hard to swallow. An apology was due, and she was damn well going to get it over with. "Yes. We're dealing with a specific instance. You helped me this afternoon, and I was ungrateful and unkind. I was wrong, and when I am I like to think I can admit it." Without asking, she moved over to the counter that separated the living space from the kitchenette. "I brought you some beer."

"To drink or to wear?" he asked when she pulled out a six pack.

"Up to you." She broke down enough to smile, really smile. The flecks in her eyes brightened. Her lips softened as if by magic. Cody felt his heart stop for two full beats. "I didn't know whether you'd eaten, so I tossed in a meatball sub and some fries."

"You brought me dinner?"

Uncomfortable, she shrugged. "It's no big deal, just a sandwich." She pulled out a twelve-inch tube wrapped in white paper.

"Some sandwich."

"Yeah." She took out the foam dish that held the french fries. If it killed her, she told herself, she was going to get the words out. And it might kill her, she thought, if he kept looking at her as though he'd rather nibble on her than the sub. "I wanted to thank you for acting so quickly this afternoon. I don't know whether I'd have gotten out of the way in time or not, but that's not the issue. The fact is, you made certain I wasn't hurt, and I never really thanked you at the time. I guess I was more shaken up than I realized."

As he had been, Cody thought. He crossed over to stand beside her. She was holding the empty bag, folding and unfolding it. The gesture showed him more than words could have how much it had cost her to come. He took the bag from her and tossed it on the counter.

"You could have written that down in a nice little note and slipped it under the door. But I don't suppose that's your style." He resisted the urge to touch her hair, knowing it would be a mistake for both of them. He would only want to touch her more, and she already looked as though she'd jump out of her shoes at the first advance. Instead, he pulled a bottle out of the pack and turned it to read the label. "Want a beer?"

She hesitated only briefly. It looked as if he was going to make it easy for her after all. "Sure."

"Half a meatball sub?"

She relaxed and smiled again. "I could probably choke it down."

A truce, undeclared but understood, had been negotiated. They shared cold beer and spicy meatballs on Cody's terrace. A small in-ground spa swirled silently at their feet. Orange and red blossoms, their scent heavy, trailed up and along the high walls that closed them in. The sun was low, and the air was cooling.

"All the comforts of home," Abra mused as she sipped her beer.

Cody thought about his house, where everything was familiar, where so many walls were still unfinished and so many yards of trim were still unpainted. "Not quite home. But it's the next best thing."

Abra stretched the toes of her sneakers toward the water. Lord, she'd like to sink into that, close her eyes and let every muscle hum. With a soft sigh of regret, she dismissed the idea. "You do much traveling?"

"Enough. You?"

"Not really. Well, around the state. Up into Utah a couple of times. I like hotels."

"Really?"

She was relaxed enough to ignore his smirk. She bit into the sub and savored the blending of meat, sauce and cheese. "I like being able to take a shower and go out and come back to find fresh towels. Ordering room service and eating in bed. Stuff like that. You must like them, too." She watched him tilt back his beer. "You don't strike me as someone who'd keep doing something he didn't care for."

"I don't mind moving around." The fries were greasy and loaded with salt. Perfect. He took two. "I like knowing I've got some place to go back to, that's all."

She understood that very well, though it surprised her that he felt the sentiment—and the need. "Have you always lived in Florida?"

"Yeah. Can't say I care much for the snow-shoveling, finger-numbing weather in the north. I like the sun."

"Me too." She dug out fries. "It only rains here a handful of times a year. Rain's an event." With a grin, she finished off her half of the sub. The best meal, she had to admit, she'd had in weeks. It was hard to believe, but his company wasn't such a trial after all. She settled back to nurse her beer and wait for nightfall. "I'd like to see the ocean, though."

"Which one?"

"Any one."

Her eyes were gray in this light, he noted. Gray and a little sleepy. "It's a short flight to the West Coast."

"I know." She moved her shoulders and continued to watch the sky darken. "I always figured I needed a bigger reason to make the trip."

"Vacation?"

"I've been pushing pretty hard the last few years. This may be the age of women's liberation, but there are still walls to break down when you're an engineer who happens to be a woman."

"Why are you an engineer?"

He reached lazily for more fries, and so did she. Their fingers brushed companionably. "I always liked to figure out how things worked—or what to do to make them work better. I was good with numbers. I like the logic of them. If you put them together and figure out the formula, you're always going to come up with the right answer."

"The right answer's not always the best answer."

Crossing her legs at the ankles, she turned her head enough to study his face in the lowering light. "That's artistic thinking, which is why an architect needs a good engineer to keep him on track."

He took a lazy swallow of beer and smiled at her. "Is that what you're doing, Red? Keeping me on track?"

"It isn't easy. Take the design of the health club."

"I figured you'd get around to it."

Mellowed by the casual meal, she ignored his sarcasm. "The waterfall on the east wall. We'll overlook the fact that it's an impractical piece of fancy."

"You've got something against waterfalls?"

"This is the desert, Johnson."

"Ever hear of an oasis?"

She sighed, determined to be patient. It was a nice night. The food had been good, and the company more pleasant than she'd expected. "I'll give you your little whimsy."

"Bless you for that."

"But if you'd put it on the west wall, as I requested—"

"It doesn't work on the west wall," he said. "You need the windows on the west wall for the evening light, the sunsets. And the view's best in the west."

"I'm talking about logistics. Think plumbing."

"I leave that up to you. You think plumbing, I'll think aesthetics, and we'll get along fine."

Typical, typical, typical, she thought with a shake of her head. "Cody, my point is that this project could have been half as difficult as it is with a few minor adjustments."

The challenging light had come back into her eyes. He nearly smiled. The evening wouldn't have been complete without at least one argument. "If you're afraid of hard work, you should have found another profession."

That had her head snapping up, and her eyes, already filled with anger, narrowing. "I'm not afraid to work, and I'm damn good at what I do. It's people like you, who come along with your six-story egos, refusing to make any adjustments, who make things impossible."

He had a temper of his own, but he managed—barely—to check it. "It's not my ego that keeps me from making adjustments. If I made them, I wouldn't be doing the job I'd been hired to do."

"You call it professional integrity, I call it ego."

"And you're wrong," he said with deceptive calm. "Again."

She could have drawn in then and tried tact and subtlety—if she had thought of it. "Are you telling me it would have compromised your integrity to move that silly waterfall from east to west?"

"Yes."

"That's the most ridiculous thing I've ever heard. But typical," she said, rising to pace the tiny walled-in terrace. "God knows it's typical. Sometimes I think architects worry more about the color of paint than stress points."

He watched her as she paced. Her stride was long and loose, the kind that ate up ground from point to point easily. A woman going places, he mused. But he wasn't about to be walked over so that she could get there.

"You've got a bad habit of generalizing, Red."

"Don't call me Red," she muttered, then tugged an orange blossom off the vine. "I'll be glad when this project's finished and I'm out on my own. Then I can pick what architect I want to work with."

"Good luck. It might just be difficult for you to find one who's willing to put up with temper tantrums and nit-picking."

She whirled back. She knew she had a temper. She wouldn't deny it or apologize for it. But as to the rest... "I don't nitpick. It's not nit-picking to make a suggestion that would save laying an extra hundred feet of pipe. And only an egocentric, hardheaded architect would see it that way."

"You've got a problem, *Ms.* Wilson." He saw and enjoyed the way she stiffened at that. "You've got a low opinion of people in my profession, but as long as you pursue yours, you're stuck with us."

She mangled the flower she was holding. "Not everyone in your field's an idiot. There are some excellent architects in Arizona."

"So it's just architects from back east you don't like."

She wasn't going to let him put words in her mouth and make her sound like a fool. "I have no idea why Tim felt he had to hire a firm from out of state to begin with. But since he did, I'm doing my best to work with you."

"Your best could use some polishing up." Setting his beer aside, he rose. His face was in shadows, but she could tell by his stance that he was as angry as she was, and primed for a fight. "If you've got any other complaints, why don't you get them out now while there's just the two of us?"

She tossed the bruised flower, like a gauntlet, between them. "All right, I will. It infuriates me that you didn't bother to come out for any of the preliminary meetings. I was against hiring an East Coast firm, but Tim wouldn't listen. The fact that you were unavailable made things more complicated. Meanwhile, I've got to deal with Gray, who bites his fingernails and is always looking up codes or shuffling papers. Then you come out and swagger around like the cock of the walk, refusing to modify even one line of your precious design."

He took a step toward her, out of the shadows. He was angry, all right, she noted. It was just her luck that his temper made him more attractive. "In the first place,

I had a very good reason for missing the preliminary meetings. Good personal reasons that I don't feel obligated to discuss with you." He took another step. "The fact that your employer hired my firm over your objections is your problem, not mine."

"I prefer to think of it as his mistake, not mine."

"Fine." When he took the next step toward her, she had to fight back the urge to retreat. His eyes could be very dark, she discovered, very intense. He didn't remind her of a casual beachcomber now, or an easygoing cowboy. More like a gunslinger, she realized, but she held her ground. "As to Gray, he might be young and annoying, but he also works hard."

She felt a flush of shame and jammed her hands into her pockets. "I didn't mean…"

"Forget it." He took a final step that brought him so close that their bodies nearly brushed. Abra kept her jaw set and her eyes on his. "And I don't swagger."

She had a ridiculous urge to laugh, but something in his eyes warned her that that was the most dangerous thing she could do. Instead, she swallowed and lifted both brows. "You mean you don't do it on purpose?"

She was baiting him, plain and simple. He hadn't missed the light of amusement in her eyes. She wanted to laugh at him, and he'd be damned if she'd get away with it. "I don't do it at all. You, on the other hand, put on that hard hat and those steel-toed boots and stomp around the site trying to prove how tough you can be."

She opened her mouth in utter astonishment, then snapped it closed. "I don't stomp, and I don't have to prove anything to anyone. I'm doing the job I was trained to do."

"Then you do yours and I'll do mine."

"Fine. See you at sunup."

She started to spin toward the door, and he caught her by the arm. He didn't know what demon had prompted him to do it, to stop her when her angry exit would have been best for both of them. Now it was too late. The move was already made. Their faces were close, his hand was tight on her arm, and their bodies were turned toward each other. A half moon was rising. Outside the walls a woman's laugh ebbed and flowed as a couple strolled by beneath its light.

The friction had given birth to a spark—no, dozens of sparks, Cody thought as he felt them singe his skin. The heat from them was quick and dangerous, but still controllable. If he fanned them, they would flame. And then…

The hell with it, he thought as he closed his mouth over hers.

She was braced. She was ready. The desire and the intent had been plain to see as they'd stood there for that long, silent moment. Abra was honest enough to admit that the desire had been there all along. It had cut through her time and time again. So she was braced. She was ready.

It didn't do any good.

She should have been able to hold back her response, something she'd always been able to give or subdue as she chose. As *she* chose. It was frightening to learn in one split second that the choice wasn't always there. Response ripped out of her before a decision could be made and shattered her opinion of her own free will.

She was holding on to him without any recollection of having reached out. Her body was pressed hard against his without any memory of having moved at all. When her lips parted, it was as much in demand as in invitation. His rough answer was exactly what she wanted.

He dragged her against him, amazed that need could rise from a simmer to a boil so quickly. Another surprise. What flared between them came as much from her as from him. She hadn't protested or struggled angrily away, but had met him force for force, passion for passion. With temper adding an edge to desire, he caught her hair in his hands and took as ruthlessly as his need demanded.

He nipped at her lip. Her low, throaty moan was as arousing as the play of her tongue over his. Now he gave himself freedom, letting his hands run over her, testing, tormenting, taking. Her body shuddered against his, then pressed closer. She didn't hold back, didn't seem to believe in it.

She should think, oh, she knew she should think. But it wasn't possible when her pulse was pounding in her head and her muscles were like water. How could she think when his taste was spreading through her, filling her?

He was as breathless as she when they drew apart. She was as willing as he when they came together for one last long, lingering kiss. When they parted again they stayed close, his hands on her shoulders, hers on his arms. Anger defused, passion ignited, leaving them both weak.

"What are we going to do about this?" Cody asked her.

She could only shake her head. It was too soon to think and too late not to.

"Why don't you sit down?"

She shook her head again before he could lead her to a chair. "No. No, I don't want to sit." It was harder than she'd thought it would be to step away from him. "I've got to go."

"Not quite yet." He needed a cigarette. He fumbled in the pockets of his robe and swore when he found his hands weren't steady. It amazed and infuriated him. "We have to resolve this, Abra."

She watched the match spark and flame, then drew a steadying breath. Flames could be lit, she reminded herself, and they could be put out just as easily. "It shouldn't have happened."

"That's beside the point."

It hurt, more than a little, that he hadn't disagreed with her. But of course he couldn't, she told herself. She was right. "No, I think that is the point." In frustration she dragged both hands through her hair, and he remembered all too clearly what it had felt like tangled around his own hands. "It shouldn't have happened, but it did, and now it's over. I think we're both too sensible and too professional to let it get in the way of our working relationship."

"Do you?" He should have known she'd handle this the same way she would a fouled-up order for concrete. "Maybe you're right. Maybe. But you're an idiot if you think it won't happen again."

She had to be careful, very careful. It wasn't easy to speak calmly when her lips were still warm and swollen from his. "If it does, we'll simply have to deal with it—separately from business."

"We agree on something." Cody blew out a long stream of smoke. "What happened just now had nothing to do with business." Through the screen of smoke his eyes met hers and held them. "But that's not going to stop me from wanting you during working hours."

She felt a warning chill race up her spine. It made her straighten her shoulders. "Look, Cody, this is—was—a momentary thing. Maybe we were attracted, but—"

"Maybe?"

"All right, all right." She tried to find the right words. "I have to think of my future. We both know there's nothing more difficult, or awkward, than becoming involved with an associate."

"Life's rough," he murmured, and pitched his cigarette high over the wall. He watched the glow fly up and arc before he turned back to her. "Let's get something straight, Red. I kissed you and you kissed me right back. And it felt damn good. I'm going to want to kiss you again, and a lot more than that. What I'm not going to do is wait until it's convenient for you."

"You make all the decisions?" she snapped. "You make all the moves?"

He considered a moment. "Okay."

Fury didn't make her speechless. Taking a step forward, she poked a finger at his chest. "It's not okay, you arrogant pinhead. I kissed you back because I wanted to, because I liked it. If I kiss you again it'll be for the same reasons, not because you set the time and place. If I go to bed with you, the same rules hold. Got that straight?"

She was wonderful. Infuriating, but wonderful. He managed not to grab her. Instead, he grinned. When a woman called a spade a spade, you couldn't argue. "Straight as an arrow," he agreed. He tucked an errant strand of hair behind her ear. "Glad you liked it."

The sound that hissed out between her teeth was anything but pleased. His grin just widened. Rather than punch him in the face, she knocked his hand aside and turned for the door.

"Abra."

She yanked the door open and stood gripping the knob. "What?"

"Thanks for dinner."

The door slammed at her back, and then he did laugh. He waited ten seconds and heard the front door of the suite slam in turn. On impulse, he stripped off his robe and, turning on the timer for the spa, eased into the hot, bubbling water. He hoped it would soothe out the aches she'd left him with and clear his mind enough to let him think.

Chapter 4

Business. From now until the last tile was caulked Abra was determined to keep it strictly business between herself and Cody. Engineer to architect. They would discuss templates and curved headers, wiring and plastic pipe, concrete and thermal mass. Abra scowled at the bare bones of the health club. With luck, she thought, they would discuss nothing at all.

What had happened on that moonlit terrace was like temporary insanity. Inherited insanity, she decided as she dug her fists into her pockets. Obviously she was more like her mother than she had ever wanted to admit. An attractive man, a little stardust and *wham*! She was ready and willing to make a fool of herself.

She took the clipboard the foreman handed her, scanned the papers, then initialed them. She'd come this far without letting any congenital weaknesses muck up her life. She intended to go a lot farther. Maybe she had inherited the flaw from her mother, but unlike the sweet, eternally optimistic Jessie she had no intention of going into a romantic spin and ending up flat on her face. That moment of weakness had passed, and now it was back to business as usual.

She spent the morning running back and forth between the health club and the main building, with an occasional foray to check on the excavation work for the cabanas. The work on each section of the project was overlapping according to plan, keeping her constantly in demand to oversee, answer questions, smooth out problems.

She had a long, technical phone conversation with the mechanical engineer Thornway had assigned. He was moving more slowly than she might have liked, but his work was first-class. She made a note to go by the offices and take a good look at the dies for both the elevator and the mechanized roof over the pool.

Those were aspects of her profession she enjoyed every bit as much as the planning and figuring, and they were aspects she took every bit as seriously. She wasn't an engineer who figured her job was over once the specs were approved and the calculations checked. She'd wanted a part in the Barlow project that didn't begin and end at the drawing board. It had been given to her, and if she still winced inwardly when a shovelful of dirt was removed from the site, she had the satisfaction of being a part of its reshaping.

No one she came in contact with would have seen beneath the competent exterior to her distracted thoughts. If she was constantly on the lookout for Cody, she told herself, it was only that she didn't care to be taken unaware. By noon she had decided he wasn't going to show. Disappointment masqueraded as relief.

She took her lunch break in the trailer with a bottle of chilled orange juice, a bag of chips and blueprints. Since her conversation with the mechanical engineer she had decided there were still a few problems to work out in the dynamics of the sliding glass roof Cody wanted over the pool. She crunched into a chip while she punched a new equation into her calculator. If it weren't for the waterfall the man insisted on having run down the wall and into the corner of the pool... Abra shook her head and tried a new angle. The man was a maniac about waterfalls, she thought. She took a long swig of juice. Basically he was just a maniac. It helped to think of him that way, as a crazy architect with delusions of grandeur, rather than as a man who could kiss the common sense right out of you.

She was going to give him his damn sliding glass arch of a roof, and his waterfalls, and his spirals and domes. Then she was going to use this foolish fancy of a design to launch her own career while he went back to his humidity and his orange groves.

Nearly satisfied, Abra sketched out a few details, then ran a new set of figures. It wasn't her job to approve, she reminded herself, it was her job to make it work. She was very good at making things work.

When the door opened, she didn't bother to glance up.

"Close that quick, will you? You'll let the heat in."

"Yes, ma'am."

The lazy drawl had her head jerking up. She straightened her shoulders automatically as Cody stooped to walk through the doorway. "I didn't think we'd see you here today."

He merely smiled and stood aside to make room for Tim Thornway and the bullet-shaped form of William Walton Barlow, Sr. Awkwardly, due to the row of cabinets over her head, Abra stood.

"Abra." Though he would have preferred to have found her knee-deep in concrete or up on the scaffolding, Tim was skilled enough to use almost any situation to his advantage. "As you can see, WW," he said, "our crew lives, sleeps and eats B and B's resort hotel. You remember Ms. Wilson, our chief structural engineer."

The little man with the thatch of white hair and the shrewd eyes held out a meaty hand. "Indeed, indeed. A Barlow never forgets a pretty face."

To her credit, Abra didn't wince, not even when Cody smirked over Barlow's head. "It's nice to see you again, Mr. Barlow."

"WW thought it was time he had a look at things," Tim explained. "Of course, we don't want to interrupt the flow or slacken the pace—"

"Don't know much about putting these places up," Barlow cut in. "Know about running them. Like what I see, though." He nodded three times. "Like the curves and arches. Classy. Barlow and Barlow stands for classy operations."

Abra ignored Cody's grin and scooted out from behind the table. "You picked a hot day to visit, Mr. Barlow. Can I get you something cold? Juice, tea?"

"Take a beer. Nothing washes away the dust like a cold beer."

Cody opened the scaled-down refrigerator himself and rooted some out. "We were about to show WW the progress on the health club."

"Oh?" Abra shook her head at the offer of a beer and was amused when Tim accepted a bottle gingerly. "Good timing. I've just been working out the final details on the pool roof. I think Lafferty and I smoothed out some of the bugs over the phone this morning."

Barlow glanced down at the blueprints and at the

stacks of paper covered with figures and calculations. "I'll leave that to you. Only numbers I'm handy with are in an account book. Looks like you know your way around, though." He gestured with his bottle before taking three healthy gulps. "Thornway always said you had a head on your shoulders. Pretty shoulders, too." He winked at her.

Rather than getting her dander up, the wink made her grin. He was nearly old enough to be her grandfather and, multimillionaire or not, he had a certain rough charm. "Thank you. He always spoke highly of you."

"I miss him," Barlow said. Then he turned to the matter at hand. "Let's get on with this tour, Tim. No use wasting time."

"Of course." Tim set aside his untouched beer. "I'm giving a little dinner party for Mr. Barlow tonight. Seven. You'll escort Mr. Johnson, Abra."

Since it wasn't a question, Abra opened her mouth with the idea of making some excuse. Cody stepped smoothly in. "I'll pick up Ms. Wilson. Why don't you start over to the health club? We'll be right with you."

"Why don't you loosen that damn tie, Tim?" Barlow asked as they stepped out of the trailer. "Man could strangle in this heat."

Cody shut the door, then leaned against it. "They *are* nice shoulders. From what I've seen of them."

From an engineering standpoint, Abra couldn't have said why the trailer seemed more crowded now than it had a moment before. Turning back to the table, she began to tidy her papers. "It isn't necessary for you to pick me up this evening."

"No." He studied her, not certain whether he was amused or annoyed by her withdrawal. He hadn't slept well, and he knew the blame lay squarely on those pretty shoulders, which were now braced for an attack. "But I will."

This was business, Abra told herself, and should be handled as such. Making up her mind, she turned to face him. "All right. You'll need an address."

He smiled again, slowly this time. "Oh, I think I can find you, Red. Same way you found me."

Since he'd brought it up, Abra told herself, it would be best to deal with it. "It's good that we have a minute here. We can clear things up."

"What things?" Cody pushed away from the door. Abra backed into the table hard. "We had a mule back home on the farm," he mused as he stepped closer. "She tended to be skittish, too."

"I'm not skittish. It's simply that I think you have the wrong impression."

"I have the right impression," he told her, reaching around to toy with the end of her braid. "Of just how your body feels when it's fitted against mine. A very right and very pleasant impression."

"That was a mistake." She would have turned away to move around him, but he tightened his grip on her hair and tugged her back.

"What was?"

"Last night." She was going to handle this calmly, Abra told herself. She was basically a calm and reasonable person. "It should never have happened."

"It?" His eyes had darkened. Abra noted that, and noted, also, that there was no anger to be seen in them. She let out a little breath of relief. Obviously he was prepared to be as reasonable as she.

"I suppose we just got caught up in the moment. The best thing to do is forget it and go on."

"Okay." She saw his smile but didn't notice how cool

it was. He wasn't much of a hand at chess, but he was a killer at poker. "We'll forget last night."

Pleased at the ease with which the problem had been erased, she smiled back at him. "Well, then, why don't we—"

Her words were cut off as he dragged her against him and covered her mouth with his. Her body went rigid— from shock, she told herself. From fury. That was what she wanted to believe. Today there was none of the gentle, sensual exploration in the moonlight. This kiss was as bold and as bright as the sun that beat through the windows. And as angry, she thought as he twisted her against him and took whatever he wanted. She tried to yank free and was held fast. Those subtle muscles covered steel. Abra found herself caught up in an embrace that threatened every bit as much as it promised.

He didn't give a damn. She could stand there and talk all she wanted in that reasonable voice about mistakes. He'd made mistakes before and lived through them. She might be the biggest, she would certainly be the costliest, but he wasn't about to back off now. He remembered the way she had felt in his arms the night before, that shivering, wire-taut passion, that abrupt avalanche of emotion. Even then he'd known it was nothing he'd felt before, nothing he would feel again. Not with anyone else. He'd see them both damned before it was forgotten.

"Stop," she managed before he crushed her mouth again. She was drowning, and she knew she couldn't save herself. Drowning, she thought as she moaned against his lips. Drowning in sensations, in longings, in desires. Why was she clinging to him when she knew it was crazy? Why was she answering that hard, hungry kiss when she knew it could lead to nothing but disaster?

But her arms were around him, her lips were parted,

her heart was pounding in rhythm with his. This was more than temptation, more than surrender. What she felt now wasn't a need to give but a need to take.

When they broke apart she dragged air into her lungs and braced a hand on the table for balance. She could see now that she'd been wrong. There was anger in his eyes, anger and determination and a rough-edged desire that rooted her to the spot. Still, when he spoke, his voice was mild.

"Looks as if we have another point of reference, Red." He swung to the door. "See you at seven."

There were at least a half a dozen times that evening that Abra thought of a plausible excuse and began to dial Cody at his hotel. What stopped her each time was the knowledge that if she made the call she would be acknowledging not only that there was something between them but that she was a coward. Even if she forced herself to accept the fact that she was afraid, she couldn't allow him to see it.

She was obliged to go, she reminded herself as she rummaged through her closet once again. It was really no more than a business meeting, though they would be wearing evening dress and picking at canapés on Tim's elegant patio. It was politic and necessary to show Barlow that his architect and engineer could handle a social evening together.

She had to be able to handle it. Sexual attraction aside, Cody Johnson was her associate on this project. If she couldn't handle him—and what he seemed bound and determined to make her feel—she couldn't handle the job. No slow-talking East Coast architect was going to make her admit she couldn't handle anything that came her way.

In any case, she thought with some satisfaction as she tried to decide between two dresses, once they were there there would be so many people that they would get lost in the shuffle. It was doubtful she and Cody would have to exchange more than a few words.

When the knock came, she looked at her watch and swore. She'd been talking to herself for so long that it was time to leave and she wasn't even dressed. Tightening the belt on her robe, she went out of the cramped bedroom into the tiny living area and answered the door.

Cody took one lazy look at her short cotton robe and grinned. "Nice dress."

"I'm running behind," she muttered. "You can go on without me."

"I'll wait." Without waiting for an invitation, he walked in and surveyed her apartment.

She might be a woman who dealt in precise facts and figures, but she lived in chaos. Bright pillows were tossed on a faded couch, and piles of magazines were stacked on a mismatched chair. For someone who made her living turning facts and figures into structure and form, she didn't know the first thing about decorating space—or didn't care to, Cody mused. He'd seen her work, and had admired it. If she put her mind to it, he figured, she could turn a closet into an organized and functional living area.

The room was smaller than the bedroom of his hotel suite, but no one would have called it impersonal. Dozens of pictures jockeyed for position on a long table in front of the single window. There was a comfortable layer of dust over everything except a collection of crystals that hung at the window and caught the last of the evening light.

That, more than anything else in the room, told him

that she spent little time there but cared for what mattered to her.

"I won't be long," Abra told him. "If you want a drink or something, the kitchen's through there."

She escaped, clicking the door firmly behind her. God, he looked wonderful. It wasn't fair for him to look so sexy, so confident, so utterly perfect. She dragged her hands through the hair she had yet to attempt to style. It was bad enough that he looked so good in work clothes, but he looked even better in a cream-colored jacket that set off his sun-bleached hair and his tanned skin, and that didn't seem fair. Even dressed more formally for the evening he didn't lose the casual flair of the beach-comber or the masculine appeal of the cowboy. How was she supposed to fight off an attraction when every time he showed up he was that much more attractive?

The hell with it, she thought as she faced her closet again. She was going to handle him and the attraction she felt. That meant she wasn't going to wear that plain and proper blue suit after all. If she was going to play with fire, she decided, she was going to have to dress for it.

Cody found her kitchen in the same unapologetic disarray as the living room. One wouldn't have called it dirty. Something normally had to be put to use to get that way, and it was obvious that she wasn't a woman who spent a lot of time over a stove. The fact that she had a tin of cookies and a canister full of tea bags set on two of the burners made that clear.

He found a bottle of wine in the refrigerator, along with a jar of peanut butter and one lonely egg. After a search through the cupboards he located two mismatched wineglasses and a paperback copy of a horror novel by a well-known writer.

He took a sip of the wine and shook his head. He hoped he'd have a chance to teach her a little about vintages. Carrying both glasses into the living room, he listened to the sounds of movement from the bedroom. Apparently she was looking for something and pulling out every drawer she owned in the search. Sipping gingerly, he studied her photographs.

There were some of her, one a formal shot showing that she'd been very uncomfortable in pink organdy. There was another with her standing beside an attractive blonde. Since the blonde had Abra's hazel eyes, Cody wondered if she might be an older sister. There were more of the blonde, one in what might have been a wedding dress, and another of Abra in a hard hat. There were pictures of men scattered throughout, the only one he recognized being of Thornway senior. He sipped again, wondering if any were of her father, then turned. The noises in the bedroom had stopped.

"I poured some wine," he called out. "Want yours?"

"No… Yes, damn it."

"I'll go with the yes." Walking over, Cody pushed open the bedroom door.

There was something about a long, slender woman in a black dress, Cody decided. Something that made a man's mouth water. The dress dipped low in the front, and the plunge was banded with silver in a design that was repeated again at the hem, where the skirt skimmed above her knees. The glitter was designed to draw the eye before it moved down the length of slim legs clad in sheer, smoky stockings. But it was the back that was troubling Abra. She was struggling to fasten the hooks, which stopped at her waist.

"Something's stuck."

His heartbeat, Cody thought, and he waited for it to

pick up speed again. If she'd attracted him in a hard hat and a sweaty T-shirt, that was nothing compared to what she was doing to him now.

"Here." He stepped over sturdy work boots and a pair of glossy black heels that were no more than a few leather straps.

"They design these things so that you have to fight your way in and out of them."

"Yeah." He handed her both glasses and tried not to think about how much more interesting it would be to help her fight her way out of this particular scrap of black silk. "You've got the hooks twisted."

She let out an impatient breath. "I know that. Can you fix it?"

He glanced up, and their eyes met in the mirror above her dresser. For the first time since he'd seen her, she had put on lipstick. Her mouth looked slick and ripe and inviting. "Probably. What are you wearing?"

She sipped because her throat was suddenly dry. "That should be obvious. A black dress with faulty hooks."

"I mean the scent." He dipped a little closer to her neck.

"I don't know." She would have moved away, but his fingers were busy at the waist of her dress. "Something my mother bought me."

"I'm going to have to meet your mother."

She sipped again. "Are you finished back there?"

"Not nearly." He skimmed his fingers up her back and had the pleasure of watching her reaction reflected in the mirror. "You're very responsive, Abra."

"We're very late," she countered, turning.

"Then a couple of minutes more shouldn't matter." He slid his hands lightly around her waist. In defense, she pressed both glasses against his chest. He took them patiently and set them on the dresser behind her. "You have lousy taste in wine."

"I know the difference between white and red." She lifted her hands to his shoulders as he circled her waist again. His grip was loose, just the slight pressure of his fingertips against her. But she didn't shift aside.

"That's like saying I'm a man and you're a woman. There's a lot more to it than that." He bent his head to nibble at her lips. He'd been right. They were inviting. Very inviting. "A whole lot more."

"With me things are one way or another. Cody." She arched away as she felt the floor tilt under her feet. "I'm not ready for this."

A yes or no he would have dealt with swiftly. But there was a desperation in her words that made him pull back. "For what?"

"For what's happening." There were times for flat-out honesty. "For you and what I'm feeling."

His eyes skimmed over her face and came back to hers. She'd given him the leverage. They both knew it. Rather than applying weight, he gave her space. "How long do you need?"

"That's not a question I can answer." Her fingers tightened on his shoulders as his hands moved up and down her back. "You keep backing me into corners."

"So I do," he murmured. He moved aside and waited while she stepped into her shoes. "Abra." When she looked at him again, he took her hand. "This isn't the end of it. I have a feeling the end's a long way off."

She was absolutely certain he was right. That was what worried her. "I have a policy," she said carefully. "I like to know what the end looks like before I begin.

I can't see a nice clean finish with you, Cody, so I'm not altogether sure I want to take you on—so to speak."

"Red." He brought her hand to his lips, leaving her flustered. "You already have."

By the time they arrived at the Thornway estate, the party was in full swing. The buffet was loaded with spicy Mexican cuisine, and wine and margaritas flowed. Beyond the spreading white-and-pink ranch house that Tim had had built for his bride was a sweep of carefully manicured lawn dotted with a few rustling palms. A pool glittered at the tip of a slight slope. Near it was a pretty gazebo shielded by trailing vines just beginning to bloom.

The scent from the side garden was as sweet as the moonlight.

There was a crowd mingling on the glassed-in terrace and the lawn. The cream of Phoenix society had turned out. Abra had already decided to find herself a nice quiet corner. She was always pleased to build for the upper crust, but she didn't have a clue how to socialize with them.

"A Chablis," Cody explained as he handed Abra a glass. "California. Nice clean color, sharp aroma and very full-bodied."

Abra lifted a shoulder as she sipped. "It's white."

"And your dress is black, but it doesn't make you look like a nun."

"Wine's wine," she said, though her palate told her differently.

"Honey—" he trailed a finger down the side of her throat "—you have a lot to learn."

"There you are." Marci Thornway, Tim's wife of two years, glided up. She wore a heavily embroidered white silk caftan, and around her neck was a jeweled collar that glittered in the moonlight. She gave Abra a pat on the hand, then lifted her sapphire-blue eyes to Cody. Her voice dripped like Spanish moss. "I suppose I can understand why you were late."

"Marci Thornway, Cody Johnson."

"The architect." Marci slipped a proprietary hand through Cody's arm. "Tim's told me all about you—except he didn't mention you were so attractive." She laughed. It was a musical sound that suited her silvery blond looks and her petite frame. "But then, husbands have to be forgiven for not telling their wives about handsome men."

"Or men about their beautiful wives."

Abra made a face behind Marci's back and began to spoon up a cheese enchilada.

"You're from Florida, aren't you?" With a little sigh, Marci began leading Cody away. "I grew up in Georgia, a little town outside of Atlanta. Sometimes I swear I could pine away from missing it."

"Little magnolia blossom," Abra muttered, and turned directly into Barlow. "Oh, excuse me, Mr. Barlow."

"That's WW to you. Ought to put more on your plate, girl. Here, try these tortillas. Don't forget the guacamole."

Abra stared down at the food he had heaped on her dish. "Thanks."

"Why don't you have a seat with me and keep an old man company in the moonlight?"

Abra wasn't sure what she'd expected of this evening, but it hadn't been to enjoy a sweet and funny hour with one of the richest men in the country. He didn't, as she had half feared, make a pass, but flirted like an old family friend across the comfortable distance of thirty-five years.

They sat on a bench by the rippling waters of the pool and talked about their mutual love of movies. It was the one vice Abra allowed herself, the only pure recreation she didn't consider a waste of time.

If her attention wandered from time to time, it wasn't because she found Barlow boring, it was because she spotted Cody off and on—more often than not in Marci Thornway's company.

"Selfish," Barlow decided as he finished off his drink. "Ought to let you mingle with the young people."

Feeling guilty about her lapse, she gave him a warm smile. "Oh, no, I like talking to you. To tell you the truth, WW, I'm not much on parties."

"Pretty thing like you needs a young man to fuss over her."

"I don't like to be fussed over at all." She saw Cody light Marci's cigarette.

Barlow was nothing if not shrewd. He followed the direction of Abra's gaze. "Now there's a pretty little thing," he observed. "Like spun glass—expensive and easy to look at. Young Tim must have his hands full."

"He's very devoted to her."

"Been keeping your architect close company this evening."

"*Your* architect," Abra said. Because she didn't like the way that sounded, she smiled. "They're both from the East—Southeast. I'm sure they have a lot in common."

"Mmm." Plainly amused, Barlow rose. "Like to stretch my legs. How about walking around the garden?"

"All right." She made a point of keeping her back to Cody as she took Barlow's arm and strolled off.

What the hell kind of game was she playing? Cody wondered as he watched Abra disappear with Barlow. The man was old enough—more than old enough—to be her father. She'd spent the entire evening cozying up to the man while he'd been trying to untangle himself from the wisteria vine called Marci Thornway.

Cody recognized a woman on the prowl, and the porcelain-cheeked Marci was definitely sending out signals—ones Cody wasn't the least bit interested in receiving. Even if he hadn't already set his sights on Abra, he wouldn't have felt the slightest tug from a woman like Marci. Married or not, she was trouble. Tim was welcome to her.

He wouldn't have judged Abra to be the kind of woman to flatter an old man, to smile and flirt with one with an eye to what it could gain her. There was no mistaking the fact that Barlow was smitten with her, or that she had just wandered off into the roses with one of the *Fortune* 500's best.

Cody lit a cigarette, then narrowed his eyes against the smoke. There was no mistaking the fact that she had wanted him. He might have initiated the kiss—might even have backed her into a corner, as she'd said—but her response had been full-blown. No one kissed like that unless she meant it.

Yet she'd pulled back. Each time. He'd thought it was because she was cautious, maybe even a little afraid of how strong the connection between them had become. And maybe he was a fool, and she held him off because she wanted to snag a bigger fish.

Almost as soon as the thought took root, he ripped it out. It was unfair, he told himself. He was allowing himself to think that way because he was frustrated—because he wanted Abra more than he had ever wanted anyone. And, most of all, because he didn't know what the hell to do about it.

"Excuse me." He cut Marci off in midsentence, sent her a quick smile and strode off toward the garden.

He heard Abra's laughter, a low whispering sound that made him think of the mist on the lake near his home. Then he saw her, standing in the beam of one of the colored lanterns the Thornways' staff had hung all over the garden. She was smiling, twirling a red blossom in her fingertips. The same kind of flower, Cody noted, that she had mangled on his terrace only the night before.

"There's not much meat," Barlow was saying as he grinned at her, "but what's there is choice."

She laughed again, then slipped the stem of the flower into his lapel.

"I beg your pardon."

Both Barlow and Abra turned—guiltily, Cody thought—at the sound of his voice.

"Well, Johnson, been enjoying yourself?" Barlow gave him a quick slap on the shoulder. "Enjoy yourself more if you took a stroll in the moonlight with someone as pretty as our Abra here. Young people don't take enough time for romance these days. Going to see if I can dig up a beer."

For a broad man, he moved quickly enough and Abra found herself alone in the festively lit garden with Cody. "I should probably go mingle—" she began, but she stopped short when Cody blocked her path.

"You haven't felt the need to mingle all evening."

Her main thought was to get out of the garden and away from him, so she just gave him a vague smile. "I've been enjoying WW. He's great company."

"I noticed. It's an unusual woman who can jump from man to man so smoothly. My compliments."

The smile turned into a look of blank confusion.

Cody found a match and cupped his hand over the flame as he lit a cigarette. "He might be in his sixties, but two or three hundred million melt the years away, I imagine."

Abra stared at him for nearly a full minute. "Maybe you should go out and come in again. Then I might understand what you're talking about."

He tossed aside the match. In heels she was eye to eye with him. "I think I'm clear enough. Barlow's a very rich man, widowed for about ten years, and one who obviously appreciates a young, attractive woman."

She nearly laughed, but then she saw the disdain in his eyes. He was serious, she realized. It was incredibly insulting. "You could say he's certainly a man who knows how to treat a woman. Now, if you'll excuse me."

He grabbed her arm before she could storm past him. "I don't find any excuse for you, Red, but that doesn't stop me from wanting you." He pulled her around until they were once again face-to-face. "Can't say that I care for it, but there it is. I want you, and whatever goes on in that calculating head of yours I intend to have you."

"You can go straight to hell, Johnson." She jerked her arm away, but she wasn't through. "I don't care what you want, or what you think of me, but because I like Mr. Barlow too much to let you go on thinking he's some kind of senile fool, I'll let you in on something. We had a conversation tonight, the way some people do in social situations. We happened to hit it off. I wasn't coming on to him, nor he to me."

"What about that crack I heard when I walked up?"

"What?" She hesitated a minute, and then she did

laugh. But her eyes were cold. "That was a line from a movie, you simpleton. An old Tracy Hepburn movie. Mr. Barlow and I both happen to be fans. And I'll tell you something else." Temper lost, she shoved him, taking him back two steps. "If he *had* been coming on to me, it would've been none of your business. If I want to flirt with him, that's my business. If I want to have an affair with him—or anyone else—you don't have jack to say about it." She shoved him again, just for the satisfaction. "Maybe I prefer his kind of attention to the grab-and-go treatment I get from you."

"Now hold on."

"You hold on." Her eyes glowed green in the light from the lanterns. "I have no intention of tolerating this kind of insult from you, or anyone. So keep clear, Johnson, if you want that face of yours to stay in one piece."

She stormed off, leaving Cody singed. He let out a breath between his teeth as he dropped the cigarette onto the path and crushed it out.

"You had that one coming, Johnson," he muttered, rubbing the back of his neck. He knew what it was to dig a hole, and he knew he'd dug this one deep. He also knew that there was only one way out.

Chapter 5

He thought about flowers. Somehow Cody didn't think Abra was the type of woman to melt at the sight of a few roses. He considered a straight-out apology, the kind of no-frills shoot-from-the-hip *I'm sorry* one friend might offer another. But he didn't think Abra saw him as a friend, exactly. In any case, the ice she was dishing out would freeze the words before they got from his mouth to her ear. So he gave her the only thing he thought she would accept for the time being. Space.

They worked together over the next two weeks, often shoulder to shoulder. The distance between them was as great as that between the sun and the moon. Consultations were often necessary, but Abra always arranged it so that they weren't alone. With a skill he was forced to admire, she used Charlie Gray as a buffer. It couldn't have been easy, but she avoided Cody altogether whenever possible. Understanding the need for a cooling-off period, he did nothing to change the situation. Twice he made brief trips, once to the home office in Fort Lauderdale and once to work out a few bugs in a medical complex in San Diego.

Each time he returned he stuck a toe in the waters of Abra's temperament and found them still frigid.

With his hard hat in place and his eyes shielded by tinted glasses, Cody watched the glass of the dome being lowered into place.

"A nice touch. A class touch." Barlow looked up, grinning at the light that came through the glass in red-and-gold spears.

"WW." Cody relaxed a bit when the glass settled on the opening like a cap on a bottle. "Didn't know you were back in town."

"Doing some spot-checking." Barlow mopped his face with a handkerchief. "Hope they get that cooling system going."

"It's on today's schedule."

"Good. Good." Barlow turned around, wanting to take in the entire sweep of building. It pleased him. It had the look of a castle, noble and impregnable, yet at the same time was unabashedly modern. He strolled over to study the glass arch of roof that brought the mountain into the lobby. He approved of the dramatic touch here, where guests would check in and out. First and last impressions, he thought. Young Johnson was making certain they would be lasting ones. Landscapers would plant a few desert shrubs and cacti, then let nature take over. All along the west wall were wide arching windows that let in the vast arena of desert and butte. To the west, men were connecting pipe and laying the stone pool for the waterfall.

"I'll say this, boy—you deliver." It was the kind of blunt compliment Barlow gave only when it was deserved. "I'll admit I had some bad moments over the blueprints and the mock-ups, but my son saw something in all this. I went with his judgment, and I can say now he was right. You've made yourself something here, Cody. Not every man can look back on his life and say the same."

"I appreciate that."

"I'm going to want you to show me the rest." He slapped Cody on the back. "Meantime, is there a place a man can get a beer around here?"

"I think we can arrange it." Cody led the way outside to an ice chest and dug out two cans.

Barlow drank deeply and sighed. His thinning hair was covered by a straw hat with a paisley band. A porch hat, Cody's mother would have called it. It had the effect of making the millionaire look like a retired tobacco farmer.

"I'll be sixty-five my next birthday, and there's still nothing quite like a cold beer on a hot afternoon." Barlow glanced toward the health club and caught a glimpse of Abra. "Well, maybe one thing." With a quick bray of laughter he sat down on the ice chest and loosened his collar. "I like to think of myself as a student of human nature. Figure I made most of my money that way."

"Mmm-hmm," Cody responded absently. He, too, had spotted Abra. She was wearing baggy bib overalls that should have made her appear sexless. They didn't. Cody kept remembering how she'd looked in the little black dress.

"Seems to me you're a man with more on his mind than steel and glass." Barlow swigged his beer with simple appreciation. "Wouldn't have something to do with a long-legged engineer, would it?"

"Might." Cody sent him a mild look as he took out

his cigarettes. He offered Barlow one, but the older man shook his head.

"Had to give them up. Damn doctors yammering at me. Took a liking to her," he continued, switching back easily to the subject of Abra. "'Course, most men take a liking to good looks, but she's got brains and grit. Might have scared me off in my younger days." He grinned and took off his hat to fan his face. "Seemed to me you two had a tiff at that do we had at Tim Thornway's."

"You could call it that." Cody sipped and considered. "I was jealous of you."

"Jealous?" Barlow had lifted the can to his lips. Now he had to set it on the ground for fear he'd drop it as he roared with laughter. Cutting loose, he rocked back and forth on the chest, mopping his streaming face with his handkerchief. "You just knocked twenty years off me, boy. I gotta thank you." He sucked in air, then let it out again in a wheeze. "Imagine a good-looking sonofabitch like you jealous of an old man." He caught his breath and leaned back, still grinning. "A rich old man. Well, well, I don't suppose the little lady took kindly to that."

"The little lady," Cody drawled, "came very close to knocking out my teeth."

"Told you she had grit." Barlow stuffed his handkerchief back in his pocket, then picked up his beer. Life still had some surprises, he thought. Thank God. "Fact is, I had her in mind for my son." At Cody's look, he chuckled and dropped the hat back on his head. "Don't get your dander up now, boy. A man can only take so much excitement in one day. 'Sides, decided against it when I saw the way she looked at you."

"That simplifies things."

"Between you and me, anyway," Barlow pointed out.

"Otherwise, I'd say you were about waist-deep in quick-sand."

"Pretty accurate estimate." Cody tossed his empty can in a trash barrel. "Any suggestions?"

"Better find yourself a rope, son, and haul your tail out."

"My father always used flowers," Cody mused.

"Couldn't hurt." Wincing at a few creaks in his joints, Barlow rose. "Neither would groveling." He noted Cody's expression and laughed again. "Too young for groveling yet," he said. "But you'll learn." He gave Cody a thump on the back. "Yes, indeed, you'll learn."

He wasn't about to grovel. Absolutely not. But he thought it might be time to give the flowers a shot. If a woman hadn't cooled off some in two weeks, she wasn't going to cool off at all—at least not without a little help.

In any case, Cody told himself, he owed her an apology. He laughed a little to himself as he shifted the tiger lilies to his other hand. It seemed as if they'd been bouncing apologies back and forth since the first minute they'd met. Why break the pattern? he mused as he stood in front of her door. If she didn't accept it now, he'd just stick around and drive her crazy until she did.

Each of them seemed to excel at driving the other crazy.

Besides, he'd missed her. It was as simple as that. He'd missed arguing with her about the project. He'd missed hearing her laugh the way she could when her guard was down. He'd missed the strong, uninhibited way her arms would come around him.

He glanced at the flowers in his hand. Tiger lilies were a pretty fragile rope, but they were better than none at all. Even if she tossed them in his face, it would be a change from the stiff politeness she'd dished out since the evening at Tim's. He knocked and wondered what he was going to say to get his foot in the door.

It wasn't Abra who answered, but the blonde from the photographs. She was a small, rosy-cheeked woman Cody guessed was about forty. She was dressed very simply, in a copper-colored jumpsuit that complemented her hair and her eyes, which were so much like Abra's. Cody smiled at her, as much for that as for the fact that, in her porcelain way, she was a knockout.

"Well, hello." She smiled back at him and offered a hand. "I'm Jessie Peters."

"Cody Johnson. I'm a—an associate of Abra's."

"I see." She gave him a slow, sweeping study that was laced with feminine approval. "Come in. I always love meeting Abra's...associates. Would you like a drink? Abra's in the shower."

"Sure." He remembered Abra's wine. "Something cold, if you have it."

"I've just made some lemonade. Fresh. Make yourself at home." She disappeared into the adjoining kitchen. "Was Abra expecting you?"

"No." He glanced around, noting that the apartment had had a swift but thorough tidying.

"A surprise, then. I love surprises." She walked back in with two tall glasses crackling with ice. "Are you an engineer?"

"I'm an architect."

Jessie paused for a moment. Then a smile wisped around her mouth. "*The* architect," she murmured, gesturing for Cody to sit. "I believe Abra's mentioned you."

"I'll bet." He set the flowers on the newly dusted table.

"She didn't mention you were so attractive." Jessie

crossed her legs and settled back. "But it's like her to keep a thing like that to herself." She ran a fingertip down her glass as she summed him up. Her hand was pretty and fragile-looking, like the novelty magnet in Abra's car. There was a diamond on her finger, a small one in a rather ornate setting, but no wedding band. "You're from the East?"

"That's right. Florida."

"I never think of Florida as the East," she commented. "I always think of Disney World."

"Did I hear the door? I— Oh." Abra came out of the adjoining bedroom. She was wearing baggy white pants and an oversize sweatshirt with a pair of battered-looking sandals. Her hair was still damp and curled from the shower.

"You have company." Jessie rose and gathered up the flowers. "Bearing gifts."

"Yes, I see." Abra dug her hands into the deep pockets of her pants.

With her bright smile still in place, Jessie buried her face in the blooms. She recognized tension and romance. As far as she was concerned, one was wasted without the other. "Why don't I put these in water for you, sweetheart? You don't happen to have a vase, do you?"

"Somewhere."

"Of course."

Abra waited until Jessie went into the kitchen to search for it. Cautious, she kept her voice low. "What do you want?"

"To see you."

Abra's hands tightened into fists in her pockets when he rose. "You've done that. Now, if you'll excuse me, I'm busy this evening."

"And to apologize," Cody continued.

She hesitated, then let out a long breath. She had gone to him once with an apology, and he had accepted. If there was one thing she understood, it was how difficult it was to try to mend fences temper had broken.

"It's all right," she said, and managed what she hoped was a casual smile. "Let's forget it."

"Wouldn't you like an explanation?" He took a step forward. She took one backward.

"I don't think so. It might be best if—"

"I found one." Jessie came back in holding a milk bottle. "So to speak. Actually, I think they look charming in this, don't you?" She set the flowers in the center of the coffee table, then stepped back to admire them. "Don't forget to change the water, Abra. And it wouldn't hurt to lift the vase up when you dust."

"Mom…"

"Mom? You've got to be kidding." The genuine astonishment in Cody's voice had Jessie beaming.

"That's the nicest compliment I've had all day," she said. "If I didn't love her so much, I'd deny it." Raising up on her toes, she kissed Abra's cheek, then brushed lightly at the faint smear of lipstick she left behind. "You two have a nice evening. Don't forget to call me."

"But you just got here."

"I've a million things to do." Jessie gave her daughter's hand a squeeze, then offered her own to Cody. "It was lovely meeting you."

"I hope I see you again, Mrs. Peters."

"Jessie." She smiled again. "I insist that all handsome men call me Jessie." The sweep of her lashes was the gesture of a practiced flirt. "Good night, sweetheart. Oh, you're almost out of dish detergent."

Abra let out a huff of breath when the door closed.

"Are you sure that's your mother?"

"Most of the time." Abra tunneled her fingers through her hair. Jessie always left her feeling bewildered. "Look, Cody, I appreciate you coming by to clear the air."

"Now clear out?"

"I don't want to be rude. I think both of us have used up our share of rudeness for this year, but it would simplify things if we kept our contact limited to working hours."

"I never said I wanted things simple." He took a step closer. Her eyes stayed warily on his as he toyed with the damp ends of her hair. "But if you do, fine. I look at you and I want. It doesn't get much simpler than that."

"For you." If it was difficult not to step away, it was much more difficult not to step forward. "I don't want to get into all of the reasons, but when I told you that I wasn't ready I was being perfectly honest. Added to that is the fact that we just don't get along very well. We don't know each other. We don't understand each other."

"All right. So we'll get to know each other."

"You're simplifying."

"Isn't that what you just said you wanted?"

Feeling trapped, she turned away and sat down. "Cody, I told you, I have reasons for not wanting to get involved with you, with anyone."

"Let's just stick with me." He sat across from her. For the life of him he couldn't understand why he was so keyed up. He had very little time or energy to put into a relationship at this point in his life. He certainly wasn't looking for one. He corrected himself. Hadn't been. This one, one he couldn't seem to resist, had crashed onto his head. "Okay, Wilson, why don't we look at this logically? Engineers are logical people, right?"

"We are." She wished the flowers weren't sitting so bright and lovely between them.

"We have to work together for a few months yet. If there's tension between people, they don't work well. If we keep walking on eggshells around each other the way we have been the last couple weeks, the project's going to suffer."

"Okay, you have a point." She smiled. "But I'm not going to go to bed with you to ease the tension."

"And I thought you were dedicated." He sat back and braced his ankle on his knee. "If that's out…" He raised a questioning brow.

"Definitely."

"How about pizza and a movie?"

She started to speak, then stopped. She was logical. She was trained to take facts to the correct conclusion. "Nothing else?"

"That would depend."

"No." Shaking her head, Abra lifted her mother's untouched lemonade. "I prefer to deal in absolutes. If we agree to get to know each other, to try to develop a professional and a personal relationship, I have to know that the personal relationship will remain on a certain level. So we set ground rules."

He lifted a brow. "Should I get out my notepad?"

"If you like," she said mildly. "But I think we can keep it simple. We can see each other, as friends, as associates. No romantic situations."

Amused, Cody watched her. "Define 'romantic situation.'"

"I think you get the picture, Johnson. You're right in the sense that we are working closely together. If either one of us is in a snit, the work suffers. A personal understanding and respect can only lead to better professional communication."

"You ought to write that down for the next staff meeting." He held up a hand before she could snap at him. "Okay, we'll give it a shot your way. Pals." He leaned over and offered his hand. When she took it, he grinned. "Guess I'll have to take back the flowers."

"Oh, no. You gave them to me before we set the rules." She rose, pleased with herself. "I'll buy the pizza. You spring for the movie."

It was going to work. Over the next few days Abra congratulated herself on taking a potentially volatile situation and making it into a pleasant arrangement. There were times, inevitably, that they rubbed each other the wrong way on the job. When they saw each other after working hours, they met as casual friends to enjoy a meal or a show. If she caught herself longing for more after she dropped Cody at his hotel or he left her at her apartment, she smothered the need.

Little by little she learned more about him, about the farm he had grown up on, about his struggle to finish his education. He didn't speak of the financial hardships or the backbreaking hours he'd had to put in, but she was able, as their time together went on, to hear what he didn't say through what he did.

It changed her view of him. She'd seen him as a pampered, privileged partner in a top architectural firm. She hadn't considered the fact that he had worked his way up to where he was in much the same way she had. Abra admired ambition when it was married with drive and old-fashioned hard labor.

She was more careful than he about giving away pieces of her private life. She spoke easily about her years with Thornway and about her admiration for the man who had given her her chance. But she never mentioned her family or her childhood. Though he noted the shield, Cody made no attempt to pierce it. What was growing between them was still fragile. He had no intention of pushing harder until a firm foundation had been laid.

If Abra was pleased with herself and the arrangement, Cody was growing more and more frustrated. He wanted to touch her—a fingertip to her cheek, a hand to her hair. He knew that if he made even so gentle a move the tenuous thread that was spinning between them would snap. Time and again he told himself to back off completely, to call a halt to their platonic evenings. But he couldn't. Seeing her, spending time with her, had become a habit too strong to break.

Still, he was beginning to think that whoever had said half a loaf was better than none hadn't known anything about real hunger.

Hands on hips, Abra stood and watched the crew of engineers and mechanics work on the mechanism for the sliding roof. The envelope for the glass was completed, and the glass itself would be installed at the end of the week. The sun beat mercilessly down on the smoothed concrete while she worried over her design like a mother hen.

"Darling!"

"Mom?" Her concentration broken, Abra managed to smooth her frown into a smile. "What are you doing here?"

"You talk about this place so much, I thought it was time I came to see for myself." She tilted her hard hat at a jaunty angle. "I talked Mr. Blakerman into giving me just a smidgen longer for my lunch hour." She linked arms with her daughter as they stood in the stream of sunlight. "Abra, this place is fabulous. Absolutely fabulous. Of course, I don't know anything about these things, and all those little places over there look like a bunch of stick houses in heaps of dirt."

"Those are the cabanas."

"Whatever. But that big building I saw when I drove in. Incredible. It looks like a castle out of the twenty-fourth century."

"That about sums it up."

"I've never seen anything like it before. It's so alluring, so majestic. Just the way I've always thought of the desert."

Abra glanced back at her mother. "Really?"

"Oh, yes. I can tell you, when I first saw it I could hardly believe my own little girl had a part in something so, well…grand." She beamed as she inspected the empty pool, which was even now being faced with mosaic tiles. She didn't miss the tanned, muscular arms of the laborers, either. "Why, it's shaped like a half-moon. How clever. Everything's curved and arched, isn't it? It makes for a relaxed tone, don't you think? Just the right effect for a resort."

"I suppose," Abra murmured, hating to admit that she was beginning to see the appeal of it herself.

"What goes up there?"

Frowning again, Abra looked up through the roof at the hard blue sky. "Glass, movable glass. It'll be tinted to filter the sunlight. When it's opened, the two panels will separate and slide into the curve of the walls."

"Wonderful. I'd love to see it when it's finished. Do you have time to show me around, or should I just wander?"

"I can't leave just now. If you can—"

"Oh, look, there's your architect." Jessie automatically smoothed her skirt. She had already zeroed in on the shorter, broader man who was walking beside Cody. "And who's that distinguished-looking man with your beau?"

"He's not my beau." Abra took a swift look around to be certain no one had heard Jessie's remark. "I don't have or want a beau."

"That's why I worry about you, sweetheart."

Patience, Abra told herself. She would be patient. "Cody Johnson is my associate."

"Whatever you say, darling. But who's that with him?"

"That's Mr. Barlow. It's his resort."

"Really?" Jessie was already aiming a smile at Cody and holding out both hands. "Hello again. I was just telling Abra how much I like your design. I'm sure this is going to be the most beautiful resort in the state."

"Thank you. William Barlow, this is Abra's mother, Jessie Peters."

"Mother?" Barlow's bushy brows rose. He'd already tried, and failed, to suck in his stomach. "I didn't know Abra was only sixteen."

Jessie gave a delighted laugh. "I hope you don't mind my popping in like this, Mr. Barlow. I've been dying to see what Abra's been working on so long and hard. Now that I have, I'm convinced it's been worth it."

"We're very pleased with Abra's work. You can be proud of her."

"I've always been proud of Abra." Her lashes swept down, then up. "But tell me, Mr. Barlow, how did you ever imagine putting a resort here, and such a beautiful one?"

"That's a long story."

"Oh." Jessie sent a rueful look at Abra. "Well, I know I'm keeping everyone from their work. I'd hoped Abra could give me a little tour, but that will have to wait."

"Perhaps you'll allow me to show you around."

"I'd love it." Jessie put a hand on Barlow's beefy arm. "But I don't want to be in the way."

"Nonsense." Barlow gave her hand a quick pat. "We'll just leave everything in capable hands and have a nice stroll."

They started off, with Jessie sending a fleeting smile over her shoulder.

"There she goes again," Abra muttered.

"Hmm?"

"Nothing." With her hands jammed into her pockets, Abra turned away to watch her men. It disturbed her, and always had, to watch her mother in action. "We should have the wiring and supports finished by the end of the day."

"Good. Now do you want to tell me what's bugging you?"

Bad-temperedly she shrugged off the hand he put on her shoulder. "I said nothing. We had some problems with the angle."

"You've worked it out."

"At considerable time and expense."

They were going to fight. Knowing it, Cody rubbed the bridge of his nose between his thumb and forefinger. "Don't you get tired of singing the same song?"

"With a slight change in degrees—"

"It would have changed the look, and the feel."

"A fly stuck on the glass wouldn't have noticed the changes I wanted."

"I would have noticed."

"You were being obstinate."

"No," Cody said slowly, struggling to pace his words well behind his temper. "I was being right."

"Stubborn. The same way you were being stubborn when you insisted we had to use solid sheets of glass rather than panes."

Without a word, Cody took her arm and dragged her away.

"What the hell are you doing?"

"Just shut up." With Abra dragging her heels, he pulled her down the steps into the empty pool. Laborers glanced over, tiles in hand, and grinned. Taking her face in his hands, he pushed her head back. "What do you see?"

"Sky, damn it. And if you don't let go you're going to see stars."

"That's right. Sky. That's what I want you to see. Whether the roof's open or whether it's closed. Not panes of glass, not a window, not a roof, but sky. It's my job to imagine, Wilson, and yours to make it work."

She shrugged out of his hold. The sides of the pool rose around them. If the water had been added, it would have been well over her head. For now the pool was like an arena.

"Let me tell you something, hotshot. Not everything that can be imagined can be engineered. Maybe that's not what people like you want to hear, but that's the way it is."

"You know the trouble with you, Red? You're too hung up to dream, too buttoned into your columns and calculations. Two and two always make four in your head, no matter how much better life might be if once in a while it came up five."

"Do you know how crazy that sounds?"

"Yeah. And I also know it sounds intriguing. Why

don't you take a little time out to wonder why not instead of always assuming the negative?"

"I don't assume anything. I just believe in reality."

"This is reality," he said, grabbing her. "The wood, the glass, the steel, the sweat. That's reality. And damn it, so is this."

He clamped his mouth onto hers before either of them had a chance to think. Work around them stopped for ten humming seconds. Neither of them noticed. Neither of them cared. Abra discovered that, though the pool was indeed empty, she was still in over her head.

She'd wanted this. There was no denying it now, not when his lips were hot and demanding on hers. She curled her fingers into his work shirt, but not in protest. In possession. She held him close as the need spiraled high inside her, very fast and, yes, very real.

He hadn't meant to touch her this way, to take what he had tried to convince himself she would give him in her own time. Patience had always been an integral part of his nature—the knowing when, the knowing how. But with her none of the old rules seemed to apply.

Perhaps if her response hadn't been so complete, if he hadn't tasted desire warm and waiting on her lips, he could have pulled back. But, like Abra, he was in over his head and sinking fast. For the first time in his life he wanted to sweep a woman up and away like some knight on a white charger. He wanted just as badly to drag her to the ground and have her like a primitive warrior reaping the spoils of victory. He wanted, like a poet, to light the candles and set the music. Most of all, he wanted Abra.

When he drew her away, she was dazed and speechless. He had kissed her before and sent the passion swimming. But there was something different, something deeper, something desperate, about this. For a moment she could only stand and stare at him, giddy with the knowledge that a woman could fall in love anywhere, anytime, even when she had barricaded her heart against it.

"That real enough for you?" Cody murmured.

She only shook her head as the buzzing in her brain cleared and separated into sounds. The whirl of drills, the slap of trowels, the murmur of men. The color rose into her cheeks quickly, and with it a combination of fury, embarrassment and self-reproach.

"How dare you do something like that here?"

He hooked his thumbs in his pockets when he realized he was still angry enough to do something rash and regrettable. "You got someplace else in mind?"

"Keep away from me, Johnson," she said under her breath. "Or you'll find yourself hauled up on sexual harassment charges."

His eyes remained very calm and very level. "We both know that what happened here has nothing to do with harassment, sexual or otherwise. It's personal, Red, and keeping my distance isn't going to make it go away."

"Fine," she said, going toe-to-toe with him. The argument interested the men around them almost as much as the kiss had. "If it's personal, let's keep it that way. Off the job, Johnson. I'm on Thornway time, and I don't intend to waste it arguing with you."

"Good."

"Good," she echoed, scrambling up the steps and out of the pool.

Cody rocked back on his heels as she stormed out of the building. They would both be off the clock soon enough.

Chapter 6

It was nearly five when Abra stopped by the trailer to splash cold water on her face. After her scene with Cody it seemed as if everything that could go wrong had. A part for the elevators had proved defective, and then there had been another tiff between Rodriguez and Swaggart. One of the carpenters had gotten a splinter in his eye, and Tim had dropped by the site to moan about the budget.

It had all started with her mother's visit, Abra thought as she wiped her dripping face with a towel. It wasn't fair to blame Jessie, but no matter when, no matter where, she was a woman who trailed complications behind her, then waited for other people to clear them up.

Maybe it wasn't right to resent the fact that her mother had hit it off so well with Barlow or to worry about the fallout. But history had a habit of repeating itself. The last thing Abra wanted added to her plate was the possibility of a romance between the owner of the project and her very susceptible mother.

Better to worry about her, Abra decided as she gathered up a load of files to take home. Jessie's varied and colorful love life was much safer to fret over than her own.

She didn't have a love life, Abra reminded herself. She didn't want a love life. Her plans, personal and professional, were all mapped out. She wasn't about to let some high-handed Florida cowboy botch them up.

What the hell had he been thinking of?

The moment the thought ran through her head, she grimaced and kicked the door open. She knew very well what he'd been thinking of, because she'd been thinking of exactly the same thing.

Rockets exploding, volcanoes erupting, tornadoes swirling. It was difficult to think of anything but power and chaos when she was in Cody's arms.

Was it that way for him, too? she wondered as she locked the trailer door. Did he lose part of himself when they came together? Did everything and everyone fade away until they seemed—no, until they *were* totally unimportant?

Of course not, she decided, and gave in enough to rest her forehead against the side of the trailer. He was just another good-looking man with a glib tongue and clever hands. The world was full of them. God knew her mother had made a science out of the search and discovery.

Not fair, Abra thought again as she straightened. Jessie's life was Jessie's life. It wasn't fair to Cody, either, she admitted, shifting the files and starting toward her car. He had initiated the kiss, but she had done nothing to stop it. That made her behavior every bit as outrageous and unprofessional as his.

She should have stopped it. A dozen times through

the rest of the day she'd asked herself why she hadn't. It hadn't been shock, it hadn't even been overpowering lust. Though she would have preferred to lay the blame on either one. It had been... Just for a moment it had been as though something strange and wonderful and completely unexpected had happened. There had been more than need, more than passion, more than desire.

There had been a bang. Those rockets again, she thought ruefully, looking at the buttes, which were shadowed in the lowering sun. But with this bang something had shaken loose. She'd almost believed she had fallen in love.

Which was nonsense, of course. She dug in her pocket for her keys. She was far too levelheaded to take that route ever again. Nonsense or not, the idea was giving her some bad moments.

So, she wouldn't think about it. There were plenty of other problems to occupy her mind, and most of them were in the files she carried. With a little effort and a lot of concentration she could dig out the calculations, work the equations and find the solutions. Finding a solution to Cody was out of her sphere, so she would leave it alone and spare herself the headache.

She turned her head at the sound of a car and had another bad moment when she recognized the sporty little toy Cody had rented. He pulled up beside her, his car spewing dust, just as she yanked her own car door open.

He'd done his own share of thinking that afternoon and he'd come to his own decisions. Before she could slide behind the wheel, he was out and taking her arm.

"Let's go."

"I was just about to."

"We'll take my car."

"You take your car." She turned back to her own.

He took her keys and the files, pocketing the first and tossing the second into the back of his convertible. "Get in."

"What do you think you're doing?" Shoving him aside, she reached in to retrieve her files. "If you think I'm going anywhere with you, you need brain surgery."

"We always do it the hard way, don't we?" he said, and scooped her up.

"You are crazy." She nearly got an elbow into his ribs before she was dumped into the passenger seat. Fuming, she grabbed for the handle. His hand closed like a vise over hers as he waited for her to toss the hair out of her eyes and glare up at him. He leaned down close, and his voice was very soft.

"You get out of this car, Wilson, and I'll make you sorry."

"Give me my keys."

"Not a chance."

She considered the possibility of wrestling the keys from him. She was mad enough, but she knew when she was outweighed. Eyes narrowed, she met him look for look. "Fine. Then I'll walk up to the road and hitch a ride."

"You already have a ride." He stepped back to walk about the hood. Abra pushed the door open. She'd no more than gotten to her feet when he shoved her back again.

"You don't scare me, Johnson."

"I should. We're off the clock, Abra, and we've got business of our own. Personal business." Reaching down, he fastened her safety belt. "I'd keep that on. It could be a rough ride."

By the time she'd fumbled the catch open, he'd slid

behind the wheel. Wordlessly he jammed her belt back in its slot before he sent the car spinning up the road.

"What are you trying to prove?"

He turned off the construction road onto the highway. "I'm not sure yet. But we're going someplace quiet until I figure it out." Dust rose in plumes behind the car. It would take some time for it to settle. "The way I look at it, our first plan didn't pan out, so we go back to the drawing board."

Someplace quiet turned out to be his hotel. Abra's reaction was to slam out of the car and head across the parking lot. Cody simply picked her up and tossed her over his shoulder. Her stream of abuse trailed behind them to his door.

Cody unlocked it and pushed it open, then took the precaution of bolting it before dropping Abra into a chair.

"Want a drink?" he asked. Abra glared at him. "Well, I do." He went to the bar and opened a bottle of wine. "A chardonnay this time. Gold highlights, a bright flavor, a bit tart. You'll like it."

She could probably have made it to the door in a dash, but she was through running. Instead, she rose very slowly, very deliberately, out of the chair. "Do you know what I would like?" she asked in a surprisingly silky voice. The tone of it alerted him even as he drew out the cork. "Do you know what I would *really* like? To see you hanging by your thumbs over a large, open fire." She advanced toward him while he poured two glasses. "A big fire, Johnson, with just enough breeze to draw the smoke away so it wouldn't dull your senses." She slapped her palms on the bar and leaned her face close to his.

"Why don't you try the wine instead?"

She snatched for the glass, but he was quicker. His fingers wrapped firmly around hers. "Red," he said in a reasonable tone, "if you pour this on me, I'm going to have to beat you up."

She jerked the glass away and downed the contents in one swallow. "Thanks for the drink." She made it to the door, dignity intact, but he was there beside her before she could unlock it.

"You'll never learn to appreciate good wine that way." Pulling her back, he shoved her into a chair. "Now sit," he told her. "We can talk this through or I can go with my more primitive instincts. Up to you."

"We have nothing to talk about."

"Fine." As quickly as he'd pushed her into the chair, he hauled her out of it. She managed one sputter of protest before she was swirled into his arms.

He kissed her as though he meant to go on kissing her forever. His mouth was hard, but skilled rather than punishing as it demanded and received response. One hand was caught in her hair, while the other roamed freely. Up and over her it stroked in one long, firm line of possession, discovering her slenderness, her softness, her weaknesses and her strengths. He'd never touched her like this before, and the result stunned both of them.

She was so alive. He could all but feel her pulse through his fingertips. An energy fueled by passion raced through her, leaving him dazed and desperate. There was no one else who had ever set off this combination of needs and sensations inside him.

No one had ever made her feel this way. No one. It terrified her. It delighted her. It was easy, almost too easy, to forget the rules she had set up for their relationship, the reason for them, and the anger he had set boiling in her only moments before. There was only now and the way her body experienced dozens of tiny explosions wherever he touched—wherever she wanted him to go on touching. With a murmur of confused pleasure, she shifted against him and offered more.

Behind them, the phone began to ring. They ignored it and listened to the pounding of their own hearts.

Cody broke away to bury his face in her hair and catch his breath. Another first, he thought. He couldn't think of another woman who had left him breathless.

He held her at arm's length to study her face. Her eyes were big and clouded and very green. He decided she looked every bit as stunned as he felt. If they moved on impulse now, their already shaky foundation would crumble.

"We'd better talk."

She nodded and sank into a chair, wondering if the strength would ever seep back into her legs. "Okay."

Turning to the bar, he poured more wine into her glass. His hand wasn't steady. Cody wondered if he'd find the energy to laugh about that later. He gave her a glass, then took his own to the chair facing hers.

She looked at him then, as she had refused to before. His hair was ruffled by the fast ride in the open car. Hours in the sun had streaked it and deepened his tan. Still, he didn't make her think of a laid-back beach-comber now. There was a sense of movement about him even when he was sitting—arrested, held in check, but ready. The energy was there, and a power she'd already experienced firsthand. If they crossed swords again while this mood was on him, she would lose.

After a long breath, she sipped. "You wanted to talk."

He had to laugh. It helped somehow to diffuse the worst of his tension. "Yeah. That was the idea."

"I don't appreciate being hauled in here this way."

He settled back but discovered that relaxing wasn't as easy as it had once been. "Would you have come if I'd asked nice?"

Her lips curved briefly. "No. But that doesn't give you the right to turn into a Cro-Magnon and haul me off by the hair."

The image of dragging Abra into a cave had a certain appeal at the moment, but she had a point. "It's not my usual style. Want an apology?"

"I think we've already passed around enough of those. You wanted to talk." She thought she was on firmer ground now. "Since I'm here, we'll talk."

"You look great in overalls, Red."

With a shake of her head, she started to rise. "If that's all—" But he held up a hand.

"I think it's fair to say that the plans we laid out about keeping our personal relationship impersonal are pretty well washed up."

Abra stared into the wine in her glass. When facts were facts, she wasn't one to evade them. "I guess that's fair."

She didn't look too thrilled by the admission, he thought, fumbling for a match. He nearly swore at his own clumsiness. Even when he dragged smoke into his lungs, all he could taste was her. "So, where do we go from here?"

She looked up then. Her eyes were calm again, calm and direct. Whatever fears were swirling inside her were carefully controlled. "You seem to have all the answers."

"Abra—" He stopped himself, knowing it would do no good to lose his temper again or to demand more than she was ready to give. "You'd like to keep things simple." He took a sip of his wine. "Do I have that right?"

Simple? she thought wildly. Things would never be

simple again. Her fingers tightened on the stem of her glass, and she deliberately relaxed them. He looked so in control. "Yes. I can't imagine that either of us have time for complications at this point in our lives."

Complications. He nearly sprang out of the chair and grabbed her to show her just how complicated things already were. She looked so composed. "Then we'll deal with the facts. Fact one, I want you." He saw something—passion, fear, hope—flicker in her eyes. "Fact two, you want me." He took a moment to crush out his cigarette. "Now, if we work with those two factors and add the information that neither of us are kids, that we're both responsible adults who are smart enough to approach a relationship intellectually, as well as emotionally, we should come up with, as you said, a simple answer."

She didn't want to be intellectual. She didn't want to be smart. It had taken his practical recitation of the facts to make her realize that she just wanted to open up her arms and her heart and take him in. The hell with facts and plans and simple answers.

That was Jessie talking, Abra reminded herself as she cooled her dry throat with the wine. What worked for Jessie was never going to work for her.

She looked at Cody over the rim of her glass. He seemed so relaxed, so at ease. She couldn't see the tension that had his muscles stretched and humming like wire. She only saw the faint amusement in his eyes and the easy way he sprawled in the chair.

"Want me to run through it again for you, Red?"

"No." She set the glass aside and folded her hands. "A simple answer. We have an affair."

He didn't like the cool way she said it, as though it meant no more than the letters it took to make up the word. Yet when you cut through to the core of it, wasn't that what he wanted? To be with her. Still, it hurt, and that amazed him.

"When do you want to get started?"

His curt response had her curling her fingers hard into her palms. She had opened the door, Abra reminded herself. Now it was time to face it. "I think it's best we understand each other first. We don't let our personal life interfere with the job."

"God forbid."

Taking a deep breath, she pressed on. "It's important that we go into this knowing there are no strings, no regrets, no long-term demands. In a few weeks you'll go back to Florida and I'll stay here. It won't do either of us any good to pretend otherwise, or to act as though what we're beginning isn't going to end."

"That's clear enough," he said, toying with the idea of strangling her for being so cool, so aloof, when all he wanted to do was make love with her until they both stopped breathing. "Obviously you've been through this before."

She didn't answer. She didn't have to. Before she lowered her eyes he saw them go bleak.

"What's this?" Rising, he moved over to crouch beside her. "Someone break your heart, Red?"

"I'm glad you're amused," she began, but he cut her off by touching a hand to her cheek.

"I'm not." He curled his fingers around hers before bringing them to his lips. "I don't expect to be the first man in your life, but I'm sorry someone hurt you. Was it bad?"

The last thing she'd expected from him was sensitivity. It brought tears to her eyes that had much less to do with the past than with the present. "I don't want to talk about it."

Some wounds scar over, he thought, and others fester. He intended to find out just how deep this one had cut, but he could wait. "All right. Let's try this. Have dinner with me."

She blinked back her tears and managed a smile. "I'm not dressed to go out to dinner."

"Who said anything about going out?" Leaning over, he teased her lips with his. "Didn't you say something about liking hotels because you could order room service and eat dinner in bed?"

"Yeah." She laid a hand on his face and let herself drift with the kiss.

"I'll let you use my shower and drop the towels on the floor."

Her lips curved against his. It was going to be all right. She could almost believe it. "Sounds like a pretty good deal."

"You won't get a better one." Still holding her hand, he brought her to her feet. "You didn't mention anything about promises in your blueprints."

"I guess I missed that one."

"Then I get to make you one."

"Cody—"

He touched his lips to hers. It was his gentleness that stopped her words. It was her softness that made him speak. "Just one. I won't hurt you, Abra."

He meant it. She could see that clearly when she looked into his eyes. Too late, she thought, leaning her cheek against his. The heart she had tried so hard to hold on to was lost to him irrevocably. He was bound to hurt her now, though he would try not to. She could never let him know.

When the phone rang this time, they both heard it. Still holding Abra against him, Cody reached down for the receiver.

"Johnson." He listened a moment while he skimmed his lips over Abra's temple. "Lefkowitz, anyone ever tell you you're a pain in the neck?" Reluctantly he let Abra go and gave his attention to the phone. "You were put in charge there because we thought you could handle complications like that. You got the specs? Well, read them." Swearing, he shifted the phone to his other hand. "I hear what you're saying. Give me the number and I'll deal with it from here. Modify those blueprints and I'll break your fingers. Clear? Good. I'll take the first plane out."

When he hung up, Abra offered him his wine. "You're real smooth, Johnson."

"I leave tact and diplomacy to my partner, Nathan."

"Good thing." She toyed with her own glass and tried to be casual. "Taking a trip?"

"San Diego. Why we thought a pinhead like Lefkowitz could handle a job like that is beyond me. The man redefines the word *inept*." He moved to the closet and pulled out a small bag. "Some hotshot engineer's telling him he has to make changes in the design, and now a supplier's balking and he hasn't got the sense to bash their heads together and get on with it."

"Your design?" she asked, grinning.

"Mostly." He grabbed her braid and tugged hard enough to make her squeal. "Why don't you come with me, Wilson? You can point out all the reasons the engineer's right and I'm wrong, and then I can show you the ocean."

It was tempting—so tempting that she nearly said yes before she remembered she had a job to do. "I can't.

There's no way both of us can leave the project." She turned away and tried not to show how much it mattered. "So, how long will you be gone?"

"A day or two—unless I murder Lefkowitz and stand trial. Abra." He put his hands on her shoulders and drew her gently back against him. "Is it against the rules for you to miss me?"

She turned around, covering one of his hands with hers. "I'll try to work it in."

He pulled her against him and kissed her until they were both clinging. He had an image of sinking onto the bed with her and letting the night take care of itself but, like Abra, he understood responsibility too well.

"I have to toss a few things into a bag and get to the airport. I'll drop you back by your car."

"Sure."

When she stepped back, he kept his hands on her shoulders. It was funny, he thought. Never before in his life had he thought twice about hopping a plane or moving from place to place. Somehow, in the last few minutes, he'd grown roots. "I owe you a shower—and room service."

He wasn't going off to war, Abra reminded herself. It was a business trip. There would come a time when he would board a plane and fly out of her life. This wasn't it. "We'll settle accounts when you get back."

It took three days, and that infuriated him. The only thing that saved Lefkowitz was the fact that the resolutions took more time and trouble than Cody had anticipated. Now he was cooling his heels in another hotel room and waiting until it was time to catch his plane. His bag was packed, but there was one item he carried in his pocket—a choker he'd bought for Abra. Cody took it out now and studied it.

It had been a whim, a glance in a jeweler's window as he'd walked to an appointment. They weren't icy white diamonds, but delicate blue-green "fancy" stones the color of the sea. The moment he'd seen them, he'd thought of her.

Closing the lid, he dropped the box back into his pocket. He didn't suppose it was the kind of token two people involved in a casual affair exchanged. The problem for him—maybe for both of them—was that his feelings for Abra were anything but casual.

He hadn't been in love before, but he recognized the symptoms.

She wasn't ready to hear it, he mused. For that matter, he wasn't ready to say it. Words like *love* changed the scope of lives, the same way a single window could change the scope of a wall.

And it might pass. He knew people who fell in and out of love as if they were bobbing for apples. That wasn't for him. If it was true, and if it was real, he intended to make it last. He didn't design without making certain the building would stand the test of time. How could he do less with his own life?

With a glance at his watch, he noted that he had more than two hours before his flight. Dropping onto the bed, he plucked up the phone and called Abra. When he heard the connection click, he opened his mouth to speak. Her smooth recorded voice sounded in his ears.

"You've reached Abra Wilson. I'm sorry I can't take your call right now, but if you'll leave a message and the date and time you called, I'll get back to you as soon as possible. Thanks."

He was scowling at his watch and wondering why

the hell she wasn't home when the recorder beeped. "Hi. You sound good, Red, but I'd rather talk to you in person. Listen, if you get in before seven, give me a call here at the hotel. I, ah… I hate these damn things. Don't get crazy or anything, but I missed you. A lot. Get home, will you?"

He hung up and, unsatisfied, dialed another number. The voice that answered was feminine—and real. "Hi, Jack. Cody."

"Cody. Did you get me the stuff I wanted on Monument Valley?"

"Nice to talk to you, too, Jack."

"Sorry." She laughed and changed her tone. "Cody, how the heck are you? It's great to hear from you."

"Thanks. By the way, I mailed off about ten pounds of pamphlets, pictures, souvenir books and assorted historical information on Arizona."

"My life for you. I'm halfway through the revisions on *Lawless* and I needed some more information. I do appreciate it."

"Anytime. I like being tight with a famous novelist."

"I'm not famous yet. Give me a few more months. The historical isn't coming out until May. How's Arizona?"

"It's fine, but right now I'm in San Diego."

"San Diego?" He heard the sound of pots clattering and envisioned her in the kitchen creating some exotic meal. "Oh, that's right, I forgot. Cody… I wonder if you could pick me up some—"

"Give me a break, Jackie. Are you fat yet?"

He could almost see her running a hand over her growing belly. "Getting there. Nathan went with me last week for my exam and heard the baby's heartbeat."

She chuckled again, warmly. "He hasn't been the same since."

"Is he there?"

"You just missed him. I wanted some fresh dill for dinner. He had the idea that my going out and buying it would tire the baby, so he went himself."

"Nathan wouldn't know dill from dandelions."

"I know." There was a wealth of love in those two words. "Isn't it wonderful? When are you coming back?"

"I don't know. I'm, ah…considering staying out here until the project's finished."

"Really?" She paused a moment. "Cody, do I detect a purpose other than creative control?"

He hesitated. Stupid, he thought. He hadn't called to discuss the medical complex or the resort or any other project. He'd called to talk to a friend. "There's a woman."

"No! Just one?"

He had to smile. "Just one."

"Sounds serious."

"Could be."

Because she knew him, Jackie saw through his casual air. "When am I going to meet her? You know, give her the third degree, look her over, pick her apart? Is she another architect? Wait, I know. She's a graduate student moonlighting as a cocktail waitress."

"She's an engineer."

It was several seconds before Jackie could speak. "Are you kidding? You hate them more than Nathan does. Good grief, it must be love."

"Either that or sunstroke. Listen, Jack, I wanted to let Nathan know I'd cleaned things up here and I'm heading back to Phoenix."

"I'll let him know. Cody, are you happy?"

He paused a moment, discovering there wasn't a yes-or-no answer to that. "That's going to depend on the engineer. I'll give it to you straight. I'm crazy about her, but she's dragging her heels."

"If she messes with you, I'm going to fly out and break her slide rule."

"Thanks. That ought to keep her in line. I'll keep in touch."

"You do that. And, Cody, good luck."

It was nearly nine before Abra got in. She'd had a nice, long, talky meal with her mother. That sort of thing always left her of two minds. The first was amusement, pure and simple. Jessie was great company, funny, absurd and easy to be with. No one made a better friend.

The other was worry. Those same qualities made Jessie what she was, a free spirit, a take-it-as-it-comes woman who danced from man to man without collecting any bruises. Her newest partner was W. W. Barlow—or, as her mother had taken to calling him, Willie.

Jessie had been full of him during dinner. How sweet he was, how cute, how attentive. Abra knew the signs. Jessie Wilson Milton Peters was in for another run.

Rubbing the back of her neck, Abra tossed her purse aside and stepped out of her shoes as she crossed the living room. How was she supposed to keep a professional outlook on the job if her mother was having an affair with the owner? With a laugh, she scanned the mail she'd brought in with her, then tossed that aside, as well. How was she supposed to keep that same outlook if she herself was having an affair with the architect of record?

Life had gotten very complicated in a very short time. She would back out if she could. One of the things she was best at was untangling herself from uncomfortable situations. The trouble was, she was almost sure she was in love with him. That made it more than a situation—it made it a crisis. She'd thought she was in love once before, but...

There were no buts, Abra told herself. Just because this was more intense than anything she'd ever known, just because she couldn't seem to go more than five minutes without thinking of him, that didn't make this any different from what had happened to her years before.

Except that this time she was older and smarter and better prepared.

No one was ever going to do to her what Jamie Frye had done. She was never going to feel that small or that useless again. If love was a crisis, she could deal with it the same way she dealt with any crisis on the job. Calmly, thoroughly, efficiently. It would be different with Cody, because they were meeting on equal terms, with the rules set out clearly for both of them to read. And he was different. That much she was sure of. He wasn't shallow and insensitive, as Jamie had proved himself to be. Hardheaded, maybe. Infuriating, certainly. But there was no cruelty in him. And, she believed, no dishonesty.

When he hurt her, which she had already accepted he would do, it would happen suddenly and without intent. Hurts healed; she knew that well. She would have no reason to look back on whatever time they had together with regret or self-recrimination.

Abra shook herself. She had to stop thinking about him, or she would work herself into the blues because he wasn't there. What she needed was a nice strong cup of coffee and an hour at the drawing board.

She changed into a basketball jersey for comfort,

then settled down with the hot coffee, her mind open to ideas. It was then that she noticed the message light blinking on her answering machine.

Pressing the button, Abra bit into one of the stale cookies she'd dug out of a cupboard. The first call was from a college friend she hadn't seen for weeks. Abra made a note to return the call in the morning. The second was from Tim's secretary, setting a meeting for Monday morning. Grumbling a bit, Abra scrawled a reminder on her calender. Then she heard Cody's voice and forgot everything else.

"...if you get in before seven..."

Abra looked at her watch and sighed. It was well past that. He probably had late meetings. Even if she called the hotel she wouldn't reach him. Cupping her chin, she listened to his voice.

"...I missed you. A lot."

Ridiculously pleased, she rewound the tape and listened to the entire message again. Even though she called herself a fool, she rewound it a second time, then a third.

She worked a little and dreamed a lot during the next hour. Her coffee grew cold. Abra ran figures, then planned out how she would welcome Cody home. She'd have to go out and buy something wonderful. Tomorrow was Saturday. Surely he'd be home by the next evening, or by Sunday morning at the latest. That meant hours, and perhaps even an entire day, without the pressure of work to interfere.

She would stop by one of those fancy little boutiques the first thing in the morning and buy some glorious concoction of silk and lace. Something sexy and soft and irresistible. She'd go have a facial. Wasn't Jessie always touting the wonders of her beauty salon? Not just a fa-

cial, Abra decided. She'd go for the works. Hair, nails—
what there were of them—skin, everything. When Cody
got back, she'd look fantastic. Definitely black silk, she
decided. A skimpy teddy or a sheer, elegant chemise.

She'd need some wine. What the devil was that brand
he'd told her about? She'd have to throw herself on the
mercy of the clerk in the wine shop around the corner.
And flowers. Rising, Abra looked at her bedroom for the
first time in days. Good God, she was going to have to
clean up. Candles. She probably had candles somewhere.
Caught up in her own fantasy, she began to gather up
clothes and shoes. When a knock interrupted, she tossed
an armful in the closet and slammed it closed.

"All right, I'm coming." Where in the hell was her
robe? She found it crumpled under the bed and struggled one arm into it as she ran to the door. "Who is it?"

"Three guesses."

"Cody?"

"Right the first time," he told her as she pulled at the
security chain. She yanked open the door and stared at
him. Grinning, he took a long, lazy look.

Her hair was tied back with a broken shoestring. The
makeup she'd applied for dinner with her mother had
long since been scrubbed off. Her robe dangled open,
revealing the oversize basketball jersey, which skimmed
her thighs.

"Hiya, Red. Wanna shoot some hoops?"

Chapter 7

Abra blinked, wondering if he was a mirage. "What are you doing here?"

"Standing in the hallway. Are you going to let me in?"

"Yes, but—" She stepped back, and he came in and dropped his flight bag on the floor. Mirages didn't look this good. Or smell this good. Confused, she glanced back toward the bedroom and the phone machine. "I just got your message. You didn't say you were back."

"I wasn't." Since she didn't seem to be in any hurry to do so, he shut the door himself. "Now I am."

She thought of the plans she had been making. Taking a quick look around her jumbled apartment, Abra ran a helpless hand through her hair. "You should have told me you were coming back tonight. I wasn't— I'm not ready."

"What's the matter, Wilson?" To please himself, he put his hands on her shoulders, then ran them slowly up and down her arms, gradually pushing her robe aside.

She was definitely giving him a whole new perspective on athletic wear. "Got another man under the bed? In the closet?"

"Don't be stupid." Frustrated, she pulled back. She knew her face was scrubbed as clean as a baby's. And her hair—she didn't need a mirror to know that was hopeless. Then there was the green-and-white jersey. Hardly the sophisticated, seductive lingerie she'd envisioned. "Damn it, Cody, you should have let me know you were coming."

He checked an impulse to gather her up and shut her up. Maybe he'd let himself get carried away thinking she'd be as glad to see him as he was to see her. And maybe he shouldn't have assumed she'd be waiting patiently and alone for him to come back.

"I might have," he said slowly, "if I'd gotten you instead of a recording. Where were you?"

"When? Oh." Her mind still racing, she shook her head. "I was out to dinner."

"I see." He stuck his hand in his pocket, and it knocked against the jeweler's box. He didn't have any claims on her. *The hell he didn't.* "Anyone I know?"

"My mother," she said absently. "What are you grinning at?"

"Nothing."

Her chin came up as she snatched at the sleeve of her robe. "I know how I look, Johnson. If you'd given me any warning at all I could have done something about it. The place is a wreck."

"It's always a wreck," he pointed out. It was all beginning to seep in. She'd wanted to set the stage, and he'd come in ahead of his cue.

"I could have cleaned up a little." Scowling, she kicked a shoe aside. "I only have lousy wine."

"Well, in that case, I'd better go." He turned away, then turned back as if he'd had a sudden thought. "Before I do, I have something to say about the way you look."

Abra folded her arms, and the glint was back in her eyes. "Watch your step."

"I guess there's only one way to handle this honestly." He stepped toward her and put a friendly hand on her shoulder. "You do want us to be honest with each other, don't you, Abra?"

"Maybe," she muttered. "Well, to a point."

"I've got to tell you something, and you should be tough enough to take it."

"I can take it." She started to shrug his hand away. "I wish you'd—"

Whatever she wished would have to wait. He jerked her forward and crushed her mouth with his. She tasted heat, waves of it that only increased when her lips parted on a half moan. In one quick movement he stripped the robe from her, then took his hands up and under the thin jersey to explore naked skin and subtle curves. Gasping, she strained against his rough hands. Then she was clinging, her knees buckling, as he sent her arrowing to the edge.

"Cody..."

"Shut up," he murmured before he pressed his lips to her throat.

"'Kay." She could manage no more than a moan as his fingers dug into her hips. Her head was spinning, but underneath the dazed pleasure was an urgency every bit as great as his. She tugged at his jacket as they began to work their way across the room. "I want you," she whispered, yanking his shirt up and over his head. In one quick, possessive stroke, she ran her hands up his chest. "Now."

Her desperate murmur triggered explosions inside him. He'd thought he'd be ready for them, but anticipation and reality were worlds apart. Desire became raw, impatient, primitive. For both, the bedroom was too far away. When they tumbled onto the couch he was still half dressed, with each of them fighting to free him. Her hands were wild, digging into him, dragging over him, while she reared up to keep her mouth fused with his. He could feel the heat radiating from her, driving him farther and farther from sanity.

With a sudden oath, he pulled the jersey down, yanking it to her waist so that he could bury his mouth at her breast. With an abandonment she'd never known before, she arched against him, pressing him closer, welcoming the dangerous scrape of teeth and tongue.

The lights burned around them. In the apartment overhead someone turned a stereo up loud, and the bass vibrated in a low, passionate rhythm. The delicate fragrance she'd splashed on an hour before mingled with the musky scent of desire.

She was going to drive him crazy. That was all Cody could think as he followed the trail of her jersey down, farther down the smooth, taut skin of her torso. Everywhere he touched, everywhere he tasted, she responded with a ripe, huge pleasure that astonished him. She pulled at his hair, and the shuddering breaths she drew in were nearly sobs.

They'd waited too long—a lifetime. Now they were together—no more evasions, no more excuses. Only impatience.

When clothing was finally stripped away, her long, graceful limbs twined around him. She could no lon-

ger think, nor did she wish to. She wanted only to feel.
She wanted to murmur to him, something, anything that
would tell him what was happening inside her. But the
words wouldn't form. She had never wanted like this,
never needed like this. Her body felt like a furnace that
only he could stoke higher. There was a tremendous
ache building. Instinctively she reached out, half in delight, half in defense. As if he understood, he drove her
to a shuddering climax.

She gasped out his name and she felt herself falling,
endlessly, weightlessly. Even as she spiraled down he
caught her and sent her soaring again.

He could see her in the lamplight, her skin sheened
with moisture, her eyes dazed and open. Her hair was
spread out on the rug where they'd rolled. He tried to
say her name, but the air in his lungs burned like fire,
and the word flamed out like a curse when he crushed
her lips one last time.

He watched her peak again, felt her fingers dig ruthlessly into his back. Driven to the limit, he plunged into
her. She rose up to meet him with a speed that tore at
his already-tattered control.

Fast, hard, hot, they raced together to a place neither
of them had ever been.

Weakened, stunned, Cody collapsed onto her. He had
neither the energy nor the clearheadedness to separate
what had happened to him into individual actions, re-
actions, sensations. It was as though one huge bubble
of emotion had enclosed him and then burst, leaving
him drained.

She was as soft as water beneath him, her breathing
slow and shallow. He felt her hand slide off his back and
fall limply to the rug. Beneath his lips her heart beat

quickly, and he closed his eyes and let himself drift with the sound and the rhythm.

They didn't speak. Even if words had been possible, he wouldn't have known which ones to use to tell her what she had done to him. Done for him. He only knew that she belonged to him now and that he would do whatever was necessary to keep her.

Was this what love did? she wondered. Did it fill you with wild energy, then leave you so fragile that you thought you would dissolve from your own breathing? Anything she had ever felt before paled to insignificance compared to what she had experienced with Cody.

Everything had been new and almost unbearably intense. She hadn't had to think or plan or decipher. She'd only had to act on her own needs—needs she had successfully ignored until the first time he'd touched her.

It seemed he understood and accepted that. Just as it seemed he understood and accepted her. No one else ever had—not like this.

Was it love, she asked herself, or just the most overpowering of desires? Did it matter? She felt his fingers tangle in her hair and closed her eyes. It mattered—too much. Just a touch and she was tempted to toss away everything she believed, everything she'd planned, if only he would touch her again.

There was no point in denying what she felt for him, and she didn't have the courage to think about what he might feel for her.

He pressed a kiss to her throat. "You okay?"

"I don't know." It was an honest answer, she thought as she dragged in a deep, greedy breath. "I think so." Clearing her throat, she opened her eyes again. They were on the floor, she realized, wondering how they'd managed it. "How about you?"

"Fine. As long as I don't have to move for the next week or two." He turned his head so that he could nuzzle lazily at her neck. "Still mad?"

"I wasn't mad." The trace of his tongue along her already-sensitized skin had her shifting beneath him. "I just wanted things to be set up."

"Set up?" He shifted lazily to her ear.

"Yes. I was planning..." She let her words trail off as he skimmed his fingertip over her nipple. She started to say his name, but the word ended on a sigh as his lips teased hers.

"Amazing," he murmured as her slow, sinuous movements had him hardening inside her. "Absolutely amazing."

She was as astonished as he when passion leaped out again and took control.

Sometime during the night they fell into the bed, but they didn't sleep. It was as though in the few weeks they had known each other a mountain of needs had built and tonight it had come tumbling down in an avalanche. There was no music, no flicker of candles, no seduction of silk and lace. They came together without frills, without illusions.

Energy fed on energy, desire on desire. In the darkest hour of the night they fell into an exhausted sleep, only to wake with the first light of dawn hungry for more. Passions, though satisfied again and again, remained raw until, in a tangle of limbs, they slept.

She awoke with the sun full on her face and the bed empty beside her. Groggy, she stroked a hand over the sheet, murmuring.

"Cody?" Sighing, she opened her eyes and saw that she was alone.

Abra sat straight up, looking quickly around the room. She couldn't have dreamed it, she thought. No one could have dreamed that. Rubbing her hands over her face, she tried to think.

Could he have left her? Sometime during the morning could he just have strolled out as easily as he'd strolled in? And what if he had? she asked herself as she leaned back against the headboard. They had said no strings, no commitments. Cody was free to come and go as he chose, just as she was.

If it hurt, if it left her feeling empty and miserable, it was no one's fault but her own. The trouble, Abra thought, was that she always wanted more than she had. Closing her eyes, she reminded herself that she had just been given a night no woman would ever forget. If it wasn't enough, the lack was in her.

"I was hoping you'd wake up with a smile on your face," Cody said from the doorway.

Abra's eyes flew open. In a nervous gesture she gathered the rumpled sheet to her breasts. "I thought you'd gone."

He walked over and, easing down on the mattress, offered her a cup of coffee. "Gone where?"

"I..." Feeling foolish, she sipped at the coffee and scalded her tongue. "Just gone."

His eyes darkened briefly, but then he shrugged. "You still have a very poor opinion of me."

"It's not that. I just thought you probably had things to do."

"Yeah." He shifted, sliding a leg onto the bed. He was damned if he could remember a night with a woman ever making him feel so light-headed. And awkward. Taking his time, he sipped. "Your coffee's stale, you know."

"I never seem to have time to make it in the morning." She drank again. Small talk. That seemed the best way out, and the safest. "I'd, ah, offer you breakfast, but—"

"I know. There's nothing in the kitchen but a banana and a bag of corn chips."

"There's cookies," she muttered.

"I thought they were rocks." Deliberately he put a hand under her chin. "You want to look at me?"

She did, while her free hand moved restlessly on the sheets. "I'd have gotten a few things if I'd known you were coming back."

"I don't think bacon and eggs is the issue here. Why don't you tell me what the problem is, Red?"

"There's no problem." She struggled for a casual tone. She was an adult, she reminded herself. As such she should be able to handle the morning after. But what did you say to a man in the full light of day when he'd taken you to the darkest depths of your own passions? She could hardly tell him that there had been no one who had given her so much—or taken so much.

"Would you rather I'd gone?"

"No." She said it too quickly, and she swore silently. So much for small talk, she thought, and any pretense of sophistication. "Listen, I don't know what I'm supposed to do next, what I'm supposed to say or how I'm supposed to act. I haven't had a lot of practice at this kind of thing."

"No?" Thoughtful now, he took the coffee from her and set it aside. "How much have you had?" It wasn't a question he'd known he would ask. He'd told himself that her past life was just that—her life. But he wanted to know if there was anyone, anyone at all, who had shared what he had experienced during the night.

"I don't think this is a joke."

He grabbed her shoulders before she could roll out of bed. "Am I laughing? I get the feeling you're judging what's happening here by something that happened before. I don't like it."

"Sorry," she said stiffly.

"Not good enough." He kept his hold firm so that she couldn't yank away. "This guy, the one who bounced your heart around…tell me about him."

Angry color rose to her cheeks as she tried to push him away. "I don't see that that's any of your business."

"You see wrong. Nothing new."

She struggled with the temper she was very close to losing. "I haven't asked you about any of the women you've been involved with."

"No, but you could if you thought it was important. I think this is."

"Well, you're wrong. It's not important."

But it was important. He saw it in her eyes, heard it in her voice. Both tempted him to be gentle with her. If comfort had been the answer, he would have offered it. Sometimes life and love were tough.

"If that's true, why are you upset?"

"I'm not upset."

"I thought we said something about being honest."

"Maybe we did. We should also have said something about not poking around in past relationships."

"Fair enough." He gave her a long, level look. "Unless they seep over into this one. If I'm going to be compared to someone else, I want to know why."

"You want to hear about him? Fine." She pulled away, taking the sheet with her to wrap around her body. "He was an architect." She sent Cody a humorless smile.

"Is that your basis for comparison?"

"You're the one who says I'm comparing," she countered. "You could say I have a habit of tumbling into bed with architects. I was just out of college and working full-time at Thornway. I'd been given a shot as assistant to the engineer on a small project. James was the architect. He'd just moved from Philadelphia. He was very smooth, very smart." She moved her shoulders. "I wasn't."

It was hurting her, and he found he couldn't take it. Rising, he dipped his hands into the trousers he'd pulled on earlier. "All right. I get the picture."

"No." She pulled the sheet more securely around her as they faced each other over the bed. "You wanted to hear about it, and I'm going to tell you. We started seeing each other, and I got stars in my eyes. Looking back, I can't say he promised anything, but he let me believe what I wanted. I'd always wanted to be first with someone. You know, the person someone thinks about before they think about anyone or anything else."

"Yes, I know." He would have gone to her then if he'd thought she'd accept it.

Because he sounded as though he did, she calmed down a bit. "I was very young, and I still believed things like that happened, so when he told me how much he wanted me I was ready to take him on any terms. When I went to bed with him, I was smelling orange blossoms."

"And he wasn't."

"Oh, it was more than that." She laughed, pushing the hair back from her face. "I'd like to think if it was only a matter of me wanting more than I could have I'd have swallowed hard and gone on. I'm not a whiner, Cody."

"No." Anything but, he thought. "What happened?"

"I was packing to go on a weekend trip with him. It was going to be very romantic, very intimate. A ski weekend up north—snow, roaring fires, long nights. I was certain he was going to propose. I was already picturing white picket fences. Then I had a visitor. It's funny." Her voice quieted as she looked beyond him to something only she could see. "I was nearly out the door. I don't like to think what would have happened if I'd been a little quicker. The visitor turned out to be his wife, a wife he hadn't bothered to tell me existed."

Taking a deep breath, Abra sat down behind her drawing board. "The worst part was that she loved the bastard and was coming to see me to beg me to let him go. She was ready and willing to forgive him, if only I'd take pity on her and step aside."

Abra pressed her fingers to her eyes as the memory of that scene played back all too clearly in her head, and with it the shame, the hard, bitter shame. "I'm not the other-woman type, Cody. At first I thought she was lying. I was sure of it. But she wasn't lying. That became horribly clear."

She dropped her hands, folding them loosely together. "I just stood there and listened to her tell me about herself and the three-year-old boy they had and how she wanted to save her marriage more than anything. How they had moved out west to make a new start because there had been other incidents. Other women. I felt more horrid than I ever want to feel again. Not just used, not just betrayed, but vile, really ugly and vile. She cried and begged and I couldn't say anything at all. I'd been sleeping with her husband."

Cody eased down on the bed across from her. He had to choose his words carefully. "Would you…have become involved with him if you'd known?"

"No. I asked myself that a lot after it was all over. No, I wouldn't have…couldn't have."

"Then why are you blaming yourself for something you couldn't control? He deceived you every bit as much as he deceived his wife."

"It's not just blame. I got over that, or most of it, and I got over him." It wasn't easy, but she made herself look at him. "I've never been able to forget the fact that I opened myself up to what happened to me. I never asked him any questions. I never asked myself any questions. When you make that big a mistake once, you better be careful not to repeat it. So I concentrated on my career and left the romance to Jessie."

She hadn't been with anyone else, he realized with a kind of dull amazement. There had been no one else in her life, and when he'd come into it he'd rolled in like a bulldozer. He thought of the night. It had been wonderful, exciting, overwhelming, but he hadn't been gentle, he hadn't been tender. He hadn't shown her any of the romance she was claiming she had decided to live without.

"Abra, are you afraid you're making the same mistake with me?"

"You're not married."

"No, and there's no one else." He paused when she turned her head to look at him. "You're not a diversion or a convenience to me."

She could never explain how those words made her feel. How could she have known such a tiny flicker of hope could burn so brightly? "I'm not comparing you to James—or maybe I was, a little. It's me. I feel stupid because I don't know how to handle this kind of thing. My mother…"

"What about your mother?"

Abra rested her elbows on the drawing board and dipped her head into her hands. After a moment she straightened again. "All my life I've watched her swing from one man to another. It was always so easy for her, so light, so natural. It doesn't work for me."

He went to her to take her arm and lift her gently to her feet. "I don't want you to act any way that doesn't suit you, or be anything you're not." He brushed his lips over her brow, knowing that if he kissed her now he'd want her in the bed. She needed more than that now, whether she understood it or not. "Let's just take it from here, Red. A day at a time. I care about you. You can believe that."

"I do." She drew back. "I think I do."

He pulled her back to hug her in a way that made her eyes widen in surprise. There was something so sweet, so uncomplicated, about the gesture. "We've got the weekend ahead of us. Get dressed. I'll buy you some breakfast."

Abra was a little amazed at how easily Cody could change from the reckless lover to the casual friend. She was always surprised at how easy he made it for her to make the same transition. Breathing space, she decided as they shared a meal in a dusty diner Cody had unearthed along the highway.

She already knew his appetite—for food and other pleasures—so she barely lifted a brow when he packed away enough for two lumberjacks. It was the trip to the market, at his insistence, that left her reeling. When they returned to her apartment they were carrying what would have been for Abra a year's supply of groceries.

"What are we supposed to do with this stuff?" She dumped two bags on the counter in the kitchen, then stood back as Cody did the same.

"We eat it. At various times of the day." He began

to pull out produce. "These are what's known as the basics."

"For a dormitory, maybe." She cast a dubious eye at the pile growing on the counter. "Do you cook?"

"No." He tossed her a bag of apples. "That's why you buy stuff that doesn't need it. Or…" He pulled out a can of chow mein and a frozen pizza. "Stuff that you heat and eat. As long as you have a can opener and an oven timer, you can live like a king."

She shoved a quart of milk, the apples and whatever else came to hand in the refrigerator. Cody watched her, decided she had other, more important qualities and offered her a box of corn flakes. She put those in, as well.

"Takeout's easier," she told him.

"You have to go out for takeout." He swung her around and rained kisses all over her face. A man had to love a woman who put corn flakes in the refrigerator. "You're not going anywhere until Monday morning."

Laughing, she pushed away and dug out a loaf of bread. "I was going to go buy a black silk teddy."

"Oh, yeah?" He grinned, then gripped the baggy waist of her sweats. "For me?"

"It's too late." After slapping his hand away, she tossed the bread in a drawer.

"Let's talk about this." He wrapped his arms around her waist and pulled her back against him. "I like the way you look in black silk. That's probably why I acted like a jealous maniac at Thornway's."

"Jealous?" She let out a peal of laughter. She was sure he was joking—until she turned and saw his face. "Jealous?" she repeated. "Of Mr. Barlow?"

"Don't rub it in."

"I thought you were just being insufferable and insulting."

He winced a little, then lowered his head to bite her neck. "Forget I said it."

"I don't think so," she murmured, even as she shifted to give him more access. "From where I was standing that night you seemed to be vastly entertained by Marci Thornway."

"Give me some credit." He slipped his hands under her sweatshirt to skim them up her sides. "I know a shark when I see one. No matter how pretty the teeth are, they still rip you up. Besides…" His fingers turned in to tease her breasts. "I'm not interested in cotton candy."

He had her backed against the refrigerator and was making her tremble. "As opposed to?"

"Just you, Red." He turned his head to give her a long, soul-stealing kiss. "Just you. Tell me—" he moved his hands down to mold her hips "—have you ever done anything constructive on this counter? Chopped vegetables, canned fruit, made love?"

"On the counter?" Her eyes went wide, then fluttered closed again when he ran his tongue behind her ear. "No. I haven't done any of those things."

He was moving too fast again. In a moment he wouldn't be able to pull back and give her the time and attention he wanted to. With an effort, he stepped back and brought only her hand to his lips. "We'll have to keep that in mind. I bought you something else."

"Something else?" Her breathing was almost level when she glanced around the kitchen. "What, a twenty-pound turkey?"

"No. Actually, I picked it up in San Diego."

She smiled as she took out a carton of eggs she hoped he didn't expect her to deal with. "You bought me something in San Diego? A souvenir?"

"Not exactly. Are we finished here?"

"I certainly hope so."

"Come on, then. I'll show you."

He took her by the hand to pull her out of the kitchen and into the bedroom, where his bag sat open on a chair. Reaching in, he took out a box and handed it to her.

"A present?" She felt foolishly shy as she ran a finger over the top of the box. "That was sweet of you."

"It could be an ashtray that says San Diego Padres."

"It would still be a present." She leaned over to touch her lips to his. "Thanks."

"That's the first time you've done that," he murmured.

"What?"

"Kissed me."

She laughed and would have drawn her hand away, but he reached up to hold it against his cheek. "You have a short memory."

"No." He uncurled her fingers to press his lips to her open palm. "That's the first time you've kissed me first, before I backed you into one of those corners. And you don't even know what I bought you."

"It doesn't matter. I like knowing you were thinking of me."

"Oh, I thought of you." He dipped his head to kiss her lightly, sweetly, and her lips parted in surprise. "I thought of you a lot." He checked himself again because he wanted nothing more than to gather her into his arms and show her. She needed space and time and more care than he'd bothered to show her. So instead he grinned and sat on the arm of the chair. "I would have given it to you last night, but you couldn't keep your hands off me."

She gave him an amused look before sitting on the arm beside him. "Better late than never." Then she opened the lid and sat staring and speechless.

She had expected some little token, some funny souvenir a friend might bring another after a quick trip. The gems glittered up at her, pale as water, smooth as satin. She didn't, as many women would have, recognize the glint of diamonds. What she saw were lovely stones that caught the late-afternoon light.

"It's beautiful." The amazement was still on her face when she looked across at him. "Really beautiful. You bought this for me?"

"No, I bought it for Charlie." With a shake of his head, Cody lifted out the necklace and reached over to fasten it around her neck. "Think it'll look good on him?"

"I don't know what to say." She lifted a hand and ran it over the stones. "No one's ever given me anything so lovely."

"I guess I'll have to buy Charlie something else."

With a laugh, she sprang up to go to the mirror and look. "Oh, they are beautiful. They sparkle." Turning, she launched herself into his arms. "Thank you." She kissed him. "Thank you." And again. "Thank you."

"If I'd known it would only take a handful of glitters, I could have arranged this weeks ago."

"Laugh all you want." She pressed her cheek against his. "I really love it."

And I love you, he thought. Before too much longer, she was going to know it. "I want to see them on you," he murmured, and rose with her. With his eyes on hers, he slipped the shirt over her head. He saw the change in her face, and the invitation. He would take what she offered, but this time he would take it carefully.

"You're beautiful, Abra."

Now he saw the new change, the blank astonishment his words had brought to her. He cursed himself for a fool. Had he never bothered to tell her, or to make her believe it?

"I love the way you look in the sunlight. The first time I saw you I watched you in the sunlight."

With an easy tug he loosened the drawstring at her waist so that her pants slithered down over her hips. Now she wore only the necklace, shimmering like water around her throat. But he didn't touch her, not in any of the hot, hungry ways she'd come to expect. He framed her face as though it were made of glass and kissed her as softly as a dream.

Confused, moved to aching, she reached for him. "Come to bed."

"There's time." He kissed her again and again, lingering over it until she swayed. "This time." He peeled off his shirt so that she could feel the solid strength of his chest against her. But passion weakened now, where before it had streamed through her like fire. Her muscles trembled, then went lax. Her mind, so clear only moments before, blurred.

He only kissed her, and kissed her and kissed her.

"I don't..." Her head fell back as he deepened the kiss. "I can't..."

"You don't have to do anything. Let me show you." He swept her up, muffling her dazed protest with his lips until he lowered her to the bed.

His gentleness filled her until her limbs were too weighted to move. She would have clasped him to her and given him everything, but he linked his hands with hers and caressed her with his lips alone. Soft, moist, patient. Her mind began to float, then to soar with a pleasure far beyond the physical.

No one had ever treated her as though she were fragile, or delicate, or beautiful. He made love to her now in a way she hadn't known existed. In a way she would never forget. If the night had been flash and fire and the darkest of passions, this was quiet and cool and wonderfully light. She trembled over the first edge, then drifted like a feather in the softest of breezes.

She was exquisite. He'd seen the passion and the strength—felt them—but he hadn't seen, hadn't touched on, her fragility or her openness to love. Whatever he had felt before, in the heat of desire, was nothing compared to the intimacy of giving. Her body flowed like a river under his hands, warmed like a flower beneath his lips. When she murmured his name, the sound rippled over him, touching some deep hidden core. It was the only voice he ever wanted to hear.

He murmured to her. She heard him, responded, but she couldn't understand the words. Sensation layered over sensation, wrapping her in a cocoon of pleasure. There was the feel of his hands, the strength of them as they stroked over her skin. There was the taste of his mouth whenever he searched for hers, the warm, drugging taste of it. Over lids too heavy to lift, the sunlight beat so that vision, like her mind, was a red mist. Time spun out, inconsequential. For Abra, years might have passed without her noticing.

She felt the brush of his hair as he roamed over her, caught the scent of his skin as he skimmed over hers. If there were other things in the world, they had stopped being important. If night fell or the sun rose, it hardly mattered. Not as long as he was with her and showing her what there could be to love.

When he slipped inside her, she let out a long sigh of welcome. Still, he moved slowly, slowly, taking her gently up the wave, riding the crest. Trapped in the world he had opened up to her, she rose to meet him, matching rhythms, merging bodies.

Promises were made, though she didn't know it. A bond, solid and firm, was formed.

His own breath grew shallow as he dug for control. He'd thought she'd driven him wild in the night. And she had. Now, in surrender, she had taken him beyond even that. His muscles trembled, then steadied with a sweet, dark ache, and his pulse beat in hammer blows at the back of his neck. He was driven to taste her again. Her breath whispered into his mouth as their lips met. Hers softened, opened, offered.

Then she opened her eyes, her lashes lifting in one long, languid movement. Though she couldn't know it, she had never been more beautiful than at that moment. Though she couldn't know it, from that moment on he was completely and irrevocably hers.

She spoke his name, and they slipped over the top together.

Chapter 8

It wasn't so hard, this being in love. Abra thought it through as she swung her car into the parking lot at Thornway. She didn't have to act differently, live differently, be different. She wasn't required to change her life so much as open it up. Perhaps she hadn't thought it was possible for her to do even that, but Cody had proved her wrong. For that, if only for that, she would always be grateful.

If she could love him without changing who she was, didn't that mean that when the time came for him to leave she could pick up and go on as she had before? She wanted to believe it. She had to believe it.

With her keys jingling in her hand and her step very light, she crossed the lot to the building. The sun wasn't really shining brighter this morning. She knew that. But in her heart it glowed more golden, more beautiful, than ever before.

It was all a matter of perspective, she told herself as she passed through the lobby, heading toward the elevators. She knew all about perspective and planning and coming up with a workable structure.

A love affair could be engineered just like anything else. They cared about each other, enjoyed each other, respected each other. That was a solid foundation. They shared a common love of building. Even if they came at it from different angles, it was a base of sorts. From there it was a matter of adding the steel and the struts. After the weekend they had shared, Abra felt confident that progress had been made. Without the tension of work interfering, they had discovered pleasures in and out of bed.

She liked him. That seemed almost too elementary, but to her it was a revelation. It wasn't only a matter of need, attraction, falling in love. She liked who he was, how he thought, how he listened. Companionship wasn't something she'd looked for from him, any more than she'd looked for passion. In one weekend she'd discovered she could have both.

Abra pushed the button for the elevator and smiled as she remembered the way they had sprawled on her couch and watched a Cary Grant festival on television. Or the way they'd put together a meal of pizza and gingersnaps. Or the way they'd tumbled into her rumpled bed on Sunday afternoon with the radio playing jazz and the breakfast dishes neglected.

He'd made her happy. That in itself was more than she'd ever expected from a man. They were building a relationship, solid and strong. When it was time to walk away from it, she would be able to look back and remember something wonderful that had come into her life.

When the elevator doors opened, she stepped through, then felt hands encircle her waist.

"Going up?"

As the doors shut, Cody spun her around and captured her mouth with his. She held on the way he'd hoped she would. She answered the kiss the way he'd needed her to. It was hardly more than an hour since he'd left her to go back to his hotel and change for the meeting, but it seemed like days.

She'd gotten to him, he thought as he pressed her back against the side of the car. In all ways, in every way, she'd gotten to him. He was only just beginning to plan how to deal with the results.

"You taste good, Red." He lingered over her lips a moment, nibbling before he pulled back far enough to look at her. "And I like your face."

"Thanks." She lifted her hands to keep some sensible distance between them. "You were quick getting here."

"I only had to change. I could have done that at your place if you'd let me bring some things over."

She wasn't ready for that. If he lived there, really lived there over the next few weeks, the apartment would be much too empty when he left. She smiled and glanced up to check the progress of the car. They were still at lobby level. With a shake of her head she pushed the button both of them had forgotten.

"I'd hate for you to give up room service, and that neat little spa."

"Yeah." He knew she was evading him. No matter how intimate they became, she still refused to take the next step and close the final gap. He gave himself a moment to control his frustration, then pushed the button to stop the car between floors.

"What are you doing?"

"I want to ask you something before we go back to work. It's personal." He trailed a finger from the base of her neck to her waist. "As I remember, one of the rules is no mixing business with pleasure."

"That's right."

"Have dinner with me."

With a long sigh, Abra reached out to start the elevator again. Cody circled her wrist before she could press the button. "Cody, you didn't have to trap me in an elevator to ask me to have dinner."

"So you will?"

"Unless I'm stuck between the fourth and fifth floors."

"At my hotel," he added, bringing her wrist to his lips. As always, it delighted him when her response came out in a rush. "And stay with me tonight."

The fact that he had asked rather than assumed made her smile. "I'd like that. What time?"

"The sooner the better."

She laughed as she pushed the button for Tim's floor. But her pulse would be hammering for some time to come. "Then we'd better get to work."

Tim was waiting for them with a tray of coffee and Danish, which Abra ignored. It took only moments for her to recognize the signs of stress, though Tim was as jovial and expansive as ever. She was forced to stem her own impatience as details of the plans were brought out and gone over yet again. If she wasn't on the site by ten, she would miss another inspection.

When Tim set up a flow chart that diagrammed the construction sequence and the estimated dates of completion, she settled back and gave up. She'd be lucky to be on the job by noon.

"As you can see," Tim continued, "the blasting and the foundation were completed on schedule. Where we began to fall behind was on the roofing."

"There's no real problem there." Cody lit a cigarette as he studied the chart. "We were well within the usual grace period of twenty percent. In fact, it looks like we're no more off than five."

"We have another lag with the plumbing of the health club."

"No more than a day or two," Abra put in. "We'll be able to make it up with the cabanas. At this pace the resort will be built and operational within our time frame."

Tim was staring at the figures and projections. "It hasn't even been three months into construction and we're nearly ten percent behind." Tim held up a hand before Abra could speak. "Added to that is the budget. Unless we're able to take some cost-cutting methods, we're going to go over."

"The budget's not my province." Cody topped off his coffee, then filled Tim's cup. He'd seen the builder down three in the last half hour. Ulcers were made from less, he thought mildly. "And it's not Abra's. But I can tell you that from my own figures, and taking a look at the do list, you're going to come in as close to budget as it's possible."

"Cody's right. We've had no major hitches on this job. It's run more smoothly than any I've been involved with. The supplies have been delivered on time and in good order. If we've run over on a few things, such as the pool roof and the parallel windows in the main building, it's been minimal. I think that you—" She broke off when the phone rang.

"Excuse me." Tim picked up the receiver. "Julie, I want you to hold my calls until— Oh. Yes, of course." Tim pulled at the knot of his tie, then reached for his coffee. "Yes, Marci. Not yet. I'm in a meeting." He drew a long breath as he listened. "No, there hasn't been time.

I know that." He gulped more coffee. "I will. By this afternoon. Yes, yes, I promise. You…" He let his words trail off, rubbing the back of his neck. "Fine, that's fine. I'll look at them when I get home. By six. No, I won't forget. Bye."

He set down the phone. Abra thought his smile was a bit forced when he turned back to them.

"Sorry about the interruption. We're planning a little trip for next month and Marci's excited about it." He gave the chart an absent glance. "You were saying?"

"I was going to point out that I think you can be very pleased with the way this job's been going." Abra paused a moment, no longer sure Tim was listening.

"I'm sure you're right." After a long breath, Tim beamed at both of them. "I want to make sure I'm on top of things. I appreciate the input." He came around the desk. "I know I'm keeping you both from your work, so we won't drag this out any longer."

"Got any idea what that was all about?" Cody asked Abra as Tim closed the door behind them.

"I'm not sure." Thoughtfully she walked toward the elevators. "I guess he's entitled to be nervous. This is the first big job he's taken on solo. Everything else he's done was already in the works when his father died."

"Thornway has a good reputation," Cody commented as they stepped inside and started down. "What's your opinion of Thornway junior?"

"I don't like to say." Uneasy about the meeting, Abra stared at the wall of the elevator. "I was very close to his father. I really loved him. He knew the building trade inside out, every angle, every corner, and he was… It was personal with him, if you know what I mean."

"I do."

"Tim's not the man his father was, but they're big shoes to fill."

They crossed the lobby and started out to the parking lot together. "How tight do you figure he bid this job?"

"Close. Maybe too close." She narrowed her eyes against the sun as she thought the problem through. "But I can't believe he'd be reckless enough to risk taking a loss on something of this size. The penalty clause is a whopper, that I do know." She fished out her keys, frowning. "Enough to put the fear of God into anyone. It's offset by a bonus if the job comes through ahead of schedule."

"So maybe he's counting too heavily on the bonus." With a shrug, Cody leaned against Abra's car. "Seems to me his wife is an expensive tax deduction."

She gave a quick, unladylike snort. "That's a nice way to talk about a man's wife."

"Just an observation. That little dog collar she had on the other night would have set old Tim back five or six thousand."

"Thousand?" Her interest piqued, Abra stopped in the act of sliding into her car. "Was it real?"

Pulled back from his speculations, he grinned. "You're awfully cute, Red."

She almost snapped at him, but curiosity got the best of her. "Well, was it?"

"Women like that don't wear glass and paste."

"No, I suppose not," she murmured. But five thousand—she just couldn't conceive of it. That much money would go a long way toward buying a new car, or a piece of equipment, or—she could think of a dozen uses for five thousand dollars more reasonable than wasting it on something a woman wore around her neck.

"What are you thinking?"

"That he must be crazy." Then she moved her shoulders, dismissing it. "But the man's entitled to spend his money however he chooses."

"Maybe he considers it an investment." At Abra's puzzled look, Cody thought back to the night of the party and Marci's frank and unmistakable come-on. "You could say some women need a lot of incentive to stay with one man."

Because that thought made her think uncomfortably—and perhaps unfairly—of Jessie, Abra brushed it aside. "Well, it's certainly his problem. In any case, we don't have time to stand here gossiping about Tim and his wife."

"Just speculating." But he, too, brushed the subject aside. "Listen, I've got to make a stop on the way to the job. Can you follow me?"

She glanced at her watch. "Yeah, but why—?"

"There's something I have to pick up. I could use your help." He kissed her, then slid behind the wheel of his own car.

Ten minutes later, Abra drove in behind him at Jerry's Tire Warehouse. "What are you getting here?"

"A new suit. What do you think?" He pulled her out of the car and through the door. The place was a sea of tires—blackwalls, whitewalls, steel-belted radials. It smelled of rubber and grease. Behind a scarred counter piled with thick catalogs was a bald man wearing half glasses.

"Morning, folks," he shouted over the hissing and blowing of pumps and lifts. "What can I do for you?"

"See that?" Cody turned and pointed at Abra's car through the plate-glass window. "Tires, all around, and a spare."

"But I—" Before Abra could finish, the clerk was

thumbing through the catalogs. He'd summed up Abra's car with one glance.

"We have some very nice budget products."

"I want the best," Cody told him, making the clerk's eyes gleam behind his dusty lenses.

"Cody, this is—"

"Well, well." Obviously seeing his commission soar, the clerk began to write out an invoice. "I have something in stock that should do very nicely."

Cody glanced down at the invoice, noted the brand and nodded. "Can you have it ready by five?"

The clerk looked at his watch and his daily list. "Just."

"Good." Plucking the keys out of Abra's hand, Cody tossed them. "We'll be back."

Before she could complete a sentence, Abra found herself being pulled back outside. "Just what do you think you're doing?"

"Buying you a birthday present."

"My birthday's in October."

"Then I'm covered."

She managed—barely—to dig in her heels. "Listen, Cody, you have absolutely no right making decisions like this for me. You can't just—just drag somebody into a tire warehouse, for God's sake, and order tires."

"Better here than the supermarket." He put his hands on either side of her head, resting them on the roof of his car. "And I didn't drag somebody in there. I dragged somebody important to me, somebody that I won't see driving around on four tires that gave up the last of their rubber six months ago. You want to fight about that?"

Because he'd taken the wind out of her sails, she only frowned. "No. But I would have taken care of it. I've been planning to take care of it."

"When?"

She shifted her feet. "Sometime."

"Now it's done. Happy birthday."

Giving up, she leaned forward and kissed him. "Thanks."

Abra came home that evening in a dead rush. She'd missed the inspector again, but the foundations for the first set of cabanas had passed without a hitch. She'd been able to see the sliding roof in operation, and at long last the elevators were riding smoothly.

The meeting with Tim had given her some problems, enough that she had made a point of checking the foremen's daily lists. Her description of Tim to Cody had made her feel guilty. To combat that, she had decided to take a personal interest in every facet of the job. The extra time had pushed the end of her workday to six, and then she'd eaten up nearly an hour more picking up her car.

"Never ready when they say they'll be ready," she mumbled as she sprinted up the stairs of her building. When she reached her landing, she saw one more delay at her door.

"Mom. I didn't know you were coming by."

"Oh, Abra." With a little laugh, Jessie dropped a piece of paper back in her purse. "I was just going to leave you a note. Running a bit late?"

"I feel like I've been running all day." She unlocked the door and pushed it open.

"Have I come at a bad time?"

"No— Yes. That is, I'm heading back out again in a few minutes."

"I won't be long, then." Jessie gave an automatic sigh at the sight of Abra's living room. "Were you held up at work?"

"First." Abra shot straight into the bedroom. She wasn't going to have dinner with Cody in work boots and dusty jeans. "Then I had to pick up my car."

Straightening up as she went, Jessie trailed behind her. "Did it break down again?"

"No, I was getting tires. Actually Co—a friend of mine bought me tires."

"Someone bought you tires—for a present?"

"Uh-huh." She pulled out a nile-green jumpsuit. "What do you think of this?"

"For a date? Lovely. You've always had a good sense of color. Do you have any gaudy earrings?"

"Maybe." Abra pulled open a drawer and began to search.

"Why did someone buy you tires?"

"Because mine were shot," Abra said absently as she pawed through cotton underwear and sweat socks. "And he was worried that I'd have an accident."

"He?" Jessie's ears perked up. She stopped tidying Abra's clothes and smiled. "Why, that's the most romantic thing I've ever heard of."

With a snort, Abra lifted out one silver earring with copper beading. "Tires are romantic?"

"He was worried about you and didn't want you to be hurt. What's more romantic than that?"

Abra dropped the earring back in her drawer as her lips pursed. "I didn't think about it that way."

"That's because you don't look on the romantic side of things often enough." Anticipating the reply, Jessie held up a hand. "I know, I know. I look on that side too often. That's the way I am, sweetheart. You're much more like your father was—practical, sensible, straightforward. Maybe if he hadn't died so young…" With a shrug of her slender shoulders, Jessie plumped the pillows on the bed. "That's water over the dam now, and I can't help being the kind of woman who enjoys and appreciates having a man in her life."

"Did you love him?" The moment she asked, Abra shook her head and began to search for an overnight bag. "I'm sorry. I didn't mean to ask you that."

"Why shouldn't you?" With a dreamy sigh, Jessie folded a discarded blouse. "I adored him. We were young and broke and totally in love. Sometimes I think I've never been happier, and I know it's a part of my life I'll never forget and will always be grateful for." Then the dreamy look was gone, and she set the blouse aside. "Your father spoiled me, Abra. He took care of me, cherished me in a way every woman needs to be cherished. I suppose I've looked for parts of him in every man I've ever been involved with. You were just a baby when he died, but I see him when I look at you."

Slowly Abra turned. "I never realized you felt that way about him."

"Because it's been so easy for me to form other relationships?" With competent movements, Jessie began to make the bed. "I don't like being alone. Being part of a couple is as necessary to me as your independence is to you. Flirting is like breathing to me. I'm still pretty." Smiling, she fluffed her hair as she bent to take a quick look in the mirror. "I like being pretty. I like knowing that men think I'm pretty. If your father had lived, things might have been different. The fact that I can be happy with someone else doesn't mean I didn't love him."

"It must have sounded as though I were criticizing. I'm sorry."

"No." Jessie smoothed the bedspread. "I know you don't understand me. The truth is, I don't always understand you. That doesn't mean I don't love you."

"I love you, too. I'd like you to be happy."

"Oh, I'm working on it." With a chuckle, Jessie moved around the bed to set Abra's sneakers in the closet. "I'm always working on it. That's one of the reasons I came by. I wanted you to know I was going out of town for a couple of days."

"Oh? Where?"

"Vegas. Willie's going to show me how to play black-jack."

"You're going away with Mr. Barlow?"

"Don't get that look," Jessie said mildly. "Willie is one of the sweetest men I've ever met. In fact, he's fun, considerate and a complete gentleman. He's arranged for separate suites."

"Well." Abra tried hard to accept the news. "Have a nice time."

"I will. You know, honey, if you put away all these things on your dresser you'd be able to find them when you— Oh, my." Her eye fell unerringly on the necklace. "Where did you get this?"

"It was a present." Abra smiled as Jessie scooted in front of the mirror with the necklace held around her throat. "It's pretty, isn't it?"

"It's a great deal more than that."

"I really love it."

"I don't think you should leave it lying around."

"I've got the box around here somewhere." She rummaged. "I think I'll wear it tonight."

"If it were mine, I'd never take it off. You said a present." Jessie turned from the mirror. "From whom?"

"A friend."

"Come on, Abra."

Evading only made it into something that it wasn't,

Abra reminded herself. She said lightly, "Cody picked it up for me when he went to San Diego."

"Well, well..." Jessie let the choker drip from one palm to the other like a stream of stars. "You know, sweetheart, this is the kind of gift a man gives his wife. Or his lover."

As her color rose, Abra made a production of brushing her hair. "It was a thoughtful token from a friend and associate."

"Associates don't give associates diamond chokers."

"Don't be silly. They're not real."

Jessie was silent for three heartbeats. "My only daughter, and she has such a huge gap in her education."

Amused, Abra glanced around. "Diamonds are white, these aren't. Anyway, it's ridiculous to think he'd bring me diamonds. It's a lovely necklace with beautiful colored stones."

"Abra, you're a very good engineer, but sometimes I worry about you." Picking up her bag, Jessie searched out her compact. "Glass," she said, holding up the mirror. "Diamonds." She scraped the stones across the mirror, then held it up.

"It's scratched," Abra said slowly.

"Of course it's scratched. Diamonds do that. And what you have here is about five carats. Not all diamonds are white, you know."

"Oh, my God."

"You're not supposed to look terrified." Abra stood stock-still, and Jessie hooked the choker around her neck. "You're supposed to look delighted. I know I am. Oh, my, they're stunning on you."

"They're real," she murmured. "I thought they were just pretty."

"Then I think you'd better finish getting ready so that

you can go thank him properly." Jessie kissed her cheek. "Believe me, sweetheart, it's just as easy to accept the real thing as it is a fake. I should know."

He was getting edgy waiting for her. He wasn't a man who kept his eye on time, but he'd looked at his watch over and over during the last ten minutes. It was after eight. The way he figured it, she should have been able to get home, toss a few things in a bag and be on his doorstep by 7:45.

So where was she?

You're getting crazy, he told himself, dropping into a chair to light a cigarette. Maybe this was normal behavior for a man in love. He'd like to think so. It was better than wondering whether he was the first and only one to go off the deep end.

He was doing this exactly the way she'd asked. While they'd been on the job he'd been completely professional. The fact that they'd nearly fallen into a shouting match twice should have reassured him. At least he hadn't lost his artistic perspective. He still thought of her as a damn annoying engineer once her hard hat was in place.

But they were off the clock now, and he was only thinking of Abra.

She looked beautiful while she slept. Soft, vulnerable, serene. He'd watched her Sunday morning until he'd been driven to touch her. He was even charmed—God help him—by the chaos of her apartment. He liked the way she walked, the way she sat, the way she got nose-to-nose with him when she started to shout.

All in all, Cody decided, he was sunk. So when she knocked he was up and at the door in three seconds flat.

"It was worth it." He relaxed the minute he saw her.

"What was?"

"The wait." Taking her arm, he drew her inside. Before he could lower his head for a kiss he saw the look in her eyes. "Something wrong?"

"I'm not sure." Feeling her way carefully, Abra stepped past him. There was a table set near the terrace doors, with candles waiting to be lit and wine chilled and ready to be opened. "This is nice."

"We can order whenever you like." He took her bag and set it aside. "What's the problem, Red?"

"I don't know that there is— Well, yes, there is, but it's probably just for me. If I'd had any idea…but I don't know a lot about these things and didn't realize what it was at the time. Now that I do, I'm not sure how to deal with it."

"Uh-huh." He sat on the sofa and gestured for her to join him. "Why don't you run that through for me one more time, adding the details?"

She dropped down beside him, clasping her hands firmly in her lap. As beginnings went, that had been pitiful. "All right. It's this." She unlinked her hands long enough to touch the choker at her throat.

"The necklace?" With a frown, he reached out to trace it himself. "I thought you liked it."

"I did. I do." She was going to ramble again. To hold it off, she took a deep breath. "It's beautiful, but I thought it was glass or… I don't know, some of those man-made stones. My mother was by a little while ago. She's going to Las Vegas with Mr. Barlow."

Cody rubbed his temple, trying to keep up. "And that's the problem?"

"No, at least not this one. My mother said these were diamonds even though they aren't white."

"That jibes with what the jeweler said. So?"

"So?" She turned her head to stare at him. "Cody, you can't give me diamonds."

"Okay, give me a minute." He sat back, thinking it through. He remembered her reaction to the gift, her pleasure, her excitement. It made him smile, all the more now that he understood she had thought it only a glass trinket. "You're an interesting woman, Wilson. You were happy as a lark when you thought it was a dime-store special."

"I didn't think that, exactly. I just didn't think it was…" She let her words trail off, blowing out a long, frustrated breath. "I've never had diamonds," she told him, as if that explained it all.

"I like the idea that I gave you your first. Are you hungry?"

"Cody, you're not listening to me."

"I've done nothing but listen to you since you walked in. I'd rather nibble on your neck, but I've been restraining myself."

"I'm trying to tell you I don't know if it's right for me to keep this."

"Okay. I'll take it back." She sat there, frowning, while he reached around to the clasp.

"But I want it," she muttered.

"What?" It was hard to keep the smile from his voice, but he managed it. "Did you say something?"

"I said I want it." Disgusted, she sprang up and began to pace. "I'm supposed to give it back. I was going to. But I want to keep it." She paused long enough to frown at him. "It was a lousy thing for you to do, to put me in a position like this."

"You're right, Red." He rose, shaking his head. "Only a creep would go out and buy something like that and expect a woman to enjoy it."

"That's not what I meant and you know it." She paused again, this time to glare. "You're making me sound stupid."

"That's all right. It's no trouble."

She was nearly successful in stifling a giggle. "Don't be so smug. I've still got the necklace."

"Right you are. You win again."

Recognizing defeat, she turned and linked her hands around his neck. "It's beautiful."

"Sorry." He rested his hands on her hips. "Next time I'll try for cheap and tacky."

She tilted her head to study his face. He was amused, all right, she decided. It was hard not to admit he deserved to be. "I guess I should thank you for the tires, too."

He enjoyed the way her lips rubbed warm over his. "You probably should."

"My mother said they were a very romantic gift."

"I like your mother." He skimmed his hands up the length of her and down again as she traced the shape of his mouth with her tongue.

"Cody..."

"Hmm?" He lifted his hands to her face to frame it as he began to drift toward desire.

"Don't buy me any more presents, okay? They make me nervous."

"No problem. I'll let you buy dinner."

Her fingers were combing through his hair as she watched him through lowered lashes. "Are you really hungry?"

This time when she kissed him the punch of power all but brought him to his knees. "Depends," he managed.

"Let's eat later." She pressed closer.

Chapter 9

"Cody, will you get that?"

Abra sat on the side of the bed, pulling on her work boots. The knock at her door had her scowling at her watch. It wasn't often she had visitors at seven o'clock in the morning, and she was already cutting it close if she wanted to be on the site before eight.

Cody came out of the kitchen with a cup of coffee in one hand. His hair was still damp from the shower and his shirt only half buttoned when he opened the door to Abra's mother.

"Oh, hello." There was an awkward pause before Jessie smiled at him.

"Morning." Cody stepped back to let her in. "You're up early."

"Yes, I wanted to catch Abra before she left. Then I have a dozen things to do." Jessie cleared her throat as she pleated the strap of her purse. "Is she around?"

"In the other room." Cody wasn't quite sure how a

man handled his lover's mother at 7:00 a.m. "Would you like some coffee?"

"Actually, I'd— Oh, there you are." She turned her nervous smile on Abra.

"Mom." The three of them stood there for a moment, forming an awkward triangle. Abra found that she didn't know what to do with her hands, so she stuck them in her pockets. "What are you doing out at this hour?"

"I wanted to see you before you left for the day." She hesitated again, then looked at Cody. "I would love a cup of coffee."

"Sure." Setting down his own, he stepped through to the kitchen.

"Abra, could we sit down a moment?"

Without a word, Abra took the chair across from the sofa. Certainly her mother wasn't going to lecture her about having a man in her apartment. "Is something wrong?"

"No, no, nothing's wrong." She took a deep breath, then accepted the cup Cody brought out to her.

"Why don't I leave you two alone?"

"No." Jessie spoke quickly, then managed a smile. Now that the initial discomfort had passed, she was glad, very glad, that her daughter had someone in her life. Someone, she thought as she studied his face, who obviously cared for her very much.

"Please, sit down, Cody. I'm sorry I've interrupted your morning, and I'm sure you both want to get to work. This won't take long." She drew a second, longer breath. "I've just gotten back from that trip with Willie."

Because she'd already resigned herself to that, Abra smiled. "Did you lose the family fortune at the craps table?"

"No." Perhaps it was going to be easier than she'd

thought, Jessie decided. She plunged ahead. "I got married."

"You what?" The shock brought Abra straight up in her chair. "In Vegas? To whom?"

"Why, to Willie, of course."

Abra said nothing for ten humming seconds. When she spoke, she spoke slowly, spacing each word. "You married Mr. Barlow in Las Vegas?"

"Two days ago." She held out her hand to show off a twin set of diamonds. "When we decided it was what we wanted, there didn't seem any reason to wait. After all, neither of us are children."

Abra stared at the glittering rings, then back at her mother. "You—you hardly know him."

"I've gotten to know him very well over the last couple of weeks." No, it was going to be hard, Jessie realized as she watched Abra's face. Very hard. "He's a wonderful man, sweetheart, very strong and steady. I'll admit I didn't expect him to ask me, but when he did I said yes. We were right there, and there was this funny little chapel, so…we got married."

"You should be getting good at it by now."

Jessie's eyes flashed, but her voice remained mild. "I'd like you to be happy for me. I'm happy. But if you can't, at least I'd like you to accept it."

"I should be getting good at that, too."

The pleasure went out of Jessie's face. "Willie wanted to come with me this morning, but I thought it best that I told you myself. He's very fond of you, speaks very highly of you as a woman and as a professional. I hope you won't make this difficult for him."

"I like Mr. Barlow," Abra said stiffly. "And I suppose I shouldn't be surprised. I'll wish you luck."

An ache passed through Jessie's heart. "Well, that's

something." She rose, worrying the rings on her finger. "I have to go in early and type up my resignation."

"You're quitting your job?"

"Yes, I'll be moving to Dallas. Willie's home is there."

"I see." Abra rose, as well. "How soon?"

"We're flying out this afternoon so I can meet his son. We'll be back in a few days to tie up details." She would have stepped toward her daughter, but she thought it best to give her time. "I'll call you when we get back."

"Fine." There was no affection in the word, only a brusque dismissal. "Have a nice trip."

Cody moved to the door to open it, then touched Jessie's arm before she could pass through. "Best wishes, Jessie."

"Thank you." Jessie was grateful the office would be empty when she arrived. She could have a good, healthy cry. "Take care of her, will you?" she murmured, and walked away.

Cody shut the door, then turned to see Abra standing in exactly the same spot. "A little rough on her, weren't you?"

"Stay out of it." She would have stormed into the bedroom, but he was quick enough to grab her arm.

"I don't think so." She was as rigid as ice, and just as cold. Except for her eyes. They boiled with emotion. "What's the problem here, Abra? Don't you figure your mother's free to marry whomever she chooses?"

"Absolutely. She's always been free. I want to finish getting ready for work."

"No." He kept his grip firm. "You're not going to work or anywhere until you get this out of your system."

"All right. You want me to get it out of my system? I'll get it out. She never changes." He heard the despair under the fury and gentled his hold. "It's the same pattern with her, over and over and over. First there was Jack, my father. He died before his twenty-fifth birthday." She pulled her arm free, then snatched a picture from the table. "He was the love of her life, to hear her tell it."

Feeling his way, he spoke carefully. "He's been gone a long time. She's entitled to go on living."

"Oh, she's gone right along. *Speeding* right along. It's been hard to keep up. Husband number two. Bob." She plucked up another picture. "I was, oh, about six when she decided she was free to marry him. That one lasted two, maybe three years. Hard to keep track." She dropped those pictures to grab another. "Then we have Jim. Let's not forget Jim, husband number three. Now before him, there were three or four others, but she never got around to marrying them. Jim managed a convenience store. They met over a carton of soft drinks and were married six months later. And that's about how long they were together afterward. Jessie doesn't really count Jim. She didn't bother to keep his name.

"Then there was Bud. Good old Bud Peters. I don't seem to have a picture of him, but this is Jessie on the day they were married."

Abra swooped it up, knocking several other photographs on their faces. "Bud sold shoes and liked to putter around the house. He wasn't a man to set the world on fire, but I liked him. I guess Jessie liked him, too, before they were together almost seven years. That's a record." She set the photo back. "Good old Bud Peters holds the record."

Cody took her shoulders, massaging them gently. "It's her life, Red."

"It was my life, too," she said passionately. "Damn

it, it was my life, too. Do you have any idea what it's like never knowing what last name your mother's going to use, or wondering which 'uncle' is going to be your next stepfather? What house or apartment you're going to live in? What school?"

"No." He thought of the steady and stable marriage of his parents, of the close-knit unit that was his family. "No, I don't. But you're a grown woman now. Your mother's marriage doesn't have to affect you."

"It's the same pattern, over and over. Don't you see? I've watched her fall in and out of love faster than a high-school cheerleader. And every time she gets married or divorced she says the same thing. This is going to be best for all of us. But it was never best, not for me. Now she comes here to tell me about this after it's already done. I always heard about these things after the die was cast."

He held her tighter. "If she's had poor judgment, Abra, it doesn't mean she doesn't love you."

"Oh, she loves me." Now that the venom was out, she felt hollow. Her voice sagged, and her resistance with it. "In her way. It was just never the way I needed. It's okay." She pulled back. The tears that had threatened were under control now, and so was she. "You're right. I'm overreacting. I'll talk to her, to them both, when they get back." She pushed her hands over her face and back into her hair. "I'm sorry, Cody. I took it out on you."

"No, you didn't. You just let it out."

"I guess I'm being stupid. And selfish."

"No, you're not. Just human." He stroked a hand over her cheek, wondering just how badly those early years had hurt her and how many hurts were left. "Come here." As he spoke, he pulled her into his arms and held her, just held her, until she relaxed against him. "I'm crazy about you."

He couldn't see the rush of emotions that came into her eyes. "Really?"

"Absolutely. I've been thinking that when things settle here you ought to come east—for a while," he added, not wanting to scare her off. "You can take a look at the house I'm building, give me a hard time about the design. Look at the ocean."

If she went east with him, would she ever be able to leave again? She didn't want to think about that, about endings and goodbyes. "I think I'd like that." With a sigh, she rested her head on his shoulder. "I'd like you to show me the ocean. I haven't had a chance to show you the desert yet."

"We could go AWOL today."

Her lips curved against his throat before she stepped back. He'd helped. By being there to lean on he'd helped her stand up again. "I don't think so. It wouldn't be right for me to neglect my mother's new husband's resort."

She was in a much better frame of mind by the time they reached the site. Without Cody—without his just being there—Abra knew she might have stayed depressed and angry for days. He was good for her. She wished she knew how to tell him *how* good without putting pressure on their relationship.

So far he seemed perfectly content to follow the blueprints she'd set up. There had been no promises, no talk of the future, no pretense about happy-ever-after. The invitation to visit back east had been casual enough that she felt safe in accepting.

Now, as so often happened on the site, he went his way and she hers. Later they would share the night.

She was coming to count on that, to depend on it, Abra thought as she made her way to the cabanas. It wasn't wise, it wasn't safe, but then there had to be some risks involved.

"Tunney." Abra nodded to the electrical foreman, then stood, hands on hips, studying the framework of the cabanas. "How's it going?"

"Pretty good, Ms. Wilson." He rubbed the back of his hand over his mouth. He was a big man who was running to fat, and he was sweating freely. As he watched Abra he took out a bandanna and wiped his face. "I thought you were still busy at the health club."

"I wanted to check things here." She stepped closer. Tunney kept at her shoulder. "You think the wiring's going to be done on schedule? Thornway's a little nervous."

"Yeah, sure. You might want to take a look at those units over there." He gestured to a section across what would be a courtyard. "The carpenters are really moving on it."

"Umm-hmm." Because she'd yet to find time to go through a unit, she walked forward. "I haven't checked with— Damn." She snagged her boot on a curled scrap of wire. "These places need to be squared away. Safety inspector would slap our wrists for that."

She would have reached down for the wire herself, but Tunney was ahead of her. "You gotta watch your step." He tossed the scrap into a trash drum.

"Yeah. This delivery just come in?" Abra gestured to three huge spools of wire. "As long as the suppliers keep ahead of us, we'll be fine." Absently she leaned against one of the spools.

She liked the look of the site, liked the ring of buttes and mesas constructed by time and nature that cupped the spreading growth conceived by man's imagination and sweat. This was building to her. This was what had drawn her. When a person could stand under the wide arch of sky and see progress—the right kind of progress—it brought hope, as well as satisfaction.

Though she hadn't told him yet, she'd begun to see and understand Cody's vision. A little magic, a little fantasy, here in one of the harshest and most beautiful spots in the country. There were still coyotes in the hills, snakes in the rocks, but man belonged here. When the resort was finished, it wouldn't simply merge with the desert, it would celebrate it.

That was what he had seen. That was what she was coming to understand.

"It's going to be quite a place, isn't it?"

"Guess it is." He was shifting his weight from one foot to the other as he watched her.

"Ever take a weekend in one of these places, Tunney?"

"Nope." He wiped his face again.

"Me either." She smiled at him. "We just build them, right?"

"Guess so."

He wasn't the most expansive of men, and she sensed his impatience. "I'm keeping you from your work," she said. She tried to straighten, but the end of the wire caught at her jeans. "God, I'm a klutz today." She bent to free it before Tunney could reach her. Frowning, she pulled the length of wire out and ran it between her fingers. "Did you say this just came?"

"Right off the truck. Hour ago."

"Damn. Have you checked it?"

He looked down as she crouched to examine the wire. "No. Like I say, it was just off-loaded."

"Check it now." She waited while he bent beside her to take the cable in his hand.

"This ain't fourteen-gauge."

"No, it's not. I'd say twelve."

"Yes, ma'am." His face puckered as he straightened. "That'd be right."

Swearing, she walked over to the other reels. "These are all twelve, Tunney."

Breathing between his teeth, he pulled out his clipboard. "Fourteen-gauge on the order sheet, Ms. Wilson. Looks like somebody screwed up the delivery."

"I should have known it was too good to last." She straightened, wiping her palms on her thighs. "We can't use this, it's substandard. Call the supplier and see if they can deliver the fourteen-gauge right away. We don't want to fall behind."

"No, we sure don't. Easy mistake, though. Unit numbers almost match." He showed her the numbers on his invoice, then pointed to those stamped on the spool. "Can't tell twelve from fourteen by just looking."

"It's a good thing you can tell by feel, or else we might have had a mess on our hands." She shaded her eyes with her hands as she looked toward the cabanas. "Any chance some might have slipped by you?"

He balled the bandanna back in his pocket. "I've been in the business eighteen years."

"Right. Still, you might—" She broke off when she heard a crash of glass and a scream. "Oh, my God." She raced across the distance to the health club, following the sound of men shouting.

She was breathing hard by the time she reached it. Pushing her way through, she spotted Cody leaning over the bleeding body of one of the workers.

Her heart rose up to block her throat. "How bad?"

She thought she recognized him vaguely. He was young, maybe twenty, with a long sweep of dark hair and a tough, tanned body.

"Can't tell." Cody's voice was curt. The only thing he was sure of was that the kid was breathing. For now. "An ambulance is on the way."

"What happened?" Her boots crunched over vicious shards of broken glass as she moved to kneel beside him.

"Seems like he was on the scaffold inside, finishing some wiring. Lost his balance, took a bad step, I don't know. He went right through the window." Cody looked up, and his mouth was grim as fury and frustration ripped through him. "He fell a good twenty feet."

She wanted to do something, anything. "Can't we get him off this glass?"

"His back could be broken, or his neck. We can't move him."

Minutes later, when they heard the siren, Abra sprang into action. "Cody, get in touch with Tim. Let him know what happened. You men get back, give them room to do whatever they have to do." She wiped at the clammy skin of her brow. "What's his name?"

"It's Dave," somebody called out. "Dave Mendez."

When the ambulance pulled up, Abra waved the men back. "How about family?"

"He's got a wife." One of the men who'd seen the fall drew jerkily on a cigarette. What had happened to Mendez could have happened to any of them. "Her name's Carmen."

"I'll take care of it," Cody told her as they watched the paramedics strap Mendez to a backboard.

"Thanks. I'm going to follow the ambulance in. Somebody should be there." Because her stomach was rolling, Abra pressed a steadying hand to it. "As soon as

I know anything, I'll be in touch." After a quick word to one of the ambulance attendants, she raced for her car.

Thirty minutes later she was in a waiting room, pacing uselessly.

There were other people scattered through the room. One woman waited patiently, almost placidly, with her nose in a paperback. Abra continued to pace and wondered how anyone could sit in a hospital without going slowly crazy.

She didn't even know Mendez, and yet she knew him very well. She worked with men like him every day of her professional life. It was men like him who made reality out of what she and Cody put on paper.

He wasn't family, and yet he was. As she paced the room she prayed for him.

"Abra."

"Cody." She turned, hurrying forward. "I didn't think I'd see you."

"I brought the kid's wife in. She's signing some papers."

"I feel so useless. They won't tell me much of anything." She dragged her hands through her already-tousled hair. "How's his wife?"

"Terrified. Confused. She's trying to hold on. God, I don't think she's more than eighteen."

With a nod, Abra went back to pacing. "I'll hang around with her. She shouldn't wait alone. Did you call Tim?"

"Yes. He's upset. He said to keep him posted."

Abra opened her mouth, then shut it again. In Thornway's day, if an employee was badly hurt, he came himself. "Maybe I could talk to the doctor now." She started out of the room just as a young, pregnant woman stepped in.

"Señor Johnson?"

Cody slipped an arm around her shoulders. She was trembling as he led her to a chair. "Abra, this is Carmen Mendez."

"Mrs. Mendez." Abra reached out to take both of her hands. They were very small, like a child's—and very cold. "I'm Abra Wilson, the engineer on the project. I'm going to stay with you, if you like. Is there anyone else you want me to call?"

"Mi madre." Tears flowed down her face as she spoke. "She lives in Sedona."

"Can you give me the number?" Abra asked gently.

"Sí." But she only sat there, weeping silently.

Moving to the couch, Abra put an arm around her and began to speak in low, fluent Spanish. Nodding and twisting a tattered tissue, Carmen answered. After a moment, Abra patted her shoulder, then gestured to Cody.

"They've been married less than a year," Abra said in an undertone as they moved to the corridor. "She's six months pregnant. She was too upset to really understand what the doctor told her, but they've taken Mendez to surgery."

"Want me to see what else I can find out?"

She leaned forward to kiss his cheek. "Thanks. Oh, her mother's number." Pulling a notebook from her pocket, she scribbled in it.

Abra went back to Carmen, sitting with her, offering what comfort she could. When Cody returned he brought little new information. They spent the next four hours waiting with a television murmuring in a wall bracket nearby.

Cody poured coffee from the pot kept on a warming plate in the waiting room, and Abra urged cups of tea on Carmen. "You should eat," she murmured, closing her hand over Carmen's before she could protest. "For the baby. Why don't I get you something?"

"After they come. Why don't they come?"

"It's hard to wait, I know." The words were hardly out of her mouth when she saw the doctor, still in his surgical scrubs. Carmen saw him, too, and her fingers tightened like a vise on Abra's.

"Mrs. Mendez?" He walked over to sit on the table in front of her. "Your husband's out of surgery."

In her fear she lost her English and sent out a stream of desperate Spanish.

"She wants to know how he is," Abra said. "If he's going to be all right."

"We've stabilized him. We had to remove his spleen, and there was some other internal damage, but he's very young and very strong. He's still critical, and he lost a considerable amount of blood from the internal injuries and the lacerations. His back was broken."

Carmen closed her eyes. She didn't understand about spleens and lacerations. She only understood that her David was hurt. "*Por favor*, is he going to die?"

"We're going to do everything we can for him. But his injuries are very serious. He's going to be with us for a while. We'll monitor him closely."

"I can see him?" Carmen asked. "I can see him now?"

"Soon. We'll come for you as soon as he's out of Recovery."

"Thank you." Carmen wiped her eyes. "Thank you. I will wait."

Abra caught the doctor before he stepped back into the corridor. "What are his chances?"

"To be candid, I would have said they were very poor when you brought him in. I had my doubts that he'd survive the surgery. But he did and, as I said, he's strong."

She would have to be content with that. "Will he walk?"

"It's early to say, but I have every hope." He flexed his fingers, which were obviously still cramped from surgery. "He'll need extensive therapy."

"We'll want him to have whatever he needs. I don't think Mrs. Mendez understands about the insurance. Thornway has excellent coverage of medical expenses."

"Then I'll tell you frankly there'll be plenty of them. But with time and care he'll recover."

"That's what we want. Thank you, Doctor."

Abra leaned against the doorway and let her body go limp.

"You okay?"

She reached for Cody's hand. "Pretty good now. I was scared. He's so young."

"You were wonderful with her."

Abra glanced back to where Carmen sat on the couch composing herself. "She just needed someone to hold her hand. If I were in her position, I'd hate to wait alone. They're just kids." Weary, she rested her head on Cody's shoulder. "She was telling me how happy they were about the baby, how they were saving for furniture, how good it was that he had steady work."

"Don't." Cody brushed a tear from her lashes. "They're going to be fine."

"I felt so helpless. I hate feeling helpless."

"Let me take you home."

She shook her head, surprised by the sudden draining fatigue. "I don't want to leave her yet."

"We'll wait until her mother gets here."

"Thanks. Cody?"

"Yeah?"

"I'm glad you hung around."

He put his arms around her. "Red, sooner or later you're going to figure out that you can't get rid of me."

Later, when the sun was going down, Cody sat in a chair in her apartment and watched her as she curled up on the couch and slept. She'd exhausted herself. He hadn't known she could. He hadn't, he added as he lit a cigarette and let his own body relax, realized a good many things about her.

The explosion he'd witnessed after her mother's announcement that morning had told him a great deal. It hadn't been just the one incident, the one betrayal, that had made her so wary of relationships. It was her whole life.

How difficult would it be to trust yourself, to trust a man, after living in broken home after broken home? Damn near impossible, the way Cody figured. But she was with him. Maybe she still set up boundaries, but she was with him. That counted for something.

It was going to take time—more than he'd planned on—but he was going to see that she stayed with him.

Rising, he walked over to her and gathered her up in his arms.

"What?" Roused, she blinked her eyes open.

"You're worn out, Red. Let me tuck you in."

"I'm okay." She nuzzled her head in the curve of his shoulder. "I just needed a nap."

"You can finish it in bed." When he laid her down, she curled into almost the same position she'd been in on the couch. Sitting at the foot of the bed, Cody unlaced her shoes.

"I was dreaming," she murmured.

"About what?" He sat her shoes on the floor, then unbuttoned her jeans.

"I don't know exactly. But it was nice." She sighed, hoping she could find her way back to the dream. "Are you seducing me?"

He looked at the long line of her legs and at her narrow hips, which were bare but for a brief triangle of practical cotton. "Not at the moment."

She rubbed her cheek against the pillow, comfortably drowsy. "How come?"

"Mostly because I like seducing you when you're awake." He drew the sheet over her and bent to kiss the top of her head. He would have stepped back, but she reached for his hand.

"I'm awake." Her eyes were still closed, but her lips curved. "Almost."

He sat on the bed again, contenting himself with stroking her hair. "Is that a request?"

"Umm-hmm. I don't want you to go."

Cody pulled off his boots, then slipped into bed to hold her. "I'm not going anywhere."

Her arms curled around him as she settled her body against his. Then she lifted her lips to his. "Will you love me?"

"I do," he murmured, but she was already drifting with the kiss.

The light lowered, softened, glowed gold. She moved to him with the ease and familiarity of a longtime wife. Her fingers grazed him, exciting as the touch of a new lover. They didn't speak again, didn't need to.

Her lips were warm, softened by sleep, as they moved over his. Her taste was more than familiar now, it was a part of him, something he could draw in like his own breath. He lingered there, nibbling, then demanding, teasing, then taking, while she worked her way down the buttons of his shirt.

She wanted to touch him, to feel his strength beneath her hand. It was strange that she felt safe here, in his arms, when she'd never realized she needed safety. Protected, wanted, cared for, desired. He gave her all that, and she'd never had to ask. His heart beat fast and steady. The pulse of it against her was like an echo of her own.

This was what she had dreamed of—not just the pleasure, not only the excitement, but the simple security of being with the man she loved.

Cradling his face in her hands, she tried to show him what she was afraid to tell him.

She was overwhelming. Even though the loving was slow, almost lazy, she took his breath away. There seemed to be no bounds to her generosity. It flowed from her like honey, warm and thick and sweet.

No hurry. No rush. The shadows washed the room until the gold faded to a soft, soft gray. There was no sound but his lover's sigh and the quiet shifting of her body over the sheets. He looked at her as evening fell and the light faded. Her eyes, aroused now, no longer sleepy, were like the shadows—darkening, deepening.

Very slowly, as though some part of him knew he would need to remember this moment on some cold, lonely day, he combed his fingers through her hair until her face was unframed. Then he just looked and looked, while the breath trembled through her parted lips. Slowly, almost painfully, he lowered his head, his eyes on hers, watching, watching, until their lips parted, separated and were drawn back together.

With a small, helpless sound she pulled him closer, almost afraid of what his tenderness was doing to her. But the demand didn't come, only the gift. There were tears in her eyes now, and an ache in her throat, as the beauty weakened her. She spoke again, but only his name, as the emotions that were flooding her poured out.

Then they were clinging together, as survivors of a storm might cling to one another. It was as if they couldn't touch enough, couldn't take enough. Wrapped tight, mouths seeking, they rolled over the bed. Sheets tangled and were ripped aside. Their tenderness was replaced by a greed that was every bit as devastating.

With their fingers locked, their needs fused, she rose over him, sliding down to take him into her. When he filled her she arched back, crying out. Not helplessly, but triumphantly.

Caught in the last light of day, they swept each other toward dusk and the welcoming night.

Chapter 10

"I appreciate you going with me."

Cody spared Abra a brief look as he stopped the car in front of the hotel where W. W. Barlow and his new wife were staying. "Don't be stupid."

"No, I mean it." She fiddled nervously with her choker as the valet hurried to open her door. "This is my problem. A family problem." After stepping out on the curb, she took a deep breath and waited for Cody to join her. "But I'd have hated to face this dinner alone."

It continued to surprise him to find these traces of insecurity in her. This same woman who was afraid to share a quiet dinner with her mother had once stepped carelessly between two angry construction workers with fists like cinder blocks. With a shake of his head he pocketed his parking stub, then took her arm to lead her into the lobby.

"You're not alone. Still, there's no reason to go into this believing it's going to be some sort of trial by fire."

"Then how come I can already feel the heat?" she mumbled as they crossed the lobby.

"You're not being interviewed by the State Department, Wilson. You're having dinner with your mother and her new husband."

She couldn't prevent a short laugh. "And I've had tons of experience." She paused again at the entrance to the dining room. "Sorry. No snide remarks, no sarcasm and no pouting."

He cupped her face, amused by the way she had straightened her shoulders and brought up her chin. "All right. But I had planned to pout at least through the appetizers."

She laughed again, and this time she meant it. "You're good for me."

His fingers tightened as he dipped his head to give her a hard, unexpected kiss. "Red, I'm the best for you."

"Good evening." The maître d' was all smiles. He evidently had a weakness for romance. "A table for two?"

"No." Cody let his hand slip down to take Abra's. "We're joining the Barlows."

"Of course, of course." That seemed to perk him up even more. "They've just been seated. If you'll follow me?"

It was early for dinner, so the restaurant was all but empty. Salmon-colored tablecloths and turquoise napkins were pressed and waiting for the patrons who would trickle in over the next two hours. A miniature fountain shaded by palms rose up in the center. The candles on the tables had yet to be lit, as the sun still filtered through the windows. As the maître d' had said, the newlyweds were already seated. They were holding hands. Barlow spotted them first and sprang out of his chair. Abra couldn't be sure, but she thought his smile seemed a bit sheepish.

"Right on time." He grabbed Cody's hand for a quick, hearty shake. "Glad you could make it." He hesitated a moment before turning to Abra. He was wearing an obviously pricey Fioravanti suit, but he still looked like anyone's favorite uncle. "Am I allowed to kiss my new stepdaughter?"

"Of course you are." Trying not to wince at the term, she offered a cheek, but found herself gripped in a huge, hard bear hug. Instinctively at first, then with more feeling than she'd expected, she returned it.

"Always wanted a daughter," he mumbled, making a production of pulling out her chair. "Never expected to get one at my age."

Not certain what she should do next, Abra leaned over to kiss her mother's cheek. "You look wonderful. Did you enjoy your trip?"

"Yes." Jessie twisted the napkin in her lap. "I'm going to love Dallas as much as Willie does. I hope— we hope—you'll find time to visit us there."

"Always a room for you there." Barlow tugged at his tie, mangling the tidy Windsor knot. "Make it your home whenever you want."

Abra clasped and unclasped her purse. "That's kind of you."

"Not kind." Giving up his tie, Barlow smoothed what was left of his hair. "Family."

"You would like a drink before you order?" The maître d' hovered, clearly pleased to have one of the wealthiest men in the country at one of his tables.

"Champagne. Dom Perignon '71." Barlow laid a hand on Jessie's. "We're celebrating."

"Very good, sir."

Silence descended immediately, awkwardly. Cody had a quick flash of his own family meals, with everyone talking over everyone else. When Abra's hand found his under the table, he decided to give them all a little help. "I hope you'll be able to come by and check on the project before you go back to Dallas."

"Why, yes, yes. Planned to." Barlow gripped the lifeline gratefully.

Sitting back, Cody began to steer the conversation over easy ground.

Why, they're nervous, too, Abra realized as all three of them struggled to hit the right tone, find the right words. Everyone could have walked on eggshells without causing a crack. Only Cody was relaxed, hooking an arm over the back of his chair and taking the reins the others gladly relinquished. Jessie continued to twist her napkin, though she managed the occasional forced smile. Barlow ran his finger under his collar constantly, clearing his throat and reaching out to touch Jessie's hand or arm or shoulder.

Reassuring each other, Abra thought. Because of her. It made her feel small and selfish and mean-spirited. Whatever happened between Barlow and her mother, they cared for each other now. Holding back her approval or acceptance helped nothing and hurt everyone. Including her.

There seemed almost a communal sigh of relief when the wine was served. The fussy little show began with the display of the label. The cork was removed with only a whisper of sound, and a swallow was offered to Barlow for tasting. Once it was approved, wine was poured in all the glasses.

"Well, now." Barlow sent his nervous smile around the table as bubbles raced to the surface.

"I'd like to propose a toast," Cody began.

"No, please." Abra stopped him with a hand on his arm. During the strained silence, Jessie linked fingers with Barlow. "I'd like to." She couldn't think of any clever words. She'd always been better with figures. "To your happiness," she said, wishing she could do better. She touched her glass to her mother's, then to Barlow's. "I hope you'll love my mother as much as I do. I'm glad you found each other."

"Thank you." Jessie sipped, struggled to compose herself, then gave up. "I must go powder my nose. Excuse me a minute."

She hurried off, leaving Barlow grinning and blinking his eyes. "That was nice. Real nice." He took Abra's hand, squeezing tightly. "I'm going to take good care of her, you know. Man doesn't often get a chance to start over at my age. Going to do it right."

Abra rose to move over and rest her cheek against his. "See that you do. I'll be back in a minute."

Barlow watched her take the same route as Jessie. "Guess if I were any prouder I'd bust my seams." He lifted his glass and took a long gulp. "Quite a pair, aren't they?"

"You could say that." He was feeling enormously proud himself.

"Ah, now that we've got a minute… Jessie tells me you and Abra are…close."

Cody lifted a brow. "Going to play papa, WW?"

Embarrassed, Barlow shifted in his chair. "Like I said, I never had a daughter before. Makes a man feel protective. I know Jessie would like to see that girl settled and happy. She thinks Abra's feelings might be serious. If yours aren't—"

"I love her." There. He'd said it out loud, and it felt

wonderful. Cody savored it for a moment, finding it as rich and exciting as the wine. He hadn't expected it to feel good, hadn't expected the words to come so easily. As if experimenting, he said it again. "I love her. I want to marry her." The second part came as a surprise to him. It wasn't that he hadn't thought of the future, with her as a part of it. It wasn't that he hadn't thought of them spending their lives together. But marriage, the solidity of it, the absoluteness of it, came as a surprise. He found it a pleasant one.

"Well, well..." Doubly pleased, Barlow lifted his glass again. "Have you asked her?"

"No, I... When the time's right."

With a bray of laughter, Barlow slapped him on the back. "Nothing more foolish than a young man in love. Unless it's an old one. Let me tell you something, boy. You try to plan these things out—right time, right place, right mood—they never get done. Maybe you're not old enough to think about how precious time is, but take it from me, there's nothing worse than looking back and seeing how much you wasted. That girl...my daughter—" he puffed out his chest "—she's a prize. You'd better grab on before she slips away from you. Have another drink." He topped off Cody's glass. "Marriage proposals come easier if you're loose. Had to get damn near drunk to manage both of mine."

With an absent nod, Cody lifted his glass, and wondered.

Abra found Jessie in the ladies' lounge, sitting on an overstuffed white chair and sniffling into a hankie. Abra cast a helpless look around, then sat beside her.

"Did I say something wrong?"

Jessie shook her head and dabbed at her eyes. "No. You said everything right and made me so happy." She sobbed as she turned to throw her arms around Abra's neck. "I was so nervous about tonight, so afraid you'd sit there hating me."

"I've never hated you. I couldn't." Abra felt her own eyes filling. "I'm sorry. I'm sorry I made things so hard on you before."

"No, you didn't. You never have. You've always been the one thing in my life I could count on. I've always asked too much of you. I have," she insisted when Abra shook her head. "I know I've let you down, over and over again, and I regret it. But I can't go back and change it." She drew back, and her smooth cheeks were streaked with tears. "To be honest, I don't know if I would if I had the chance. I've made mistakes, sweetheart, and you've had to pay for them." She dried Abra's cheeks with her damp handkerchief. "I never thought of you first, and you have the right to resent me for that."

Sometimes she had, and sometimes the resentment had edged toward despair. Tonight wasn't the night to think of it. Instead, she smiled. "Do you remember the time, I was about ten or eleven and that boy up the street—Bob Hardy—pushed me off my bike? I came home with my knees all bloody and my shirt torn."

"That little bully." Jessie's pretty mouth thinned. "I wanted to give him a good smack."

The idea of Jessie smacking anyone, even a grubby delinquent, made Abra's smile widen. "You cleaned me all up, kissed all the scrapes and promised me a new shirt. Then you marched right off to Mrs. Hardy."

"I certainly did. When I— How do you know? You were supposed to be in your room."

"I followed you." Delighted with the memory, Abra grinned. "I hid in the bushes outside the door and listened."

Jessie's color was a bit heightened when she meticulously replaced the hankie in her purse. "You heard what I said to her? Everything?"

"And I was amazed." With a laugh, Abra took her mother's hand. "I didn't know you had even heard those kind of words, much less that you could use them so… effectively."

"She was a fat old witch." Jessie sniffed. "I wasn't going to let her get away with raising a mean, nasty boy who pushed my little girl around."

"By the time you'd finished with her she was eating out of your hand. That night she brought that mean, nasty boy to the door by his ear and made him apologize. I felt very special."

"I love you just as much now. More, really." Gently she brushed Abra's hair from her temples. "I never knew quite how to deal with a child. It's so much easier for me to talk to a woman."

Because she was beginning to understand, Abra kissed her cheek. "Your mascara's running."

"Oh, no." Jessie took one look in the mirror and shuddered. "What a mess. Willie will take one look and run for cover."

"I doubt that, but you'd better fix it before we miss out on that champagne." Abra settled back comfortably to wait.

"That wasn't so bad." Cody stripped off his tie the moment they stepped into Abra's apartment.

"No, it wasn't." She kicked off her shoes. She felt good, really good. Perhaps her mother's marriage would go the way of her others. Perhaps it wouldn't. But they had crossed a bridge tonight. "In fact, it was nice. Champagne, caviar, more champagne. I could get used to it." When he wandered to the window to look out, she frowned at his back. "You seem a little distracted. Cody?"

"What?" He turned back to stare at her. She was wearing a white sundress sashed at the waist with a vivid green scarf. She never failed to knock him out when she was wearing something slim and feminine. Who was he kidding? She knocked him out when she was wearing dirty overalls.

A little confused by the way he was staring, Abra tried a smile. "I know I was pretty wrapped up in myself this evening, but I did notice how quiet you got. What's wrong?"

"Wrong? Nothing. I've…got some things on my mind, that's all."

"The project? Is there a problem?"

"It's not the project." Hands in his pockets, he crossed over to her. "And I don't know if it's a problem."

She felt her hands go cold. His eyes were very dark, very intense, very serious. He was going to end it, she thought, her heart trembling. He was going to end it now and go back east. Moistening her lips, she prepared herself. She'd promised herself that she would be strong when this moment came, that she wouldn't ruin what they'd had by clinging when it was over. Quite simply, she wanted to die.

"Do you want to talk about it?"

He glanced around the apartment. It was, as always, in chaos. There was no candlelight or mood music. He didn't have a rose or a diamond ring to give her. Then again, he was hardly the down-on-one-knee, hand-on-heart type. "Yeah. I think we should—"

The phone interrupted him, making him swear and Abra jolt. As if in a dream, she moved to answer. "Hello.

I… Oh, yes. Yes, he's here." Her face blank, she offered Cody the receiver. "It's your mother."

A little skip of fear raced through him as he took the phone. "Mom? No, it's no problem. Is everything all right?"

Abra turned away. She heard snatches of his conversation, but they floated in and out of her head. If he was going to break it off, she had to be strong and accept it. As Cody had only minutes before, she walked to the window and stared out.

No, it was wrong. The whole idea was wrong and had always been wrong. She loved him. Why the hell did she have to accept that it was going to end? And why was she automatically assuming that he was going to leave? It was hateful, she thought, closing her eyes. Hateful to be so insecure over the only thing, the only person, who really mattered.

"Abra?"

"Yes?" She turned quickly, torn. "Is everything all right?"

"Everything's fine. I gave my family this number, as well as the one at the hotel."

"That's all right." Her smile was strained around the edges.

"My father had some trouble—heart trouble—a couple of months ago. It was touch and go for a while."

Compassion came instantly and wiped out her nerves. "Oh, I'm sorry. Is he okay now?"

"Looks like." He took out a cigarette, unsure how to balance his relief about his father with his nerves over Abra. "He went in for more tests today and got a clean bill of health. My mother just wanted to let me know."

"I'm so glad. It must be terrifying…" She let her words trail off as another thought sank in. "A couple of months ago? About the time we were having our preliminary meetings?"

"That's right."

On a long breath, she shut her eyes. She could see herself perfectly, standing in the trailer on that first day and berating him for being too spoiled and lazy to leave his orange grove.

"You should have poured that beer over *my* head."

The grin helped. He walked over to tug on her hair. "I thought about it."

"You should have told me," she muttered.

"It wasn't any of your business—at the time." Taking her hand, he brought it to his lips. "Times change. Abra—"

This time the phone had him snarling.

"Yank that damn thing out of the wall, will you?"

Chuckling, she moved away to answer. "Hello. Yes, this is Abra Wilson. Mrs. Mendez? Yes, how is your husband? That's good. No, it wasn't any trouble at all. Mr. Johnson and I were glad to do it." She shifted the phone to her other ear as Cody moved behind her to nibble on her neck. "Tonight? Actually, I... No. No, of course not, not if it's important. We can be there in about twenty minutes. All right. Goodbye."

Puzzled, Abra replaced the receiver. "That was Carmen Mendez."

"So I gathered. Where can we be in about twenty minutes?"

"The hospital." Abra glanced around for the purse she'd tossed aside when they'd come in. "She sounded very strange, very nervous, yet she said that Mendez was out of Intensive Care and doing well enough. She said he needed to talk to us right away."

Since she was already putting on her shoes, Cody decided she'd made up her mind to go. "One condition."

"Which is?"

"When we get back we don't answer the phone."

They found Mendez flat on his back in a semiprivate room with his wife sitting beside him, clinging to his hand.

"It was good of you to come."

Cody noticed that Mendez's knuckles were white. The curtains between the beds were drawn. The other patient had the television on, and the squealing sounds of a car chase poured out.

"I'm glad you're doing better." Abra laid a hand on Carmen's shoulder, squeezing lightly as she studied the man in the bed. He was young, too young, for the lines of pain and trouble around his eyes. "Is there anything you need? Anything we can do for you?" She broke off, surprised and embarrassed to see his eyes fill with tears.

"No, *gracias*. Carmen told me how good you were, staying with her, taking care of all the papers and the questions."

Carmen leaned over him, murmuring in Spanish, but the words were too soft for Abra to hear.

"Sí." He moistened his lips, and though his back brace prevented him from moving, Abra thought he was set as if for a blow. "I thought I would die, and I could not die with sins on my soul. I told Carmen everything. We have talked." His eyes shifted so that he could see his wife and her nod of encouragement. "We have decided to tell you." He swallowed, closing his eyes for a moment. "It didn't seem so bad, and with the baby coming we needed the money. When Mr. Tunney asked me, I knew in my heart it was wrong, but I wanted good things for Carmen and the baby. And myself."

Uneasy, Abra moved closer to the bed. Across the prone body of Mendez, she and Cody exchanged one brief look.

Cody kept his voice calm. "What did Tunney ask you?"

"Only to look the other way, to pretend not to notice. Much of the wire we use on the project is not up to code."

Abra felt her stomach sink and her blood go cold. "Tunney offered to pay you to install substandard wire?"

"*Sí*. Not all, not everywhere. Not all of the men could be trusted—not to be trusted," he said lamely. "When a delivery would come, he would assign a few of us to work with the twelve-gauge. We would be paid in cash every week. I know I can go to jail— We know. But we have decided to do what is right."

"David, this is a very serious accusation." But Abra was remembering the reels of wire she had examined herself. "That wiring was inspected."

"*Sí*. It was arranged to have the same inspector. He is paid, also. When he comes, you and Mr. Johnson are to be busy somewhere else in case you would notice something."

"How could Tunney arrange—" Abra closed her eyes. "David, was Tunney following orders?"

Mendez squeezed his wife's hand again. This was what he feared most. "*Sí*, he has orders. From Mr. Thornway." Murmuring, Carmen lifted a cup to his lips so that he could wet his dry lips.

"There is more than the wiring. I hear things. Some of the concrete, some of the steel, some of the rivets. Some," he explained. "Not all, you see? I think when I am asked that Mr. Thornway is a big builder. He is powerful, important, so this must be the way. When

I tell Carmen, she is ashamed of me and says it is not our way."

"We will give back the money." Carmen spoke for the first time. Her eyes were as they had been on the day of the accident, very young and very afraid, but her voice was strong.

"I don't want you to worry about that now." Abra rubbed a hand over her temple. "Or anything else. You did the right thing. Mr. Johnson and I will take care of it. We may need to talk to you again, and you'll have to go to the police."

Carmen put an unsteady hand on her rounded stomach. "We will do what you say. *Por favor*, Señorita Wilson, my David is not a bad man."

"I know. Don't worry."

Abra stepped out of the room, feeling as though she had taken a long, nasty fall. "What are we going to do?"

"We're going to go see Tim." He put his hands on her shoulders. "I'm going to call Nathan. He needs to know about this."

She nodded, walking away as he headed to a bank of phones.

They didn't speak on the drive to Thornway's house. Abra could only think of the business Thornway had built, brick by brick, the reputation he had earned, the pride he had felt and had given her the chance to feel. In one flash the son he had handed it to had tossed it aside.

"I should have guessed," she murmured at length.

"How?" He was dealing with his own demons, and with the crumbling of his own dreams.

"The day Mendez was hurt. I was with Tunney. There had just been a delivery, and I happened to check it. It was twelve-gauge." She turned her head to look at him. "He spun me a tale about someone screwing up the invoice numbers. We were talking when the accident happened, and I never took it any further. Damn it, Cody, I never even thought of it again."

"You wouldn't have had any reason to suspect him. Or Thornway." He pulled up in front of Tim's house. "Why don't I handle this? You can wait here."

"No." She pushed open the car door. "I have to be there."

Moments later they were waiting in Tim's spacious foyer.

Elegant in a dinner jacket, Tim came down the steps. "Abra, Cody. This is a surprise. I'm afraid you just caught us. Marci and I are on our way out. She's still dressing."

"You'll have to be late," Cody said curtly. "This can't wait."

"Sounds serious." Tim checked his watch before gesturing them into his library. "I can always squeeze out a few minutes. Marci's never on time anyway." He went to a small ebony bar. "What can I get you?"

"An explanation." Abra took a step toward him, needing to see his eyes. "As to why you've been using substandard equipment on the Barlow project."

His hand shook once, and the whiskey spilled before he steadied it and poured. That was all she needed to be sure of the truth. "What in the world are you talking about?"

"I'm talking about materials that don't come up to code. I'm talking about payoffs and kickbacks and bribes." She grabbed his arm when he started to lift his drink, and her fingers dug in. "I'm talking about ruining a reputation your father spent his life building."

Whiskey in hand, Tim turned. Though the room was cool, there was already a light film of sweat beading above his mouth. "I have no idea what this is all about, but I don't appreciate being accused of any illegalities." He tossed back the whiskey, then poured another. "I realize my father had an affection for you, Abra, and that you feel a certain personal interest in my company. But that doesn't excuse this."

"Be careful." Cody's voice was too soft and too mild. "Be very careful what you say to her, or I may just decide to go with my instincts and break your arms."

The sweat was dripping now, hot and sticky down his back. "I don't have to stand here in my own house and be threatened."

Cody simply shifted in front of the door before Tim could storm out. "You're going to stand here and be a lot more than threatened. The game's up. We know about the materials, about the inspectors you bribed, about the laborers who were paid off to install and keep their mouths shut. Funny thing, Tim, it turns out that some of them have consciences."

"This is ridiculous. If someone's been skimming on the material, I intend to find out about it. You can be sure I'll initiate an investigation."

"Fine." Abra put a hand on his arm and looked him in the eye. "Call the building commissioner."

"I'll do just that."

"Do it now." Abra tightened her grip when he tried to pull away. "I imagine you have his home number. We can have a little meeting right here tonight."

Tim reached for his glass again. "I have no intention of disturbing the commissioner at home on a Saturday evening."

"I think he'd be very interested." Abra recognized the fear in his eyes and gave him one last push. "While you're at it, why don't you call Tunney, too? The commissioner's going to want to talk to him. Somehow I don't think Tunney's a man who'd be willing to take the fall alone."

Saying nothing, Tim sank into a chair. He drank again, this time in small sips, until the glass was empty. "We can work something out." He leaned forward, his hands braced on his knees. "It's business, you understand. I took a few shortcuts. Nothing that has to matter."

"Why?" She'd needed to hear him say it. Now that he had, her anger drained away. "Why would you risk everything for a few extra dollars?"

"A few?" With a laugh, he snatched the bottle from beside him and poured more whiskey. He'd already had too much and too quickly, but he badly needed more. "Thousands. It came to thousands. You skim here, cut through there, and before you know it there are thousands. I needed it." The liquor steadied his hand as he drank. "You don't know what it's like being the son, being expected to do things as well as they were always done. Then there's Marci." He glanced up as though he could see her in the room above his head. "She's beautiful, restless, and she wants. The more I give, the more she wants. I can't afford to lose her." He dropped his face into his hands. "I bid too low, way too low, on this project. I thought I could pull it off somehow. I had to. There are debts, debts to the wrong kind of people. Ever since I took over, things have been going wrong. I lost fifty thousand on the Lieterman project."

He glanced up when Abra said nothing. "It wasn't the first time. For the past nine months the business has been dropping into the red. I had to make it up. This was the best way. Cut a few corners, sweeten a few pots. If I brought this in under budget and on time I'd be in the black again."

"And when there was an electrical fire?" Cody put in. "Or the supports gave way? What then?"

"It didn't have to be that way. I had to take the chance. I had to. Marci expects to live a certain way. Am I supposed to tell her we can't go to Europe because the business is in trouble?"

Abra looked at him and felt only pity. "Yes. You're going to have to tell her a lot more than that now."

"Work isn't going to start again on Monday, Tim." Cody waited until he brought his head back up. "It's not going to start at all until after a full investigation. You bit this off, now you're going to have to swallow it. You can call the building commissioner, or we can."

Tim was getting drunk. It helped somehow. "You haven't told anyone?"

"Not yet," Abra said. "You're right that I felt close to your father and that I feel a responsibility to the business. I wanted you to have a chance to make this right yourself."

Make it right? Tim thought desperately. How in God's name could he make it right? One official inspection and everything would be over. "I'd like to speak with Marci first. Prepare her. Give me twenty-four hours."

Cody started to object, but Abra touched his arm. The wheels were already in motion, she thought. Another day wasn't going to stop what had begun. She could give him a day, because she'd cared for his father. "You'll set up a meeting at your office? For all of us?"

"What choice do I have?" His words were slurred now by drink and self-pity. "I'm going to lose everything, aren't I?"

"Maybe you'll get back your self-respect." Cody took Abra's hand. "I want to hear from you by nine tomorrow night, or we'll make that call."

Outside, Abra pressed her fingers to her eyes. "Oh, God, it's awful."

"It's not going to get better."

"No." She straightened and glanced back at the house. The light was still burning in the library. "This was going to be my last job for them. I never expected it to end like this."

"Let's go."

Tim heard their car start up and sat listening as the sound of the engine died away in the night. His wife, his beautiful, selfish wife, was primping upstairs. In a fit of rage, he hurled his glass across the room. He hated her. He adored her. Everything he'd done had been to make her happy. To keep her. And if she left him…

No, he couldn't bear to think of it. He couldn't bear to think of the scandal and the accusations. They would crucify him, and he would lose his business, his home, his status. His wife.

Maybe there was still a chance. There was always a chance. Stumbling to the phone, he dialed a number.

Chapter 11

Perhaps it was the strain of the evening, or the discomfort of witnessing another's despair and humiliation, but they needed each other. They fell into bed in a kind of fury, saying nothing, looking for what they could bring to each other to block out the lingering anger and disillusionment.

Together they had built something strong—or thought they had. Now they had learned that it had been built on lies and deceits. If they tangled together quickly, reaching, taking, it was to assure themselves that what they had built privately was no lie.

This was real, solid, honest. She could feel it as his mouth closed hungrily over hers, as their tongues met, as their bodies fitted together. If he needed to forget what existed outside this room, this bed, for just one night, she understood. She needed it, too, and so she gave herself utterly.

He wanted to comfort her. She had looked so stricken when Tim had collapsed into confession. It was personal with Abra, and he knew, though she had said nothing, that she was taking part of the failure as her own. He wouldn't have it. But the time for straight talk was in the morning, when her feelings weren't so raw. For now, for a few hours, he would give her release in passion.

Her scent. He remembered watching her dab it on before dinner, absently, as an afterthought. It had faded as the night had worn on, and now it was no more than a whisper along her skin, and all the more intimate for that. He drew it in as he let his mouth glide over her throat and down to where her skin became impossibly soft, impossibly delicate.

Her hair. She had taken a brush through it quickly, impatiently. She was never fully satisfied with the way it looked. He thought it glorious. Now, as he combed a hand through it, he could luxuriate in the wildness of it. When she rolled over, stretching her body over his as if she couldn't get enough of him, her hair streamed over her shoulders and dipped to his.

Her lips. She had added color to them, worried it off, then replaced it. They were naked now, smooth as silk, soft as rain. He had only to touch his to them for them to part in welcome. If he asked more, she gave more.

Now, with him trapped beneath the tangle of her hair and her agile body, she took her mouth over him, giving him pleasure, seeking her own. There was an excitement in having the freedom to explore the man she loved. To touch him and feel him tremble. To taste him and hear him sigh.

The light in the hallway was still burning, so she could see him, the lean lines, the firm muscles. And his eyes. She could see his eyes as she brought her lips back to his. They were so dark, so completely focused on her.

She could sense something different but was unable

to understand it. One moment he was impatient, almost brutal, in his loving. The next he held her, kissed her, as if she were precious and fragile. However his hands took, however his lips demanded, she belonged to him. Passions layered so tightly with emotions that she couldn't separate desire from love. There was no need to.

When he filled her, she found both.

It was later, much later, when she woke, disturbed by some sound or some dream. Murmuring, she shifted, reaching out—and found him gone.

"Cody?"

"I'm right here."

She saw him then, standing by the window. The end of his cigarette glowed red in the dark. "What's wrong?"

"Nothing. Can't sleep."

Sitting up, she pushed her hair away from her face. The sheet slid down to pool at her waist. "You can come back to bed. We don't have to sleep."

He laughed and tapped out his cigarette. "I never thought I'd meet a woman who could wear me out."

She threw a pillow at him. "Is that supposed to be a compliment?"

"Just an observation." He came over to sit on the side of the bed. "You're the best, Red." He wasn't talking about sex. Because she understood that, she smiled and fumbled for something to say.

"I'm glad you think so." As her eyes adjusted to the dark, she frowned. "You're dressed."

"I was going to go for a drive. I didn't know whether or not to wake you."

"Of course you should have. Where were you going?"

He took her hand, carefully, as though weighing it.

"I have to see it, Abra. I might be able to get it out of my head for a few hours once I do."

Her fingers curled into his. "I'll go with you."

"You don't have to. It's late—early, I guess."

"I want to. Will you wait for me?"

"Sure." He brought her hand to his lips. "Thanks."

The air was cool and breathlessly clear. Overhead, the sky was a dark, calm sea pierced by stars. There was no traffic to dodge, only a long ribbon of road, banked first by houses and shops, then by nothing but acres of empty desert. With the windows down and the engine no more than a purr, Abra heard the lonesome call of a coyote.

"I've never driven through here at this time of night." Abra turned to look out the window at the distant buttes, which were no more than dark shadows rising and spreading. "It's so quiet. It makes you wonder."

"Wonder what?"

"That it's been this quiet, just this quiet, for centuries. I guess if we do it right it'll be just this quiet for centuries more."

"People in our business are supposed to see undeveloped land and think immediately of how it can be put to use."

She frowned a little and searched in her purse for a band or a string to tie back her hair. "Do you?"

He was silent for a moment, enjoying the drive, the quiet, the company. "There are places along the Intracoastal where the brush is so dense you can't see beyond the first foot. It's not quiet, because it's as thick with life as it is with leaves. The waterway cuts through— that's man's contribution—but some things are meant to stay as they are."

She was smiling again as she pulled her hair into a ponytail. "I like you, Johnson."

"Thanks, Wilson. I like you, too." He rested his arm on the back of the seat so that he could toy with the ends of her hair. "You said something before about the Barlow project being your last one with Thornway."

"Yeah. I've been thinking about it for a long time. After Tim took over I decided it was time to do more than think. I wish..." But it was no use wishing she had already cut her ties with the firm.

Because he understood, he massaged the tension at the back of her neck. "You got another offer?"

"No. I haven't exactly announced my resignation, but I'm not looking for another offer." She was afraid he would think her foolish, so she began to fiddle with the dial of the radio. Music poured out, as clear as the air. "I'm going to freelance, maybe start up my own business. A small one." She shut off the radio and shot him a look. "I've been putting money aside for a while now, to see me through the rough spots."

"Do you want out on your own or do you just want a change of scene?"

She considered for a moment, then shook her head. "Both, I guess. I owe a lot to Thornway. Thornway senior," she explained. "He gave me a chance, let me prove myself. Over the past year or so, things have changed. I didn't know...never had any idea Tim was into something like this, but I was never comfortable with the way he did business." Her eyes were drawn to the east, where the sky was just beginning to lighten. "He always looked at the ledger sheets instead of the overall project, the payroll instead of the men who were earning the wage. Nobody goes into business without the idea of making money, but when it's the only thing..."

"When it's the only thing you end up in a situation like the one we're in now."

"I still can't believe it," she murmured. "I thought I knew him, but this— Cody, how can a man risk everything, everything he's been given, to please a woman?"

"I'd say he loves her, obviously more than he should."

"Maybe she loves him. Maybe all the jewelry, the cars and the cruises didn't matter."

He ran a finger down the back of her neck. "They mattered, Red. With a woman like that, they always matter. It's a safe bet that when all this hits Marci Thornway takes the high road."

"That's cruel. She's still his wife."

"Remember the night of the party? She was his wife then, too, but she invited me to...let's say she invited me to spend an afternoon with her."

"Oh." Whatever sympathy she had felt for Marci Thornway vanished. "You turned her down?"

"It wasn't a hardship. Besides, I had other things on my mind. In any case, I don't think we can dump the whole mess in Marci's lap. Tim wanted too much too soon. Maybe he'd been given too much all along. Apparently he's been going after success in all the wrong ways."

"He mentioned owing money to the wrong kind of people," Abra said.

"He wouldn't be the first businessman to make a connection with organized crime. He won't be the first to lose because of it. What's this?" As they approached the turnoff for the site, he spotted another car. It hesitated at the crossroads, then swept to the right and sped away.

"I don't know." Abra frowned at the receding taillights. "Probably kids. A lot of times construction sites end up as lovers' lanes."

"Maybe, but it's late for teenagers to be out necking." He slowed to negotiate the turn.

"Well, we're here to look around, anyway. If they were vandals we'll find out soon enough."

He parked the car by the trailer. In silence they stepped out of opposite sides and stood. The main building, with its dome and spirals, was shadowed in the predawn light. Like a sculpture, it rose up out of rock, a product of imagination. The interior was rough, and the landscaping had yet to be started, but Abra saw it now as Cody had.

In this very fragile light it looked more fanciful, yet somehow more solid, than ever before. It didn't meld with the rock and sand, nor did it harmonize. Rather, it stood with and against and for—a celebration of man's ingenuity.

Standing apart, not yet connected by the flower-bordered paths, was the health center. Castlelike, it grew out of the thin, greedy soil, its arches and curves adding a richness, even a defiance, to the stark strength of the landscape. The early light struggled over the eastern rise and sprinkled on the walls.

They stood, hands lightly linked, and scanned what they had had a part in creating.

"It's going to have to come down," Cody murmured. "All or most of it."

"That doesn't mean it can't be built again. We can build it again."

"Maybe." He slipped an arm around her shoulders. The sun had yet to rise, and the air held the clean-edged chill of the desert night. "It's not going to be easy, and it's not going to be quick."

"It doesn't have to be." She understood now, as she never had, just how much of himself he had put into this.

These weren't just walls, weren't just beams and supports. This was his imagination, his contribution and, though only one who built could feel it, his heart. She turned to put her arms around him. "I guess it's time I told you the truth."

He kissed her hair, and the scent was warm, sun-drenched, though the air was cool with dawn. "About what?"

"About this place." She tilted her head up but didn't smile. He saw that her eyes were gray, like the light in the east. "I was wrong and you were right."

He kissed her, taking his time about it. "That's nothing new, Red."

"Keep it up and I won't tell you what I really think."

"Fat chance. You always tell me what you think whether I want to hear it or not."

"This time you will. You may even be entitled to gloat."

"I can't wait."

She drew away to dip her hands into her pockets and turn a slow circle. "It's wonderful."

"What?" With a hint of a smile, he gripped her shoulder. "Must be the lack of sleep, Wilson. You're light-headed."

"I'm not joking." She pulled away to face him again. "And I'm not saying this to make you feel better—or worse, for that matter. I'm saying it because it's time I did. For the past few weeks I've been able to see what you envisioned here, what you wanted to say, how you wanted to say it. It's beautiful, Cody, and maybe it sounds overdone, but it's majestic. When it's finished— and it will be finished one day—it's going to be a work of art, the way only the best buildings can be."

He stared at her as the sun peeked over the ridges

of rock and brought the first hints of daylight. "I know I'm supposed to gloat, but I can't seem to manage it."

"You can be proud of this." She rested her hands on his shoulders. "I'm proud of this, and of you."

"Abra…" He skimmed his knuckles over her cheek. "You leave me speechless."

"I'd like you to know that when it comes time to rebuild I want to be a part of it." Tilting her head, she smiled. "Not that there shouldn't be a few adjustments."

He laughed and yanked her close. He'd needed this. "There had to be that."

"Minor ones," she continued, holding on to him. "Reasonable ones."

"Naturally."

"We'll discuss them." She bit his ear. "Professionally."

"Sure we will. But I'm not changing anything."

"Cody…"

"I haven't told you that you're one of the best." Now it was her turn to look astonished. "As engineers go."

"Thanks a lot." She pulled back. "I feel better. How about you?"

"Yeah, I feel better." He ran a finger down her cheek. "Thanks."

"Let's take a look around, then. It's what we came for."

Arm in arm, they walked toward the main building. "The investigation's going to be rough," Cody began. It was easier to talk about it now. "It could mess up your plans to start your own business. At least for a while."

"I know. I guess I've been trying not to think about that. Not yet."

"You'll have Barlow behind you. And Powell and Johnson."

She smiled as he pulled open the door. "I appreciate that. I never asked you what Nathan said."

"He said he'd be on the first available plane." He paused just inside the door and looked.

The walls were up, the drywall smeared with compound and sanded smooth. Empty buckets were turned over, some of them bridged with boards to make casual seats. The elevators that had given Abra such grief were resting at ground level. The forms for the curving stairs were in place, the windows secured. Instead of the buzz and whine of tools, there was a silence, an echoing one that reached from the scarred subflooring to the brilliantly colored dome.

As they stood there she knew how he felt, even how he thought, because her own frustration at the futility of it all rose.

"It hurts, doesn't it?"

"Yeah." But he'd had to come and work his way through it. Minute by minute, it was becoming easier. "It'll pass, but I've got to say I don't want to watch when they start tearing it out."

"No, neither do I." She walked in a little farther and set her purse on a sawhorse. It did hurt. Maybe it would help for them to look beyond the immediate future to a more distant one. "You know, I've always wanted to come into a place like this as a patron." She turned with a smile because she felt they both needed it. "I'll make you a deal, Johnson. When it's done and your damn waterfalls are running, I'll treat you to a weekend."

"There's a resort I designed in Tampa that's already open."

She lifted a brow. "Does it have waterfalls?"

"A lagoon, in the center of the lobby."

"Figures. It's too dark to see much in here."

"I've got a flashlight in the car." He rocked back on his heels. "I'd like to take a closer look, make sure whoever was down here wasn't poking around where they shouldn't have been."

"Okay." She yawned once, hugely. "I can sleep tomorrow."

"I'll be right back."

She turned back into the room when he had gone. It was a waste, a terrible one, she thought, but it all hadn't been for nothing. Without this project, these buildings, she might never have met him. They said you didn't miss what you'd never had, but when she thought of Cody Abra was certain that was wrong. There would have been a hole in her life, always. She might not have known why, but she would have felt it.

Building had brought them together, and it would bring them together again. Maybe it was time she stopped sitting at the drawing board and planning out her personal life. With Cody, it might be possible to simply take, to simply act. With Cody, it might be possible to admit her feelings.

Scary, she thought, and with a nervous laugh she began to wander. She'd have to give the idea a lot of thought.

He cared for her. He might care enough to be glad if she told him she would relocate in Florida. They could go on there the way they had here. Until... She couldn't get beyond the *until*.

It didn't matter. She would deal with *until* when she got there. The one thing she was certain of was that she wasn't going to let him walk away.

With a shrug, she glanced up at the dome. The light was trickling through, thin but beautifully tinted by the glass. Pleased, she circled around. It was lovely the way it fell on the flooring, seeped into the corners. She could almost imagine the tinkling of the waterfall, the thick, cozy chairs circled around the clear pool.

They'd come back here one day, when the lobby was filled with people and light. When they did, they would remember how it had all started. His vision, and hers.

Daydreaming, she wandered toward the pipes that ran down the walls. Fanciful, yes, but certainly not foolish. In fact, she could— Her thoughts broke off as she stared down.

At first she wondered how the drywall finishers could have been so careless as to waste a trowelful of compound. And then not to clean it up, she thought as she crouched down to inspect it. A finger of light fell over it, making her look again, then look more closely and reach out to touch.

The moment she did, her heart froze. Scrambling up, she raced for the door, screaming for Cody.

He found the flashlight in the glove compartment, then tested it as a matter of course. It was probably useless to look around. It was probably just as useless to want to rip off a few panels of drywall and see for himself.

What did it matter if the place had been vandalized at this point? Correcting the wiring would have been difficult and time-consuming enough, but if the concrete and the steel were substandard, it all had to come down.

The anger bubbled up again, enough that he nearly tossed the flashlight back into the car. He'd come this far, he reminded himself. And Abra with him. They would look, and then they would leave. After the next day, what had once been his would be completely out of his hands.

His thoughts were running along the same lines as

Abra's when he started back. Without the building—whatever Tim had done to sabotage it—he would never have met her. Whatever happened here, the moment the mess was turned over to the proper authorities he was going to tell her exactly what he wanted. Needed.

The hell with that, he decided, quickening his pace. He was going to tell her now, right now, on the spot where it had all started. Maybe it was fitting, somehow, to ask her to marry him inside the half-finished building that had brought them together. The idea made him grin. What could be more fitting?

When he heard her scream the first time, his head whipped up. His heart stopped, but he was already running when she screamed again. He was close enough, when the explosion ripped, that the wall of hot air punched him like a fist and sent him flying in a rain of glass and rock and sheared metal.

The fall left him dazed—five seconds, ten. Then he was up and racing forward. He didn't feel the gash on his temple where something sharp and jagged had spun by close enough to tear his flesh. He didn't realize that the fall and those few seconds of numbness had saved his life.

All he saw were the flames licking greedily out of the windows the explosion had blown apart. Even as he reached what had been the doorway there were other explosions, one after another until the dawn echoed like a battlefield.

He was screaming for her, so strangled by fear that he couldn't hear his own voice, couldn't feel his own heart pumping out the panic. Something else blew, and a chunk of two-by-four shot out like a bullet, missing him by inches. The wall of heat drove him back once, searing his skin. Coughing, choking, he dropped to his knees and crawled inside.

There was more than fire here. Through the thick screen of smoke he could see where walls had crumbled, where huge chunks of ceiling had fallen in. As he fought his way in he could hear the sickening sound of steel breaking free and crashing down.

Blindly he heaved rubble aside, slicing his hand diagonally from one side of the palm to the other. Blood trickled into his eyes, which were already wet from the sting of smoke and fear.

Then he saw her hand, just her hand, almost covered by a pile of rubble. With a strength born of desperation, he began to heave and toss while the fire raged around him, roaring and belching and consuming. Over and over he called out her name, no longer aware of where he was, only that he had to get to her.

She was bleeding. In the turmoil of his mind he couldn't even form the prayer that she be alive. When he gathered her up, her body was weightless. For a moment, only a moment, he lost control enough to simply sit, rocking her. Slowly, with the terror clawing inside him, he began to drag her out.

Behind them was an inferno of unbearable heat and unspeakable greed. It was a matter of minutes, perhaps seconds, before what was still standing collapsed and buried them both. So he prayed, desperately, incoherently, while his shirt began to smoke.

He was ten feet beyond the building before he realized they were out. The ground around them was littered with steel and glass and still-smoldering wood. Every breath he took burned, but he fought his way to his feet, Abra in his arms, and managed another five yards before he collapsed with her.

Dimly, as if through a long, narrow tunnel, he heard the first sirens.

There was so much blood. Her hair was matted with it, and one arm of her shirt was soaked red. He kept calling to her as he wiped the worst of the grime and soot and blood from her face.

His hand was shaking as he reached out to touch the pulse in her throat. He never heard the last thundering crash behind him. But he felt the faint thready beat of her heart.

Chapter 12

"You need some attention, Mr. Johnson."

"That can wait." The panic was down to a grinding, deadly fear in the center of his gut. "Tell me about Abra. Where have you taken her?"

"Ms. Wilson is in the best of hands." The doctor was young, with wire-framed glasses and a shaggy head of dark hair. He'd been on the graveyard shift in the ER for a week, and he was looking forward to eight hours' sleep. "If you lose much more blood, you're going to pass out and save us all a lot of trouble."

Cody lifted him off his feet by the lapels of his coat and slammed him against the wall. "Tell me where she is."

"Mr. Johnson?"

Cody heard the voice behind him and ignored it as he stared into the eyes of the first-year resident. "Tell me where she is or you'll be bleeding."

The resident thought about calling for security, then decided against it. "She's being prepped for surgery.

I don't know a great deal about her condition, but Dr. Bost is heading the surgical team, and he's the best."

Slowly Cody let him down, but he maintained the grip on his coat. "I want to see her."

"You can throw me up against the wall again," the young doctor said, though he sincerely hoped it wouldn't come to that, "but you're not going to be able to see her. She needs surgery. You're both lucky to be alive, Mr. Johnson. We're only trying to keep you that way."

"She's alive." Fear was burning his throat more than the smoke inhalation.

"She's alive." Cautiously the doctor reached up to remove Cody's hands. "Let me take care of you. As soon as she's out of surgery I'll come for you."

Cody looked down at his hands. Blood was already seeping through the bandage the ambulance attendant had fashioned. "Sorry."

"Don't mention it. From what the paramedics said, you've had a rough time. You've got a hole in your head, Mr. Johnson." He smiled, hoping charm would work. "I'll stitch it up for you."

"Excuse me." The man who had spoken earlier stepped forward and flashed a badge. "Lieutenant Asaro. I'd like to speak with you, Mr. Johnson."

"You want to speak with him while he's bleeding to death?" Feeling a bit more in control, the doctor pulled open a curtain and gestured toward an examining room. "Or would you like to wait until he's patched up?"

Asaro noticed a chair near the examining table. "Mind?"

"No." Cody sat on the table and peeled off what was left of his shirt. Both his torso and his back were lashed with burns and lacerations that made Asaro wince.

"Close call, I'd say."

Cody didn't respond as the doctor began to clean the gash at his temple.

"Mind telling me what you and Miss Wilson were doing out there at dawn?"

"Looking around." Cody sucked in his breath at the sting of the antiseptic. From a few rooms down came a high, keening scream. "She's the engineer on the job. I'm the architect."

"I got that much." Asaro opened his notebook. "Don't you figure you see enough of the place during the week?"

"We had our reasons for going tonight."

"I'm going to give you a shot," the doctor said, humming a little through his teeth as he worked. "Numb this up."

Cody merely nodded to the doctor. He didn't know if he could get any more numb. "Earlier this evening we were informed that there had been discrepancies on the job. Substandard materials used."

"I see. You were informed?"

"That's right." Cody divorced his mind from his body as the doctor competently stitched the wound. "I'm not going to name the source until I discuss it, but I'll tell you what I know."

Asaro set pencil to paper. "I'd appreciate it."

Cody went through it all—the discovery, the confrontation with Tim Thornway, the confession. His anger at the deception had faded. The only thing on his mind now was Abra. He continued, speaking of the car they had seen leaving the site, their assumption that it had been teenagers taking advantage of a lonely spot.

"You still think that?" Asaro asked.

"No." He felt the slight pull and tug on his hand as his flesh was sewed together. "I think somebody planted explosives in every building on that site and blew it all to hell. It's a lot tougher to identify substandard material when there's nothing much left of it."

"Are you making an accusation, Mr. Johnson?"

"I'm stating a fact, Lieutenant. Thornway panicked and had his project destroyed. He knew Abra and I were going to the building commissioner tomorrow if he didn't. Now we can bypass that."

"How so?"

"Because as soon as Abra's out of surgery I'm going to find him and I'm going to kill him." He flexed the fingers of his bandaged hand and was vaguely relieved when they moved. He spared the doctor a brief glance. "Finished?"

"Almost." The resident continued without breaking rhythm. "You've got some glass in your back and a few nice third-degree burns."

"That's an interesting story, Mr. Johnson." Asaro rose and pocketed his book. "I'm going to have it checked out. A little advice?" He didn't wait for Cody to answer. "You should be careful about making threats in front of a cop."

"Not a threat," Cody told him. He felt the sting as the resident removed another shard of glass. He welcomed it. "There's a woman upstairs who means more to me than anything in the world. You didn't see how she looked when we got her here." His stomach tightened, muscle by muscle. "You know her only crime, Lieutenant? Feeling sorry enough for that bastard to give him a few hours to explain all of this to his wife. Instead, he might have killed her."

"One more question. Did Thornway know you were going to visit the site?"

"What difference does it make?"

"Humor me."

"No. It wasn't planned. I was restless." He broke off to press his fingers to his burning eyes. "I wanted to look at it, try to resign myself. Abra came with me."

"You ought to get yourself some rest, Mr. Johnson." Asaro nodded to the doctor. "I'll be in touch."

"We're going to check you in for a day or so, Mr. Johnson." The doctor wrapped the last burn before picking up a penlight to shine it in Cody's eyes. "I'll have the nurse give you something for the pain."

"No. I don't need a bed. I need to know what floor Abra's on."

"Take the bed, and I'll check on Miss Wilson." The look in Cody's eye had the resident holding up a hand. "Have it your way. You might not have noticed, but there are people around here who like my time and attention. Fifth-floor waiting room. Do yourself a favor," he said when Cody slid gingerly off the table. "Stop by the pharmacy." He scrawled a prescription on a pad, then ripped the sheet off. "Have this filled. Your being in pain's not going to help her."

"Thanks." Cody pocketed the prescription. "I mean it."

"I'd say anytime, but I'd be lying."

He didn't fill the prescription, not because the pain wasn't grim but because he was afraid that whatever he took might knock him out.

The waiting room was familiar. He'd spent hours there with Abra only days before, while David Mendez had been in surgery. Now it was Abra. He remembered how concerned she'd been, how kind. There was no one there now but himself.

Cody filled a large plastic cup with black coffee, scalded his already-raw throat with it and began to pace.

If he could have risked leaving her alone for a time, he would have gone then to find Thornway, to pull him out of that nice white house and beat his face to a pulp on that well-groomed lawn.

For money, Cody thought as he downed the rest of the burning coffee. Abra was lying on an operating table fighting for her life, and the reason was money. Crushing the cup in his hand, he hurled it across the room. The pain that tore through his shoulder had him swearing in frustration.

She'd screamed for him. Cody dragged a hand over his face as the memory of the sound ripped through him every bit as savagely as the glass. She'd screamed for him, but he hadn't been fast enough.

Why had she been alone in there? Why hadn't he sent her back to the car? Why hadn't he simply taken her home?

Why? There were a dozen whys, but none of the answers changed the fact that Abra was hurt and he was—

"Cody." Her hair mussed and her face drawn, Jessie ran into the room. "Good God, Cody, what happened? What happened to Abra?" She took his hands, not noticing the bandage as she squeezed. "They said there was an accident at the site. But it's Sunday morning. Why would she be out there on Sunday morning?"

"Jessie." Barlow hurried in behind her to take her hand and lead her to a chair. "Give him a chance. You can see the boy's been hurt."

Jessie's lip was trembling, and she had to bite it to steady it. She saw the bandages and the burns, and she saw the look on his face, which spoke more clearly than words of shock and fear. "Dear Lord, Cody, what happened? They said she's in surgery."

"You sit, too." Taking charge, Barlow eased Cody

into a chair. "I'm going to get us all some coffee here, and you take your time."

"I don't know how she is. They wouldn't let me see her." He was going to break down, he realized, if he didn't find something to hold on to. Reaction had taken its time seeping through, but now it struck like an iron fist. "She's alive," he said. It was almost a prayer. "When I pulled her out, she was alive."

"Pulled her out?" Jessie held the cup Barlow urged on her with both hands. Still, the coffee swayed and trembled. "Pulled her out of what?"

"I was outside, on my way back. Abra was in the building when it exploded."

"Exploded?" The coffee slipped out of her hands and onto the floor.

"The fire went up so fast." He could see it, he could feel it. As he sat in the chair, in his mind he was still back in the building, blinded by smoke and searching for her. "I got through, but I couldn't find her. The place was coming down. There must have been more than one charge. She was trapped under the rubble, but when I got her out she was alive."

Barlow put a hand on Jessie's arm to calm her, and to quiet her. "I want you to take it slow, Cody. Start at the beginning."

It was like a dream now. The pain did that, and the fear. He started with the call from Carmen Mendez and continued until they had wheeled Abra, unconscious, away from him.

"I should have pushed him," Cody murmured. "I should have picked up the phone and called the authorities myself. But he was drunk and pitiful and we wanted to give him a chance to salvage something. If I hadn't wanted to go out there, to look at it, to—I don't know, soothe my pride?—she wouldn't be hurt."

"You went in after her." Jessie rubbed the heels of her hands hard over her face. "You risked your life to save hers."

"I have no life without her."

The time for tears would have to wait. She rose to take his hand. "You know, most of us never find anyone who loves us that much. She's always needed it, and I always fell short. You're not going to lose her."

"I don't suppose you'd listen to an old man and stretch out on the couch over there?" When Cody shook his head, Barlow stood. "Thought not. Got to make a few phone calls. Won't be long."

So they waited. Cody watched the clock as the minutes ticked by. When Nathan and Jackie came in ahead of Barlow an hour later, he was too numb to be surprised.

"Oh, honey…" Jackie went to him immediately, her small, sharp-featured face alive with concern. "We heard almost as soon as the plane touched down. What can we do?"

He shook his head but held on. It helped somehow just to hold on to someone who knew him. "She's in surgery."

"I know. Mr. Barlow explained everything out in the hall. We won't talk about it now. We'll just wait."

Nathan dropped a hand on his shoulder. "I wish we could have gotten here sooner. If it helps any, Thornway's already been picked up."

Cody's eyes focused, then hardened. "How do you know?"

"Barlow did some checking. The police went by to

question him. The minute he was told that you and Abra had been in the explosion he fell apart."

"It doesn't matter." Cody stood up and went to the window. It didn't matter whether Thornway was in jail or in hell. Abra was in surgery, and every second was an eternity.

Nathan started forward, but Jackie laid a hand on his arm. "Let me," she murmured. She stepped up quietly beside him, waiting for him to gather his control. "She's the engineer, isn't she?"

"Yeah. She's the engineer."

"And I don't have to ask if you love her."

"I haven't even told her." He laid his forehead on the glass because he was tempted to punch his fist through it. "It was never the right time or the right place. Jack, when I pulled her out—" He needed another minute to force himself to say it out loud. "When I pulled her out, I thought she was dead."

"She wasn't. She isn't." She laid a hand gently on his wrist. "I know I have this rotten optimism that can be annoying, but I don't believe you're going to lose her. When she's better, are you getting married?"

"Yeah. She doesn't know that, either. I have to talk her into it."

"You're a good talker, Cody." She touched his cheek, then turned his head so that she could study his face. He was deadly pale, with bruises under eyes that were still swollen and red-rimmed from smoke. "You look terrible. How many stitches?"

"Didn't count."

She turned over his hands, barely managing to suppress a shudder. "Did they give you something for the pain?"

"Some prescription." Absently he touched his pocket.

"Which you didn't fill." At least this was something she could do, Jackie decided, plucking it out of his pocket. "I'm going down to have it filled now, and when I bring it up you're going to take it."

"I don't want—"

"You don't want to mess with me," Jackie told him. She kissed his cheek before she strode out of the waiting room.

He took the pills to placate her, then drank the coffee-pot dry to offset the drowsiness. Another hour passed, and then another. His pain dulled to a throb, and his fear sharpened.

He recognized the doctor as the same one who had operated on Mendez. Bost came in, swept a glance over the group huddled in chairs and couches and approached Jessie.

"You're Mrs. Barlow, Miss Wilson's mother?"

"Yes." She wanted to rise but found her legs wouldn't straighten. Instead she put one hand in her husband's and the other in Cody's. "Please, tell me."

"She's out of surgery. Your daughter hasn't regained consciousness yet, and she's lost a great deal of blood. We were able to stop the hemorrhaging. She has some broken ribs, but fortunately her lungs weren't damaged. Her arm was broken in two places, and she has a hairline fracture below the right knee."

Foolishly Jessie remembered kissing scraped elbows and knees to make them better. "But they'll heal?"

"Yes. Mrs. Barlow, we're going to do a series of X-rays and a CAT scan."

"Brain damage?" Cody felt his blood dry up. "Are you saying she has brain damage?"

"She suffered a severe blow to the head. These tests are standard. I know they sound ominous, but they're our best defense against whatever other injuries she may have."

"When will you have the results?" Jessie asked.

"We'll run the tests this afternoon. They'll take a couple of hours."

"I want to see her." Cody stood, sending Jessie a brief, apologetic glance. "I have to see her."

"I know."

"She won't be awake," the doctor explained. "And you'll have to keep it brief."

"Just let me see her."

He wasn't sure what was worse—all those hours of speculation or the actuality of seeing her lying so still, so pale, with bruises standing out so harshly on her cheeks and the tubes hooking her to a line of impersonal machines.

He took her hand, and it was cool. But he could feel the pulse beating in her wrist, echoed by the monitors next to her.

There was no privacy here. She would hate that, he thought. Only a wall of glass separated her from the quiet movement of nurses and technicians in ICU. They'd given her a bed gown, something white with faded blue flowers. He resented the idea that dozens of others had worn it before.

She was so pale.

His mind kept leaping back to that, though he tried to fix it on other, inconsequential things. The faded gown, the beep of the monitors, the hush of crepe soles on the tiles beyond the glass.

Where was she? he wondered as he sat and kept her hand in his through the bars on the side of the bed. He didn't want her to get too far away. He didn't know what to say to bring her closer.

"They won't let me stay, Red, but I'll be hanging around in the waiting room until you wake up. Make it soon." He rubbed a hand absently over his chest as it tightened. "You came through okay. They want to take some more tests, but they don't amount to much. You've got a nasty bump on the head, that's all."

Please, God, let that be all.

He fell silent again, counting the monotonous beeps of the monitors.

"I was thinking we could take that trip back east once you're out of here. You can work on your tan and nag me about stress points." His fingers tightened uncontrollably on hers. "For God's sake, Abra, don't leave me."

He thought—or perhaps it was only a wish—that her fingers pressed just for an instant against his hand.

"You've got to get some rest, Cody."

He'd been staring at the same paragraph of the newspaper for twenty minutes. Now he looked up and saw Nathan. "What are you doing back here?"

"Putting my foot down with you." Nathan sat on the couch beside him. "I left Jack at the hotel. If I can't go back and tell her I convinced you to take a break, she's going to insist on coming out herself."

"I'm doing better than I look."

"You'd have to be to still be conscious."

"Be a pal, Nathan." He gave himself the luxury of sitting back and closing his eyes. "Don't push."

Nathan hesitated. He wasn't the kind of man who interfered in other people's lives. There had been a time when he'd chosen not to become involved at all. That had been before Jackie. "I remember saying almost the same thing to you once when I was confused and upset. You didn't listen, either."

"You were being too stubborn to admit your own feelings," Cody said. "I know what my feelings are."

"Let me buy you something to eat."

"I don't want to miss Bost."

"How about an update on Thornway?"

Cody opened his eyes. "Yeah."

"He made a full confession." Nathan waited while Cody lit a cigarette. The ashtray was already littered with them. "He admitted to substituting materials, the payoffs, the bribes. He claims he was drunk and in a state of panic after you and Abra confronted him. He made the call to arrange the arson with some kind of crazed idea that no one would be able to prove anything against him if the project was destroyed."

"Didn't he think there would be an investigation?" Cody expelled a quick stream of smoke. "Did he think we'd all just keep quiet about it?"

"Obviously he didn't think."

"No." Too drained even for anger, Cody stared across the room, where Jessie dozed on Barlow's shoulder. "And because he didn't think, Abra was almost killed. Even now she could be—" He couldn't say it. He couldn't even think it.

"He's going to spend a lot of years paying for it."

"No matter how many," Cody murmured, "no matter how much, it won't be enough."

"Still up and around, Mr. Johnson?" The young resident walked in, looking as though he'd slept in a packing crate. "I'm Dr. Mitchell," he explained to Nathan. "I patched your friend up, oh—" he glanced at his watch

"—about eight hours ago." He looked back at Cody. "Hasn't anybody chained you to a bed yet?"

"No."

Mitchell sat and stretched out his legs. "I pulled a double shift, but I still don't feel as bad as you look."

"Thanks."

"That was a free medical opinion. I ran into Dr. Bost up in the lab." He looked longingly at Cody's cigarette, reminded himself he was a doctor and subdued the urge to ask for one. "He was just finishing up with the results of Miss Wilson's tests."

Cody said nothing, could say nothing. Very slowly he leaned forward and crushed out the cigarette.

"It looks good, Mr. Johnson."

His mouth was dry, too dry. He couldn't find the saliva to swallow. "Are you telling me she's all right?"

"We're moving her from critical to guarded condition. The scan and the X-rays don't indicate brain damage. She's got one whopper of a concussion, to couch things in unprofessional terms. Bost should be down in a few minutes to give you the details, but I thought you could use a little good news. She came to briefly," he continued when Cody remained silent. "She recited her name and address, remembered who was president and asked for you."

"Where is she?"

"It's going to be a little while before you can see her. She's sedated."

"That's her mother." Cody rubbed a hand over his face. "Her mother's sitting over there. Will you tell her? I've got to take a walk."

"I've got a bed with your name on it," Mitchell said, rising with Cody. "The best way to stay close to your lady is to check into our little hotel. I can recommend the chicken surprise."

"I'll keep that in mind." Cody found his way out and walked.

Abra wanted to open her eyes. She could hear things, but the sounds ran through her mind like water. There was no pain. She felt as though she were floating, mind and body, inches off the ground.

She remembered. If she forced her mind to focus, she remembered. There was the sun shooting in red-and-gold fingers through the dome, and a sense of content-ment, of purpose. Then came the fear.

Had she screamed for him? She thought she had, but that had been before that horrible noise had thundered around her. There was another memory, but it was un-clear and dreamlike. She had gone flying— Something like a hot, invisible hand had scooped her up and hurled her through the air. Then there had been nothing.

Where was he?

She thought, was almost certain, that he'd been with her. Had she spoken to him, or was that a dream, too? It seemed to her that she'd opened her eyes and seen him sitting beside her. There had been a bandage on his face, and his face had been drawn and pale. They'd spoken. Hadn't they spoken? With the drugs clouding her mind, she struggled to remember and was frustrated.

Jessie. Her mother had been there, too. She'd been crying.

Then there were strangers' faces. They'd peered down at her, shone lights in her eyes, asked her fool-ish questions. Did she know her name? Of course she knew her name. She was Abra Wilson and she wanted to know what was happening to her.

Maybe she was dead.

She'd lost track of time, but so had Cody. He'd spent every minute he'd been permitted to, and as many more as he could fight for, beside her. Two days had crawled by. She'd been conscious off and on, but the medication had kept her drowsy and often incoherent.

By the third day he could see that she was struggling to focus.

"I can't stay awake." For the first time he heard petulance in her voice, and he was cheered by it. Until now she had accepted everything without complaint. "What are they giving me?"

"Something to help you rest."

"I don't want any more." She turned her head so that she could look at him. "Tell them not to give me any more."

"You need to rest."

"I need to think." Annoyed, she tried to shift. She saw the cast on her arm and fought to remember. It was broken. They'd told her it was broken. There was a cast on her leg, too. She'd been confused at first, wondering if she'd been in a car accident. But it was becoming easier to remember now.

"The buildings. They're gone."

"They don't matter." He pressed his lips to her fingers. "You gave me a scare, Red."

"I know." She was beginning to feel now. Whenever she was awake for this long she began to feel. The pain reassured her. "You're hurt."

"Couple of scrapes. You're having pain." He was up immediately. "I'll get the nurse."

"I don't want any more medicine."

Patiently he leaned over and kissed her just below

the bruise on her cheekbone. "Baby, I can't stand to watch you hurt."

"Kiss me again." She lifted a hand to his cheek. "It feels better when you do."

"Excuse me." The nurse bustled in, all business. "It's time for the doctor to examine you now, Miss Wilson." She shot Cody a look. He'd given her more than his share of aggravation over the past few days. "You'll have to wait outside."

"Yes, ma'am."

"I'm not taking any more medication," he heard Abra say. "If you've got any needles on you, you'd better lose them."

For the first time in days, he laughed. She was coming back.

In another week she was frantic to get out. The night nurse caught her trying to hobble into the corridor. Cody ignored her pleas to smuggle her into the elevators. The doctor scotched her compromise suggestion of outpatient care.

Abra found herself trapped, her arm covered with plaster, her leg in a cast to the knee. She'd gone through phases of anger and self-pity. Now she was just bored. Miserably bored.

When she awoke from a nap she'd taken in self-defense, she saw a woman in her room. She was small and obviously pregnant and had a wild mop of red hair. As Abra looked, she shifted around the arrangements of flowers and plants.

"Hello."

"Hi." Jackie turned and beamed a smile. "So you're awake. Now Cody's going to yell at me because I chased him downstairs to the cafeteria. He's gone from lean to skinny in a week. He'll be gaunt in another couple of days." She walked over to the bed and made herself comfortable beside it. "So how are you feeling?"

"Pretty good." It was easy to smile. "Who are you?"

"Oh, sorry. I'm Jack. Nathan's wife?" She glanced around. "Even with the flowers, hospitals are depressing, aren't they? Bored?"

"Stiff. It's nice of you to come, though."

"Cody's family. That makes you family, too."

Abra glanced toward the doorway. "How is he?"

"He gets better as you get better. We were worried about both of you for a while."

Abra glanced back and studied Jackie's face. She'd had a lot of time to study faces in the last week. This one was friendly and—thank God—cheerful. She'd spoken of Cody as family, and Abra was certain she'd meant it.

"Will you tell me something?" Abra began. "Straight?"

"I'll try."

"Will you tell me what happened? Every time I try to talk to Cody about it he changes the subject, evades or gets angry. I can remember most of it, but it's patchy."

Jackie started to evade, as well, but then she looked into Abra's eyes. Eyes that strong, she decided, deserved the truth. "Why don't you tell me how much you remember?"

Satisfied, Abra relaxed. "We'd gone out to the site, then into the main building. It was still dark, so Cody went out to the car for a light. I was looking around. You know about the switch in materials?"

"Yes."

"When I was alone and looking around, I saw what I took at first for a bunch of drywall compound. It was plastic explosive. I ran for the door." She half lifted her casted arm. "I didn't get there."

Jackie realized she'd been right about the strength. It wasn't fear she saw but determination, laced with what she imagined was a healthy dose of frustration.

"Cody was still outside when the building went up. He managed to get through and find you. I don't know the details about that—he doesn't talk about it—but it must have been terrifying. He managed to drag you out. He told me he thought you were dead."

"It must have been horrible," Abra murmured. "Horrible for him."

"Abra, he's blaming himself for what happened to you."

"What?" She shifted, fought off a twinge of pain and struggled to sit up straighter. "Why should he?"

"He has the idea that if he had dropped the ax on Thornway straight off…if he hadn't wanted to go out there that night…if he hadn't left you alone in the building. If."

"That's stupid." She found the control button and brought the head of the bed up.

"What's stupid?"

Jackie glanced over as Cody walked in. She rose and moved over to pat his cheek. "You are, honey. I'll leave you two alone. Where's Nathan?"

"Took a side trip to the nursery."

She laughed and patted her belly. "I'll join him."

"I like her," Abra said when they were alone.

"Jack's hard not to like." He handed her a rose, careful, as he had been careful for days, not to touch her. "You've got a roomful of flowers, but I thought you might like to have one to hold."

"Thanks."

His eyes narrowed. "Something wrong?"

"Yes."

"I'll get the nurse."

"Sit down." She gestured impatiently toward the chair. "I wish you'd stop treating me like an invalid."

"Okay. Want to take a quick jog around the block?"

"You're a riot."

"Yeah." But he didn't sit. Restless, he roamed the room, stopping off by the table, which was loaded with flowers. "You got some new ones."

"Swaggart and Rodriguez. They called a truce long enough to bring me carnations. They were fighting when they left."

"Some things never change."

"And some things do. You used to be able to talk to me, and to look at me when you did."

He turned. "I'm talking to you now. I'm looking at you now."

"Are you angry with me?"

"Don't be ridiculous."

"I'm not being ridiculous." She pushed herself up, wincing. Cody's jaw tightened. "You come in here every day, every night."

"I must be furious to do that." He walked to her with some idea of helping her settle comfortably.

"Stop it." She took an ill-tempered swipe at his hand. "I can do it myself. A broken arm's not terminal."

He nearly snapped back at her before he bit down on temper. "Sorry."

"That's it. *That's it.* You won't even fight with me." She gestured with her cast, which was crisscrossed with signatures. "All you do is pat me on the head or hover over me or ask me if I need anything."

"You want to go a couple rounds, fine. We'll take it up when you're on your feet."

"We'll take it up now, damn it. Right now." She pounded a frustrated fist on the bed. She couldn't even get out of bed by herself and pace off the rage. "You've treated me like some kind of slow-witted child these last few days, and I've had enough. You won't even talk to me about what happened."

"What do you want?" The strain that had stretched his emotions to the breaking point finally snapped. "Do you want me to tell you what it was like to see that building go up and know you were inside? Do you want me to describe to you what it was like to crawl through what was left, looking for you? Then to find you half buried, bleeding and broken?" His voice rose as he strode toward her, and he gripped the rail along the side of the bed, his fingers white. "Do you want me to go over how I felt waiting in this damn place, not knowing if you were going to live or die?"

"How are we going to get beyond it if we don't?" She reached for his hand, but he snatched it away. "You were hurt, too." Her own temper and frustration broke free. "Don't you know how it makes me feel to see your hand, your face, and know it happened because you went back for me? I want to talk about it, damn you. I can't stand lying here and trying to reconstruct it."

"Then stop." He waved his hand and sent a pitcher flying. There was some small satisfaction in hearing the plastic hit the wall. "It's over and it's done. When you get out of here we're not going to look back. You're never going to put me through anything like this again. Do you understand?" He whirled back to face her. "I can't stand it. I want you out of here. I want you back with me. I love you and I'm sick of lying in bed at night and sweating through what might have happened."

"What didn't happen," she shouted. "I'm here, I'm alive, because you saw to it. You didn't cause this, you jerk. You saved my life. I love you too much to sit here and watch this eat at you. It's going to stop, Johnson. I mean it. If you can't come in here and treat me normally, don't come at all."

"Stop this." A nurse hurried in. "We can hear you arguing all the way down—"

"Get out!" both of them shouted in unison.

She did, shutting the door behind her.

"You want me to leave, I'll leave." Cody stalked toward the bed again, this time sending the railing down with a crash. "But not before I have my say. Maybe I do blame myself for this. And that's my business. You're not going to sit there and tell me how I should feel or what I should feel. I've played along with your way of doing things too long already."

Abra set her chin. "I don't know what you're talking about."

"No strings, no commitment, no long-term plans. Isn't that the way you set things up?"

"We agreed—"

"I'm through agreeing, and I'm through waiting until the time's right, the place is right, the mood's right. Did you hear what I said a few minutes ago? I said I loved you."

"You didn't say it." Abra frowned down at her hands. "You yelled it."

"Okay, I yelled it." He sat beside her, barely controlling the urge to shout again. "Now I'm saying it, and I'm saying you're going to marry me. And that's the end of it."

"But—"

"Don't." His temper vanished so abruptly that he could only press his fingers to his eyes. "Don't push me now."

"Cody, I—"

"Just shut up, will you?" He dropped his hands, thinking—hoping—he'd regained control. "It wasn't supposed to be like this, a shouting match with you flat on your back. It seems whenever we plan things out it doesn't work. So here it is, Red—no plans, no design. I need you. I want you to marry me, to come back East and live your life with me."

She looked up and took a long breath. "Okay."

With a half laugh, he rubbed his hands over his face. "Okay? That's it?"

"Not exactly. Come here." She held out her arm and took him to her. For the first time in days he held her as if he meant it. "You probably heard what I said a little while ago, about being in love with you."

"You didn't say it." His lips curved with a combination of pleasure and relief as he pressed them to her neck. She was warm and very much alive, and she was with him. "You yelled it."

"It's still true." She eased him back so that she could look at his face. "I'm sorry."

"For what?"

"For putting you through all of this."

"It wasn't your fault," Cody told her.

"No, it wasn't." She smiled, curling the fingers at the end of her cast into the fingers at the end of his bandage. "It wasn't yours, either. It's not something I'd like to go through again, but it did push you to ask me to marry you."

"I might have done it anyway." He grinned and brushed his lips over her fingers. "Maybe."

She lifted a brow. They'd crushed the rose between them. Carefully Abra smoothed out the petals. "I have a confession. I was going to come East whether you wanted me or not."

He drew away to study her face. "Is that right?"

"I thought that if I got in your way often enough you'd get used to it. In my head I told myself I was going to let you walk away, but in my heart… I wasn't going to give you a chance."

He leaned closer to kiss her. "I wasn't going anywhere."

Epilogue

Cody scrawled the information on the registration form. Behind the desk, the slope of rock was dotted with cacti just beginning to bloom. Light streamed through the arch of glass. The clerk beamed at him.

"Enjoy your stay with us, Mr. Johnson."

"I intend to." He turned, pocketing the key.

People moved in and out of the lobby, many of them in tennis clothes. Some strolled down the wide, curving staircase, others glided up and down in the silent elevators. Overhead the dome let in the sun in a fantasy of color. He watched it spread over the tile floor. A waterfall tumbled musically into a small rock pool. Smiling, he walked over to it, and to the woman who stood watching the race of water.

"Any complaints?"

Abra turned, tilting her head to study his face. "I still remember how many feet of pipe we needed to give you your little whim."

He took her chin in his hand. "It makes a statement."

"So you always said." She'd tell him later how lovely she thought it was. "Anyway, thanks to me, it's functional." Resting her head on his shoulder, she turned back to watch the water.

"What's wrong?"

"You'll think I'm stupid."

"Red, I think you're stupid half the time." He sucked in air when her elbow connected with his ribs. "Tell me anyway."

"I miss the kids."

With a laugh he spun her around and kissed her. "That's not stupid. But I bet I can take your mind off them for a while—once we walk over to our cabana."

"Maybe." She smiled challengingly. "If you really work at it."

"I figure a second honeymoon should be even better than the first."

She linked her hands around his neck. "Then let's get started."

"In a minute." He drew her hands away to take them in his own. "Five years ago we stood in here at dawn. The place was empty, and neither of us could be sure it would ever be finished."

"Cody, it doesn't do any good to remember all that."

"It's something I'll never forget." He brought her hands to his lips. "But there's something I never told you. I was going to ask you to marry me here, that morning."

The surprise came first, even after nearly five years of marriage and partnership. Then came the pleasure and the sweetness. "I guess it's too late now. You're already stuck with me."

"Too late for that." Ignoring the people around them, he gathered her close. They might have been alone, as they had been alone that morning years before. "It's not too late for me to tell you that you're the best part of my life. That I love you more now than I did five years ago."

"Cody." She pressed her lips to his. The feeling was as strong as ever, the taste as alluring. "I'm so happy to have you, to have the family. Coming back here now makes me realize how lucky I am." She traced the faint scar along his temple. "We could have lost everything. Instead, we have everything." For a moment she held him tight. Then, breaking away, she smiled. "And I like your waterfall."

"Praise indeed, from an engineer. Here." He took a coin out of his pocket. "Make a wish."

"I don't need wishes." She tossed it over her shoulder. "Just you." The coin sank slowly into the pool as they walked away together.

* * * * *